SHARPE'S HONOUR

RICHARD SHARPE AND THE
VITORIA CAMPAIGN,
FEBRUARY TO JUNE 1813

Bernard Cornwell

VIKING

VIKING
Viking Penguin Inc.,
40 West 23rd Street,
New York, New York 10010, U.S.A.

First American edition
Published in 1985

LIBRARY OF CONGRESS CATALOGING IN PUBLICATION DATA
Cornwell, Bernard.
Sharpe's honour.
1. Peninsular War, 1807–1814—Fiction.   I. Title.
PR6053.O75S535   1985   823'.914   84-40474
ISBN 0-670-80389-8

Printed in the United States of America
by The Book Press, Brattleboro, Vermont
Set in Baskerville

SHARPE'S HONOUR
is for
Jasper Partington and Shona Crawford Poole,
who marched from the very start.

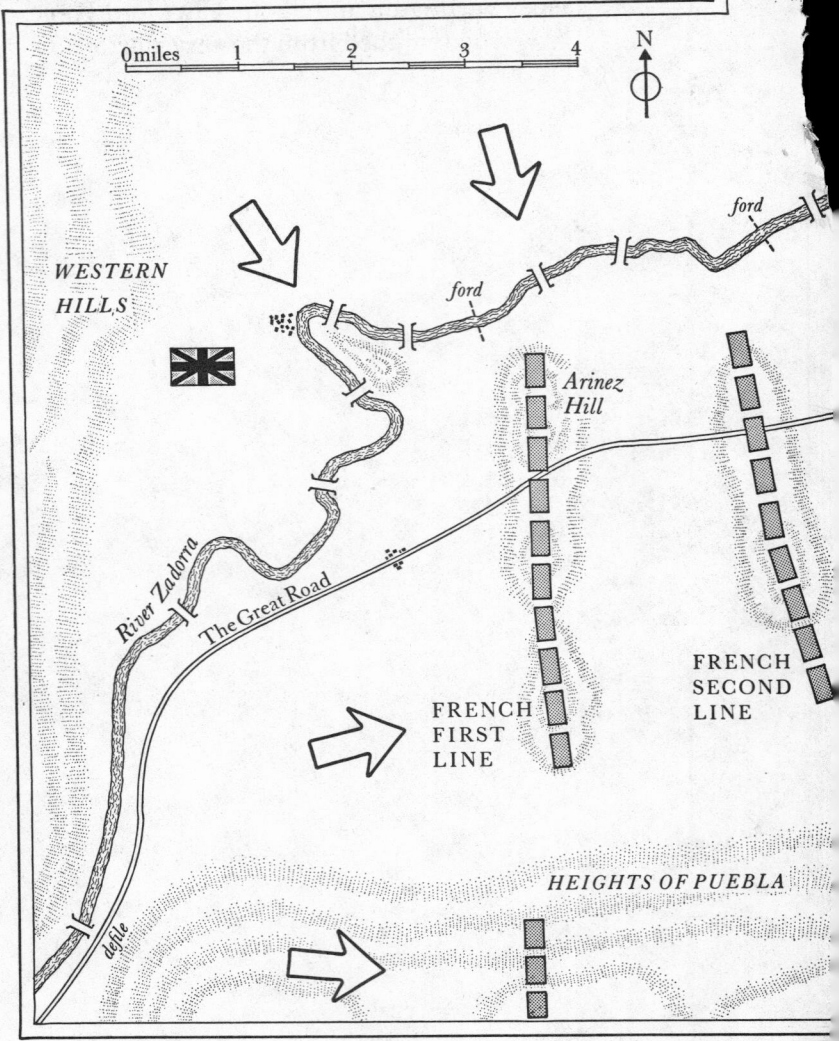

BATTLE OF VITORIA
June 21st. 1813

French positions and directions of British attacks

0 miles 1 2 3 4

N

WESTERN HILLS

ford

ford

Arinez Hill

River Zadorra

The Great Road

FRENCH FIRST LINE

FRENCH SECOND LINE

HEIGHTS OF PUEBLA

defile

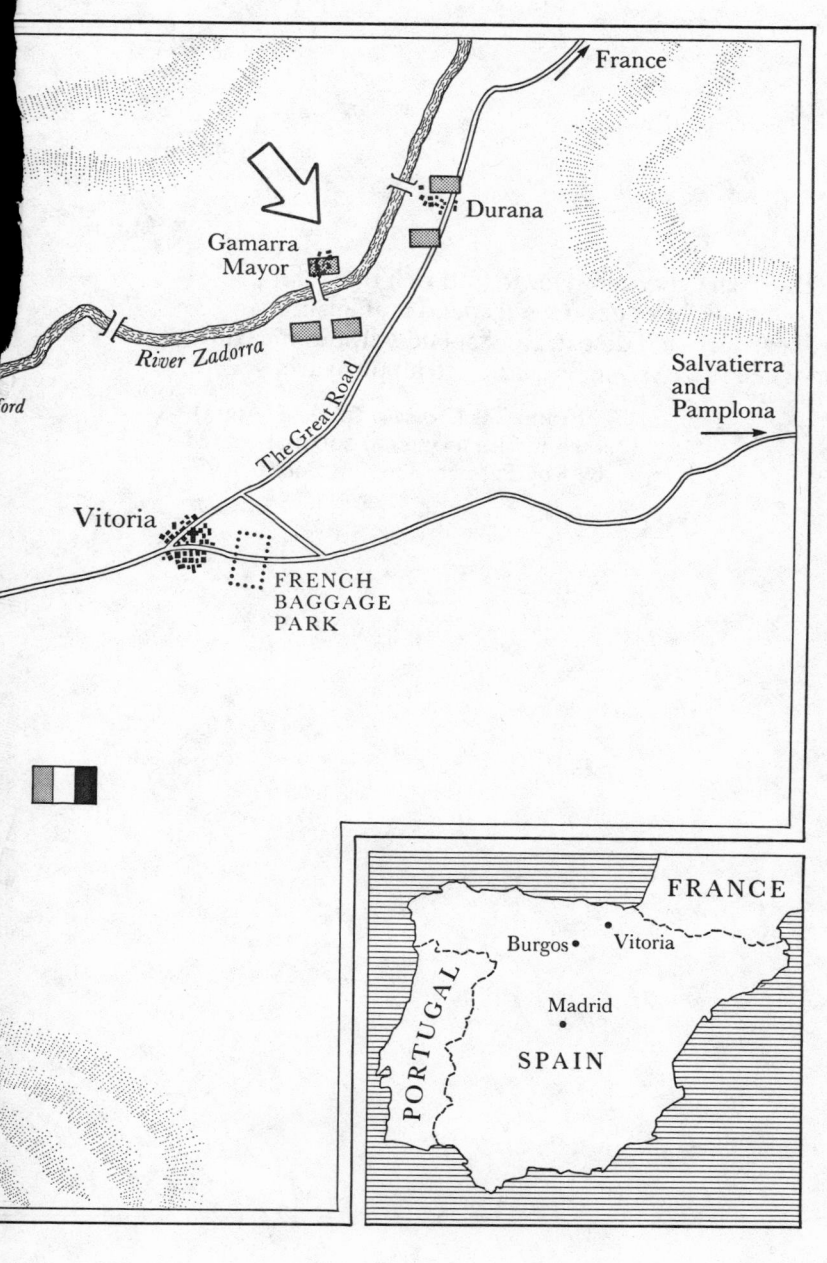

France

Durana

Gamarra
Mayor

River Zadorra

ford

The Great Road

Salvatierra
and
Pamplona

Vitoria

FRENCH
BAGGAGE
PARK

FRANCE

Burgos • • Vitoria

PORTUGAL

Madrid
•

SPAIN

We'll search every room for to find rich treasure,
And when we have got it we'll spend it at leisure.
We'll card it, we'll dice it, we'll spend without measure,
And when it's all gone, bid adieu to all pleasure.

From: *The Grenadier's March* (Anon),
Quoted in THE RAMBLING SOLDIER, edited
by Roy Palmer, Penguin Books, 1977.

PROLOGUE

There was a secret that would win the war for France. Not a secret weapon, nor some surprise strategy that would send the enemies of France reeling in defeat, but a sleight of politics that would drive the British from Spain without a musket being fired. It was a secret that must be kept, and must be paid for.

To which end, on a pitiless winter's day in 1813, two men climbed into the northern hills of Spain. Whenever the road forked they took the lesser path. They climbed by frost-hardened tracks, going ever higher into a place of rocks, eagles, wind, and cruelty, until at last, at a place where the far sea could be seen glittering beneath a February sun, they came to a hidden valley that smelt of blood.

There were sentries at the valley's head; men wrapped in rags and pelts, men with muzzle-blackened muskets. They stopped the travellers, challenged them, then incongruously knelt to one of the horsemen, who, with a gloved hand, made a blessing over their heads. The two men rode on.

The smaller of the two travellers, the keeper of this secret of secrets, had a thin, sallow face that was pockmarked by the old scars of smallpox. He wore spectacles that chafed the skin behind his ears. He stopped his horse above a rock amphitheatre that had been made when this valley was mined for iron. He looked with his cold eyes at the scene below him. 'I thought you didn't fight the bulls in winter.'

It was a crude bullfight, nothing like the splendour of the entertainment provided in the barricaded plazas of the big cities to the south. Perhaps a hundred men cheered from the sides of the rock pit, while, beneath them, two men tormented a black, angry bull that was slick with the blood drawn from its weakened neck muscles. The animal was weak anyway, ill fed through the winter, and its charges were pitiful, easily evaded, and its end swift. It was not killed with the traditional sword, nor with the small knife plunged between its vertebrae, but by a poleaxe.

A huge man, clothed in leather beneath a cloak of wolf's fur, performed the act. He swung the great axe, its blade glittering in the weak sun, and the animal tried to swerve from the blow, failed, and it bellowed one last useless challenge at the sky as the axe took its life and cut down, through bone and pipes and sinews and muscles, and the men about the rock pit cheered.

The small man, whose face showed distaste for what he saw, gestured at the axeman. 'That's him?'

'That's him, Major.' The big priest watched the small, bespectacled man as if enjoying his reaction. 'That's *El Matarife*.' The nickname meant "the Slaughterman".

El Matarife was a frightening sight. He was big, he was strong, but it was his face that caused fear. He was bearded so thickly that his face seemed half man and half beast. The beard grew to his cheekbones, so that his eyes, small and cunning, appeared in a slit between beard and hair. It was a bestial face that now looked up, over the dead bull, to see the two horsemen above him. *El Matarife* bowed mockingly to them. The priest raised a hand in reply.

The men about the rock pit, Partisans who followed the Slaughterman, were calling for a prisoner. The carcass of the bull was being dragged up the rocks, going to join the three other dead animals that had left their blood on the white-frosted stone.

The small man frowned. 'A prisoner?'

'You can hardly expect *El Matarife* not to have a welcome for you, Major? After all it's not every day that a Frenchman comes here.' The priest was enjoying the small Frenchman's discomfiture. 'And it might be wise to watch, Major? To refuse would be seen as an insult to his hospitality.'

'God damn his hospitality,' the small man said, but he stayed nonetheless.

He was not impressive to look at, this small Frenchman

whose glasses chafed his skin, yet the appearance was deceptive. Pierre Ducos was called Major, though whether that was his real rank, or whether he held any rank in the French army at all, no one knew. He called no man "sir", unless it was the Emperor. He was part spy, part policeman, and wholly politician. It was Pierre Ducos who had suggested the secret to his Emperor, and it was Pierre Ducos who must make the secret come true and thus win the war for France.

A fair-headed man, dressed only in a shirt and trousers, was pushed past the bulls' carcasses. His hands were tied behind his back. He was blinking as though he had been brought from a dark place into the sudden daylight.

'Who is he?' Ducos asked.

'One of the men he took at Salinas.'

Ducos grunted. *El Matarife* was a Partisan leader, one of the many who infested the northern hills, and he had lately surprised a French convoy and taken a dozen prisoners. Ducos pushed at the earpiece of his spectacles. 'He took two women.'

'He did,' the priest said.

'What happened to them?'

'You care very much, Major?'

'No.' Ducos' voice was sour. 'They were whores.'

'French whores.'

'But still whores.' He said it with dislike. 'What happened to them?'

'They ply their trade, Major, but their payment is life instead of cash.'

The fair-headed man had been taken to the base of the rock pit and there his arms were cut free. He flexed his fingers in the raw, cold air, wondering what was to happen to him in this place that stank of blood. There was a mood of expectant enjoyment among the spectators. They were quiet, but they grinned because they knew what was to happen.

A chain was tossed to the pit's floor.

It lay there, links of rusting iron in the bull's blood which had steamed in the cold. The prisoner shivered. He took a step back as a man picked up one end of the chain, but then submitted quietly as the links were tied to his left forearm.

The Slaughterman, his huge beard flecked with the blood of the bull, picked up the other end of the chain. He looped it about his own left arm and laughed at the prisoner. 'I shall count the ways of your death, Frenchman.'

The French prisoner did not understand the Spanish words. He did understand, though, the knife that was tossed to him; a long, wicked-bladed knife that was identical to the weapon in the hands of *El Matarife*. The chain that linked the two men was ten feet long.

The priest smiled. 'You've seen such a fight?'

'No.'

'There is a skill to it.'

'Undoubtedly,' Ducos said drily.

The skill was all with the Slaughterman. He had fought the linked knife fight many times, and he feared no opponent. The Frenchman was brave, but desperate. His attacks were fierce, but clumsy. He was pulled off balance by the chain, he was tormented, he was cut, and with every slice of *El Matarife's* knife the count was shouted out by the watching partisans. '*Uno!*' greeted a slash that opened the Frenchman's forehead to his skull. '*Dos!*' saw his left hand slit between his fingers. The numbers mounted.

Ducos watched. 'How long does it go on?'

'Perhaps fifty cuts?' The priest shrugged. 'Maybe more.'

Ducos looked at the priest. 'You enjoy it?'

'I enjoy all manly pursuits, Major.'

'Except one, priest,' Ducos smiled.

Father Hacha looked back at the pit. The priest was a big man, as big as *El Matarife* himself. He showed no distress as the prisoner was slashed and cut and flayed. Father Hacha was, in many ways, an ideal partner to Major Pierre Ducos. Like the Frenchman he was part spy, part policeman, and wholly politician, except that his politics were those of the Church, and his skills were given to the Spanish Inquisition. Father Hacha was an Inquisitor.

'Fourteen!' the Partisans shouted, and Ducos, startled by the loudness of the shout, looked back at the pit.

El Matarife, who had not been touched by the prisoner's knife, had, with exquisite skill, taken out his opponent's left eye. *El Matarife* fastidiously wiped the tip of his blade on his leather sleeve. 'Come, Frenchman!'

The prisoner had his left hand clapped over his ruined eye. The chain tightened, the links making a small noise in the pit, and the tension of the chain dragged his hand away from the blood and pain. He was shaking his head, half sobbing, knowing that the ways of his death would be long and painful. Such was always the death of the French when captured by the Partisans, and such were the deaths of the Partisans caught by the French.

The Frenchman pulled back on the chain, trying to resist the pressure, but he was powerless against the huge man. Suddenly the chain was thrashed, the Frenchman fell, and he was dragged about the floor of the pit like a landed fish. When the Spaniard paused, the Frenchman tried to get up, but a boot hammered into his left forearm, breaking the bones, and the pulling began again and the watching Partisans laughed at the squeals of pain as the chain pulled on the broken limb.

Ducos' face showed nothing.

Father Hacha smiled. 'You're not upset, Major? He is your countryman.'

'I hate all unnecessary cruelty.' Ducos pushed again at the spectacles. These were new glasses, fetched from Paris. His old ones had been broken on Christmas Day by a British officer called Richard Sharpe. That insult still hurt Ducos, but be believed, with the Spanish, that revenge was a dish best eaten cold.

At the count of twenty, the Frenchman lost his right eye.

At the count of twenty-five, he was sobbing for mercy, unable to fight, his ragged, dirty trousers bright with new blood.

At the count of thirty, his breath misting as he sobbed, the prisoner was killed. *El Matarife*, disgusted with the lack of fight in the man, and bored with the entertainment, slit his throat, and went on cutting until the head came away in his hand. He threw the head to the dogs that had been beaten away from the dead bulls. He unwound the chain from his left forearm, sheathed the wet knife, and looked again at the two horsemen. He smiled at the priest. 'Welcome, brother! What have you brought me?'

'A guest.' The priest said it forcibly.

El Matarife laughed. 'Take him to the house, Tomas!'

Ducos followed the Inquisitor through rocks stained red by the iron ore to a house built of stone with blankets for windows and doors. Within the house, warmed by a fire that filled the damp walls with smoke, a meal waited. There was stew of gristle and grease, loaves, wine, and goat's cheese. It was served by a scared, thin faced girl. *El Matarife*, bringing into the damp warmness of the small room the stink of fresh blood, joined them.

El Matarife clasped the priest in his arms. They were brothers, though it was hard to see how the same womb could have given birth to two such different men. They were alike in their size, but in nothing else. The Inquisitor was subtle, clever, and delicate where *El Matarife* was crude, boisterous, and savage. The Partisan leader was the kind of man despised by Pierre Ducos, who admired cleverness and hated brute strength, but the Inquisitor would not give the Frenchman his help unless his brother was taken into their confidence and used in their scheme.

El Matarife spooned the greasy stew into his mouth. Gravy dripped onto his huge beard. He looked with his small, red-rimmed eyes at Ducos. 'You're a brave man, coming here.'

'I come with your brother's protection.' Ducos spoke Spanish perfectly, as he spoke a half dozen other languages.

El Matarife shook his head. 'In this valley, Frenchman, you are under my protection.'

'Then I am grateful.'

'You enjoyed seeing your countryman die?'

Ducos kept his voice mild. 'Who would not enjoy your skill?'

El Matarife laughed. 'You'd like to see another die?'

'Juan!' The Inquisitor's voice was loud. He was the elder brother, and his authority cowed *El Matarife*. 'We have come for business, Juan, not pleasure.' He gestured to the other men in the room. 'And we will talk alone.'

It had not been easy for Pierre Ducos to come to this place, yet such was the state of the war that he had agreed to the Inquisitor's demands.

Ducos had agreed to sit at this table with his enemy because the war had turned sour for France. The Emperor had invaded Russia with the greatest army of modern times, an army which, in one winter, had been destroyed. Now northern Europe threatened France. The armies of Russia, Prussia, and Austria scented victory. To fight them, Napoleon was taking troops from Spain, at the very time when the English General Wellington was increasing his forces. Only a fool was now confident of a French military victory in Spain, and Pierre Ducos was no fool. Yet if the army could not defeat the British, politics might.

The thin girl, shivering with fear of her master, poured raw wine into silver mounted horn cups. The silver was chased with the wreathed "N" of Napoleon, booty taken by the Slaughterman in one of his attacks on the French. Ducos waited until the girl had gone, then, in his quiet, deep voice, he spoke of politics.

In France, in the luxury of the chateau of Valençay, the Spanish King was a prisoner. To his people Ferdinand VII was a hero, the lost King, the rightful King, a symbol of their pride. They fought not just to expel the French invader, but to restore their King to his throne. Now Napoleon proposed to give them back their King.

El Matarife paused. He was slicing the goat's cheese with the knife that had tormented and killed the prisoner. 'Give him back?' He sounded incredulous.

'He will be restored to the throne,' Ducos said.

Ferdinand VII, the Frenchman explained, would be sent back to Spain. He would be sent in majesty, but only if he signed the Treaty of Valençay. That was the secret; the Treaty, a treaty which, to Ducos' clever mind, was an idea of genius. It declared that the state of war that had unfortunately arisen between Spain and France was now over. There would be peace. The French armies would withdraw from Spain and a promise would be made that hostilities would not be resumed. Spain would be a free, sovereign country with its own beloved King. Spanish prisoners in French camps would be sent home, Spanish trophies restored to their regiments, Spanish pride burnished by French flattery.

And in return Ferdinand had only to promise one thing; that he would end the alliance with Britain. The British army would be ordered to leave Spain, and if it hesitated then there would be no forage for its horses, food for its men, or ports for its supply ships. A starved army was no army. Without a shot being fired, Wellington would be forced from Spain and Napoleon could take every one of France's quarter million soldiers in Spain and march them against the northern foes. It was a stroke of genius.

And, of necessity, a secret. If the British government even dreamed that such a treaty was being prepared then British gold would flow, bribes be offered, and the populace of Spain roused against the very thought of peace with France.

The Treaty, Ducos allowed, would not be popular in Spain. The common people, the peasants whose lands and women had been ravaged by the French, would not welcome a peace with their bitterest enemy. Only their beloved, absent King could persuade them to accept it, and their King hesitated.

Ferdinand VII wanted reassurance. Would the nobility of Spain support him? Would the Spanish Generals? What, most important of all, would the Church say? It was Ducos' job to provide those answers for the King, and the man who would give Ducos those answers was the Inquisitor.

Father Hacha was clever. He had risen in the Inquisition by his cleverness, and he knew how to use the secret files that the Inquisition kept on all Spain's eminent men. He could use his fellow Inquisitors in every part of Spain to collect letters from such men, letters that would be passed to the imprisoned Spanish King and assure him that a peace with France would be acceptable to enough nobles, churchmen, officers, and merchants to make the Treaty possible.

To all this *El Matarife* listened. He shrugged when the story finished, as if to suggest that such politics were not his business. 'I am a soldier.'

Pierre Ducos sipped wine. A gust of wind lifted one of the damp blankets at a window and fluttered the tallow candle that lit their meal. He smiled. 'Your family was rich once.'

El Matarife stabbed his cheese flecked knife at the Frenchman. 'Your troops destroyed our wealth.'

'Your brother,' and Ducos' voice held a hint of mockery, 'has put a price upon the assistance he will give me.'

'A price?' The bearded face smiled at the thought of money.

Ducos smiled back. 'The price is the restoration of your family's fortune, and more.'

'More?' *El Matarife* looked at his brother.

The priest nodded. 'Three hundred thousand dollars, Juan.'

El Matarife laughed. He looked from his brother to the Frenchman and he saw that neither smiled, that the sum was true, and his laughter died. He stared belligerently at Ducos. 'You're cheating us, Frenchman. Your country will never pay that much. Never!'

'The money will not come from France,' Ducos said.

'Where then?'

'From a woman.' Ducos spoke softly. 'But first there has to be a death, then an imprisonment, and that, *El Matarife*, is your part of this.'

The Partisan leader looked at his brother for confirmation, received it, and looked back at the small Frenchman. 'A death?'

'One death. The woman's husband.'

'The imprisonment?'

'The woman.'

'When?'

Pierre Ducos saw the Partisan's smile and felt the surge of hope. The secret would be safe and France saved. He would buy, with three hundred thousand Spanish dollars that were not his to spend, the future of Napoleon's empire.

'When?' the Partisan asked again.

'Spring,' Ducos said. 'This spring. You will be ready?'

'So long as your troops leave me alone.' *El Matarife* laughed.

'That I promise.'

'Then I will be ready.'

The bond was sealed by a handshake. The secret would be safe, the Treaty that would defeat Britain made, and, in the course of it, Pierre Ducos would accomplish his revenge on the Englishman who had broken his spectacles. When the spring came, and when the armies prepared to fight a war that would, within a year, be made redundant by the secret treaty, a man called Richard Sharpe, a soldier, would die.

CHAPTER 1

Major Richard Sharpe, on a damp spring day when a cold wind whipped down a rocky valley, stood on an ancient stone bridge and stared at the road which led southwards to a low pass in the rocky crest. The hills were dark with rain.

Behind him, standing at ease, with their musket locks wrapped with rags and the muzzles plugged with corks to stop the rain soaking into the barrels, stood five companies of infantry.

The crest, Sharpe knew, was five hundred yards away. In a few moments there would be enemy on that crest and his job was to stop them crossing the bridge. A simple job, a soldier's job. It was made easier because the spring of 1813 was late, the weather had brought these border hills nothing but rain, and the stream beneath the bridge was deep, fast, and impassable. The enemy would have to come to the bridge where Sharpe waited or not cross the watercourse at all.

'Sir?' D'Alembord, Captain of the Light Company, sounded apprehensive, as if he did not want to provoke Major Sharpe's ill temper.

'Captain?'

'Staff officer coming, sir.'

Sharpe grunted, but said nothing. He heard the hooves slow behind him, then the horse was in front of him and an excited cavalry Lieutenant was looking down on him. 'Major Sharpe?'

A pair of dark eyes, hard and angry, looked from the Lieutenant's gilt spurs, up his boots, up the rich, mud-spattered, blue woollen cloak till they met the excited staff officer's eyes. 'You're in my way, Lieutenant.'

'Sorry, sir.'

The Lieutenant hastily moved his horse to one side. He had ridden hard, making a circuit of difficult country, and was proud of his ride. His mare was restless, matching the rider's exhilarated mood. 'General Preston's compliments, sir, and the enemy is coming your way.'

'I've got picquets on the ridge.' Sharpe said it ungraciously. 'I saw the enemy a half hour since.'

'Yes, sir.'

Sharpe stared at the ridge. The Lieutenant was wondering whether he ought to quietly ride away when suddenly the tall Rifleman looked at him again. 'Do you speak French?'

The Lieutenant, who was nervous of meeting Major Richard Sharpe for the first time, nodded. 'Yes, sir.'

'How well?'

The cavalryman smiled. *Tres bien, Monsieur, je parle . . .*'

'I didn't ask for a god-damned demonstration! Answer me.'

The Lieutenant was horrified by the savage reproof. 'I speak it well, sir.'

Sharpe stared at him. The Lieutenant thought that this was just such a stare that an executioner might give a plump and once-privileged victim. 'What's your name, Lieutenant?'

'Trumper-Jones, sir.'

'Do you have a white handkerchief?'

This conversation, Trumper-Jones decided, was becoming increasingly odd. 'Yes, sir.'

'Good.' Sharpe looked back to the ridge, and to the saddle among the rocks where the road came over the skyline.

This had become, he was thinking, a bastard of a day's work. The British army was clearing the roads eastward from the Portuguese frontier. They were driving back the French outposts and prising out the French garrisons, making the roads ready for the army's summer campaign.

And on this day of fitful rain and cold wind five British Battalions had attacked a small French garrison on the River Tormes. Five miles behind the French, on the road that would be their retreat, was this bridge. Sharpe, with half a Battalion and a Company of Riflemen had been sent by a circuitous night march to block the retreat. His task was simple; to stop the French long enough to let the other Battalions come up behind and finish them off. It was as simple as that, yet now, as the afternoon was well advanced, Sharpe's mood was sour and bitter.

'Sir?' Sharpe looked up. The Lieutenant was offering him a folded linen handkerchief. Trumper-Jones smiled nervously. 'You wanted a handkerchief, sir?'

'I don't want to blow my nose, you fool! It's for the surrender!' Sharpe scowled and walked two paces away.

Michael Trumper-Jones stared after him. It was true that fifteen hundred French were approaching this small force of less then four hundred men, but nothing that Trumper-Jones had heard of Richard Sharpe had prepared him for this sudden willingness to surrender. Sharpe's fame, indeed, had reached England, from whence Michael Trumper-Jones had so recently sailed to join the army, and the closer he had come to the battle lines, the more he had heard the name. Sharpe was a soldier's soldier, a man whose approval was eagerly sought by other men, whose name was used as a touchstone of professional competence, and apparently a man who now contemplated surrender without a fight.

Lieutenant Michael Trumper-Jones, appalled at the thought, looked surreptitiously at a face made dark by sun and wind. It was a handsome face, marred only by a scar that pulled down Sharpe's left eye to give him a mocking, knowing expression. Trumper-Jones did not know it, but that scar-pulled expression would disappear with a smile.

What astonished Trumper-Jones most was that Major Richard Sharpe bore no marks of rank, neither sash nor epaulettes; indeed nothing except the big battered cavalry sword at his side indicated that he was an officer. He looked, Trumper-Jones thought, the very image of a man who had taken the first French Eagle captured by the British, who had stormed the breach at Badajoz, and charged with the Germans at Garcia Hernandez. His air of confidence made it hard to believe that he had started his career in the ranks. It made it even harder to believe that he would surrender his outnumbered men without a fight.

'What are you staring at, Lieutenant?'

'Nothing, sir.' Trumper-Jones had thought Sharpe was watching the southern hills.

Sharpe was, but he had become aware of the Lieutenant's gaze, and he resented it. He hated being pointed out, being watched. He was comfortable these days only with his friends. He was also aware that he had sounded unnecessarily harsh to the young cavalry officer. He looked up at him. 'We counted three guns. You agree?'

'Yes, sir.'

'Four pounders?'

'I think so, sir.'

Sharpe grunted. He watched the crest. He hoped the two questions would make him appear friendlier to the officer, though in truth Sharpe did not feel friendly to any strangers these days. He had been oppressed since Christmas, swinging between violent guilt and savage despair because his wife had died in the snows at the Gateway of God. Unbidden into his mind came the sudden picture of the blood at her throat. He shook his head, as if to drive the picture away. He felt guilty that she had died, he felt guilty that he had been unfaithful to her, he felt guilty that her love had been so badly returned, he felt guilty that he had let his daughter become motherless.

He had become poor through his guilt. His daughter, still not two years old, was growing up with her uncle and aunt, and Sharpe had taken all his savings, that he had stolen from the Spanish government in the first place, and given them to Antonia, his daughter. He had nothing left, except his sword, his rifle, his telescope, and the clothes on his back. He found himself resenting this young staff officer with his expensive horse and gilt scabbard furnishings and new leather boots.

There was a murmur in the ranks behind him. The men had seen the small figures who suddenly appeared on the southern crest. Sharpe turned round. ''Talion!' There was silence. ''Talion! 'Shun!'

The mens' boots crashed on the wet rocks. They were in two ranks, stretched across the mouth of the small valley which carried the road northwards.

Sharpe stared at them, knowing their nervousness. These were his men, of his Battalion, and he trusted them, even against this outnumbering enemy. 'Sergeant Huckfield!'

'Sir!'

'Raise the Colours!'

The men, Lieutenant Michael Trumper-Jones thought, grinned most unfittingly for such a solemn moment, then he saw why. The "Colours" were not the usual flags of a Battalion, instead they were scraps of cloth that had been tied to two stripped birch trunks. The rain made them hang limp and flat, so that from any distance it was impossible to see that the flags were nothing more than two cloaks tricked out with yellow facings torn from the jackets of the soldiers. At the head of the two staffs were wrapped more of the yellow cloth to resemble, at least at a distance, the crowns of England.

Sharpe saw the staff officer's surprise. 'Half Battalions don't carry Colours, Mr Trumper-Jones.'

'No, sir.'

'And the French know that.'

'Yes, sir.'

'So what will they think?'

'That you have a full Battalion, sir?'

'Exactly.' Sharpe looked back to the south, leaving Michael Trumper-Jones curious as to why this deception was a necessary preliminary to surrender. He decided it was best not to ask. Major Sharpe's face discouraged casual questions.

And no wonder, for Major Richard Sharpe, as he stared at the southern ridge, was thinking that this river valley was a miserable, unfitting, and stupid place to die. He wondered, sometimes, if in death he would meet Teresa again, would see her thin, bright face that had always smiled a welcome; a face that, as her death receded, had lost the detail in his memory. He did not even have a picture of her, and his daughter, growing up in her Spanish family, had no picture of her mother or her father.

The army, Sharpe knew, would march away from Spain one day, and he would march with it, and his daughter would be left to life, just as he had been left orphaned as a small child. Misery begets misery, he thought, and then he remembered the consolation that Antonia's uncle and aunt were better, more loving parents than he could have been.

A gust of wind slapped rain over the valley, obscuring the view and hissing on the stones of the bridge. Sharpe looked up at the mounted staff officer. 'What do you see, Lieutenant?'

'Six horsemen, sir.'

'They haven't got cavalry?'

'Not that we saw, sir.'

'That's their infantry officers then. Buggers will be planning our deaths now.' He smiled sourly. He wished this weather would end, that the sun would warm the land and push the memory of winter far behind him.

Then the skyline, where it was crossed by the road, was suddenly thick with the blue uniforms of the French. Sharpe counted the companies as they marched towards him. Six. They were the vanguard, the men who would be ordered to rush the bridge, but not till the French guns had been fetched into place.

That morning Sharpe had borrowed Captain Peter d'Alembord's horse and had ridden the French approach route a dozen times. He had put himself into the place of the opposing commander and had argued with himself until he was certain what the enemy would do. Now, as he watched, they were doing it.

The French knew that a large British force was behind them. They dared not leave the road, abandoning their guns to take to the hills, for then they would be meat for the Partisans. They would want to blast away this road-block swiftly, and their tools for the job would be their guns.

A hundred and fifty yards beneath the crest, where the road twisted for the last time towards the valley floor, there was a flat platform of rock that would make an ideal

24

artillery platform. From there the French could plunge their canisters into Sharpe's two ranks, could twitch them bloody, and when the British were scattered and torn and wounded and dying, the infantry would charge the bridge with their bayonets. From the convenient rock platform the French guns could fire over the heads of their own infantry. The platform was made for the task, so much so that Sharpe had put a working party there this morning and made them clear the space of the boulders that might inconvenience the gunners.

He wanted the French guns there. He had invited the French to put their guns there.

He watched the three gun teams inch their way down the steep road. Infantrymen helped brake the wheels. Lower and lower they came. It was possible, he knew, that the guns might be brought to the flat land across from the bridge, but to stop that he had posted his handful of Riflemen from the South Essex Light Company on the river bank. The French would have seen them there, would fear the spinning accuracy of the bullets, and would, he hoped, choose to place the guns out of the rifles' range.

They so chose. Sharpe watched with relief as the teams swung onto the platform, as the weapons were unlimbered, and as the ready ammunition was brought forward.

Sharpe turned. 'Unstop your muzzles!' The two red-coated ranks pulled the corks from their musket barrels and unwrapped the damp rags from the locks. 'Present!'

The muskets went into the mens' shoulders. The French would see the movement. The French feared the speed of British musket fire, the well drilled rhythm of death that had scoured so many battlefields of Spain.

Sharpe turned away from his men. 'Lieutenant?'

'Sir?' Michael Trumper-Jones answered in a squeak. He tried again in a deeper voice. 'Sir?'

'Tie your handkerchief to your sabre.'

'But, sir . . .'

'You will obey orders, Lieutenant.' It was not said so loudly as to reach any ears other than Trumper-Jones', but the words were harshly chilling.

'Yes, sir.'

The six attack companies of the French were two hundred and fifty yards away. They were in column, their bayonets fixed, ready to come forward when the guns had done their work.

Sharpe took the telescope from his haversack, extended the tubes, and looked at the guns. He could see the canisters, the tin cans that spread their balls in a fan of death, being carried to the muzzles of the three guns.

This was the moment when he hated being a Major. He must learn to delegate, to let other men do the dangerous, hard work, yet at this moment, as the French gunners made the last adjustments to the gun trails, he wished he was with the Company of Riflemen that he had been given for this day's work.

The first canister was pushed into a barrel.

'Now, Bill!' Sharpe said it aloud. Michael Trumper-Jones wondered if he was supposed to reply and decided it was best to say nothing.

To the left of the road, from the high rocks that dominated the track, white puffs of smoke appeared. Seconds later came the crack of the rifles. Already three of the gunners were down.

It was a simple ambush. A company of Riflemen hidden close to where the guns would be forced to unlimber. It was a ploy Sharpe had used before; he supposed he would use it again, but it always seemed to work.

The French were never ready for Riflemen. Because they did not use rifles themselves, preferring the smoothbore musket that fired so much quicker, they took no precautions against the green-jacketed men who used cover so skilfully, and who could kill at three or four hundred paces. Half the gunners were down now, the rocks were thick with rifle smoke, and still the cracks sounded and the bullets span into the gun teams. The Riflemen, changing their positions to aim past the smoke of their previous shots, were shooting the draught horses so the guns could not be moved and killing the gunners so the immobilised guns could not be fired.

The enemy rearguard that was on the road behind the guns was doubled forward. They were formed beneath the rocks and ordered upwards, but the rocks were steep and the Riflemen nimbler than their heavily laden opponents. The French attack did, at least, stop the Riflemen firing at the gunners, and those artillerymen who survived crawled out from the shelter of their limbers to continue the loading.

Sharpe smiled.

There was a man in those hills called William Frederickson, half German, half English, and as fearsome a soldier as any Sharpe knew. He was called Sweet William by his men, perhaps because his eye patch and scarred face were so horrid. Sweet William let the surviving gunners uncover themselves, then he ordered the Riflemen to the right of the road to open fire.

The last gunners dropped. The Riflemen, reacting to Frederickson's shouts, switched their aim to the mounted officers of the infantry. The enemy, by a few, well-aimed rifle shots, had been denied artillery and thrown into sudden chaos. Now was the time for Sharpe to unleash his other weapon. 'Lieutenant?'

Michael Trumper-Jones, who was trying to hide the damp white flag that drooped from his sabre tip, looked at Sharpe. 'Sir?'

'Go to the enemy, Lieutenant, give them my compliments, and suggest that they lay down their weapons.'

Trumper-Jones stared at the tall, dark-faced Rifleman. 'That they surrender, sir?'

Sharpe frowned at him. 'You're not suggesting that we surrender, are you?'

'No, sir.' Trumper-Jones shook his head a little too emphatically. He was wondering how to persuade fifteen hundred Frenchmen to surrender to four hundred wet, disconsolate British infantrymen. 'Of course not, sir.'

'Tell them we've got a Battalion in reserve here, that there's six more behind them, that we've got cavalry in the hills, that we've got guns coming up. Tell them any god-damned lie you like! But give them my compliments and suggest that enough men have died. Tell them they have time to destroy their Colours.' He looked over the bridge. The French were scrambling up the rocks, yet still enough rifle shots, muffled by the damp air, sounded to tell Sharpe that men died wastefully in the afternoon. 'Go on, Lieutenant! Tell them they have fifteen minutes or I will attack! Bugler?'

'Sir?'

'Sound the Reveille. Keep it sounding till the Lieutenant reaches the enemy.'

'Yes, sir.'

The French, warned by the bugle, watched the lone horseman ride towards them with his white handkerchief held aloft. Politely, they ordered their own men to cease firing at the elusive Riflemen in the rocks.

The smoke of the fight drifted away in a shower of windblown rain as Trumper-Jones disappeared into a knot of French officers. Sharpe turned round. 'Stand easy!'

The five companies relaxed. Sharpe looked to the river bank. 'Sergeant Harper!'

'Sir!' A huge man, four inches taller than Sharpe's six feet, came from the bank. He was one of the Riflemen who, with Sharpe, had been stranded in this Battalion of redcoats as part of the flotsam of war. Although the South Essex wore red and carried the short-range musket, this man, like the other Riflemen of Sharpe's old Company, still wore the green uniform and carried the rifle. Harper stopped by Sharpe. 'You think the buggers will give in?'

'They haven't got any choice. They know they're trapped. If they can't get rid of us within the hour, they're done for.'

Harper laughed. If any man was a friend of Sharpe's it was this Sergeant. They had shared every battlefield together in Spain and Portugal, and the only thing that Harper could not share was the guilt that haunted Sharpe since his wife's death.

Sharpe rubbed his hands against the unseasonal cold. 'I want some tea, Patrick. You have my permission to make some.'

Harper grinned. 'Yes, sir.' He spoke with the raw accent of Ulster.

The tea was still warm in Sharpe's cupped hands when Lieutenant Michael Trumper-Jones returned with the French Colonel. Sharpe had already ordered the fake Colours to be lowered and now he went forward to meet his forlorn enemy. He refused to take the man's sword. The Colonel, who knew he could not take this bridge without his guns, agreed to the terms. He took consolation, he said, in surrendering to a soldier of Major Sharpe's repute.

Major Sharpe thanked him. He offered him tea.

Two hours later, when General Preston arrived with his five Battalions, puzzled because he had heard no musketry ahead of him, he found fifteen hundred French prisoners, three captured guns, and four wagons of supplies. The French muskets were piled on the roadway. The plunder they had brought from their garrisoned village was in the packs of Sharpe's men. Not one of the South Essex, nor one of Frederickson's Riflemen, was even wounded. The French had lost seven men, with another twenty-one wounded.

'Congratulations, Sharpe!'

'Thank you, sir.'

Officer after officer offered him congratulations. He shook them off. He explained that the French really had no choice, they could not have broken his position without guns, yet still the congratulations came until, shy with embarrassment, he walked back to the bridge.

He crossed the seething water and found the South Essex's Quartermaster, a plump officer named Collip who had accompanied the half battalion on its night-time march.

Sharpe backed Collip into a cleft of the rocks. Sharpe's face was grim as death. 'You're a lucky man, Mr Collip.'

'Yes, sir.' Collip looked terrified. He had joined the South Essex only two months before.

'Tell me why you're a lucky man, Mr Collip?'

Collip swallowed nervously. 'There'll be no punishment, sir?'

'There never would have been any punishment, Mr Collip.'

'No, sir?'

'Because it was my fault. I believed you when you said you could take the baggage off my hands. I was wrong. What are you?'

'Very sorry, sir.'

In the night Sharpe and his Captains had gone ahead with Frederickson's Riflemen. He had gone ahead to show them the path they must take, and he had left Collip, with the Lieutenants, to bring the men on. He had gone back and discovered Collip at the edge of a deep ravine that had been crossed with harsh difficulty. Sharpe had led the Riflemen over, climbing down one steep bank, wading an ice-cold stream that was waist deep with the water of this wet spring, then scrambling up the far bank with dripping, freezing clothes.

When he returned for the five companies he had found failure waiting for him.

Mr Collip, Quartermaster, had decided to make the crossing easier for the redcoats. He had made a rope out of musket slings, a great loop that could be endlessly pulled over the chasm, and on the rope he had slung across the ravine all the mens' weapons, packs, canteens, and haversacks. On the last pass the knotted slings had come undone and all the South Essex's musket ammunition had gone down into the stream.

When the French approached the bridge only Sharpe's Riflemen had ammunition. The French could have taken the bridge with one volley of musketry because Sharpe had nothing with which to oppose them.

'Never, Mr Collip, ever, separate a man from his weapons and ammunition. Do you promise me that?'

Collip nodded eagerly. 'Yes, sir.'

'I think you owe me a bottle of something, Mr Collip.'

'Yes, sir. Of course, sir.'

'Good day, Mr Collip.'

Sharpe walked away. He smiled suddenly, perhaps because the clouds in the west had parted and there was a sudden shaft of red sunlight that glanced down to the scene of his victory. He looked for Patrick Harper, stood with his old Riflemen, and drank tea with them. 'A good day's work, lads.'

Harper laughed. 'Did you tell the bastards we didn't have any ammunition?'

'Always leave a man his pride, Patrick.' Sharpe laughed. He had not laughed often since Christmas.

But now, with this first fight of the new campaign, he had survived the winter, had made his first victory of the spring, and he looked forward at last to a summer untrammelled by the griefs and tangles of the past. He was a soldier, he was marching to war, and the future looked bright.

CHAPTER 2

On a day of sunshine, when the martins were busy making their nests in the old masonry of Burgos Castle, Major Pierre Ducos stared down from the ramparts.

He was hatless. The small west wind lifted his black hair as he stared into the castle's courtyard. He fidgeted with the earpieces of his spectacles, wincing as the curved wire chafed his sore skin.

Six wagons were being dragged over the cobbles. The wagons were huge, lumbering fourgons, each pulled by eight oxen. Tarpaulins covered their loads, tarpaulins roped down and bulging with cargo. The tired oxen were prodded to the far end of the courtyard where the wagons, with much shouting and effort, were parked against the keep's wall.

The wagons had an escort of cavalrymen who carried bright-bladed lances from which hung red and white pennants.

The garrison of the castle watched the wagons arrive. Above their heads, at the top of the keep, the tricolour of France flapped sullenly in the wind. The sentries stared out across the wide countryside, wondering whether the war would once again lap against this old Spanish fortress that guarded the Great Road from Paris to Madrid.

There was a rattle of hooves in the gateway and Pierre Ducos saw a bright, gleaming carriage come bursting into the courtyard. It was drawn by four white horses that were harnessed to the splinter-bar with silver trace chains. The carriage was driven too fast, but that, Ducos decided, was typical of the carriage's owner.

She was known in Spain as *La Puta Dorada*, "the Golden Whore".

Beside the carriage, where it stopped beneath Ducos' gaze, was a General of cavalry. He was a youngish man, the very image of a French hero, whose gaudy uniform was stiffened to carry the weight of his medals. He leaped from his horse, waved the coachmen aside, and opened the carriage door and let down the steps with a flourish. He bowed.

Ducos, like a predator watching its victim, stared at the woman.

She was beautiful, this Golden Whore. Men who saw her for the first time hardly dared believe that any woman was so beautiful. Her skin was as white and clear as the white pearl shells of the Biscay beaches. Her hair was golden. An accident of lip and bone, of eye and skin had given her a look of innocence that made men wish to protect her. Pierre Ducos could think of few women so little in need of protection.

She was French. She was born Helene Leroux and she had served France since her sixteenth year. She had slept in the beds of the powerful and brought from their pillows the secrets of their nations, and when the Emperor had taken the decision to annex Spain to his Empire, he had sent Helene as his weapon.

She had pretended to be the daughter of victims of the Terror. She had married, on instructions from Paris, a man close to the Spanish King, a man privy to the secrets of Spain. She was still married, though her husband was far off, and she bore the title that he had given her. She was the Marquesa de Casares el Grande y Melida Sadaba. She was lovely as a summer dream and as treacherous as sin. She was *La Puta Dorada*.

Ducos smiled. A hawk, high above its victim, might have felt the same satisfaction that the bespectacled French Major felt as he ordered his aide to send his compliments to the Marquesa with a request, which, from Pierre Ducos, was tantamount to an order, that her Ladyship come to his presence immediately.

La Marquesa de Casares el Grande y Melida Sadaba, smelling of rosewater and smiling sweetly, was ushered into

33

Major Ducos' bare room an hour later. He looked up from the table. 'You're late.'

She blew a kiss from her lace-gloved hand and walked past him to the bastion. 'The country looks very pretty today. I asked your deliciously timid Lieutenant to fetch me some wine and grapes. We could eat out here, Pierre. Your skin needs some sun.' She shaded her face with a parasol and smiled at him. 'How are you, Pierre? Dancing the nights away, as ever?'

He ignored her mockery. He stood in the doorway and his deep voice was harsh. 'You have six wagons in this fortress.'

She pretended awe. 'Has the Emperor made you his wagonmaster, Pierre? I must congratulate you.'

He took a folded piece of paper from his waistcoat pocket. 'They are loaded with gold and silver plate, paintings, coins, tapestries, statues, carvings, and a wine cellar packed in sawdust. The total value is put at three hundred thousand Spanish dollars.' He stared at her in silent triumph.

'And some furniture, Pierre. Did your spy not find the furniture? Some of it's rather valuable. A very fine Moorish couch inlaid with ivory, a japanned écritoire that you'd like, and a mirrored bed.'

'And doubtless the bed in which you persuaded General Verigny to guard your stolen property?' General Verigny was the cavalry officer whose men had guarded the wagons on their journey from Salamanca.

'Stolen, Pierre? It all belongs to me and my dear husband. I merely thought that while Wellington threatens to defeat us I would remove our few household belongings into France. Just think of me as a simple refugee. Ah!' She smiled at Ducos' aide who had brought a tray on which stood an opened bottle of champagne, a single glass, and a dish of white grapes. 'Put it on the parapet, Lieutenant.'

Scowling, Ducos waited till his aide had gone. 'The property is loaded on French army wagons.'

'Condemned wagons, Pierre.'

'Condemned by General Verigny's Quartermaster.'

'True.' She smiled. 'A dear man.'

'And I will countermand his condemnation.'

She stared at him. She feared Pierre Ducos, though she would not give him the satisfaction of showing her fear. She recognised the threat that he offered her. She was running from Spain, running from the victory that Wellington threatened, and she was taking the wealth with her that would make her independent of whatever tragedies befell France. Now Ducos menaced that independence. She plucked a grape from the bunch. 'Tell me, Pierre, do you order your breakfast with a threat? If you want something of me, why don't you just ask? Or is it that you want to share my plunder?'

He scowled at that. No one could accuse Pierre Ducos of greed. He changed the subject. 'I wanted to know how you felt about your husband returning from America.'

She laughed. 'You want me to go back to his bed, Pierre? Don't you think I've suffered enough for France?'

'Does he still love you?'

'Love? What an odd word from you, Pierre.' She stared up at the tricolour. 'He still wants me.'

'He knows you're a spy?'

'I'm sure someone's told him, aren't you? But Luis doesn't take women seriously, Pierre. He'd think I was a spy because I was unhappy without him. He thinks that once he's back and I'm neatly tucked up beneath his glass dome then everything will be all right again. He can grunt all over me and then weep to his confessor. Men are so stupid.'

'Or do you choose stupid men?'

'What a boudoir conversation we are having.' She smiled brilliantly at him. 'So what do you want, Pierre?'

'Why has your husband come home?'

'He doesn't like the climate in South America, Pierre. It gives him wind, he says. He suffers from wind. He once had a servant whipped who laughed when he broke it.'

'He's gone to Wellington.'

'Of course he has! Luis is Spain's new hero!' She laughed. Her husband had led a Spanish army against rebels in the

Banda Oriental, the area of land north of the River Plate. The rebels, seeing Spain humiliated by France, were trying to wrest their independence from the Spanish. To the Marquesa's surprise, indeed, to the surprise of many people, the Marqués had defeated them. She flicked a grape pip over the parapet. 'He must have outnumbered them by a hundred to one! Or perhaps he broke wind in their faces? Do you think that's the answer, Pierre? A grape?' She smiled at his silence and poured herself champagne. 'Tell me why you summoned me here with your usual charm and consideration.'

'Your husband wants you back?'

'You know he does. I'm sure you intercept all his letters. His lust exceeds his patriotism.'

'Then I want you to write a letter to him.'

She smiled. 'Is that all? One letter? Do I get to keep my wagons then?' She asked the question in a small girl's voice.

He nodded.

She watched him, suspecting a bargain so easily made. Her voice was suddenly hard. 'You'll let me move my property to France for one letter?'

'One letter.'

She shrugged. 'You'll give me papers?'

'Of course.'

She sipped the champagne. 'What do I write?'

'Inside.'

He had written the letter and she had only to copy it onto the writing paper that bore the crest of her husband's family. She admired Ducos' efficiency in stealing the paper so that it was prepared for her. He gave her the only chair in the room, a freshly cut quill, and ink. 'Do improve the phrasing, Helene.'

'That won't be difficult, Pierre.'

The letter told a harrowing tale. It replied to a letter from the Marqués and said that she wanted nothing more than to join him, that her joy at his return had filled her with longing and expectation, but that she feared to come to him so long as he was under Wellington's command.

She feared because there was an English officer who had

pursued her most vilely, insulted her and her husband, who had heaped every indignity upon her. She had complained, she said, to the English Generalissimo, yet nothing could be done because the offending officer was a friend of Wellington's. She feared for her virtue, and until the officer was removed from Spain she feared to come to her husband's side. The officer, she wrote, had already attempted to violate her once, in which attempt he had been defeated only by his drunkenness. She did not feel safe while the vile man, Major Richard Sharpe, lived. She signed the letter, carefully dabbing drops of champagne onto the ink so that the writing appeared tear-stained, then smiled at Ducos. 'You want them to fight a duel?'

'Yes.'

She laughed. 'Richard will slaughter him!'

'Of course.'

She smiled. 'Tell me, Pierre. Why do you want Richard to kill my husband?'

'It's obvious, isn't it?'

If her husband, a Grandee of Spain and a sudden, unlikely hero, was killed by an Englishman, then the fragile alliance between Spain and England would be stretched dangerously. The alliance was one of expedience. The Spanish had no love for the English. They resented that they needed a British army to expel the French. It was true that they had made Wellington the Generalissimo of all their armies, but that was a recognition of his talent, and the necessity of the act had only made their need of him more apparent. She watched Ducos dry the ink with sand. 'You do know that there won't be a duel, don't you?'

'There won't?' He shook the sand onto the floor.

'Arthur won't allow them.' "Arthur" was Wellington. 'What will you do then, Pierre?'

He ignored the question. 'You know this could be Major Sharpe's death warrant?'

'Yes.'

'It doesn't worry you?'

She smiled prettily. 'Richard can look after himself,

Pierre. The gods smile on him. Besides, I'm doing this for France, am I not?'

'For your wagons, dear Helene.'

'Ah yes. My wagons. When do I get my pass for them?'

'For the next convoy north.'

She nodded and stood up. 'You really believe they'll fight, Pierre?'

'Does it matter?'

She smiled. 'I'd rather like to be a widow. A rich widow. *La Viuda Dorada*.'

'Then you must hope Major Sharpe obliges you.'

'He always has in the past, Pierre.' She filled the room with her perfume.

He folded the letter. 'Are you fond of him?'

She put her head to one side and seemed to think about it. 'Yes. He has the virtue of simplicity, Pierre, and loyalty.'

'Hardly your tastes, I would have thought?'

'How little you know my tastes, Pierre. Am I dismissed? May I return to my pleasures?'

'Your seal?'

'Ah.' She took off a ring that she wore above her lace glove and handed it to him. He pressed it into hot wax and gave the signet back to her.

'Thank you, Helene.'

'Don't thank me, Pierre.' She stared at him with a slight, mocking smile on her face. 'Do you open the Emperor's letters to me, Pierre?'

'Of course not.' He frowned at such a thought, while inside he was wondering how Napoleon sent such letters so that they avoided his men.

'I thought not.' She licked her lips. 'You know he's still fond of me.'

'I believe he stays fond of all his lovers.'

'You're so very sweet, Pierre.' She turned her folded parasol in her hands. 'You know he thinks of me as quite an expert on Spanish matters? He asks my advice even?'

'So?' Ducos stared at her.

'I must congratulate you, Pierre. I told the Emperor that your idea for the Treaty was magnificent.' She smiled at the shock on his face. 'Truly, Pierre! Magnificent. That was the very word I used. Of course, I told him we might beat Wellington first, but if we didn't? Magnificent!' She smiled a victor's smile. 'So you're not going to stop my little wagons crossing the border, are you?'

'I have already made my promise.'

'But to whom, sweet little Pierre? To whom?' She said the last two words as she opened the door. She smiled again. 'Good day, Major. It was such a small pleasure.'

He listened to her heels on the stone of the passage and felt bitterly angry. Napoleon, always a fool for a pair of legs in a bed, had told the Golden Whore about Valençay? And now she dared to threaten him? That if her puny wagons did not reach France then she would betray her country by revealing the Treaty's existence?

He walked onto the ramparts. The letter she had written was in his hand, and it was the key to the Treaty. Today he would give it to the Inquisitor, and tomorrow the Inquisitor, with his brother, would start the journey westwards. Within three days, he decided, the matter would be irreversible, and within another two weeks he would sew up that pretty mouth for ever.

He watched her greet General Verigny beneath him, watched her climb with the General into her carriage, and he thought with what joy he would see that whore brought low. She dared to threaten him? Then she would live to regret the threat throughout eternity.

He turned back to his office. He would defy her. He would save France, defeat Britain, and dazzle the world with his cleverness. For a few seconds, standing with his back to the magnificent view from Burgos' ramparts, he imagined himself as the new Richelieu, the new bright star in France's glory. He could not lose, he knew it, for he had calculated the risks, and he would win.

CHAPTER 3

'Tents!' Sharpe spat the word out. 'God-damned bloody tents!'

'For sleeping in, sir.' Sergeant Patrick Harper kept a rigidly straight face. The watching men of the South Essex grinned.

'Bloody tents.'

'Clean tents, sir. Nice and white, sir. We could make flower gardens round them in case the lads get homesick.'

Sharpe kicked one of the enormous canvas bundles. 'Who needs god-damned tents?'

'Soldiers, sir, in case they get cold and wet at night.' Harper's thick Ulster accent was rich with amusement. 'I expect they'll give us beds next, sir, with clean sheets and little girls to tuck us up at night. And chamberpots, sir, with God save the King written on their rims.'

Sharpe kicked the heap of tents again. 'I'll order the Quartermaster to burn them.'

'He can't do that, sir.'

'Of course he can!'

'Signed for, sir. Any loss will be deducted from pay, sir.'

Sharpe prowled round the great heap of obscene bundles. Of all the ridiculous, unnecessary, stupid things, the Horse Guards had sent tents! Soldiers had always slept in the open! Sharpe had woken in the morning with his hair frozen to the ground, had woken with his clothes sopping wet, but he had never wanted a tent! He was an infantryman. An infantryman had to march, and march fast, and tents would slow them down. 'How are we supposed to carry the bloody things?'

'Mules, sir, tent mules. One to two companies. To be issued tomorrow, sir, and signed for.'

'Jesus wept!'

'Probably because he didn't have a tent, sir.'

Sharpe smiled, because he was enjoying himself, but this sudden arrival of tents from headquarters posed problems he did not need. The tents would need five mules to carry them. Each mule could carry two hundred pounds, plus thirty more pounds of forage that would keep the animal alive for six days. If they marched on a campaign like last summer's then he would have to assume that forage would be short and extra mules would have to carry extra forage. But the extra mules would need feed too, which meant more mules still, and if he assumed a march of six weeks then that was nine hundred extra pounds of forage. That would need four to five more mules, but those mules would need an extra seven hundred pounds of feed which would mean four more mules, who would also need forage; and so on, until the ridiculous but accurate conclusion was reached that it would take fourteen extra mules simply to keep the five tent-carrying mules alive! He kicked another tent. 'Christ, Patrick! It's ridiculous!'

It was three days since the French had surrendered to them in the hills. They had marched north from the bridge, suddenly leaving the approaches to Salamanca and coming into an area of hills and bad tracks. Waiting for them was the bulk of the army, and a white-grey pile of god-damned tents. Sharpe scowled. 'We'll leave them in store.'

'And have them stolen, sir?'

Sharpe swore. What Harper meant, of course, was that the storekeeper would sell the tents to the Spanish, claim that they were stolen, and have them charged to the Battalion's accounts. 'You know the storekeeper?'

'Aye.' Harper sounded dubious.

'How much?'

'Handful.'

Sharpe swore again. He could doubtless get five pounds out of the Battalion accounts to bribe the storekeeper, but the job would be a nuisance. 'He's no friend of yours, this storekeeper?'

'He's from County Down.' Harper said it meaningfully. 'Sell his own bloody mother for a shilling.'

'You've got nothing on the bastard?'

'No.' Harper shook his head. 'He's tighter than an orangeman's drum.'

'I'll get you the handful.' He could sell one of the mules that would arrive tomorrow, claim it died of glanders or God knows what, and see if anyone dared question him. He shook his head in exasperation, then grinned at the big Sergeant. 'How's your woman?'

'Grand, sir!' Harper beamed. 'Blooming, so she is. I think she'd like to cook you one of those terrible meals.'

'I'll come for one this week.' Isabella was a small, dark Spanish girl whom Harper had rescued from the horror at Badajoz. Ever since that terrible night she had loyally followed the Battalion, along with the other wives, mistresses and whores who formed a clumsy tail to every marching army. Sharpe suspected that Harper would be marrying before the year's end.

The huge Irishman pushed his shako back and scratched at his sandy hair. 'Did your dago find you, sir?'

'Dago?'

'Officer; a real ribbon-merchant. He was sniffing about this morning, so he was. Looked as if he'd lost his purse. Grim as a bloody judge.'

'I was here.'

Harper shrugged. 'Probably wasn't important.'

But Sharpe was frowning. He did not know why, but his instinct, that kept him alive on the battlefield, was suddenly warning him of trouble. The warning was sufficient to destroy the small moment of happiness that insulting the tents had given him. It was as if, on a day of hope and peace, he had suddenly smelt French cavalry. 'What time was he here?'

'Sunrise.' Harper sensed the sudden alertness. 'He was just a young fellow.'

Sharpe could think of no reason why a Spanish officer should want to see him, and when something had no reason, it was liable to be dangerous. He gave the tents a parting kick. 'Let me know if you see him again.'

'Aye, sir.' Harper watched Sharpe walk towards the Battalion's headquarters. He wondered why the mention of the gaudy-uniformed Spaniard had plunged Sharpe into such sudden tenseness. Perhaps, he thought, it was just more of Sharpe's guilt and grief.

Harper could understand grief, but he sensed that Sharpe's mood was not simple grief. It seemed to the big Irishman that his friend had begun to hate himself, perhaps blaming himself for his wife's death and the abandonment of his child. Whatever it was, Harper thought, he hoped that soon the army would march against the French. By that bridge, when the infantrymen had not a shot between them, Harper had seen the old energy and enthusiasm. Whatever Sharpe's sadness was, it had not stopped his ability to fight.

'He needs a good battle,' he said to Isabella that night.

She made a scornful sound. 'He needs another wife.'

Harper laughed. 'That's all you women think about. Marriage, marriage, marriage!' He had been drinking with the other Sergeants of the Battalion and had come back late to find the food she had cooked for him spoilt.

She pushed the burnt eggs about the pan as if hoping that by rearranging them she would improve their looks. 'And what's wrong with marriage?'

Harper, who could sense marriage on his own horizon, decided that discretion was the best part of valour. 'Nothing at all. Have you got any bread?'

'You know I have. You fetch it.'

There were limits to discretion, though. A man's job was not to fetch bread, or be on time for a meal, and Harper sat silent as Isabella grumbled about the billet and as she complained to him about the landlady, and about Sergeant Pierce's wife who had stolen a bucket of water, and told him that he should see a priest before the campaign began so as to make a good confession. Harper half listened to it all. 'I smell trouble ahead.'

'You're right.' Isabella scooped the eggs onto a tin plate.

'Big trouble if you don't fetch the bread.' When she spoke English she did it with a northern Irish accent.

'Fetch it yourself, woman.'

She said something that Harper's Spanish was not good enough to understand, but went to the corner of the room and unearthed the hidden loaf. 'What kind of trouble, Patrick?'

'He's bored.'

'The Major?'

'Aye.' Harper deigned to cut the loaf with his rifle's bayonet. 'He's bored, my love, and when he's bored he gets into trouble.'

Isabella poured the ration wine. 'Rainbows?'

Harper laughed. He was fond of saying that Major Sharpe was always chasing the pot of gold that lay at the end of every rainbow. He found the pots often enough, but, according to Harper, he always discarded them because the pots were the wrong shape. 'Aye. The bugger's chasing rainbows again.'

'He should get married.'

Harper kept a diplomatic silence, but his instinct, like Sharpe's, suddenly sensed danger. He was remembering Sharpe's sudden change of mood that day when he had mentioned the ribbon-merchant, and Harper feared because he knew Richard Sharpe was capable of chasing rainbows into hell itself. He looked at his woman, who waited for a word of praise, and smiled at her. 'You're right. He needs a woman.'

'Marriage,' she said tartly, but he could see she was pleased. She pointed her spoon at him. 'You look after him, Patrick.'

'He's big enough to look after himself.'

'I know big men who can't fetch bread.'

'You're a lucky woman, so you are.' He grinned at her, but inside he was wondering just what it was that had alarmed Sharpe. Like the prospect of marriage that he sensed for himself, he sensed trouble coming for his friend.

* * *

'Ah, Sharpe! No problems? Good!' Lieutenant Colonel Leroy was pulling on thin kid-leather gloves. He had been a Major till a few weeks before, but now the loyalist American had achieved his ambition to command the Battalion. The glove on his right hand hid the terrible burn scars that he had earned a year before at Badajoz. Nothing could hide the awful, puckered, distorting scar that wrenched the right side of his face. He looked into the morning sky. 'No rain today.'

'Let's hope not.'

'Tent mules coming today?'

'So I'm told, sir.'

'God knows why we need tents.' Leroy stooped to light a long, thin cigar from a candle that, on his orders, was kept alight in Battalion headquarters for just this purpose. 'Tents will just soften the men. We might as well march to war with milkmaids. Can you lose the bloody things?'

'I'll try, sir.'

Leroy put on his bicorne hat, pulling the front low to shadow his thin, terrible face. 'What else today?'

'Mahoney's taking Two and Three on a march. Firing practice for the new draft. Parade at two.'

'Parade?' Leroy, whose voice still held the flat intonation of his native New England, scowled at his only Major. Joseph Forrest, the Battalion's other Major, had been posted to the Lisbon Staff to help organize the stores that poured into that port. 'Parade?' Leroy asked. 'What god-damned parade?'

'Your orders, sir. Church parade.'

'Christ, I'd forgotten.' Leroy blew smoke towards Sharpe and grinned. 'You take it, Richard, it'll be good for you.'

'Thank you, sir.'

'Well, I'm off!' Leroy sounded pleased. He had been invited to Bridge headquarters for the day and was antici-pating equal measures of wine and gossip. He picked up his riding crop. 'Make sure the parson gives the buggers a rousing sermon. Nothing like a good sermon to put men in a frog-killing mood. I hear there was a ribbon-merchant looking for you?'

'Yes.'

'What did he want?'

'He never found me.'

'Well tell him "no", whatever he wants, and borrow money off him.'

'Money?'

Leroy turned in the doorway. 'The adjutant tells me you owe the Mess sixteen guineas. True?' Sharpe nodded and Leroy pointed the riding crop at him. 'Pay it, Richard. Don't want you dying and owing the god-damn Mess money.' He walked into the street to his waiting horse, and Sharpe turned to the table of paperwork that waited for him.

'What the devil are you grinning at?'

Paddock, the Battalion clerk, shook his head. 'Nothing, sir.'

Sharpe sat to the pile of work. Paddock, he knew, was grinning because Leroy had told Sharpe to pay his debts, but Sharpe could not pay them. He owed the laundry-woman five shillings, the sutler two pounds, and Leroy, quite rightly, was demanding that Sharpe buy a horse. As a Captain, Sharpe had not wanted a horse, preferring to stay on his boots like his men, but as a Major the added height would be useful on a battlefield, as would the added speed. But a good horse was not to be had for under a hundred and thirty pounds and he did not know where the funds were to come from. He sighed. 'Can't you forge my bloody signature?'

'Yes, sir, but only on pay forms. Tea, Major?'

'Any breakfast left?'

'I'll go and look, sir.'

Sharpe worked through the papers. Equipment reports and weekly reports and new standing orders from Brigade and Army. There was the usual warning from the Chaplain-General to keep an eye on subversive Methodists that Sharpe threw away, and a General Order from Wellington that reminded officers that it was mandatory to remove the hat when the Host was being carried by a priest through a street to a dying man. Do not upset the Spanish was the message of that order and Sharpe noted its receipt and wondered again who the ribbon-merchant was.

He signed his name three dozen times, abandoned the rest of the paper-work, and went out into the spring sunlight to check the picquets and watch the recruits, shipped out from England, fire three rounds of musket fire. He listened to the officer of the day's usual complaint about the ration beef and dodged round the back of the houses to avoid the Portuguese sutler who was looking for his debtors. The sutler sold tobacco, tea, needles, thread, buttons, and the other small necessities of a soldier's life. The South Essex's sutler, who had a small stable of ugly whores, was the richest man with the Battalion.

Sharpe avoided the man. He wondered if the sutler would buy the tent mule, though he knew the man would only pay half value. Sharpe would be lucky to get fifteen pounds from the sutler, less the two pounds he owed and less the five pounds to bribe the storekeeper. Paddock, the clerk, would have to be bribed into silence. Sharpe supposed he would get seven or eight pounds from the deal, enough to keep the Mess happy. He swore. He wished the army was marching and fighting, too busy to worry about such small things as unpaid bills.

The fight at the bridge had been a false alarm. He guessed that it had been meant as a feint, a means to persuade the French that the British were retracing last year's steps and marching on Salamanca and Madrid. Instead the Battalion had force-marched north to where the main part of the British army gathered. The French were guarding the front door into Spain and Wellington was planning to use the back. But let it start soon, Sharpe prayed. He was bored. Instead of fighting he was worrying about money and having to organize a church parade.

The General had ordered that all Battalions that lacked their own chaplain should receive one sermon at least from a priest borrowed from another unit. Today it was the turn of the South Essex and Sharpe, sitting on Captain d'Alembord's spare horse, stared at the ten companies of the South Essex as they faced the man of God. Doubtless they were wondering why, after years free of such occasions, they should suddenly be hectored by a bald, plump man telling them to count their blessings. Sharpe ignored the sermon. He was wondering how to persuade the sutler to buy a mule when the man already had a half dozen to carry his wares.

Then the ribbon-merchant came.

The Reverend Sebastian Whistler was enumerating God's blessings; fresh bread, mothers, newly brewed tea, and such like, when Sharpe saw the eyes of the Battalion look away from the preacher. He looked himself and saw, coming to the field where the church parade was tactfully held away from Spanish Catholic eyes, two Spanish officers and a Spanish priest.

The ribbon-merchant rode ahead of his two companions. He was a young man uniformed so splendidly, so gaudily, that he had earned the nickname given by the British troops to any fine dandy. The young man wore a uniform of pristine white, laced with gold, decorated with a blue silken sash on which shone a silver star. His coat was edged with scarlet, the same colour as his horse's leather bridle. Hanging from his saddle was a scabbard decorated with precious stones.

The Battalion, ignoring the Reverend Sebastian Whistler's injunctions that they should be content with their humble lot and not covet wealth that would only lead them into temptation, watched the superbly uniformed man ride behind the preacher and pause a few paces from Sharpe.

The other two Spaniards reined in fifty yards away. The priest, mounted on a big, fine bay, was dressed in black, a hat over his eyes. The other man, Sharpe saw, was a General, no less. He was a burly, tall Spaniard in gold laced finery who seemed to stare fixedly at the Rifle officer.

The young man in the gorgeous white uniform had a thin, proud face with eyes that looked disdainfully at the Englishman. He waited until the sermon was finished, until the RSM had brought the parade to attention and shouldered its muskets, then spoke in English. 'You're Sharpe?'

Sharpe replied in Spanish. 'Who are you?'

'Are you Sharpe?'

Sharpe knew from the ribbon-merchant's deliberate rudeness that his instinct had been right. He had sensed trouble, but now that it was here he did not fear it. The man spoke with scorn and hatred in his voice, but a man, unlike a formless dread, could be killed. Sharpe turned away from the Spaniard. 'Regimental Sergeant Major!'

'Sir?'

'A general officer is present! General salute!'

'Sir!' RSM MacLaird turned to the parade, filled his lungs, and his shout bellowed over the field. ''Talion! General salute!'

Sharpe watched the muskets fall from the shoulders, check, slam over the bodies, then the right feet went back, the officers' swords swept up, and he turned and smiled at the Spaniard. 'Who are you?'

The Spanish General, Sharpe saw, returned the salute. MacLaird shouted the shoulder arms and turned back to Sharpe. 'Dismiss, sir?'

'Dismiss the parade, Sergeant Major.'

The white uniformed Spaniard spurred his horse forward into Sharpe's line of vision. 'Are you Sharpe?'

Sharpe looked at him. The man's English was good, but Sharpe chose to reply in Spanish. 'I'm the man who'll slit your throat if you don't learn to be polite.' He had spoken softly and he saw his words rewarded by a tiny flicker of fear in the man's face. This officer was covering his nervousness with bravado.

The Spaniard straightened in his saddle. 'My name is Miguel Mendora, Major Mendora.'

'My name is Sharpe.'

Mendora nodded. For a second or two he said nothing, then, with the speed of a scorpion striking, he lashed with his right hand to strike Sharpe a stinging blow about the face.

The blow did not land. Sharpe had fought in every gutter from London to Calcutta and he had seen the blow coming. He had seen it in Mendora's eyes. He swayed back, letting the white-gloved hand go past. He saw the anger in the

49

Spaniard, while inside himself he felt the icy calm that came to him in battle. He smiled. 'I have known piglets with more manhood than you, Mendora.'

Mendora ignored the insult. He had done what he was ordered to do and survived. Now he looked to his right to see the dismissed soldiers straggling towards him. They had seen him try to strike their officer, and their mood was at once excited and belligerent. Mendora looked back to Sharpe. 'That was from my master.'

'Who is?'

Mendora ignored the question. 'You will write a letter of apology to him, a letter that he will use as he sees fit. After that, as you are no gentleman, you will resign your commission.'

Sharpe wanted to laugh. 'Your General is who?'

Major Mendora tossed his head. 'The Marqués de Casares el Grande y Melida Sadaba.'

And suddenly the memory of that flawless beauty that masked the flawed woman flooded into him so that the excitement came searing back. Helene! It was with Helene that he had betrayed Teresa, and he knew that the revenge for that betrayal had come to this field. He wanted to laugh aloud. Helene! Helene of the hair of gold, of the white skin on her black sheets, the woman who had used him in the service of death, but who, he thought, had perhaps loved him a little.

He stared past Mendora at the General. He had thought, from Helene's description, that her husband would be a short, fat man. Fat he was, but it was a burly, muscular fatness. He looked tall. The excitement was still on Sharpe. The Marquesa was the most beautiful creature he had ever seen, a woman he had loved for a season, then lost. He had thought her gone forever, but now here was her husband back from the Spanish colonies with the horns on his head. Sharpe smiled at Mendora. 'How have I offended your master?'

'You know how, *señor*.'

Sharpe laughed. 'You call me *señor*? You've found your manners?'

'Your answer, Major?'

So the Marqués knew he had been cuckolded? But why in God's name pick on Sharpe? There must be a half-Battalion of men he would have to fight to retrieve his honour that had been held so lightly by Helene. Sharpe smiled. 'You will get no letter from me, Major, nor my resignation.'

Mendora had expected the answer. 'You will name me your second, *señor?*'

'I don't have a second.' Sharpe knew that Wellington had forbidden all duels. If he took the risk, that was his foolishness, but he would not risk another man's career. He looked at the Marqués, judging that such a heavy-set man would be slow on his feet. 'I choose swords.'

Mendora smiled. 'My master is a fine swordsman, Major. You will stand more chance with a pistol.'

The soldiers were gawping up at the two mounted officers. They sensed, even though they could not hear the words, that something dramatic took place.

Sharpe smiled. 'If I need advice how to fight, Major, I will seek it from a man.'

Mendora's proud face looked with hatred at the Englishman, but he held his temper. 'There is a cemetery on the southern road, you know it?'

'I can find it.'

'My master will be there at seven this evening. He will not wait long. I hope your courage will be sufficient for death, Major.' He turned his horse, looking back at Sharpe. 'You agree?'

'I agree.' Sharpe let him turn away. 'Major!'

'*Señor?*'

'You have a priest with you?'

The Spaniard nodded. 'You're very observant for an Englishman.'

Sharpe deliberately switched back into English. 'Make sure he knows the prayer for the dead, Spaniard.'

A shout came from the watching men. 'Kill the bugger, Sharpie!'

The shout was taken up, grew louder, and some wit began shouting 'a ring! a ring!', the usual cry when a fight broke out in Battalion lines. Sharpe saw the look of fury cross Mendora's face, then the Spaniard put his spurs to his horse and galloped it at a knot of men who scattered from his path and jeered at his retreating back. The Marqués de Casares el Grande y Melida Sadaba and his attendant priest galloped after him.

Sharpe ignored the shouts of the men about him. He watched the three Spaniards go and he knew, on pain of losing all that he had gained in this army, that he should not go to the cemetery and fight the duel. He would be cashiered; he would be lucky, if he won, not to be accused of murder.

On the other hand, there was a memory of La Marquesa, of her skin against the sheets, her hair on the pillow, her laughter in the shadowed bedroom. There was the thought that the Spanish Major had tried to strike him. There was his boredom, and his inability to refuse a challenge. And, above all, there was the sense of unfinished business, of a guilt that demanded its price, of a guilt that ordered him to pay that price. He shouted at the men for silence and looked through the ragged crowd of soldiers to find the man he wanted. 'Harps!'

Patrick Harper pushed through the men and stared up at Sharpe. 'Sir?'

Sharpe took the sword from his slings. It was a sword that Sergeant Harper had re-fashioned for him while Sharpe lay in Salamanca's hospital. It was a cheap blade, one of many made in Birmingham for Britain's Heavy Cavalry, nearly a yard of heavy steel that was clumsy and ill-balanced except in the hands of a strong man.

Sharpe tossed the sword to the Irishman. 'Put an edge on it for me, Harps. A real edge.'

The men cheered, but Harper held the sword unhappily. He looked up at Sharpe and saw the madness on the dark, scarred face.

Sharpe remembered a face of delicate beauty, the face of a woman whom the Spanish now called the Golden Whore. Sharpe knew he could never possess her, but he could fight for her. He could give up all for her, what else was a warrior to do for a beauty? He smiled. He would fight for a woman who was known to be treacherous, and because, in an obscure way that he did not fully understand, he thought that this challenge, this duel, this risk was some expiation for the guilt that racked him. He would fight.

CHAPTER 4

'You're slow, Sharpe, very slow.' Captain Peter d'Alembord, who had taken Sharpe's place as Captain of the Light Company, had run his slim sword past Sharpe's guard and now the tip quivered an inch beneath the silver whistle holstered on Sharpe's cross belt. D'Alembord, an impressively elegant and slim man, had volunteered, with some diffidence, to 'put Sharpe over the jumps'. He had also scouted the opposition and his news was grim. 'It seems the Marqués is rather good.'

'Good?'

'Took lessons in Paris from Bouillet. They say he could beat him. Still, not to worry. Old Bouillet must have been getting on, perhaps he was slow.' D'Alembord smiled, stepped back, and raised his sword. '*En garde?*'

Sharpe laughed. 'I'll just hack the bugger to bits.'

'Hope springs eternal, my dear Sharpe. Do raise your blade, I'm going to pass it on the left. With some warning you might just be able to stop me. *Engage.*'

The blades rattled, scraped, disengaged, clanged, and suddenly, with eye-defeating speed, d'Alembord had passed Sharpe's guard on the left and his sword was poised again to split Sharpe's trunk. Captain d'Alembord frowned. 'If I darken my hair with lamp black, Sharpe, and paint a scar on my face, I might just pass for you. It's really your best hope of survival.'

'Nonsense. I'll chop the bastard into mincemeat.'

'You seem to forget that he has handled a sword before.'

'He's old, he's fat, and I'll slaughter him.'

'He's not yet fifty,' d'Alembord said mildly, 'and don't be fooled by that waist. The fastest swordsman I ever saw was fatter than a hogshead. Why didn't you choose pistols? Or twelve pounder cannons?'

Sharpe laughed and hefted his big, straight sword. 'This is a lucky blade.'

'One sincerely hopes so. On the other hand, finesse is usually more useful than luck in a duel.'

'You've fought a duel?'

D'Alembord nodded. 'Rather why I'm here, Sharpe. Life got a little difficult.' He said it lightly, though Sharpe could guess the ruin that the duel had meant for d'Alembord. Sharpe had been curious as to why the tall, elegant, foppish man had joined a mere line regiment like the South Essex. D'Alembord, with his spotless lace cuffs, his silver cutlery and crystal wine glasses that were carefully transported by his servant from camp ground to camp ground, would have been more at home in a Guards regiment or a smart cavalry uniform.

Instead he was in the South Essex, seeking obscurity in an unfashionable regiment while the scandal blew itself out in England, and an example to Sharpe of how a duel could blight a career. Sharpe smiled. 'I suppose you killed your man?'

'Didn't mean to. Meant to wing him, but he moved into the blade. Very messy.' He sighed. 'If you would deign to hold that thing more like a sword and less like a cleaving instrument, one might hold out a morsel of hope. Part of the object of the exercise is to defend one's body. Mind you, it's quite possible that he'll faint with horror when he sees it. It's positively mediaeval. It's hardly an instrument for fencing.'

Sharpe smiled. 'I don't fence, d'Alembord. I fight.'

'I'm sure it's vastly unpleasant for your opponent. I shall insist on coming as your second.'

'No seconds.'

D'Alembord shrugged. 'No gentleman fights without a second. I shall come. Besides, I might be able to persuade you not to go through with this.'

Sharpe was sheathing his sword on which Harper had put a wicked cutting edge. 'Not to go through with it?'

D'Alembord pushed open the door of the stable yard where, to the amusement of the officers' servants and grooms, they had been practising. 'You'll be sent home in disgrace, Sharpe. The Peer will have your guts for breakfast tomorrow.'

'Wellington won't know about it.'

D'Alembord looked pityingly on his superior officer. 'Half the bloody army knows, my dear Sharpe. I can't think why you accepted! Is it because the man struck you?'

Sharpe said nothing. The truth was that his pride had been offended, but it was more than that. It was his stubborn superstition that Fate, the soldier's goddess, demanded that he accept. Besides, he did it for the Marquesa.

D'Alembord sighed. 'A woman, I suppose?'

'Yes.'

The Light Company Captain smoothed a wrinkle in his sleeve. 'When I fought my duel, Sharpe, I later discovered that the woman had put us up to it. She was watching, it turned out.'

'What happened?'

The elegant shoulders shrugged. 'After I skewered him she went back to her husband. It was all rather tedious and unnecessary. Just as I'm sure this duel is unnecessary. Do you really insist on this duel, Sharpe?'

'Yes.' Sharpe would not explain, was not even sure he could explain the tangle of guilt, lust, pride and superstition that drove him to folly. Instead he sat and shouted for the Mess servant to bring tea. The servant was a Spaniard who brewed tea foully.

'I'll have rum. Has it occurred to you,' and d'Alembord leaned forward with a small frown of embarrassment on his face, 'that some people are joining this regiment simply because you're in it?'

Sharpe frowned at the words. 'Nonsense.'

'If you insist, my dear Sharpe, but it is true. There's at least two or three young fire-eaters who think you'll lead them to glory, such is your reputation. They'll be very sad if they discover your paths of glory lead but to a lady's bedchamber.' He said the last words with a wry inflexion that hinted to Sharpe that it was a quotation that he ought to know. Yet Sharpe had not learned to read till he was well into his twenties; he had read few books, and none of them poetry.

'Shakespeare?' he guessed.

'Thomas Gray, dear Sharpe. "The paths of glory lead but to the grave." I hope it's not true, for you.' He smiled. What his smile did not tell Sharpe was that Captain d'Alembord, who was an efficient, sensible man, had already tried to make sure that this folly did not lead Sharpe either to a grave or to disgrace. D'Alembord had sent Lieutenant Harry Price on one of his own fastest horses to find Colonel Leroy, fetch him back to Battalion, and order Sharpe not to fight the Spaniard. If Major Richard Sharpe was idiotic enough to will his own destruction by fighting a duel against Wellington's express orders, then Captain d'Alembord would stop him. He prayed that Harry Price would reach Brigade in time, then took his glass of rum from the steward and raised it to Richard Sharpe. 'To your cleaver, Sharpe, may it hew mightily.'

'May it kill the bastard!' Sharpe sipped his tea. 'And I hope it hurts.'

They went on horseback to the cemetery to outdistance the curious troops of the South Essex who wanted to follow and watch their Major skewer the Spanish aristocrat. D'Alembord, a natural horseman, led Sharpe on a circuitous route. Sharpe, once again mounted on one of d'Alembord's spare horses, wondered whether he should accept the younger man's advice and turn back.

He was behaving stupidly and he knew it. He was thirty-six years of age, a Major at last, and he was throwing it all away for mere superstition. He had joined the army twenty years before, straggling with a group of hungry recruits to escape a murder charge. From that inauspicious beginning he had joined that tiny band of men who were promoted from Sergeant into the Officers' Mess. He had done more. Most men promoted from the ranks ended their days as Lieutenants, supervising the Battalion stores or in charge of the drill-square. Most such men, Wellington claimed, ended as drunkards. Yet Sharpe had gone on rising. From Ensign to Lieutenant, Lieutenant to Captain, and Captain to Major, and men looked at him as one of the few, the very very few, who might rise from the ranks to lead a Battalion.

He could lead a Battalion, and he knew it. The war was not over yet. The French might be retreating throughout Europe, but no enemy army had yet pierced the French frontier. Even if this year's campaign was as successful as last year's, and pushed the French back to the Pyrenees, then there would be hard fighting if, unlike last year, the British were to force their way through those cold, high mountains. Fighting in which Lieutenant Colonels would die and leave their Battalions to new commanders.

Yet he risked it all. He twisted his horse through bright-leaved ash trees on a hill top that overlooked their destination, and he thought of the Marquesa, of her eyes on him, and he knew that he risked all for one woman who played with men, and for another who was dead. None of it made sense, he was simply driven by a soldier's superstition that said not to do this thing was to risk oblivion.

D'Alembord curbed his horse at the hill's edge. 'Dear God!' He pulled a cigar from his boot-top, struck a light with his flint and steel, and jerked his head at the valley. 'Looks like a day at the races!'

The cemetery, in Spanish fashion, was a walled enclosure built well away from the town. The hugely thick walls, divided into niches for the dead, were thronged with men. There were the colours of the uniforms of Spain and Britain, the Spanish to the west and north, the British to the south and east, sitting and standing on the wall as though they waited for a bullfight. D'Alembord twisted in his saddle. 'I thought this was supposed to be private!'

'So did I.'

'You can't go through with it, Sharpe!'

'I have to.' He wondered whether another man, an old friend like Major Hogan or Captain Frederickson, could have persuaded him to stop this idiocy. Perhaps, because d'Alembord was a newcomer to the Battalion, and was a

58

man of that easy elegance which Sharpe envied, Sharpe was trying to impress him.

D'Alembord shook his head. 'You're mad, sir.'

'Maybe.'

The Captain blew smoke into the evening sky and pointed with his cigar at the sun which was low in the west. He shrugged, as though accepting the inevitability of the fight. 'You'll face up north and south, but he'll try to manoeuvre you so the sun is in your eyes.'

'I'd thought of that.'

D'Alembord ignored the ungracious acceptance of his advice. 'Assume we'll start with you in the south.'

'Why?'

'Because that's where the British troops are, and that's where you'll go to strip off your jacket.'

Somehow Sharpe had not realised how formal this would be, that he would take off his prized Rifleman's jacket and fight in his grubby shirt. 'So?'

'So he'll be attacking your left, trying to make you go right. He'll feint right and thrust left. He'll be expecting you to do the opposite. If I were you, I'd make your feint your attack.'

Sharpe grinned. He had always intended to take fencing lessons, but somehow there had never seemed to be time. In battle a man did not fence, he fought. The most delicate swordsman on a battlefield was usually overwhelmed by the anger of bayonets and savage steel, yet this evening there would be no madness beneath the battlesmoke, just cold skill and death. 'The last time I fought a skilled swordsman I won.'

'You did?' d'Alembord smiled in mock surprise.

'I got him to run his blade through my thigh. That trapped it and I killed him.'

D'Alembord stared at the Major, whose fame had reached Britain, and saw that he had been told the truth. He shuddered. 'You are mad.'

'It helps when you're fighting. Shall we go down?'

D'Alembord was searching the cemetery and roadway for a sign of Lieutenant Price bringing Colonel Leroy to the duel, but he could see no horsemen. He shrugged inwardly. 'To our fate, sir, to our fate.'

'You don't have to come, d'Alembord.'

'True, sir. I shall say I was a mere innocent misled by you.' He spurred his horse down the pastureland of the hillside.

Sharpe followed. It was a beautiful evening, a promise of summer in the blossoms beneath his horse's hooves and in the warm fragrant air. There was a scattering of high mackerel clouds in the west, each tiny cloud touched with pink as though they were puffs of cannon smoke drifting over a burning field.

The men sitting on the cemetery wall saw the two horsemen coming, recognized the green jacket, and a yell went up as though Sharpe was a prizefighter coming to hammer out a hundred bloody rounds with his naked fists. To his right, coming from the town, he saw a dark coach, windows curtained, and on its doorway, too far away to distinguish the details, was a coat of arms.

He knew that escutcheon. It had been quartered and requartered over the years as the family of Casares el Grande y Melida Sadaba had married more wealth and privilege until now, as the nineteenth century began, the crest was a patchwork of the history of the Spanish nobility. And into that family, marrying the childless widower who had been close to the Spanish throne, had come the golden-haired woman who was a traitor. La Marquesa. She would be pleased, Sharpe thought, to know that two men would face each other with drawn swords on her account.

The cheers were echoed by jeers from the Spaniards as he ducked under the arched gateway of the cemetery. The shadows of the carved graves were long. Flowers wilted in earthenware pots. An old lady, swathed and scarved in black, ignored the unseemly noise that sullied her family's resting place.

D'Alembord led Sharpe to the south side of the burial ground where they dismounted. The British troops, mixed with some of the tough soldiers of the King's German Legion, shouted at Sharpe to kill the dago, to teach the bastard a lesson, and then Sharpe heard the far side of the cemetery erupt into celebration and he turned to see his opponent walk into the burial ground. The Marqués had his long sword tucked in Spanish fashion beneath his arm. The priest was beside him, while Major Mendora walked behind. The old woman knelt to the priest who made the sign of the cross over her then touched her scarved head.

D'Alembord smiled at Sharpe. 'I shall go and make polite conversation. Try and persuade them to back down.'

'They won't.'

'Of course not. Fools never do.' D'Alembord shrugged and walked towards the party of Spaniards. Major Mendora, the Marqués' second, came to meet him.

Sharpe tried to ignore the cheering, the insults, and the shouts. There was no turning back now. In less time than it took the sun to go down, he had changed his life. He had accepted the challenge and nothing would be the same again. Only by walking away now, by refusing to fight, could he save his career. Yet to do that was to lose his pride, and deny fate.

He drew the great sword, and the action provoked another huge cheer from his supporters. Some of the South Essex, he saw, had managed to get to the place and were pushing for room on the wall's broad top. They cheered as he raised the sword and as the sunlight ran up the steel. With this blade, he thought, he had killed La Marquesa's brother. Was he now to kill her husband?

He looked up. The Marqués had taken off his gold encrusted jacket. He flexed his sword, the steel moving like a whip. He was a big man, heavily muscled, strong enough to carry his huge weight lightly. Sharpe had still not seen the man's face. He had often wondered who it was that Helene had married. He remembered that she had often spoken of her husband's piety. That, Sharpe thought, explained the tall priest who leaned in urgent conversation towards the Marqués.

D'Alembord turned and paced the weed-grown path towards Sharpe. 'You'll face north. The fight ends with death or if, in the opinion of the seconds, one man is too badly hurt to continue. Satisfied?'

Sharpe nodded. The evening was warm. He could feel the sweat prickling beneath his shirt. He handed d'Alembord his sword, undid his belt, then peeled off his jacket. He thought suddenly that the fine linen shirt he wore had been a gift from the Marquesa. He took his sword back and held it up to the sun as though some ancient god would bless it and bring him success. 'Now?'

'It seems as good a time as any.'

He walked forward, his tall French boots crunching on the stones of the path. They would fight where the paths crossed at the graveyard's centre, where the Marqués would try to turn Sharpe into the dazzling sun and run him through with the slim, shining blade.

He stopped opposite his enemy. He stared into the blank, expressionless eyes and he tried to imagine Helene marrying this man. There was a weakness in the fleshy, proud face. Sharpe tried to pin it down, tried to analyse this man whose skill he had to beat. Perhaps, he thought, the Marqués was a man born to greatness who had never felt himself worthy. That perhaps was why he prayed so hard and had so much pride.

The Marqués stared at Sharpe, seeing the man whom he believed had insulted his wife and tried to assault her. The Marqués did not just fight for Helene, nor just for his pride, but for the pride of all Spain that had been humbled by needing to make an Englishman its Generalissimo.

The Marqués remembered what the Inquisitor, Father Hacha, had said about this man. Fast, but unskilled. Sharpe, the Marqués knew, would try to kill him as if he was an ox. He twitched the fine sword in his hand. It was odd, he thought, that an Inquisitor should carry Helene's letter. He pushed the thought away.

'You are ready, my Lord?' Mendora called.

The Marqués' face gave the smallest twitch. He was ready.

'Major Sharpe?'

'Yes.'

Major Mendora flexed his sword once so that the steel hissed in the air. The Inquisitor stood with a doctor beside the Marqués' coach. D'Alembord looked hopefully towards the cemetery entrance, but it was empty. He felt the hopelessness of this idiocy, and then Mendora called them forward. 'Your swords, gentlemen?'

Sharpe's boots grated on the gravel. If he got into real trouble, he thought, then he could pretend to fall down, scoop up a handful of the stones, and hurl them to blind the big man who came cautiously forward. What had d'Alembord said? He would feint to the right and go left? Or was it the other way round?

He raised his big, straight sword and it looked dull beside the slim, polished blade that came beside it. The swords touched. Sharpe wondered if he detected a quiver in the other man's grip, but no, the blades rested quietly as Mendora drew his own sword, held it beneath the raised blades, then swept his weapon up to part the two swords and the duel had begun.

Neither man moved.

They watched each other, waiting. Sharpe's urge was to shout, as he shouted on a battlefield to frighten his opponents, but he felt cowed by the formality of this setting. He was fighting a duel against an aristocrat and he felt that he must behave as they expected him to behave. This was not like battle. This was so cold-blooded, so ritualistic, and it seemed hard to believe that in this warm evening air a man must fall to bleed his life onto the gravel.

The Marqués' sword came slowly down, reached out, touched Sharpe's blade, then flickered in bright, quick motion, and Sharpe took two steps back.

The Marqués still watched him. He had done no more than test Sharpe's speed. He would test his skill next.

Sharpe tried to shake the odd lethargy away. It seemed impossible that this was real, that death waited here. He saw the Marqués come forward again, his heavy tread no clue to the speed that Sharpe had already seen, and Sharpe went forward too, his sword reaching, and the Marqués stepped back.

The troops jeered. They wanted blood, they wanted a furious mill with their champion standing over the ripped corpse of the other man.

The Marqués tried to oblige. He came forward with surprising speed, his blade flickering past Sharpe's guard, looping beneath the heavy cavalry sword and lunging to Sharpe's right.

Sharpe countered desperately, knowing that the speed had beaten him, but with a luck he did not deserve he felt the Marqués' blade-tip lodge in the tassel hole of his sword's hilt. It seemed to stick there and Sharpe wrenched his weapon, forcing it towards the Marqués, hoping to break the man's slim blade, but the Marqués turned, drew his sword away, and the cheers of the spectators were louder. They had mistaken Sharpe's desperate counters as a violent attack.

The sun was in Sharpe's eyes. Fluently, easily, the Marqués had turned him.

The Marqués smiled. He had the speed and the skill of this Englishman, and all that mattered now was to choose the manner of Sharpe's death.

Sharpe seemed to know it, for he attacked suddenly, lunging at the big man, using all his own speed, but his blade never struck home. It rang against the slimmer blade, scraped, flashed sunlight into the spectators' eyes, and though the Marqués went back on quick feet, he was having no trouble in avoiding the attacks. Only once, when Sharpe pressed close and tried to ram his sword into the Marqués' eyes, did the Spaniard twist desperately aside and lose his composure. He regained it at once, elegantly parrying the next thrust, turning Sharpe's blade and counter-attacking from his back foot.

The counter-attack was quick as a hawk, a slashing stab of steel as the Marqués went under his guard, the point rose, and Sharpe swept his enemy's blade aside, his hand providentially moving in the right direction, but he was regretting he ever chose swords because the Marqués was a fencer of distinction, and Sharpe lunged again, hit nothing, and he saw the smile on the Marqués' face as the aristocrat coolly parried the attack.

The smile was a mistake.

God damn the aristocracy, and God damn good manners, this was a fight to the death, and Sharpe growled at the man, cursed, and he felt the anger come on him, an anger that always in battle seemed to manifest itself as cold deliberation. It was as if time slowed, as if he could see twice as clearly, and suddenly he knew that if he was to win this fight them he must attack as he had always attacked. He had learned to fight in the gutter and that was where he must take this big, smiling aristocrat who thought he had Sharpe beaten.

The Marqués came forward, his blade seeking to take Sharpe's sword one way so that he could slide the steel beneath the Englishman's guard and finish him.

'She calls you a pig, Spaniard.' Sharpe saw the flicker of surprise in the Marqués' face, heard the hiss of disapproval from Mendora. 'A fat pig, out of breath, son of a sow, porkbrain.' Sharpe laughed. His sword was down. He was inviting the attack, goading the man.

Captain d'Alembord frowned. It was hardly decent manners, but he sensed something more. Sharpe was now the master here. The Marqués thought he had the Rifleman beaten, but all he had done was to make the Rifleman fight. This no longer looked like a duel to d'Alembord; it looked like a brawl leading to slaughter.

The Marqués wanted to kill. He did not understand why the Englishman's guard was down. He tried to ignore the insults, but they raked at his pride.

'Come on, pig! Come on!' Sharpe stepped to one side, away from the sun, and the Marqués saw the Englishman lose his balance as his boot struck a large stone in the path. He saw the alarm on Sharpe's face as he flailed his sword arm to stay upright and the Marqués stamped his right foot forward, shouted in triumph, and the sword was piercing at Sharpe.

Who had known that the pretence of losing his balance would invite the straight lunge and who beat the sword aside with a shout that sounded in every part of the cemetery. He brought up his left knee, shouted again as the

Marqués squealed, and punched the heavy guard forward so that the steel thumped into the Spaniard's breastbone, threw him backwards, and the next scything blow of the sword ripped the Marqués' blade clean from his hand and Sharpe, the battle anger seething in him, brought the huge, heavy sword back for the killing blow. The shot sounded.

The Marqués knew that death was in the bright, sun blazing steel. He had never faced a force like this, a sheer animal force that snarled at him and he shook his head and wondered why the great blade did not come. For a second, as he felt his legs shaking, there was the wild hope that the Englishman was going to let him pick up his sword that had been forced out of his hand when the cavalry blade had struck the slimmer sword's ornate guard.

Then he saw the Englishman lower his sword. Saw him step back and suddenly heard the rush of hooves. The cheers about the cemetery wall had faded. The echo of the pistol shot died into silence.

Four horsemen had ducked under the gate. Now they rode towards the place where the paths crossed in the cemetery's centre. In the lead was Colonel Thomas Leroy, the inevitable cigar clenched in his mouth. In his hand was a smoking pistol. Behind him rode two Provosts, the army's policemen, and a Spanish officer.

'Major Sharpe!' Leroy's voice was harsh.

'Sir?'

'You choose an odd place to practice your sword arm.' Leroy swung from his horse and tossed the reins to d'Alembord. His ravaged, burned face made the Marqués frown with distaste. Leroy jerked his head. 'Come with me, Sharpe.'

Sharpe hesitated, but Leroy ordered it again, his voice more savage still, and Sharpe, his sword in his hand, followed his Colonel up the northern path between the intricate gravestones. 'You are a god-damned bloody fool, Sharpe.'

'Yes, sir.'

'Christ in his benighted bloody heaven!' The American seemed lost for words. He took the cigar from his lips, spat a speck of leaf onto the gravel, and stared at his Major. 'I've seen an eight year old with more damned sense! What in hell's name are you doing here?'

'A matter of honour, sir.'

'Honour!' The scarred face twisted in rage. 'Don't talk of honour, Sharpe. You're here because you're a fool!' He looked left. 'Captain d'Alembord?'

'Sir?'

'You'll oblige me by bringing your horses.'

Sharpe frowned. 'Sir!'

Leroy swung back on him, the cigar jabbed at Sharpe's face. 'Quiet! You're under orders!' Leroy saw that the Rifleman was about to protest and he jerked his head at the Provosts behind him. 'And if you disobey orders, Sharpe, I'll have you arrested. Is that clear?'

'Yes, sir.'

'Fetch your jacket. You're going.' Leroy shook his head in frustrated bitterness. 'I can't leave the god-damned Battalion for one day!'

'*Señor!*' It was Major Mendora, a sneer on his face, coming on catlike feet towards Leroy and Sharpe. 'There is a delay?'

Leroy turned to the white-uniformed man, and Sharpe saw the Spaniard recoil from the bubbled, stretched scar tissue. Leroy was trying to govern his anger. 'Major?'

'Major Sharpe cannot fight? He is afraid, perhaps?'

Leroy pushed Sharpe aside. He stared with his ravaged face at Mendora. 'Listen, you son of a whore, you prinked-up bastard. There was no duel, there is no duel, there never was a duel! This was a friendly piece of sword practice! Do you understand me?'

Mendora understood. In the face of the American's rage he simply nodded. He said nothing as Leroy tartly ordered Sharpe to follow him.

The Spanish soliders jeered as Sharpe left. They accused him of cowardice, of lacking manhood, of being afraid to fight. It was gall to Sharpe, a shame he had to endure until Leroy had led him out of earshot. Leroy scowled at him. 'Never again, Sharpe, understand?'

'Yes, sir.'

'Remember you owe me a career now.' Leroy was grim. 'One more god-damn mistake and I'll have you shipped back to god-damn England. You understand?'

'Yes, sir.'

'This is my Battalion now, Sharpe. It is going to be good. You're going to help me make it good.'

'Yes, sir.'

'And thank God Colonel Alvarez was at Brigade. He'll talk sense into that stupid fool. Nothing happened, you understand?'

'Yes, sir.'

The American seemed unimpressed by Sharpe's contriteness. 'Christ! If the Peer learned about this he'd tear you into pieces. You god-damn deserve it. You're a fool.'

'Yes, sir.'

'Now go and get drunk. Sergeant Harper says his woman's cooked you a meal. I don't want to see your ugly face till tomorrow.'

'No, sir.'

Chastened, embarrassed, humiliated by the jeers of his enemies, but his career safe, Sharpe watched Leroy ride away. The Provosts, not needed. followed the Colonel.

D'Alembord stayed with Sharpe. 'It seems our Colonel has a knack of turning up at the right time.'

Sharpe, humiliated by the tongue-lashing, nodded.

D'Alembord smiled. 'You were right.'

'Right?'

'You were about to hack the bugger into bits.'

Sharpe smiled bitterly. 'The next time I will.'

D'Alembord sighed. 'With the greatest respect, sir, don't be a god-damned idiot. You've survived a duel with your career intact. Be content.'

'I'm dishonoured.'

D'Alembord mocked him with laughter. 'Honour!' He led Sharpe off the road, up towards the ash trees on the hill. 'Honour, my dear Sharpe, is just a word behind which we hide our sins. It disappears, I find, whenever a lady's bedroom door opens.' He smiled at his Major, remembering the awesome moment when he had seen Sharpe stop trying to fence and begin to fight. He had understood then, even better than at the bridge where they had waited without ammunition, why this man was a soldier's soldier. 'Do you think if I bring some wine I might share your dinner?'

'I'm sure Harps will be pleased.'

'He'd better be, it's good wine. We can drink to your restored career in it.'

Sharpe followed him. The anger had gone, he felt foolish. Leroy was right; his job was to make the South Essex into the best it could be, and never had the time been more propitious. The Battalion had a good Colonel, and the new officers, like d'Alembord, promised well. He felt suddenly as though a hanging judge had reprieved him. He had escaped his own foolishness and he rode towards a campaign, a summer, and a future. The madness was gone, the doom lifted, and he was alive.

CHAPTER 5

That night, behind thick curtains, in a dark-panelled room lit by heavy candles that threw their flickering light on a crucifix of gold, the Marqués de Casares el Grande y Melida Sadaba prayed.

He had wondered why the Inquisitor had come to him bringing his wife's letter, curious why the letter should have so eminent a carrier, but now he understood. The Marqués' lips moved, his fingers shuffled the beads on their string, his eyes stared at the crucifix until the small, gold image seemed to shift and swim before him. He shook his head to clear his vision. 'What will happen to the Englishman?'

'Wellington will send him home.' The Inquisitor had a voice deep as the pit. 'Wellington needs the Spanish alliance.'

The Marqués groaned as he stood up from his knees. 'I should have killed him.'

'Your honour is intact. It was he who fled, not you.'

The Marqués turned to look at Father Hacha. The Inquisitor was all that a priest should be in the Marqués' estimation; he was a tall, strong man, fierce faced and grim, a warrior of God who knew that pity was a luxury in the fight against evil. The Marqués, who yearned to have the toughness he saw in the Inquisitor, frowned. 'I don't understand what made the man do it! To insult her!'

'He's English, he's from the gutter, he's heathen.'

'I should have killed him.'

'God will do it.'

The Marqués sat opposite the Inquisitor. They were in the Marqués' bedroom, taken for the night from the mayor of this small town. The candlelight shuddered on the red hangings of the bed, on the picture of the crucified Lord, and on the grim, axe-faced man of the Spanish Inquisition. The Marqués stared at the dark eyes. 'Helena will come to me?' He used the Spanish form of his wife's name.

The Inquisitor nodded. 'She must do penance, of course.'

'Of course.' The Marqués felt the stirring within him. On the table beside the bed there stood her portrait, the portrait that had travelled with him to the Banda Oriental and showed her pure skin, wide eyes, and delicate face. She had spied for the French, and that fact could not be hidden from the Marqués, but the Inquisitor had assured him that her spying was merely a woman's weakness.

'She missed you, my Lord, she was tempted by loneliness and unhappiness. She must do public penance.'

'And she will do it?'

'She is eager to be in your good graces, my Lord.'

The Marqués nodded. He had had a frank, embarrassingly frank, discussion with his grim Inquisitor. Yes, the priest had said, there were rumours about the Marquesa, but what woman did not attract rumours? And was there truth in the rumours? The priest had shaken his head. There was none.

Perhaps because Father Hacha had freely admitted that his wife had spied for the country of her birth, the Marqués believed the lie about her faithfulness. He wanted to believe it. He knew, guiltily and secretly, that it had been a fault to marry her, but what man would not have wanted to marry the frail, lovely girl? He knew he had married out of lust, out of sinfulness, and he had confessed the sin a hundred hundred times. Now, it seemed, his prayers were answered and she wanted his forgiveness and his love. He would give both to her.

He would give them because the priest had laid before him this night a glittering image of Spain's future, and a future, the Inquisitor had said, in which the Marqués would play an eminent, a vital part. 'You were always close to the old King, my Lord.'

'True.'

'His son needs you.'

Spain, the Marqués had heard, needed him. This war

against the French, the Inquisitor had said, was a mistake. True, it had been started by the French, but they now saw that their best interests lay in peace. They wanted to take their embattled armies from Spain, and only one obstacle lay before them; the British alliance.

The Inquisitor had spoken of the secret treaty. He had done it because he wanted this man's trust. The Marqués had listened. At first he had felt offence at the secret manouevering that would end with a broken promise to Britain, but as he listened more he felt the glory and excitement grow in him.

Spain, the Inquisitor had said, had been given its empire by God. That empire was the reward for defeating the Muslims in Europe. Now, because of the war against France, the empire was slipping away. The Spanish, the priest said, had a duty to their God to keep the empire. If there was peace with France then the army could go abroad as God's warriors. The secret treaty that was being forged at Valençay would give Spain peace at home and glory abroad.

That appealed to the Marqués. He had no love for the government that ruled that part of Spain not held by the French. It was, in his view, a liberal, dangerous government that would try to introduce a parliament and limit the royal power. Spain should be ruled by the King and the Church in consort, not by a shouting rabble of upstart ambition.

There was more. As he sat and listened to the Inquisitor, the Marqués heard what the Junta in Cadiz now proposed. The liberals, who ruled the country in King Ferdinand VII's absence, were trying to dismantle the power of the Church in Spain.

'Surely not!'

In answer the Inquisitor had taken from his pocket and handed to the Marqués a copy of a new law, a law that had, within the last two months, declared that the Spanish Inquisition was abolished.

It still existed in French-held Spain, that body from the protestant nightmares of the sixteenth century; the Inquisition that preached God's love with the fires of agony and the blades of torture. Now, bereft of their racks and burning irons, they were a moral police force to the Spanish people, granting licences of marriage to those who could prove they were of pure, Christrian blood, watching always those who were suspected of being Moors or Jews. They were the spies of God, the secret police of heaven, and their power was threatened. The Junta had dissolved them.

King Ferdinand VII, whose love of women was matched by his fear of God, did not agree that the Inquisition should be abolished. They might spy for God, but their reports came to the King of Spain, and no kingdom on earth had a more efficient body of informers than did the Spanish king with his loyal Inquisitors.

'If we restore His Majesty,' the Inquisitor had said, 'then we preserve our Church. Peace with France, my Lord, is Spain's only hope.'

With which sentiments the Marqués de Casares el Grande y Melida Sadaba agreed wholeheartedly. 'So what do you want of me?'

The Inquisitor told his lie smoothly. 'I want you to gain support among your friends, among the officers of the army, among your admirers, my Lord.' He shrugged. 'When the time comes, my Lord, the peasants will not be overjoyed.'

'They hate the French.'

'But they love their King. They need firm leadership, strong example, from Church and nobles. From you and I, my Lord.'

The Marqués nodded. The future was suddenly golden. His wife, whom he had married for lust, was willing to do penance. She would come back to him chastened and humbled, loving and lòyal, to be the helpmate of a man who would assist his king steer Spain into a brilliant, holy future. And to help the Marqués, to steer him, comfort him, support him, there would be this grim, tough Inquisitor with his subtle mind and sharp purpose. Suddenly the events of the day, the abortive duel and the Marqués' escape from death, seemed trivial compared to that future.

The Inquisitor smiled. 'You did us all a service today, my Lord.'

'A service?'

Father Hacha stood. 'The Englishman backed down from you. You are a hero to the army, you beat the Englishman in their sight. Where you lead, my Lord, others will now follow.'

The Marqués saw himself leading the army away from the British alliance. He saw himself welcoming King Ferdinand VII at the gates of Spain, he saw glory.

He bowed his head for the blessing of the Inquisitor who had been offered, and who had accepted, the bedroom next door. The hands of the priest were firm on the Marqués' head.

The Inquisitor, who had told lies all night, pronounced the blessing. He meant the words he spoke. He wished God to bless this man who had married so disastrously, and who was now a pawn in the struggle to defend the Inquisition. He blessed the Marqués in the name of the Father, and of the Son, and of the Holy Ghost, and he hoped that his Lordship would sleep well.

'Thank you, father.'

'I bid you a good night, my Lord.'

In his own room the Inquisitor knelt and prayed God's forgiveness for the lies he had told and the deception he had practised. God would understand. What Father Hacha did this night he did to preserve God's church. There was no more noble purpose. He rose from his knees, opened his missal, and settled down to wait for the witching hour when his brother, who was thought to be the Inquisitor's servant, would play his part to restore the glory of God's kingdom of Spain.

The Marqués' private chaplain was forced to be up every morning at half past four to waken his master at five o'clock. Then, until half past six, the two men would share private devotions. After that the Marqués would take breakfast, then go to his first Mass of the day. The chaplain's dream of heaven was a place where no one stirred from their bed until midday. He yawned.

He kissed his scapular, then draped it about his neck. He

wondered if the Inquisitor would join them this morning, and hoped not. Father Tomas Hacha rather frightened the Marqués' private chaplain; there was too much force in the man. Besides, the Inquisition was frightening anyway, its power secret and pervasive, its judgments harsh. The chaplain preferred a milder religion.

The servants who slept outside their master's room jerked awake as the chaplain's footsteps sounded on the stairs. One of them sat up, rubbing his cheek. 'Morning, father.'

'Good morning, my son.' The chaplain opened one of the shutters on the landing and saw the grey dawn spreading up from the dark hills. 'It's going to be a fine day!'

Dogs barked in the town. Somewhere a cockerel crowed. The chaplain could see, dim in the shadows of the street, the shapes of the British guns. The Spanish and British armies collected here, waiting to plunge into French-held Spain. He was glad that it was none of his business. Fighting the rebels in the Banda Oriental north of the River Plate had been bad enough, but the thought of those great guns bellowing at each other was terrifying. He turned to the Marqués' room and knocked softly on the door. He smiled at the servants. 'A quiet night?'

'Very quiet, father.'

He knocked again. One of the servants unbuttoned himself above the chamberpot on the landing's corner. 'He was up late, father. He's probably still asleep.'

'Late?'

'Father Hacha was with him.' The servant yawned as he pissed. 'Say a prayer for me, father.'

The chaplain smiled, then pushed the door open. It was dark in the room, all light blocked out by the great velvet hangings over the windows. 'My Lord?'

There was no answer from behind the curtained bed. The chaplain closed the door quietly behind him then groped uncertainly through the strange, heavy furniture until he reached the window. He reflected how wealthy these provincial merchants were who could afford such furnishings, then pulled the curtain back, flooding the room with a sickly grey light.

'My Lord? It's I, Father Pello.'

Still no sound. The Marqués' uniform was carefully hung on a cupboard door, his boots, stretchers inside, parked carefully beneath. The chaplain pulled back the curtains of the bed. 'My Lord?'

His first thought was that the Marqués was sleeping on a pillow of red velvet. His second thought was relief. There would be no prayers this morning. He could go to the kitchen and have a leisurely breakfast.

Then he vomited.

The Marqués was dead. His throat had been cut so that the blood had soaked the linen pillowcase and sheets. His head was tilted back, his eyes staring sightless at the headboard. One hand hung over the side of the bed.

The chaplain tried to call out, but no sound came. He tried to move, but his feet seemed stuck to the carpeted floor.

The vomit stained his scapular. Some of it dribbled down the dead man's plump hand. The Marqués seemed to have two mouths, one wide and red, the other prim and pale.

The chaplain called out again, and this time his voice, thickened by the vomit in his throat, came out as a terrible strangled cry. 'Guards!'

The servants came in, but to no avail. The body was cold, the blood on the linen caked hard. Major Mendora, the General's aide, came in with drawn sword, followed by the Inquisitor in his night-robe. Even the Inquisitor's strong face paled at the carnage on the bed. The Marqués of Casares el Grande y Melida Sadaba had been killed in his sleep, his throat opened, and his soul sent to the judgment of heaven where, the Inquisitor prayed aloud in his dreadful, deep voice, the soul of his murderer would soon follow for awful and condign punishment.

They came for Major Richard Sharpe at eight on the same morning. The Battalion was paraded, the companies already marching off to their tasks.

Richard Sharpe, as so often in the early morning, was in a bad mood. His mouth had the thick sourness of too much wine the night before. He was looking forward to a second breakfast and feeling only mildly guilty that his new rank gave him the freedom for such luxuries. He had scrounged some eggs from Isabella, there was a flitch of bacon that belonged to the Mess, and Sharpe could almost taste the meal already.

For once, this morning, he would not have three mens' work to do. Colonel Leroy was taking half of the companies on a long march, the others were detailed to help drag the great pontoon bridges up to the high road, ready for the march into French territory. He could, he thought sourly, catch up on his paperwork. He remembered that he must try to sell one of the new mules to the sutler, though whether that sly, wealthy man would want to buy one of the tubed, half-winded animals that had turned up from Brigade was another matter. Perhaps the sutler would buy it for its dead-weight. Sharpe turned to shout for the Battalion clerk, but the shout never sounded. Instead he saw the Provosts.

The Provosts were led, strangely, by Major Michael Hogan. He was no policeman. He was Wellington's chief of intelligence and Sharpe's good friend. He was a middle-aged Irishman whose face was normally humorous and shrewd, but who this morning looked grim as the plague.

He reined in by Sharpe. Hogan led a spare horse. His voice was bleak, unnatural, forced. 'I must ask for your sword, Richard.'

Sharpe's smile, which had greeted his friend, changed to a puzzlement. 'My sword?'

Hogan sighed. He had volunteered for this, not because he wanted to do it, but because it was a friend's duty. It was a duty, he knew, that would become grimmer as this bad day went on. 'Your sword, Major Sharpe. You are under close arrest.'

Sharpe wanted to laugh. The words were not sinking in. 'I'm what?'

'You're under arrest, Richard. As much as anything else for your own safety.'

'My safety?'

'The whole Spanish army is after your blood.' Hogan held out his hand. 'Your sword, Major, if you please.' Behind Hogan the Provosts stirred on their horses.

'What am I charged with?' Suddenly Sharpe's voice was bleak, though he was already obediently unbuckling his sword belt.

Hogan's voice was equally bleak. 'You are charged with murder.'

Sharpe stopped unbuckling the belt. He stared up at the small Major. 'Murder?'

'Your sword.'

Slowly, as if it was a dream, Sharpe took the sword from his waist. 'Murder? Who?'

Hogan leaned down and took Sharpe's sword. He wrapped the slings and belt about the metal scabbard. 'The Marqués de Casares el Grande y Melida Sadaba.' He watched Sharpe's face, reading his friend's innocence, but knowing just how hopeless things were. 'There are witnesses.'

'They're lying!'

'Mount up, Richard.' He gestured at the spare horse. The Provosts, blank faced men in red jackets and black hats, stared with hostility at the Rifleman. They carried short carbines in their saddle holsters. Hogan turned his horse. 'The Spanish say you did it. They're out for your blood. If I don't get you under lock and key they'll be dragging you to the nearest tree. Where's your kit?'

'In my billet.'

'Which house?'

Sharpe told him, and Hogan detailed two of the Provosts to fetch the Rifleman's belongings. 'Catch us up!'

Hogan led him away, surrounded by Provosts, and Sharpe rode towards more trouble then he would have dreamed possible. He was accused of murder, and he was led, in the bright sunlight of a new morning, towards a prison cell, a trial and whatever then might follow.

78

CHAPTER 6

They rode for an hour, threading the valleys towards the army's headquarters. Major Hogan, out of embarrassment and awkwardness, kept Provosts between himself and Sharpe.

At the town, which they entered by back streets, Sharpe was taken to the house where Wellington himself was quartered. He dismounted, was led to the stable yard, and locked into a small, bare room without windows. It had a stone flagged floor that, like the wall above, was stained with blood. Above the bloodstains on the limewashed wall were large rusty nails. Sharpe presumed that shot hares or rabbits had been hung there, but the conjunction of rusty nails and blood somehow took on a more sinister aspect. The only light came from above and below the ill-fitting door. There was a table, two chairs, and an insidious smell of horse urine.

The door was locked. Beyond it Sharpe could hear the boots of his guard in the stable yard. He could hear, too, the homely sounds of pails clanking, water washing down stone, and horses moving in their stalls. He sat, put his heels on the table, and waited.

Hogan had ridden fast. Once at this house he had made a brief farewell, offered no words of hope, then left Sharpe alone. Murder. Sharpe knew the penalty for that well enough, but it seemed unreal. The Marqués dead? Nothing made sense. If he had been arrested for attempting to fight a duel, he could have understood it. He could have endured one of Wellington's cold tongue lashings, but this predicament made no sense. He waited.

The sunlight that came beneath the lintel moved about the floor as the morning wore on. He smelt the burning tobacco of his sentry's pipe. He heard men laugh in the stables. The bell of the village church struck eleven and then there came the scrape of the bolt in the door and Sharpe took his heels from the table and stood upright.

A lieutenant in the blue jacket of a cavalry regiment came into the room. He blinked as his eyes went from the bright sunshine into the makeshift cell's shadow, and then he smiled nervously as he put a bundle of papers onto the table. 'Major Sharpe?'

'Yes.' Somehow the young man looked familiar.

'It's Trumper-Jones, sir, Lieutenant Michael Trumper-Jones?'

The boy expected Sharpe to recognise him. Sharpe remembered there had been a cavalry Colonel called Trumper-Jones who had lost an arm and an eye at Rolica. 'Did I meet your father?'

'I don't know, sir.' Trumper-Jones took off his hat and smiled. 'We met last week.'

'Last week?'

'At the battle, sir?'

'Battle? Oh.' Sharpe remembered. 'You're an aide-de-camp to General Preston?'

'Yes, sir.' Trumper-Jones put some papers on the table. 'And your defending officer.'

'My what?' Sharpe growled it, making Trumper-Jones step backwards towards the door which had been closed by the guard.

'I'm your defence, sir.'

Sharpe sat down. He stared at the frightened young man who looked as if he was scarce out of school. He beckoned at the vacant chair. 'Sit down, Trumper-Jones, for God's sake. Defend me from what?' He knew, but he wanted to hear it again.

Trumper-Jones came nervously forward. He put his hat on the table beside his papers and pushed a lock of light brown hair from his forehead. He cleared his throat. 'You're charged with the murder of the Spanish General Casares, the Marqués de . . .'

'I know who the hell he is.' Sharpe watched as

Trumper-Jones fidgeted with his papers. 'Is there a cup of tea in this damned place?'

The question only made Trumper-Jones more nervous. 'There's not much time, sir.'

'Time?'

'The General Court-Martial is convened for half past noon, sir. Today.' He added lamely.

'Jesus Christ!' Sharpe shouted the words. Trumper-Jones said nothing. He was nervous of the scarred Rifleman who now leaned his elbows on the table. 'Are you a lawyer, Trumper-Jones?'

'No, sir.'

'You've done this before?'

'No, sir.' He smiled weakly. 'I've only been out here a month.'

'Where's Major Hogan?'

'Don't know, sir.'

'So how do you plan to prove my innocence, Trumper-Jones?'

The young man pushed the lick of hair away from his forehead. He had a voice like d'Alembord's, but without the easy confidence. He smiled nervously. 'I fear it looks bleak, sir.'

'Tell me.'

Trumper-Jones seemed happier now that he could read from his papers. 'It seems, sir, that you are acquainted with the Marquesa de Casares el Grande . . .'

'True.'

'And that you threatened her, sir.' Trumper-Jones said it timidly.

'I did what?'

Trumper-Jones nearly jumped out of his chair. 'You threatened her . . .' He blushed. 'Well, you threatened her, sir.'

'I did no such god-damn thing!'

Trumper-Jones swallowed, cleared his throat, and gestured with a piece of paper. 'There is a letter, sir, from her Ladyship to her husband, and it says . . .'

Sharpe leaned back. 'Spare me, Lieutenant. I know the

Marquesa. Let's accept they have a letter. Go on.' So she had provoked the duel. D'Alembord had hinted at it, Sharpe had refused to believe it, but he supposed it made sense. Yet he found it hard to accept that a woman who had loved him could so easily betray him.

Trumper-Jones pushed the hair back again. 'The letter provoked a duel, sir, that you were prevented from finishing?'

'True.' It all sounded so hopeless.

'And because you were prevented from fighting, sir, the prosecution is alleging that you went to the General's quarters last night and murdered him.'

'Not true.'

'They have a witness, sir.'

'Really?' Sharpe said the word scornfully. 'Who?'

The papers rustled. 'A Captain Morillos, sir, of the Princessa Regiment. He commanded the guard on General Casares' house last night and he saw a British Rifle officer leave the house at three in the morning. The officer, he says, wore a straight sword.'

That was a nice touch, Sharpe thought. Rifle officers were issued with curved cavalry sabres, and only Sharpe wore a straight sword. He shook his head. 'And why didn't Captain Morillos stop this man?'

'He was ordered only to stop people from going into the house, sir, not from leaving it.'

'Go on.'

Trumper-Jones shrugged. 'That's it, sir. I thought, sir . . .' He stopped, nervous again.

'Well?'

'I thought, sir, that if we presented your record to the court, sir, that they must be lenient. The Eagle, sir, the Forlorn Hope at Badajoz . . .' His voice tailed away.

Sharpe smiled. 'You want me to plead guilty and trust that they won't shoot a hero, is that it?'

'Hang, sir.' Trumper-Jones blushed. 'You'll be stripped of your commission and given a criminal's death. Only, of course, if they . . .'

'If they find me guilty?'

'Yes, sir.'

Sharpe stared at the rusty nails on the wall. Of course this wasn't happening. At any moment he would wake up and feel an extraordinary relief that it was only a dream. He would laugh at it, tell Sergeant Harper that he had dreamt of being court-martialled!

Except it was not a dream. He had been abandoned to this and he could understand why. Understanding did not lessen the bitterness. A Spanish General had been murdered, and Sharpe knew well enough the fragile bond between the British and the Spanish. Spanish pride was upset that they needed the British to drive the invader from their soil, and their gratitude was made prickly by that pride. Wellington, in the wake of this blow to the alliance, was moving swiftly to offer the Spaniards a sacrifice.

Yet someone else was moving swiftly, someone who wanted Sharpe dead, and he looked at the nervous Trumper-Jones and, in a voice that sounded drained and tired, he asked him to read out his copy of La Marquesa's letter.

None of it was true, of course, but the letter existed as a damning piece of evidence. Sharpe looked at the nervous young man. 'I want paper, ink and a pen.'

'But, sir ...'

'Fetch them!'

He wrote for an hour, ignoring Lieutenant Trumper-Jones, writing to Major Hogan his own version of the night's events, describing the lies in La Marquesa's letter, warning his friend that there was a plot of some kind, he knew not what. Even if Sharpe was dead then Hogan could not say he had not been warned. Yet what was the plot? What purpose did Sharpe's death serve? He could understand the murder of the Marqués because such a murder would weaken a fragile alliance, but he saw no purpose in a plot that had his own death as its ending, nor did he believe that the Marquesa would seek his death.

He folded the letter. 'That's to go to Major Hogan.'

'Yes, sir.'

Then came the boots in the yard, the scrape of the bolt, and the sudden wash of bright sunlight as the door was opened. A Sergeant, heading Sharpe's escort, grinned at the Rifleman. 'Good luck, sir.'

Sharpe smiled, but said nothing. Luck, he thought had deserted him. He had had none since that day in the Gateway of God when Teresa died, and he remembered how, on the night before that death, he had been cursed by Obadiah Hakeswill. He had been cursed, his name buried on a stone.

Sergeant Hakeswill, who had recruited Sharpe into the army, who had succeeded in having Sharpe flogged so that the scars still marred his back, and who had become Sharpe's bitterest enemy, was dead, shot by Sharpe, and in his grave. Sharpe wondered how many hours would pass before he, too, was rolled into a shallow trench and had the dry soil of Spain shovelled onto his corpse. He followed the Sergeant to his fate.

A Major Vaughn, Welsh and suave, was the prosecuting officer. His tone, silky and musical, managed to imbue his words with a sincere regret that he had, as he said, this unfortunate duty to prosecute an officer so famed for his gallantry.

The British officers behind the table did not look at Sharpe. General Sir Edward Pakenham, the Adjutant General and Wellington's brother-in-law, presided. Three Spanish officers, their faces like masks stared at the prisoner.

Major Vaughn, despite his regrets, offered the court a swift and damning version of the night's events. Major Sharpe had been prevented from defending his honour in a duel. That failure rankled. He had gone, by night, and murdered the husband of a woman whom he had pursued vilely. He much regretted bringing in this evidence, but he had no choice, and he produced the letter written and sealed by the Marquesa.

Ned Pakenham lifted the letter as though it was plague-ridden and handed it back to Vaughn. The letter was read into the records of the Court-Martial.

Vaughn brought the letter to Sharpe. 'You recognise the

handwriting, Major? Do remember you are under oath.'

Sharpe looked up into the plump, clever face. 'La Marquesa is a Frenchwoman, a spy, and . . .'

'Thank you, Major, I only asked if you recognised the handwriting. Do you?'

He did, but he saw no sense in making things grimmer for himself than they already were. 'I can't tell.'

Vaughn walked back to his table. 'Fortunately we have witnesses who can.'

Sharpe raised his voice. 'I have another letter from . . .'

'We are concerned with this letter, Major!' Vaughn turned sharply, but Pakenham held up a hand. He looked into Sharpe's eyes for the first time since the Rifleman had entered the room.

'You have another letter from this lady?'

Sharpe nodded. He had not told Trumper-Jones of the letter because Sharpe had no faith in the young man's ability. 'She wrote to me, sir, after the death of my wife. She wanted to offer me her condolences. She regretted she would not convey them to me in person.' He could not resist a small smile. Such a letter was hardly likely to have come from a woman he had persecuted. He saw the flicker of hope on Lieutenant Trumper-Jones' face. 'I'd like that letter read into the record too, sir.'

The general officers behind the table smiled, sensing a victory for Sharpe. Pakenham leaned back. 'You have the letter, Major Sharpe?'

'It's in my pack, sir.'

'Major Vaughn?' Pakenham turned to the Welshman. 'You have no objection?'

'No, sir, none. But I must tell the court that we have already impounded the prisoner's belongings, searched them, and no such letter has been found.'

'It's in my pack!' Sharpe said stubbornly.

Vaughn sighed. 'Major Michael Hogan conducted the search, sir. No letter was discovered.'

The officers behind the table stared again at the green cloth on which their papers lay. Sharpe's sword, its scabbard and hilt battered by war, was at the table's front.

The Marqués' chaplain, through an interpreter, testified that he had found the Marqués' servants asleep outside his master's room. Perhaps, he wondered, they had been given a sleeping potion by the prisoner?

Captain Morillos, a bull of a man, gave his evidence. He had seen, in the light of a torch bracketed at the garden gate of the house, a Rifle Officer leave at three in the morning. No, he had not seen the man's face, but he had seen the English uniform and the Heavy Cavalry sword.

It was hot in the courtroom. Sharpe could feel himself sweating beneath his shirt. He listened hopelessly as Lieutenant Trumper-Jones failed to budge Captain Morillos one inch. The Captain claimed to have an intimate knowledge of uniforms and swords and was certain of what he had seen.

Sharpe had no defence other than innocence. He had eaten with Harper, Isabella, and d'Alembord, but he had left before midnight. He had slept in his billet, but he could produce no witnesses who could swear that they had watched him all night.

Major Vaughn waved a fly from the air in front of his face. 'Major Sharpe. You knew La Marquesa de Casares el Grande y Melida Sadaba?'

'Yes.'

'And that acquaintanceship,' he stressed the word delicately, 'gave rise to the challenge you accepted yesterday?'

'No.'

'No?'

'I never threatened her.'

'One is delighted to hear it.' Vaughn smiled and took two thoughtful paces into the floor's centre. 'But you did know her?'

'Yes.'

'Well? You knew her well?'

'Yes, but . . .'

'Yes is enough. Major. You were challenged by Major Mendora, aide to the General?'

'Yes.'

'And you accepted the challenge?'

86

'Yes.'

'Even though you knew that such an acceptance was counter to the General Orders of this army?'

Sharpe looked at the smug face. 'I went into the breach at Badajoz without orders, too.'

Two of the officers behind the table smiled. Vaughn just raised an eyebrow. 'Another impetuous act, Major?'

Sharpe said nothing. Vaughn sighed and walked back to his table. He straightened his papers as though he would not be needing them much longer. 'You were prevented from finishing this duel?'

'I was.'

'We should be grateful that someone was doing his duty yesterday. Presumably, Major, you felt cheated of a death?'

Sharpe frowned. 'No.'

'Ah! You were fighting a duel for exercise, perhaps?'

'I was fighting for honour.'

Vaughn said nothing. The word hung, tawdry and silly, in the embarrassment of the courtroom.

The officers of the court tried to find more evidence, but there was none. Sharpe had no witnesses. He was ordered back to his limewashed room to await the verdict.

It took only ten minutes before he was escorted back.

He was guilty.

Lieutenant Trumper-Jones, his hair dropping over one eye, made a surprisingly impassioned speech for the prisoner. He described his gallantry, enumerated his acts on the battlefield, quoted the *Times* newspaper which had called Sharpe 'Albion's stalwart son'. On the grounds of his heroism, of his contribution to this war, Trumper-Jones said, the court should show the prisoner leniency.

Major Vaughn allowed all of the gallantry. He pointed out, too, that the Spanish people had entrusted Wellington with their pride and their armies. That trust had been broken. The Spanish would suspect the good faith of an ally who let a murderer of one of their leading citizens, a gallant General who had subdued a revolt in the Banda Oriental, go unpunished. In the interests of the alliance, as well as of natural justice, he feared he must call for the most rigorous punishment. He sounded regretful, but he spoke with the confidence of a man who knew the outcome.

General Pakenham was uncomfortable. He, too, was under orders here. His eyes did not look up at the prisoner as he ordered that Major Sharpe should be stripped of his rank, and dismissed from the army. When those formalities were completed, which should be, he said, by four o'clock that afternoon, Richard Sharpe was to be escorted to the main square of the town where, in the presence of four Spanish Battalions, he would be hanged.

Reluctantly, pain in his eyes, Pakenham looked at Sharpe. 'Is there anything you have to say?'

Sharpe looked back defiantly. 'Permission to die in my Rifleman's jacket, sir.'

'Denied.' Pakenham looked as if he wanted to add that Sharpe had disgraced his uniform, but the words would not come. 'These proceedings are over.' He stood, and Sharpe was led from the courtroom, his hands tied, condemned to the gallows.

CHAPTER 7

Lord Stokeley, one of Wellington's aides-de-camp, wondered whether wine should be served to the Spanish officers who came to witness the execution.

Wellington stared at him with cold, blue eyes. 'It's an execution, Stokeley, not a god-damned christening.'

Stokeley decided it would be best not to mention that in his family refreshments were served for both functions. 'Very good, my Lord.' He decided he had never seen his master in a worse temper.

Nor had he, indeed. The damage that could be done to the tenuous alliance between British and Spanish was immense. No Spanish soldier, so far as Wellington knew, had any love for the Marqués de Casares el Grande y Melida Sadaba, but his murder had transformed him into a martyr of Spain. The damned churchmen had been quick off the mark, as usual, preaching their anti-protestant diatribes, but Wellington prided himself that he had been just as quick. The culprit had been tried, a hanging would take place, and all before the sun that had risen on the murdered man would set. The Spanish, ready to mount elaborate protests, had found the wind taken from their sails. They declared themselves satisfied with his Lordship's swift retribution.

The Spanish soldiers who were marched into the plaza of the small town were glad of the break in their routine. They had been training hard, marching long days and waking with aching bones to face more hard training. Yet this afternoon it was like a fiesta. They were marched into the plaza, Battalion after Battalion, to witness the death of an Englishman.

The gibbet was made from an army wagon that was

parked against the limewashed wall of the priest's house. There was a convenient hook high on the wall. An English Sergeant, sweating in his Provost's uniform, climbed a ladder with the rope that he looped onto the hook. The square was thick with Provosts. There was a rumour that men of the South Essex, together with some Riflemen, planned to try and rescue Richard Sharpe from the gallows. It sounded an unlikely threat, but it was taken seriously. The Provosts carried their short muskets tipped with bayonets and watched the alleys and streets that led into the plaza.

The first Spanish officers came to the headquarters. They seemed subdued. Most tactfully avoided the windows that faced the square, but Major Mendora, his bright white uniform bearing a black crepe band on its right sleeve, watched the Sergeant hang the rope in its place. Lord Stokeley wondered if the Major would care for a cup of tea? The Major would not.

The Provost Sergeant, safely off his ladder, pulled on the noose to make sure that the hook was secure. It held his weight. The rope, released from his grip, turned slowly in the small breeze.

Father Hacha, his black priest's robes stained white with dust from the square, pushed through the officers to Mendora's side. 'They should have handed him to us for punishment.'

The Major looked at the harsh faced priest. 'Sir?'

'Hanging's too quick.' His deep voice dominated the room. 'Spain won't be happy, gentlemen, till these heathens are gone from us.'

There were some murmurs of agreement, but not many. Most of the Spaniards present were glad to serve under the Generalissimo Wellington. They had learned from him how to organize an army, and the new regiments of Spain were troops that any officer could take pride in. But no one, not the most fervent supporter of the British alliance, was willing to cross an Inquisitor. The Junta might have abolished the Spanish Inquisition, but until it finally disappeared, no man wanted to have his name listed in its secret ledgers. The Inquisitor stared at the rope. 'They should have garotted him.'

Some of the Spanish soldiers in the square would have agreed with the Inquisitor. Hanging, they said, was too quick. They should have brought one of the garottes that travelled with the Spanish army, sat the Englishman in its chair, and slowly, slowly tightened the screw that would break his neck. A good executioner could draw a garotting out for an hour, sometimes relaxing the pressure of the thread to give the victim false hope, before finally turning the screw and breaking the neck as the doomed man's head snapped backwards.

Others said that a hanging could last just as long. It all depended, they said, on the drop. If the man was simply hanged, without a drop, then he could last half a day. Whatever, it was better to be in this dusty square waiting for a hanging than to be training in the hills.

'*La Puta Dorada*,' a Spanish Colonel observed, 'is now a very rich widow.' There was laughter at the thought.

'How rich?' an artillery Major asked.

'Christ knows how much he was worth! Millions.'

'She won't get the land,' someone observed. 'She won't dare show her face in Spain once the French are gone.'

'Even so,' the Colonel shrugged. 'She must be worth a few hundred thousand in coin and plate. What happens to the title?'

Major Mendora, embarrassed by the conversation, coldly named a Duke, a cousin, to whom the title reverted. He refused to give an estimate of his dead master's fortune.

The Inquisitor listened to the talk, hearing the greed and jealousy. He turned to the window and looked at the makeshift gallows on which an innocent man must die. That was regrettable, but the Inquisitor was satisfied that the Englishman, Sharpe, was a sinner whose death would not distress the Almighty. The hanging rope cast a sharp, black shadow on the limewashed wall.

The death of the Marqués was more distressing. The Marqués, at least, had been a Christian, though a weak man. Now he was in heaven where weakness was a virtue.

He had died quickly, hardly a flutter on his face as the Slaughterman, with a strong hand, had sliced his throat. The Inquisitor had prayed as his brother killed, his words soft, committing the soul to heaven as the knife cut through the tendons and windpipe and muscle and down to the great artery that had gouted blood as the Marqués' body gave one, desperate heave. The man had hardly woken as he died. *El Matarife* had eyed the golden crucifix greedily and been hurried from the room by his brother.

The Marqués' death would save Spain. It released his fortune that would go to the Church. These officers who discussed his will did so in ignorance, for now, with this one death behind him, the Inquisitor would legally take the fortune that was embarked on the Marquesa's wagons. Three hundred thousand dollars worth of fortune there alone, with millions more in land and property. He smiled.

The Inquisitor's family had been impoverished by the war, and now, with this fortune, it would rank with the greatest in Spain which was only fitting for a man who intended to be the leader behind Spain's weak King. With the fortune of Casares el Grande y Melida Sadaba behind him, the Inquisitor knew, he would rise to be a bishop, then an archbishop, and finally a cardinal. He would stand behind the throne and before the high altar. He would be powerful and Spain would be great. His ambitions, not set for himself, but for the Church and for the Inquisition, would be realised, and all for the price of one death.

And now that the Marqués was dead the Inquisitor would give to Major Ducos the assurances of support that would convince Ferdinand VII to sign his name to the secret treaty. The British would go from Spain, the French would leave peaceably, and Spain would be strong again. Its empire would be restored, its King would be glorious on a throne, and the Church would take back its power. All that for one small death. One death to give his family the money that meant power, power that would be used for God's glory. The Inquisitor forgave himself the death; it had been for God.

A murmur came from the throng of soldiers who packed

the plaza. It rose, became an excited shout, and the noise coincided with the door opening into the large room where the Spanish officers gathered. Lord Wellington, grim-faced, came into the room. He frowned at the assembled men, nodded coldly, then looked through one of the windows. His aides crowded close to him. Mendora could see the General's hands were clasped behind his back, the fingers fidgeting. The Spanish officers fell silent, embarrassed by the cold face of their commanding officer.

The prisoner, bare-headed so that the wind stirred his long, black hair, was being marched through the narrow corridor that had been made through the crowd. He was pushed up the makeshift steps to the wagon bed. He was taller than his red-jacketed guards.

He wore a grubby white shirt and the baggy white trousers of the English infantry so that, to the Spaniards watching from the headquarters, he seemed to be dressed as a penitent. The Inquisitor was saying a prayer, his deep voice harsh in the room. Wellington looked in irritation at the priest, but said nothing. Some of the Spanish officers knew that Richard Sharpe had once saved the General's life, rescued him from the bayonets of Indian troops years ago, and now the General was watching the man hanged. Yet Wellington's face, with its hooked, eagle's nose, showed no trace of emotion.

The prisoner's hands were tied. He seemed to look with disinterest at the great crowd. He was too far away for the Spanish officers to see his face clearly, yet it seemed as if he grinned at them in defiance. The watching soldiers were silent.

A second, shorter ladder had been placed against the white-washed wall and the guards pushed the prisoner towards it. He found it difficult to climb the rungs with his hands tied, but the soldiers helped him up. The Provost Sergeant climbed the longer ladder, reached out for the noose, and pushed it over the prisoner's black hair. He tightened the knot, then went back down to the wagon.

Some of the Spanish officers watched the alleyways that led into the plaza. They were thinking of the rumour that

Sharpe's men might try to rescue their officer, but there were no angry men beyond the sentries. No dogs barked, there was no tramp of feet, just the sunlight on the thick, red tiles and the wisps of smoke from kitchen fires silting the air above the town.

The condemned man was standing precariously on the ladder, the rope about his neck looping downwards. The Provost Sergeant looked at his officer.

The Lieutenant of the Provosts disliked this task, but orders were orders. Major Sharpe was to be hanged in full view of the Spanish troops. He looked up at the man standing on the ladder, his body leaning on the wall, and he caught the dark eyes in a final glance, wondered at a man who could grin at him at this moment, then the Lieutenant gave the order.

'Carry on, Sergeant.' The words came out as a croak.

The crowd gasped, then cheered.

The Provosts pulled the ladder from beneath the doomed man.

For a second the booted feet stayed on the falling rung, then they slipped off, he dropped, and the rope jerked tight. He bounced, dropped again, and then was swaying and turning from the high hook. His body seemed to arch as he dangled. His feet flailed the air, kicked the wall, and he twisted so that his unhooded face stared at the packed plaza.

The eyes bulged, the tongue pushed at the lips, the neck was grotesquely stretched to the tilted head. The Spanish watched in fascination. He jerked again, fighting upwards as if for air, and then the English Sergeant jumped up, caught one of the man's ankles, and jerked his weight down.

The extra weight snapped his neck. The Sergeant let go of the man's ankles and slowly, as the body swung, the legs drew themselves up a few inches. He was dead.

A coffin waited on the wagon bed; pine boards, rough planed, nailed together. The body was cut down. The hair had been smeared white by the limewash as the body thrashed in death.

They took the boots from the corpse, but nothing else was

worth saving. They lifted him into the coffin, but he was too tall for the box and so the Sergeant took a musket from one of his men and smashed the butt down, sweating and grunting, smashed again, and the broken shinbones let the legs be forced inside. The lid was nailed shut.

Wellington stared at the whole thing with distaste. When it was done, when the Spanish Battalions were being marched from the plaza and the pine box was being carried away, he turned his cold eyes on the assembled officers 'That's over, gentlemen. Perhaps we can now get on with this war?'

They filed silently from the room. The murder of the Marqués had failed to split the British and Spanish. The Generalissimo had made his blood sacrifice to keep the alliance alive and now there was a war to fight.

By a roadside, beneath the high mountains where the wolves roamed between grey rocks, they buried the broken-legged corpse. The Provosts heaped rocks over the shallow grave to stop predators digging up the body, and then they left it without any marker. That night a peasant put a nailed cross on the spot, not out of reverence, but to frighten the protestant spirit and keep it underground. The Inquisitor and *El Matarife*, riding north and east, passed the grave. The Slaughterman reined in. 'I should have watched him die.'

'It was better that no one saw you, Juan.'

The Slaughterman shrugged. 'I've never seen a man hanged.'

The Inquisitor looked incredulous. 'Never?'

'Never.' *El Matarife* sounded ashamed.

'Then find one and hang him.'

'I will.'

'But first look after our next business.' The priest put spurs to his horse. 'And hurry!'

They carried papers that would pass them through the British and French lines, and they carried news that would end this war and restore Spain to its old glory. The Inquisitor gave thanks to God and hurried on.

CHAPTER 8

The valley was a pass through the mountains. It was high. From its western rim, where it spilt down to a river far, far beneath, a man could see into Portugal. The hills of the Tras os Montes, the "land beyond the mountains", looked like purple-blue ridges that became dimmer and more indistinct until the horizon was a mere blur like a smear of dark water colour on a painter's canvas.

The sides of the valley were thick with thorn. The blossoms were white in the sunlight. The road, that climbed the steep pass and went through the high valley, was edged with yellow ragwort that the Spanish called St James's grass. The pasture at the valley bottom was close cropped by sheep and rabbits. Ravens nested on stone ledges, foxes hunted the thorn's margins, while wolves roamed the rock strewn hills that barred the sky in a jagged barrier.

There was a village in the high valley, but it was deserted. The doors of the cottages had been torn from their hinges and burned by one of the armies that fought in Spain.

At the western end of the valley, where the crest showed the magnificent view of the land beyond the mountains, were two great buildings. Both were ruins.

On the north side, low and squat, was an old convent. Its two cloisters still stood, though the upper cloister had been grievously torn by a great explosion that had destroyed the old chapel. The convent had long been deserted. Weeds grew on its patterned tiles, leaves choked the channels that had once carried water in its lower garden.

To the south, barring the pass, was a castle. A man could still climb to the top of the keep, or stand on the gatehouse, but it had been centuries since a lord lived in the castle.

Now it was a home for the ravens, and bats hung in its high dark rooms.

Further east, and higher still, dominating the land for miles around, was an old watchtower. That, too, could be climbed, though the winding stair led only to a broken battlement.

The high valley was called the Gateway of God. By the castle, on the grass that was littered with rabbit droppings like miniature musketballs, was a long, low mound. It was a grave, and in the grave were the bodies of the men who had died defending this pass in the winter. They had been few, and their enemies many, yet they had held the pass until relief came. They had been led by a soldier, by a Rifleman, by Richard Sharpe.

The French who had died, and there had been many, had been buried more hurriedly in a mass grave by the village. In the winter the scavenging beasts had scraped the earth from the grave and eaten what flesh they could find. Now, as the spring days turned to summer and the small stream in the Gateway of God shrank, the bones of the dead Frenchmen were littered about the village. Skulls lay like a monstrous crop of mushrooms.

In the south there was a war, armies marching to this year's campaign, but in the Gateway of God, where Sharpe had fought his war against an army, there was nothing but death and the wind moving the thorns and the skulls grinning from the cropped grass. It was a place of no use to either army, a place of ghosts and death and loneliness, a place forgotten.

The city of Burgos was where the Great Road split. The road came from the French frontier to San Sebastian, then plunged south through the mountains where the Partisans made every journey hell for the French. There was relief from ambush at Vitoria, then the road went into the hills again, going ever south, until it came to the wide plains where Burgos lay.

It was the road down which the French had invaded Spain. It was the road back up which they would retreat. At

Burgos the road divided. One branch went south to Madrid, the other south and west towards Portugal and the Atlantic. Burgos was the crossroads of invasion, the guardian of retreat, the fortress on the plains.

It was not a large fortress, yet in the last days of the summer of 1812 it had withstood a British siege. The castle was still scarred by the marks of cannon-balls and shells. In 1812 the castle had kept the British from chasing the French over the Pyrenees, and this summer, men feared, it might be called on to do the same work again against a reinforced British army.

Pierre Ducos did not care. If the soldiers lost Spain, then his secret Treaty would save France. The Inquisitor, back in Burgos, had promised that he would deliver, within the month, the letters that were even now being collected by the threatened Spanish Inquisition. The letters would convince Ferdinand VII of Spain's support of a French treaty.

The two men met, not in the castle, but in one of the town's tall, gloomy houses. Ducos winced as his spectacles rubbed his sore skin. On the advice of an army surgeon he had put axle grease behind his ears to protect against the chafing wire, but still the earpieces irritated him. At least he had the consolation of knowing that the man who had broken his other, comfortable spectacles was dead.

'Hanged,' the Inquisitor said. 'Hanged quickly.' He sounded resentful, as though he truly believed Sharpe to have been responsible for the Marqués' death.

Ducos had only one regret about Richard Sharpe's death. He wished that the Englishman had known that it was he, Ducos, who had reached out across a nation and engineered revenge. Ducos liked his victims to understand who had beaten them, and why they had been beaten. Ducos paraded his cleverness as other men displayed their medals. He took some papers from his pocket. 'La Marquesa's wagons are in the castle.'

'They will be delivered to us?'

'If you give me an address.' Ducos smiled. 'The cathedral perhaps?'

The Inquisitor did not blink at the taunt. 'My house, Major.'

'In Vitoria?'

'In Vitoria.'

'And you will give the wealth to the church?'

'What I do with the wealth is between me and God.'

'Of course.' Ducos pushed at his spectacles again. 'They will go north with the next convoy. Of course, father, the wealth is not yours. It belongs to the widow.'

'Not if she leaves Spain.'

'Which we have agreed would be unwise.' Ducos smiled. He did not want Helene bleating to the Emperor how he had cheated her of his wealth. 'So you will take care of that business?'

'When it is convenient.'

'Tonight is convenient.' Ducos pushed the papers across the table. 'Those are our dispositions. Casapalacio's men guard the western road.'

The Inquisitor took the paper and Ducos stared out of the window towards the west. Martins cut the warm air on curved wings. Beyond them, beyond the last houses of the town, the plain looked dry. He could see the village far off where the single tower of a small castle threw its long shadow. That tower was another French garrison, a place where cavalry were based to keep the Great Road clear of Partisans. Tonight, when the martins were back in their nests, and the plain was dark, La Marquesa was travelling to that tower, going to meet her lover, General Verigny.

Such a journey was safe. The land about Burgos was free of Partisans; the country was too flat and too well patrolled by the French garrisons of the plain. Yet this night there would be no safety for the Marquesa. The troops who guarded the road this night were troops who served France, but were not French. They were Spanish. They were the remnants of the army that had been recruited five years before, an army of Spaniards who believed in French ideas, in liberty, equality and fraternity; but defeat, hopelessness, and desertion had thinned their ranks. Yet there were still two Battalions of Spanish troops, and Ducos had ordered that they be given this duty this night.

The Inquisitor looked at him. 'She goes tonight?'

'As last night, and the night before. They have prodigious appetites.'

'Good.'

'And your brother?'

'He waits in the north.'

'Splendid.' Ducos stood. 'I wish you joy of it all, father.'

The Inquisitor stared up at the subtle, clever man. 'You will have your letters soon.'

'I never doubted it.' Ducos smiled. 'Give Helene my regards. Tell her I trust her marriage will be long and very happy.' He laughed, turned, and went from the room.

This night the Inquisitor arranged a marriage. Soon La Marquesa would wear, on her left hand, a wedding ring. She would not marry some Grandee of Spain, but a man who had been born in humble circumstances and lived a life of poverty and struggle. She would become a bride of Christ.

She was rich beyond avarice, yet the Marqués' will had contained one small and not uncommon stipulation which had not escaped the Inquisition's notice. If his widow took her vows as a nun, then the Marqués' wealth reverted to the church.

To which purpose she would be taken to a convent in the north country, a far, hidden, remote convent, and there she would be buried alive in the silent loneliness of the sisters while the Inquisitor, on behalf of God, took her inheritance.

It would be legal, there would be no scandal, for who could argue with a woman's decision to take the veil? Father Hacha felt the beauty of the scheme. It could not fail now. The Marqués was dead, his only legatee would become a nun, and the Inquisition would survive.

That night a carriage left Burgos at nine o'clock. It was drawn by four horses whose trace-chains were of silver. The horses were white. The carriage was dark blue, polished so that it reflected the stars, and its elegant outline was traced with lines of silver paint. Its windows were curtained.

Ahead of the carriage went four grooms, each holding a lantern. Two more lanterns were mounted high on the carriage itself. The postilions carried loaded guns.

The coachman paused at the city's edge and looked down at the Lieutenant who commanded the guardpost. 'All well ahead?'

'How far are you going?'

'Two villages.'

The Spanish Lieutenant waved the coach on. 'You'll have no trouble.' He looked at the intricate coat of arms painted on the carriage door and wondered where *La Puta Dorada* went this evening. Only an hour before an Inquisitor had passed the guardpost and the Lieutenant toyed with the fancy that she was selling it to the priests now. He laughed and turned back to his men.

The moonlight showed the road as a white, straight ribbon that lay across the plain until it came to a village just a mile from the city. There the road twisted between houses, crossed a ford, before running straight towards the lights of the cavalry outpost.

The carriage moved swiftly, each wheel putting up a plume of dust that drifted pale in the night. The lanterns flickered yellow. The smell of the town was left behind, the thick smell of rotting manure, nightsoil, horses and cooking smoke. Instead there was the scent of grass. One curtain of the carriage was pulled back and a face pressed white against the glass.

La Marquesa was angry. Pierre Ducos had refused to issue the passport that would release her wagons. He claimed it was a small thing, a clerk's mistake, but she did not believe that any clerk's mistake would deter Pierre Ducos from achieving what he wanted. She suspected he planned to take them and she had written as much to the Emperor, but it could be weeks before a reply came, if any came at all; weeks in which the wagons could disappear. This night, she decided, she would persuade General Verigny that he must steal the wagons back. He must defy Ducos, go to the castle with his men, and drag the wagons out. She knew that General Verigny, for all his medals, feared Pierre Ducos. He would need persuading and she wondered whether a hint that perhaps marriage was not so unthinkable after all might work.

The carriage slowed at a crossroads, bumped over the transverse wheel ruts, then passed a house, its windows broken and doors missing. She heard the brake scrape on the wheel rim and she knew that they approached the ford where the road snaked between houses.

The brake scraped and the carriage shuddered. She heard the coachman shouting at the horses as the carriage swayed, slowed, and halted. She frowned. She tried to see through the window, but the lantern blinded her with its flame. She lifted the leather strap and let the window fall. 'What is it?'

'A death, my Lady.'

'Death?'

She leaned out of the window. Ahead of them, just where the road twisted down to the shallow stream, a priest carried the Host for the final unction. Behind him were two altar boys. The soldiers who guarded this place had their hats off. She noticed that they were Spanish soldiers loyal to France. 'Tell him to move!' She said it irritably.

'There's a carriage coming the other way. 'We'll have to wait anyway, my Lady.'

She pulled on the strap, slamming the window up, and muffling the sound of the other carriage that rattled towards her. She settled back on the velvet cushions. God damn Pierre Ducos, she thought, and God damn Verigny's reluctance to oppose him. She thought of King Joseph, Napoleon's brother and the French puppet king of Spain. If the treaty was signed, she reflected, then Joseph would lose his throne. She wondered whether, by betraying the secret to Joseph, he might reward her by ordering the wagons released; if, that was, even King Joseph dared to defy his brother's loyal servant, Pierre Ducos.

The other carriage stopped. She heard the shout of the coachman and she presumed the soldiers wanted to search it. She smiled: no one dared search her carriage.

Then the door opened, she turned, one hand clutching

her cloak to her neck, to see a priest climbing into her carriage. 'Who are you?'

She had a pistol beneath the cushions. She pushed her right hand towards it.

The man took off his broad hat. The shielded lantern within her carriage showed a huge, strong face with eyes harder than stone. 'You are La Marquesa de Casares el Grande y Melida Sadaba?'

'I am.' Her voice was like ice. 'You?'

'Father Hacha.'

She could see men outside the coach, their shapes dim in the moonlit street. She looked back at the priest and saw that his clothes were finer than those she would have expected on an ordinary parish priest. She sensed this man's force, his strength, and his hostility. It was a pity, she thought, that such a man should give up his life to God. 'What do you want?'

'I have news for you.'

She shrugged. 'Go on.'

The Inquisitor sat on the seat opposite her. He seemed to fill the small carriage with his huge presence. His voice was deeper even than Pierre Ducos'. 'Your husband is dead.'

She stared at him. She said nothing. At each ear hung a diamond cluster. Her cloak, though the night was not cold, was edged with white fur. At her throat, where her left hand held the fur collar, were more diamonds.

'Did you not hear me?'

'I heard you.' She smiled. 'You want to be rewarded for bringing me the news? The coachman will give you a coin.'

The Inquisitor's face showed nothing. 'Adultery is a sin, woman.'

'And impudence is bad manners. Leave me, priest.'

He pointed a strong, dark hand at her. 'You are an adulterer.'

She rapped on the window and shouted at the coachman to drive on. The carriage did not move and she angrily jerked the strap from its hook so that the window crashed down. 'I said go on!'

The Spanish soldiers, uncomfortable but obedient, surrounded the carriage. With them were men in long, dark habits. She fumbled in the cushions for the pistol, but the strong hand of the Inquisitor reached for her wrist and pulled it clear. 'You are an adulterer, woman.'

She pulled away from him, but his grip was firm. She called for her servants, but the Inquisitor just smiled. 'Your servants will obey their God, as you never did. You are an adulterer, and your husband and your lover are dead.'

'My lover?'

'The Englishman.'

She had thought he meant General Verigny, now she knew he meant Richard Sharpe. She felt a pang at the news, knowing that her letter had caused his death, but her own troubles were too immediate for the pang to last. 'Let me go!'

'You are under arrest, woman.'

'Don't be impertinent!'

'You are Spanish by marriage and in the jurisdiction of this diocese.' He pulled her, making her call out in pain, but no one moved to help her.

He dragged her from the carriage and pushed her into the second coach where two women, both with lined, hard faces that were edged with white linen hoods, waited for her. She screamed at her servants for help, but they were surrounded by soldiers with muskets and monks with staves, and then the door of the coach slammed and it jerked under way. The Inquisitor sat opposite her. When she screamed again he leaned over and struck her into silence.

The Marquesa's coachman was ordered back to the town. The Spanish Major, who had been ordered to obey the summons of the Ecclesiastical court, wondered where the Golden Whore was going. He had been told not to ask, not to care, just to obey. He listened to the dark coach rattle into the night, then shouted at his men to return to their posts.

General Verigny watched from the tower, waiting for the carriage lanterns to appear on the white road. He waited as the moon sank beneath the mountains. He waited until the clocks struck two and then he knew she was not coming. He thought of sending some of his men towards Burgos to see if her carriage had run into trouble, but decided that she was probably flirting with another man instead. He cursed, wondered whether anyone would ever tame the bitch, and went to bed.

The night wind stirred the thorns of the Gateway of God. Bats flickered about the ruined keep. A cloud barred the moon. The stars were bright.

Three horsemen climbed the pass. They came slowly. They were late. They had meant to be here when it was still daylight, but it had taken them four hours to find a place to cross the last river. Their uniforms were still damp.

They stopped at the crest of the path. Nothing moved in the valley, no lights showed in the village, watchtower, convent or castle.

'Which way?'

'This way.' A man whose uniform was dark as the night led his two companions towards the ruined convent. He tied the horses to a grille beside the shattered archway, unsaddled them, then broke open a net of forage. He spread food for the horses, then led his companions into the upper cloister. He smiled. 'It's more homely than the castle.'

The older man looked about the shattered cloister. 'The French captured this?'

'Yes.' The dark-uniformed man was making a fire. 'But Sharpe took care of them.' He pointed into the ruined chapel. 'One of their guns.'

In the weed-grown ruins there was a gleam of moon on bronze where a fallen gun barrel was half covered by timber and stone.

The third man was young, so young that most would have described him as a mere boy. He did not need to shave yet. He was the only one of the three who wore no uniform, though slung on his shoulder was a rifle. He seemed nervous of the two soldiers. He watched the dark-uniformed one light a fire, doing the job with all the skill of an old campaigner.

The dark-uniformed man was fearsome. He had one eye,

105

the other covered by a black patch, and his scarred face was harsh and fierce. He was half German, half English, and his nickname in the 60th Regiment was Sweet William. He was Captain William Frederickson, the Rifleman who had ambushed the French gunners above the bridge, and who had fought, at Christmas, beneath Sharpe's command in this high valley. He had come back to the Gateway of God as a guide for Major Michael Hogan and the young, silent Spaniard.

Hogan was restless. He paced the cloister, asking questions about the battle, and staring at the castle where Sharpe had made the final stand and thrown back the last French attack. Sweet William answered his questions as he cooked the meal, though the young Spaniard noticed how the one-eyed Rifle officer was alert and listening for strange sounds beyond the ruined building.

Their meal was wine, bread, cheese, and the joints of a hare that Frederickson had shot earlier in the day and now roasted on the ramrod of his rifle. A wind came from the west, from the far ocean, making the one-eyed Rifleman lift his head and sniff. There was rain in the wind's message, a promise of a summer storm that would lash these mountains. 'We must get the horses inside once we've eaten.'

Hogan sat by the fire. He plucked at his damp trousers as if he could hasten their drying. He gestured at the nervous Spanish boy to join them, then looked round the dark shadows of the ruined convent. 'Do you believe in ghosts, Frederickson?'

'No, sir. You?'

'I'm Irish. I believe in God the father, God the son, and the Shee riding the winds.'

Frederickson laughed. He slid a joint of hare from the ramrod onto Hogan's tin plate, a second joint went onto his own plate, then he put a generous piece of meat onto the boy's plate. Hogan and the Spanish boy watched as he brought a fourth plate from his haversack and put the last piece of hare on it. Hogan began to speak, but the Rifleman grinned and motioned the Irishman into silence.

Frederickson put the plate beside him, then raised his

voice. 'I heard you two minutes ago, you noisy bastard! Come and eat!'

There was a chuckle from the cloisters. A boot sounded on a broken tile and Richard Sharpe walked from the shadows and sat beside them in the Gateway of God.

CHAPTER 9

'Who was he?'

Hogan shrugged. 'He was called Liam Dooley. He came from County Clare. He and his younger brother were going to hang for looting a church. I promised Private Dooley to let his brother live if he agreed to that little charade.' He shrugged. 'So one rogue died and two lived.'

Sharpe drank wine. He had waited in the Gateway of God for two weeks, obedient to the instructions that Hogan had given him when, in the darkness of the night of his 'execution', Hogan had sent him secretly into the north country. 'How many people know I'm alive?'

'We do,' Hogan gestured at Frederickson and the Spanish boy, 'the General, and six Provosts. No one else.'

'Patrick?'

'No.' Hogan shrugged. 'He's not happy.'

Sharpe smiled. 'I'll give him a surprise one day.'

'If you live to give it to him.' Hogan said it grimly. He licked his fingers that were smeared with the hare's gravy. 'Officially you're dead. You don't exist. There is no Major Sharpe, and there never will be unless you vindicate yourself.'

Sharpe grinned at him. 'Yes, Mr Hogan.'

Hogan frowned at Sharpe's levity. Sweet William laughed and passed Sharpe a heavy skin of wine. The freshening wind stirred the fire, blowing smoke towards the Spanish boy who was too timid to move. Hogan shook his head. 'You are a god-damned fool. Why did you have to accept his bloody challenge?'

Sharpe said nothing. He could not explain to these friends how his guilt at Teresa's death had persuaded him to fight the Marqués. He could not explain that there was sometimes a joy in taking great risks.

Hogan watched him, then reached into a pocket and brought out a folded piece of paper. 'This is yours.'

The paper crackled as Sharpe unfolded it. He smiled. It was the letter from La Marquesa that sympathised with him after Teresa's death, the letter he had wanted to produce at the Court-Martial. 'You hid it?'

'I had to, didn't I?' Hogan sounded defensive. 'Christ! We had to patch up the bloody alliance. If you'd been found not guilty then the Spanish would never have trusted us again.'

'But I wasn't guilty.'

'I know that.' Hogan said it testily. 'Of course you're not guilty. Wellington knows you're not guilty, he knows well enough that if you were going to murder someone you'd do it properly and not be caught. If he'd thought you were guilty he'd have put the rope round your neck himself!'

Frederickson laughed softly. Sharpe put the letter on the flames and the sudden gush of light lit his sun-darkened face.

Hogan watched the letter shrivel. 'So why did she write that pack of lies to her husband?'

Sharpe shrugged. He had wondered about that question for a fortnight. 'Perhaps she wanted him dead? She's bound to inherit a god-damned fortune, and I seem to remember she has expensive tastes.'

'Except in men,' Hogan said sourly. 'But if she just wanted him dead, why did she involve you? She had someone else ready to oblige her, it seems.' He was distractedly breaking a piece of bread into small crumbs. 'She must have known she was landing you into God's own trouble. I thought she cared for you?'

Sharpe said nothing. He did not believe that Helene was so careless of him, so unfeeling. He did not understand her, indeed he thought he would never understand the ways of people who lived in the great houses and took privilege as their birthright, but he did not believe that La Marquesa wished him ill.

'Well?'

Sharpe looked at the Irishman. 'I don't think she'd want me dead.'

'You killed her brother.'

Sharpe shrugged. 'Helene wasn't fond of that bastard.'

'You're sure?'

'Who in hell knows?' Sharpe laughed. 'She never seemed fond of him. He was an arrogant bastard.'

'While you, of course,' Hogan said sourly, 'are the soul of humility. So who'd want a saint like you dead?'

Sharpe smiled and shrugged. 'I don't know.'

'Perhaps,' Sweet William spoke softly, 'the French just wanted to upset the Spanish and the British, and along with it get a hero hanged?' He smiled. 'The Paris newspapers would make an hurrah about it all. Perhaps they forged the letter from the Marquesa?'

Hogan made a gesture of frustration. 'I don't know. I do know that Helene has come back to Spain. God knows why.' He saw Sharpe's sudden interest and he knew that his friend was still hooked by the golden woman.

The Spanish boy, who had not spoken since they came into the convent, reached nervously for a wineskin. Frederickson pushed one towards him.

Hogan shivered suddenly. The wind was stronger, sounding on the broken stones and whirling the sparks of the fire up into the darkness. 'And why in God's name does an Inquisitor bring her letter?'

'An Inquisitor?' Sharpe asked. 'The Spanish Inquisition?'

'Yes.'

'I thought they'd run out of people to burn years ago!'

'They haven't.' Hogan had talked long with the Marqués' chaplain and had learned some few things about the mysterious Inquisitor who had brought the incriminating letter. 'He's called Father Hacha and he's got the soul of a snake.' Hogan frowned at Sharpe. 'Helene wouldn't have caught religion, would she?'

Sharpe smiled. 'I wouldn't think so.'

'The weirdest people do,' Hogan said glumly. 'But if she

had, she'd hardly be plotting murder.' He shrugged. 'Or maybe she would. Religion does odd things to people.'

There was silence. Frederickson took a piece of broken floorboard that he had collected from the shattered chapel and put it on the fire. The Spanish boy looked from man to man, wondering what they spoke of. He stared at Sharpe. He knew all about Sharpe and the boy was worried. He wanted Sharpe to approve of him.

Hogan suddenly looked at the broken gateway. Do you know what a *torno* is?'

Sharpe took a cigar from Frederickson, leaned forward, and lit it from the flames.

'No.'

Frederickson, who loved old buildings, knew what a *torno* was, but kept silent.

'There might have been one here once.' Hogan gestured at the ruined convent gateway. 'I've only ever seen them in Spain. They're revolving cupboards built into the outer wall of a convent. You can put something into the cupboard from the outside, ring the bell, and a nun inside turns the *torno*. It has partitions so you can't see into the convent as the cupboard turns. Whatever you put there simply disappears and another part of the cupboard faces the street.' He sipped his wine. 'They use them for bastards. A girl has a baby, she can't raise it, so she takes it to the *torno*. There's no questions asked, you see. The nuns don't know who the mother is, and the mother knows the baby's in good hands. It's clean. It's better than letting the wee things die in the gutter.'

'Or join the army,' Frederickson said.

Sharpe wondered what the purpose of the story was. but knew better than to ask. The wind was driving clouds to cover the western stars.

Hogan shrugged. 'Sometimes I feel just like the person inside the convent. The cupboard turns, there's the baby on the shelf, and I don't know where it's come from, or what it's called, or who put it there, or what bastard had his joy of the girl and dropped her. It's just a little scrap of mystery, but there's one difference.' He looked from the fire to Sharpe. 'My job is to solve the mystery. The *torno* has just dumped this thing into my lap, and you're going to find out who put it there. You understand?'

Sharpe nodded. He should, he thought, be the Major of a Battalion marching to war. He should be preparing his men to stand in the musket line and blast death at an attacking army, but instead he was to be Hogan's spy. He had earned the job by his foolishness, by accepting the duel. And the result was this secret meeting in the hills and the chance to once more go close to a woman he had once thought unapproachable, a woman who had been his lover for a short, treacherous season in Salamanca. 'I understand.'

'Find out, come back, and maybe, Richard, just maybe, the General will give you your rank back.'

'Maybe?'

'Wellington doesn't like fools.' A spot of rain hissed on the fire. Hogan pulled his cloak about him. 'You'd better pray that I'm right.'

'About what?'

The Irishman stared at the fire. 'I don't understand it, Richard, I really don't. It's too elaborate! To kill a General, send an Inquisitor, mark you as the murderer? Someone thought about it all, someone planned it, and I cannot convince my addled brain that they did it just to have you hanged. Laudable as that aim is, why kill a Marqués for it? No.' He frowned in thought. 'The bastards are up to something. I can feel it in my bones, but I don't know what it is. So you find out. And if you don't find out, don't come back.'

He said the last words brutally. No one spoke. More rain hissed on the flames. One of the horses whinnied softly.

Hogan gestured at the Spanish boy. 'He's called Angel.'

Sharpe looked at the boy and nodded. Angel smiled timidly back at the Rifleman.

Hogan switched into Spanish. 'I'm lending him to you, and I want him back in one piece because he's useful. I don't care if you don't come back, but I want Angel.'

Angel smiled nervously. Hogan looked up at the sky. 'I've a horse for you as well; a better one than you deserve. And this.' He took something from his haversack and handed it to Sharpe.

It was a telescope, Sharpe's own telescope. It had been a gift to him, given ten years before when he had been commissioned as an officer. There was a small brass plate inset into the curve of the walnut barrel, and inscribed on the brass was 'In Gratitude. AW. September 23rd, 1803'.

If it was not for that day, Sharpe reflected as he took the glass, he might not be alive now. Wellington had undoubtedly remembered the day when his horse had been piked and he had been pitched forward towards the bayonets of his enemies. A Sergeant called Richard Sharpe had saved the General's life that day, beating back the enemy until the General was on his feet. It would be hard, Sharpe thought, to see a man who had saved your life condemned to hang for a crime he had not committed.

Sharpe looked at Hogan. 'You've brought my sword?'

'Yes.'

'And more ammunition?' Hogan had sent him north with only his rifle.

'Yes.'

'So what do I do with your horse and Angel?'

'You go and solve my mystery.' Hogan put snuff onto his hand, sniffed it, paused, then sneezed. For once he did not swear after the sneeze. 'I could have sent one of my own people, but you have one advantage.'

'Which is?'

Hogan looked at Sharpe, 'You know Helene. I just hope to God she'll want to see you again, and that she'll talk to you. Find her, curl up with her, find out what the hell is happening, and save your miserable career.'

Frederickson laughed. Sharpe squirted wine from the skin into his mouth.

Hogan nodded at Angel. 'Angel's your spy. Don't worry that he looks young, he's been working for me since he was thirteen. He can go where you can't go. And you have one other advantage. Helene is rather noticeable. If the two of you get within twenty miles of her, you'll hear about it. You know what the Spanish call her?'

'*La Puta Dorada.*' Sharpe said it softly It was a just enough nickname, yet its use always offended him. 'Will the Partisans help me?'

'Who knows? They think you're dead, so use another name.' He smiled mockingly. 'Don't call yourself Major Hogan, please? I suppose you'll have to look for the Partisans, but they don't have any love for the Marquesa. Still, they might help you.'

'Where would you start looking?'

'Burgos or Vitoria,' Hogan said decisively. 'Burgos because it's the crossroads of the French armies and if she's in Spain then she'll have passed through, and Vitoria because that's where the Inquisitor comes from. It's not much, God knows, but it's better than nothing.' Hogan frowned up at the sky, as if angry with the rain. 'There's one other thing.'

Sharpe grinned. 'You're saving the bad news till last?'

'If the French capture you, Richard, they'll crow their victory from every housetop in Europe. They'll prove that we cheated the Spanish with an execution, they'll parade you like a captive bear to prove Britain's perfidy. Or, if they don't do that, they'll simply kill you. You're officially dead, after all, so they've nothing to lose.' He stared at the Rifleman. 'So don't get captured.' Hogan said it with a seething intensity and, to drive the message home, repeated the words. 'Don't get captured.'

That was Hogan's fear. It had been Wellington's fear, too, when Hogan had suggested that Sharpe be sent to solve the mystery. The General had bristled at Sharpe's name. 'What if the fool gets caught, Hogan? Good God! The French will make hay of us! No. It won't do, It won't do.'

'He won't get caught, my Lord.' Hogan had already sent Sharpe to the Gateway of God, and was praying that no stray enemy cavalry patrol had already found the Rifleman.

It had taken Hogan two days to persuade the General, his only argument that no one but Sharpe could safely approach La Marquesa. The General had reluctantly agreed. He had wanted to send Sharpe back to England with orders never to show his face in the army again. 'If this goes wrong, Hogan, it'll be your hide as well as his.'

'It won't go wrong, my Lord, I promise you.'

Wellington had looked mockingly at his chief of intelligence. 'One man against an army?'

'Yes, my Lord.' And that man would win, Hogan fervently believed, because losing was not part of Richard Sharpe's world.

He watched Sharpe now, his face lit by the flames in the Gateway of God, and he wondered if Sharpe would live to come back to the army. He was sending him with just one boy deep behind the enemy lines, to find a woman who was as treacherous as she was beautiful, yet Hogan had no choice. This summer the General planned a campaign that could destroy French power in Spain, but the French knew how potent was the threat and they would be fighting back, using every weapon of treachery and subtlety that came to hand. Hogan, with an instinct for trouble far off, had fought to let Sharpe go into enemy territory. There was a mystery to be solved, and only Sharpe knew the woman whose letter had revealed that mystery. And the only hope of success was in Sharpe's belief, that Hogan knew could be utterly false, that La Marquesa had become fond of the Rifleman when they were lovers.

Yet, Hogan thought, Sharpe could be right. The Rifleman provoked great loyalty from all sorts of men and women. From generals and whores to sergeants and frightened recruits. He was a soldier's soldier, but his friends and lovers saw the vulnerability in him and it made them fond of him. Yet Hogan wondered how much fondness the Golden Whore had in her soul.

The wind gusted, shrieking like a tormented soul in the shattered cloister, and bringing a slapping, rattling burden of rain to lash the broken tiles and seethe in the embers. Hogan shivered beneath his cloak. This was a place of ghosts, the unseen Shee were riding the winds of storm, and he was sending a friend into the unknown to fight an unequal battle.

CHAPTER 10

Richard Sharpe lay on thin, wiry grass and propped his telescope on his pack. He slid the brass shutter aside from the eyepiece, adjusted the tubes, and stared in awed amazement.

He watched an army marching.

He had seen the smear of dust in the sky, rising higher as the morning moved towards midday's heat, and the dust had looked like the haze of a great grass fire in the far south.

He had ridden towards the haze, going slowly for fear of enemy cavalry patrols, and now, in the early afternoon, he lay on the low summit of a small hill and stared at the men and animals that had smudged the great plume of dust across the heavens.

The French were marching eastwards. They were marching towards Burgos, towards France.

The road itself was left for the heavy traffic, for the wagons and the guns and the carriages of the generals. Beside the road, trampling the scanty crops, marched the infantry. He moved the telescope right, the far uniforms a blur of colour in his eye, and steadied it where the road came from a small village. Tumbrils and caissons, limbers and ambulances, wagons and more wagons, the horses and oxen dipping their heads with the effort of hauling their loads under the hot Spanish sun. In the village was the tower of an old castle, its grey stone broken by spreading ivy, and Sharpe saw white smoke rising from the tower, mingling with the dust, and knew that the French had looted and now burned the tower. They were abandoning this countryside, going eastward, retreating.

He pushed the telescope left, turning it to look as far to the east as he could see, to where, like a tiny grey blur on the horizon the topmost stones of Burgos' fortress showed above some trees, and everywhere the road was crammed with men and horses. The infantry moved slowly, like men who hated to retreat. Their women and children slogged along beside them. Cavalry walked beside their steeds, under orders to save their horses' strength, while only a few squadrons, lancers mostly, whose pennants were stained white with dust, trotted on the flanks of the huge column to protect it against Spanish sharpshooters.

Sharpe rested the telescope. Without the benefit of the fine glass the French army looked like a black snake winding across the valley. He knew he saw a retreat, but he did not know why the enemy retreated. He had heard no guns like thunder in the distance that would have told him of a great battle that Wellington had won. He just watched the great beast snake in the valley, smearing the sky white, and he had no idea why it was here, or where it went, or where his own forces were.

He wriggled back from the skyline, snapped the telescope shut, and turned to the horse which he had tethered to a stone field marker. Hogan had lent him a fine, strong, patient stallion called Carbine, who now watched Sharpe and twitched his long, black, undocked tail. He was a lucky horse, Sharpe thought, because the rule in the British army was that all horses should have their tails cut short, but Carbine had been left his intact so that, at a distance, he would seem to the French to be one of their own. He had been corn fed too, strengthened through the winter to carry one of Hogan's men who would spy deep behind French lines. Now he carried Sharpe to find a lady.

Though if the Marquesa was in Burgos, Sharpe reflected as he walked towards Carbine, she would be impossible to reach. The French army was falling back on the city, and by tonight Burgos would be surrounded by the enemy. He could only hope that Angel was safe.

The boy was sixteen. His father, a cooper, had died trying to save his wife from the attentions of French Dragoons. Angel had watched his parents die, had seen his house and his father's workshop burned to cinders, and that same night, armed only with a knife, he had killed his first Frenchman. He had been lucky to escape. He had twisted into the darkness on his young legs as the bullets of the French sentries thrashed about him in the growing rye. He had told Sharpe the story diffidently. 'I put the knife in my parents' grave, *señor*.' He had buried his parents himself, then gone to find the Partisans. He had been just thirteen.

Instead of Partisans he had met one of Hogan's Exploring Officers, the men who, in full uniform, galloped their swift horses deep in enemy country. That officer had passed the boy back to Hogan and, in the last three years, Angel had carried messages between the British and the Partisans. 'I'm getting old for that now.'

Sharpe had chuckled. 'Old? At sixteen?'

'Now the French see I am a man. They think I might be an enemy.' Angel had shrugged. 'Before that I was just a boy, they took no notice of me.'

This day, as Sharpe had lain and watched the French army trudge towards Burgos, Angel had gone into the city. His horse, a gift from Hogan, had been left with Sharpe, together with the rifle that the boy carried. He refused wages from Major Hogan, wanting only his food, shelter when he was with the British, and the 'gun that kills'. He had been offered a smoothbore musket, and had scathingly rejected it. He wanted only a Baker Rifle and, now that one was his, he looked after it lovingly, polishing its woodwork and meticulously cleaning its lock. He claimed that he and the rifle had killed two Frenchmen for every year of his life.

He was incurious about his task with Sharpe. The Golden Whore meant nothing to him, and he did not care if the Marqués de Casares el Grande y Melida Sadaba was dead. Such things were boring to Angel. He cared only that he had been told that this job was important, that success would hurt his enemies, and that the search for the Marquesa would take him where there were more Frenchmen to be killed. He was glad to be working for Sharpe. He had heard that Sharpe had killed many Frenchmen. Sharpe had smiled. 'There's more to life than killing Frenchmen.'

'I know, *señor*.'

'You do?'

Angel had nodded. 'But I do not wish to marry yet.' He had looked up from the fire into Sharpe's eyes. 'You think you will chase the French over the mountains? Back to France?'

Sharpe had nodded. 'Probably.'

'I shall join your Rifles then.' He smiled. 'I shall march into Paris and remember my parents.'

Angel would not be the first Spanish youth to join the British Rifles; indeed some companies had a dozen Spaniards who had begged to be allowed into the elite ranks. 'Sweet William' Frederickson said the only problem with the Spanish recruits was getting them to stop fighting. 'They want to win the war in a day.' Sharpe, listening to Angel talk of his parents, understood the zeal with which they fought.

Sharpe rode back to the wooded valley where he would wait for Angel to return from the city. He unsaddled Carbine and tethered him to a pine trunk. He dutifully inspected the horse's hooves, wishing that Angel, who was so much more efficient at looking after the horses, was here to help, then he carried the saddle up to the small clearing that was their rendezvous.

Sharpe waited. Dusk stretched shadows among the pine trunks and a wind rattled the branches overhead. He scouted the margins of the valley in the twilight, looking for humans, but seeing only a vixen and her cubs who played a snarling game at the foot of a sandy bank. He went back to the horses, put his rifle beside him, and waited for Angel's return.

The boy came in the dawn, a grey shadow in the trees, bringing with him a cheese wrapped in vine leaves, a new loaf, and his news. Before he would say a word to Sharpe about La Marquesa he insisted on retrieving his rifle and inspecting it in the half-light as though one night's separation would have somehow changed the weapon. Satisfied, he looked up at the Rifle officer. 'She's disappeared.'

Sharpe felt a plunging of his hopes. For these four days since he had parted from Hogan he had feared that Helene would have gone back to France. 'Disappeared?'

Angel told the story. She had left the city in a carriage and, though the carriage had come back, La Marquesa had not returned. 'The French were angry. They had cavalry searching everywhere. They looked in all the villages, they offered a reward of gold, but nothing. They increased the reward, but nothing. She's gone.'

Sharpe swore, and the boy grinned.

'You don't trust me, eh?' He laughed. He was a startlingly handsome boy, curly haired and strong faced. His dark eyes shone in the light of the fire that Sharpe had lit as dawn came. 'I know where she is, *señor*.'

'Where?'

'The Convent of the Heavens, Santa Monica.' Angel held up a hand to ward off Sharpe's question. 'I think.'

'You think?'

Angel took the wine flask and drank. 'The priests took her, yes? They and the monks. Everyone knows it, but no one talks. They say the Inquisition was here.' He crossed himself, and Sharpe thought of the Inquisitor who had come with the letter for the Marqués. Angel smiled. 'They don't know where they took her, but I do.'

'How do you know?'

'Because I am Angel, yes?' The boy laughed. 'I saw a man who knows me. He tells the Partisans what troops are marching towards the hills. I trust him.' The words should have sounded odd coming from a sixteen year old, but they did not seem strange coming from this boy who had risked his life since he was thirteen. Angel took some loose tobacco from a pocket, a scrap of paper, and, in Spanish fashion, rolled a makeshift cigar. He leaned forward and the tip of the cigar flared as he sucked on a flame of the fire. 'This man says that he has heard that the woman was taken to Santa Monica, to the convent. He heard from the Partisans.' Angel blew smoke into the air. 'The Partisans are guarding the convent.'

'The Partisans?'

'*Si*. You have heard of *El Matarife*?'

Sharpe shook his head. The hills of Spain were filled with Partisan leaders who took fanciful nicknames. He tried to think what the word meant. 'A man who kills animals?'

'Yes. A slaughterman. You should have heard of him. He is famous.'

'And he guards the convent?'

Angel sucked on the disintegrating tube of tobacco. 'So it is said. He will guard the *mesa*, not the convent.'

'The table?'

'The convent is on a mountain, yes? Very high with a flat top, a *mesa*. There are few paths up, *señor*, so it is easy to guard.'

'Where is it?'

'Two days' ride? There.' He pointed to the north-east.

'Have you been there?'

'No.' Angel disgustedly threw the remains of his cigar into the fire. He had somehow not mastered the knack of twisting the paper and tobacco exactly right. 'I have heard of it though.'

Sharpe was trying to make sense, any kind of sense, from Angel's news. The Inquisition? That coincidence made the boy's tale seem true, but why should the Inquisition want to kidnap Helene? Or why, for that matter, would the Slaughterman be guarding the convent where she was held?

He asked the boy, and Angel shrugged. 'Who knows? He is not a man you can ask.'

'What kind of man is he?'

The boy frowned. 'He kills Frenchmen.' He paid the compliment dubiously. 'But he kills his own people, too, yes? He once shot twelve men of a village because the villagers had refused his men food. He rode in at the siesta time and shot them. Even Mina cannot control him.' Angel spoke of the man who had been made general of all the Partisans. Mina had been known to execute men such as *El Matarife* who persecuted their own countrymen. Angel was making himself another cigar. 'The French are scared of him. It's said that he once put the heads of fifty Frenchmen on the Great Road, one every mile through the mountains so the French would find them. That was near Vitoria where he comes from.' The boy laughed. 'He kills slowly. They say he has a leather coat made from French skins. Some say he is mad.'

'Can we find him?'

'*Si.*' Angel said it as though the question was unnecessary. 'So we ride to the mountains?'

'We ride to the mountains.'

They rode north east to where the mountains became dizzying crags, the hunting grounds of eagles, a land of awesome valleys and of waterfalls that seethed from the low clouds of morning to fall scores of feet into cold, upland streams.

They rode north east into a land where the inhabitants were few, and those inhabitants so poor and frightened that they fled when they saw two strange horsemen coming. Some of the people here, Angel said, would not even know there was a war on. 'They're not even Spanish!' He said it scathingly.

'Not Spanish?'

'They're Basques. They have their own language.'

'So who are they?'

Angel shrugged dismissively. 'They live here.' He obviously had nothing more to say about them.

Angel, it seemed to Sharpe, was fretting. They had come into these northern mountains and were far from the French. They were far from the war and, from what Angel had heard in Burgos, far from the excitement.

The rumours in Burgos said that the British had at last marched, and were attacking in the north. The French northern army was retreating and Sharpe had seen the vanguard of that army as it approached Burgos. Angel feared the campaign would be over before he could kill again. Sharpe laughed. 'It won't be over.'

'You promise?'

'I promise. How do we find *El Matarife*?'

'He finds us, *señor*. Do you think he doesn't know there's an Englishman in the hills?'

'Just remember not to call me Sharpe.'

'*Si, señor.*' Angel grinned. 'What are you called now?'

Sharpe smiled. He remembered the suave, regretful officer who had conducted his prosecution. 'Vaughn. Major Vaughn.'

He rode between high rocks, beneath the eagles, and he searched for the Marquesa and for the Slaughterman.

El Matarife, like Angel, fretted at being so far from the richer pickings that were to be had to the south. These high, deep valleys were poor, there were few French to be ambushed, and little to be stolen from the meagre villages. He had two French prisoners with him, playthings for his entertainment.

The news of the Englishman was brought to him by three of his men. *El Matarife* occupied an inn, or what passed in this miserable place for an inn, and he scowled at the three men as though they were responsible for the Englishman's coming. 'He said he wanted to speak with me?'

'Yes.'

'He did not say why?'

'Only that his General had sent him.'

El Matarife grunted. 'Not before time, eh?' His lieutenants nodded. Wellington had sent messengers to other Partisan leaders, requesting their co-operation, and the Slaughterman presumed that his turn had come.

But he could not be sure of it. In the convent, thousands of feet above the valley, was *La Puta Dorada*. She had been brought by his brother who had warned *El Matarife* that the French might search for her, but the Inquisitor had said nothing about any Englishman. *El Matarife* could understand a man searching for the woman. He had seen her in the carriage and, even dishevelled and tearful, she had been beautiful. 'Why give her to the nuns?' he had asked.

His brother had snapped at him. 'She has to take the vows, don't you understand? It must be legal! She must become a nun! She must take her vows, nothing else matters!'

The Inquisitor had left his brother with instructions that no one was to be allowed close to the convent, and that, if anyone asked about the Marquesa, her presence was to be denied. She was to be buried and forgotten and left to Christ.

Now *El Matarife* wondered whether the Englishman had come looking for the whore of gold. 'What is he called?'

'Vaughn. Major Vaughn.'

'He's alone?'

'He has a boy with him.'

One of his lieutenants saw the concern on *El Matarife's* face and shrugged. 'Just kill him. Who'll know?'

'You're a fool. Your mother sucked an ass.' *El Matarife* jabbed at the fire with a sword point. It was cold in these deep valleys, and the fire in the inn's main room did little to help. He looked back to the men who had spoken with the Englishman the night before. 'He said nothing of any woman?'

'No.'

'You're sure he's English? Not a Frenchman?'

The men shrugged.

El Matarife peered through the window, stooping so he could see to the very top of the huge, grey slab of cliff where the Convent of the Heavens was perched. The presence of La Marquesa in that cold building was supposed to be a secret, though *El Matarife* knew better than most that there were few secrets in Spain's countryside. Someone would have talked.

He could kill the Englishman, but that was a last resort. The English were the source of gold, guns and ammunition, landing them on the hidden beaches of the northern coast at night. If an Englishman was to be killed, then *El Matarife* had a suspicion that a reckoning might be made; that his men would be hunted and punished by other Partisans, yet, if he had to kill the Englishman, he would, though he would rather send the man away satisfied, suspicion allayed, so he could continue this wearisome watch uninterruptedly.

'Where is this Major Vaughn?'

'At the two bridges.'

'Bring him tonight.' The Slaughterman looked at one of his lieutenants. 'Bring the prisoners. We shall entertain our Englishman.'

'The woman too?'

'Especially her.' *El Matarife* smiled. 'If he has come for a woman then he can have her!' He laughed. He had fooled the French for four years and now he would fool an Englishman. He shouted for wine and waited for the night.

Night fell swiftly in the depths of the valley beneath the

Convent of the Heavens. When the peaks were still touched red by the last daylight it was already dark at the inn that *El Matarife* called his headquarters. In front of the inn, and lit by smoking torches, was an area of beaten earth. Sharpe and Angel, brought to the place by silent guides, were led to the lit space.

A chain was thrown onto the patch of earth. It lay there, ten feet of rusting links, and at its far end, nervous and dressed only in ragged trousers, stood a prisoner.

A Partisan picked up the chain and looped one end about the man's left wrist. He tied it clumsily, jerked on it to make sure it was secure, then stepped back. He took from his belt a long knife and tossed it at the man's feet.

One of the men who had guided Sharpe to this place grinned at the Rifleman. 'A Frenchman. You watch his death, Englishman.'

A second man stepped forward, a hulking man who shrugged off a cloak and whose appearance provoked applause from the watching Partisans. The man turned towards Sharpe and the Rifleman saw a face which, at first, seemed unnatural, as though it belonged to a creature that was half-beast and half-man. Sharpe had heard his men tell stories about the strange things that were men by day and beasts by night, and this man could have been such a thing. His beard sprouted from his cheeks, growing as high as the cheekbones, leaving only a small gap beneath his hair, a gap from which two small, cunning eyes looked at Sharpe. The man smiled. 'Welcome, Englishman.'

'*El Matarife?*'

'Of course. Our business will wait?'

Sharpe shrugged. The Partisans watched him, grinning. He sensed that this display was being given for his benefit.

El Matarife stooped, took the loose end of the chain, and wrapped it about his upper left arm. He took from his belt a long knife like that carried by the Frenchman. 'I shall count the ways of your death, pig.'

The Frenchman did not understand the words. He understood that he must fight, and he licked his lips, hefted the knife, and waited as *El Matarife* stepped backwards, lifting the chain from the ground until it was taut between them. *El Matarife* went on pulling, forcing the Frenchman to step forward. The prisoner tugged back and the Partisans laughed.

Sharpe saw that many of the Partisans, instead of watching the strange fight, watched him. They were testing him. They knew that the English treated prisoners with decency; they wanted to see what kind of a man Sharpe was. Would he flinch at the display? If he did, then he would lose face.

El Matarife looked at Sharpe, then suddenly jerked on the chain, making the prisoner stumble. The Partisan went forward, knife low, and the Frenchman desperately slashed with his own blade and it seemed to Sharpe that the Frenchman must have drawn blood, but when *El Matarife* stepped back he was untouched. The prisoner had a slashed left arm. The blood dripped from the chain.

'*Uno*,' *El Matarife* said.

'*Uno*,' his men echoed.

Sharpe watched. The Partisan leader was fast. He was skilled at this kind of fighting. Sharpe doubted whether he had ever seen a man so quick with a blade. The bearded face was smiling.

The Frenchman suddenly lunged forward, looping the chain up in an attempt to wrap it about his opponent's neck.

El Matarife laughed, stepped back, and the knife was a flicker of brightness in the flamelight.

'*Dos!*'

The Frenchman was shaking his head. There was blood on his forehead.

The chain swung between them. Once more *El Matarife* stepped back. The links made a small noise as they tightened and this time *El Matarife* went on pulling steadily, hauling the Frenchman inexorably forward. The prisoner was licking his lips. He held his knife low, but there was a puzzled look on his face. He was trying to plan this fight and *El Matarife* was content to let him plan. At this kind of fighting the Slaughterman was an expert. He feared no

126

Frenchman, no man who was not trained to the tied knife fight.

The Frenchman suddenly jerked backwards, jerked with all his weight and *El Matarife*, laughing, went fast forward so that the Frenchman, taken by surprise, fell backwards.

The Slaughterman hauled on the chain, towing the man on the ground, tugging and pulling, laughing as his prisoner thrashed like a hooked and landed fish, then *El Matarife* stepped forward, lashed out with his black-booted right foot to kick the Frenchman's left forearm.

Sharpe heard the crack of the bone and the stifled cry of the prisoner.

'*Tres*,' *El Matarife* said. He stepped away to let the Frenchman get up. The prisoner looked dizzy. He was in pain. His arm was broken and every pull on the chain would now be agony. The man looked up at his tormentor and suddenly lunged with the knife, throwing himself forward from his knees, but *El Matarife* simply laughed and moved his knife hand faster than the eye could follow.

'*Cuatro*.'

There was blood on the back of the Frenchman's hand.

Sharpe looked at the guide beside him. 'How long does it go on?'

'At least thirty cuts, Englishman. Sometimes a hundred. You don't like it, eh?' The man laughed.

Sharpe did not reply. Slowly, very slowly, so that no one could see what he did, he leaned forward and found with his right hand the lock of his rifle that was pushed into a saddle holster. Quietly and slowly he eased the cock back until he felt it seated at the full.

The Frenchman was on his feet now. He knew that he was being played with, that his opponent was a master of this kind of fighting, that the cuts would go on and on till his body was seething with pain and drenched with blood. He attacked the Slaughterman, slicing left and right, stabbing, going into a frenzy of despair, and *El Matarife*, who, despite his bulk, was as fast on his feet as any man Sharpe had seen, seemed to dance away from each attack. He was laughing, holding his own knife out of the way and then, when the Frenchman's frenzy had died, the knife seared forward.

'*Cinco!*'

There was a cheer from the crowd. The knife, with horrid accuracy, had speared into one of the prisoner's eyes. The man screamed, twisted, but the knife took his other eye just the same.

'*Seis,*' El Matarife laughed.

'*Seis!*' the men shouted.

The Spaniard beside Sharpe looked at the Rifleman. 'Now the enjoyment begins, Englishman.'

But Sharpe had pulled the rifle from the holster, brought it to his shoulder, and pulled the trigger.

The bullet went between the blinded eyes, throwing the Frenchman back, dead onto the ground that was smeared with his blood.

Then there was silence.

Sharpe pushed the weapon back into the holster and urged Carbine forward. Angel was tense with fear. A dozen men about the fighting ground had cocked their muskets as the rifle smoke drifted over the dead body.

Sharpe reined in above the bearded angry man. He bowed in his saddle. 'Now I shall be able to boast that I fought against the French alongside the great *Matarife*.'

El Matarife stared up at the Englishman who had spoiled his amusement. He knew why the Englishman had shot the man, because the Englishman was squeamish, but in doing it the Englishman had challenged *El Matarife* in front of his own men. Now, though, this Major Vaughn had offered a saving formula

El Matarife laughed. 'You hear that?' He had unlooped the chain and he gestured to his followers. 'He says he has fought beside me, eh?' His men laughed and *El Matarife* stared up at the Englishman. 'So why are you here?'

'To bring you greetings from the Generalissimo.'

'He has heard of me?' *El Matarife* had picked up a great poleaxe that he slung on his shoulder.

'Who has not heard of *El Matarife*?'

The tension had gone. Sharpe was aware that he had

failed one test by refusing to watch a blinded man being tortured, but by killing the Frenchman he had proved himself worthy of some respect. Worthy, too, of drink. He was taken into the inn, wine was ordered, and the compliments were profuse and truthless that, of necessity, had to preface the business of the night.

They drank for two hours, the main room of the inn becoming smokier as the evening wore on. A meal was provided; a hunk of goat meat in a greasy gravy that Sharpe ate hungrily. It was at the end of the meal that *El Matarife*, wrapped in a cloak of wolf's fur, asked again why the Englishman had come.

Sharpe spun a story, half based on truth, a story that told of the British army advancing on Burgos and pushing the French back on the Great Road. He had come, he said, because the Generalissimo wanted assurance that every Partisan would be on the road to harass the retreating French and help kill Frenchmen.

'Every Partisan, Englishman?'

'But especially *El Matarife*.'

El Matarife nodded, and there was nothing in what Sharpe had said to cause suspicion. His men were excited at the thought of a battle happening on the Great Road, of the plunder that would be taken, of the stragglers who could be picked off from the French march. The Slaughterman picked at his teeth with a sliver of wood. 'When will the British come?'

'They come now. Their soldiers cover the plains like a flood. The French are running away. They run towards Vitoria.' That was hardly true. Sharpe had only seen the French retreating to Burgos, and, if this year's campaign was like the last, they would make their stand at the fortress town. Yet the lie convinced *El Matarife*.

'You will tell your General that my forces will help him.' *El Matarife* waved a magnanimous hand about the room.

'He will be relieved.' Sharpe politely pushed a wineskin over the table. 'Yet he will be curious about one thing.'

'Ask.'

'There are no French in these mountains, yet you are here.'

'I hide from them, I let them think I am gone, and when they celebrate that I am gone, I return!' He laughed.

Sharpe laughed with him. 'You are a clever man.'

'Tell your General that, Englishman.'

'I will tell him that.' Sharpe could feel his eyes stinging from the thick tobacco smoke. He looked at Angel. 'We must leave.'

'Already?' *El Matarife* frowned. He was more than convinced that the Englishman had not come about the woman, and he was enjoying the flattery that impressed his men. 'You go already?'

'To sleep. Tomorrow I must ride to my General with this news. He is impatient to hear of you.' Sharpe paused as he pushed his chair back, fished in his pocket and brought out a scrap of paper. It was an order from Colonel Leroy about mending camp-kettles, but no one in this room would know that. He read it, frowned, then looked up at the Slaughterman. 'I almost forgot! You guard *La Puta Dorada*?' He could feel the tension in the room, betrayed by the sudden silence that greeted his words. Sharpe shrugged. 'It is not important, but my General asked me and I am asking you.'

'What of her?'

Sharpe screwed the piece of paper up and tossed it onto the fire. 'We heard she had been brought here.'

'You heard?'

'Whatever *El Matarife* does is important to us.' Sharpe smiled. 'You see we would like to talk to her. She must know things about the French army that would help us. The Generalissimo is full of admiration that you should have captured so important a spy.'

The compliments seemed to soothe the bearded, suspicious man. Slowly, very slowly, *El Matarife* nodded. 'You want to talk with her, Englishman?'

'For an hour.'

'Just talk?' There was appreciative laughter in the room.

Sharpe smiled. 'Just talk. One hour, no more. She is in the convent?'

El Matarife was still convinced that Sharpe's mission was to secure his help with the summer's campaign. It was a nuisance that the English had heard of the woman's presence in the mountains, but he believed the Englishman when he said he merely wanted to talk. Besides, how could one Englishman and a Spanish boy rescue her from among his men? *El Matarife* smiled, knowing that he must send this Major Vaughn away satisfied. To simply deny that the Marquesa was in these mountains was to risk that this Englishman would want to search for himself. He gestured to one of his men, who left the inn's smoky room, and turned back to Sharpe. 'You've met her before, Major Vaughn?'

'No.'

'You'll like her.' The Slaughterman laughed. 'But she's not in the convent.'

'No?'

More wine was put in front of Sharpe. The Slaughterman was smiling contentedly. 'She is here.'

'Here?'

'I heard you were coming, Englishman, and I thought I would help your General by letting you talk with her. She has much to tell you about your enemies. I waited to see if you would ask, if you had not, then I would have surprised you!'

Sharpe smiled. 'I will tell my General of your help. He will want to reward you.' He was struggling not to show his excitement, nor his consternation. The thought of Helene in the power of this beast was foul, the thought of how he was to take her away from here was daunting, yet he dared not show it. Present too in his head was the recurring fear that she would know nothing, that she would find the death of her husband as great a mystery as Sharpe, yet if he had any hopes of regaining his rank and his career, he had to ask her his questions. 'You are bringing her to this room?'

'I will give you a room to talk with her, Englishman.'

'I am grateful to you, *Matarife*.'

'A private room, Major!' *El Matarife* laughed and made an obscene gesture. 'Perhaps when you see her you will want to do more than talk, yes?'

El Matarife's gust of laughter was interrupted by a shout from outside the inn and the sound of feet running. The back door was thrown open and a voice shouted that *El Matarife* should come and come quickly.

The Slaughterman pushed towards the door, Sharpe beside him, and the room was full of men shouting for lanterns, and then Sharpe ducked under the lintel and saw a light coming from a broken down shed that was being used as a stable. Men ran towards the shed, lanterns bright, and Sharpe went with them. He pushed through them and stopped at the doorway. He wanted to vomit, so sudden was the shock, and his next urge was to draw the big sword and scythe these beasts who pressed in the small yard around him.

A girl hung in the shed. She was naked. Her body was a tracery of gleaming rivulets of blood, blood new enough to shine, yet not so new that it still flowed.

She turned on the rope that was about her neck.

El Matarife swore. He cuffed at a man who claimed that the girl had committed suicide.

The body turned, slim and white. The thighs and stomach showed dark bruises beneath the blood that had reached her ankles. Her hands were slim and pale, the nails broken, but still with flecks of red where they had once been painted. There was straw in her hair.

A dozen men shouted. They had locked the girl in here and she must have found the rope. *El Matarife's* voice drowned them all, cursing them for this stupidity, their carelessness. He looked up at the tall Englishman. 'They are fools, *señor*. I will punish them.'

Sharpe noticed how, for the first time, the Slaughterman called him *señor*. He stared up at the face that had once been lovely. 'Punish them well.'

'I will! I will!'

Sharpe turned away. 'And give her Christian burial!'

'Yes, *señor*.' The Slaughterman watched the Englishman closely. 'She was beautiful, yes?'

'She was beautiful.'

'The Golden Whore.' *El Matarife* said the words slowly,

as though he pronounced an epitaph. 'You can't talk to her now, *señor*.'

Sharpe looked at the hanging body. There were scratches on the breasts. He nodded and forced calmness into his voice. 'I shall ride south this night.' He turned away. He knew *El Matarife's* men watched him, but he would show nothing. He shouted for Angel to bring the horses.

He stopped a mile from the small village. The memory of the hanging, turning body was foul in him. He thought of his wife dead, of the blood on her throat. He thought of the torture that the dead woman in the stable had endured, of the horrid last moments of a life. He closed his eyes and shuddered.

'We go back now, *señor*?' Sharpe heard the sadness in Angel's voice that their mission had been wasted.

'No.'

'No?'

'We go to the convent.' They had seen it before the dusk, a building clinging impossibly to a plateau's edge. 'We climb there tonight.' He opened his eyes, twisted in the saddle, and stared behind him. No one had followed them from the inn.

'We go to the convent? But she's dead!'

'She's called the whore of gold.' Sharpe's voice was savage. 'Gold because of her hair, Angel, not her money. Whoever that girl was, she wasn't La Marquesa.'

But whoever the black-haired girl was whose body hung bloody and slim in the stable, she was dead, and newly dead at that, and Sharpe knew the girl had died because he had asked about La Marquesa. She had died so that Sharpe would leave this valley quietly, convinced that La Marquesa was dead. He pushed back with his heels, turning Carbine, and rode towards the dark mountain. He felt a thickness in his throat because the unknown girl was dead, and he promised her spirit, wherever it was, that he would avenge her. He rode with anger, he climbed to the Convent of the Heavens, and he planned a rescue and a battle.

CHAPTER 11

It could have been winter, so cold and misty was the plateau. At this height the mist was low cloud that threatened rain. Only the dripping leaves of the few stunted birches witnessed that summer had some to this high, strange, chilling place.

Sharpe had not slept. He had planned the fight he knew he would face once *El Matarife* discovered that he had not passed his sentinels at the two bridges. In the dawn he had scouted the plateau's edge, peering through the mist down the tumbled, precipitous slopes of the great hill.

Sharpe had not brought Angel all the way to the flat summit of the great hill. He had left the boy on the track with both rifles and careful, painstaking instructions.

Angel had been worried. 'It's a holy place, *señor*.'

'Trust me, Angel, just trust me.'

Sharpe had climbed to the plateau with the two horses, and with the fear that this dreadful, desperate deed that he planned could all be for nothing. He would fight Partisans, he would offend the Church, and all for a woman who might not have the answers to save his career and solve Hogan's mystery.

Angel had wished him luck, but the boy had been distressed. 'We have to fight them, *señor*?' He spoke of the Partisans.

'To defeat France, yes.' It was a lie, or at the very least Sharpe did not know if it was a truth. Yet Angel, who trusted the English, had believed him.

Now, as the dawn showed the grass wet on the plateau, and as the grey clouds sifted through the small trees, Sharpe galloped towards the convent. He was alone in the high place.

The Convent of the Heavens deserved its name. It was built at the highest point of this steep range of hills, a building that clung alarmingly to the edge of a precipice. It had been built in the days when the Muslims hunted the Christians north, when the prayers of Christians had to be offered in high places that could be defended by Christian swords. The walls of the convent showed no windows. They were grey like the rocks, stained by the rain, a fortress of women. There was only one door in its prison-like walls.

Sharpe knocked and waited. He knocked again, then hammered the door with a stone, making sparks fly from the square-headed iron nails that studded the great planks of wood. He could hear the sound reverberating within the building, but no answer came.

He waited. The mist drifted over the plateau. The two horses, tethered to a great stone, watched him. Their saddles were beaded with moisture.

He kicked the door, cursing, then found a larger stone that he smashed onto the timber, smashed again, until the hollow echoes were like the sound of a battery of field artillery in full fight.

There was a click.

In one of the door's two leaves was a small shutter, protected by a rusted iron grille, and the shutter had slid back. He could see an eye staring at him. He smiled and spoke in his most polite voice. 'I have come to see La Marquesa de Casares el Grande y Melida Sadaba.'

The eye blinked, the shutter slid shut, then nothing.

He waited.

There was silence from the great building. No bolts were shot back on the door, no footsteps or voices sounded from the far side. For a moment he wondered if the eye beyond the shutter had been a dream, so silent was the grey building. It seemed to have slept here for a thousand empty years and his knocking was an offence against eternity.

He found himself an even larger rock, one that he needed to lift with both hands, and he carried it to the door, measured his swing, and thumped it at the place where the

135

two leaves met. He swung it again and again, seeing the right hand leaf jar back a fraction with each blow, and the noise was huge again, echoing from the hallway within, and he wondered what Patrick Harper would think if he knew that his friend was breaking into a convent. Sharpe could almost hear the Ulster voice. 'God save Ireland.'

The rock swung and crashed, the door jerked back, and he saw an iron bar that was bent but still holding. He hammered it again, cursing with the effort, and despite the chill morning he could feel the sweat on his body and he drove the huge rock with all his strength at the weak spot and the door, at last, shattered back, the iron bar broken, and he could see into the convent.

Miles to the west, at the edge of the great plain, the army marched. Battalion after Battalion of redcoats, battery after battery of guns, all marching eastwards with the cavalry in the van searching for the retreating French.

The Marquess of Wellington, Grandee of Spain with the title of Duque de Ciudad Rodrigo, and Duque da Victoria in Portugal, looked at the northern rain clouds and scowled. 'Are they coming south?'

I think not, my Lord,' an aide said.

The General was on horseback. He had set the army in motion and he marched it eastwards. He prayed that rain would not soak the roads and slow him down. The French must not be given time to unite their armies in Spain against him. He looked at the man who rode to his left. 'Well?'

Major Hogan listed the news of the night, the messages that had come from enemy country. The news was good, so far as if went, though Hogan could not say with certainty whether the fortress at Burgos was prepared for a long siege.

'Find out! Find out!' Wellington said. 'Is that all?' His tone suggested that he hoped it was.

'One other thing, my Lord.' Hogan took a deep breath. 'It seems that the Marquesa de Casares el Grande has been arrested by the ecclesiastical authorities. We hear she's in a convent.'

Wellington stared at Hogan as if wondering why he had bothered to tell him such a trivial piece of news. Their horses walked slowly. The General frowned. 'Sharpe?' He gave a snort that was half laughter and half scorn. 'That's stopped him, eh? The vixen's gone to ground!'

'Indeed, my Lord.'

The general looked again at the clouds. The wind, such as it was, came from the east. He frowned again. 'He wouldn't be such a god-damned fool as to break into a convent, would he, Hogan?'

Hogan was of the opinion that, for the sake of a woman, Sharpe would do just that, but this did not seem to be the time to say so. 'I'm sure not, my Lord. That was not my worry.'

'What is your worry?' Wellington's tone suggested that it had better be substantial to take up his time.

'The arrest was supposed to be secret, my Lord, but inevitably rumours have spread. It seems that some French cavalry have gone north to look for her.'

Wellington laughed. 'Let them break into the convent.'

'Indeed, my Lord.'

'Rather they were there than facing us, eh? So Bonaparte's declared war on nuns, has he?'

'My concern, my Lord, was for Sharpe. If this General Verigny gets his hands on him.' Hogan shrugged.

'My God, he'd better not!' Wellington's voice was loud enough to startle some marching soldiers. 'Sharpe's got more sense than to be caught, hasn't he? On the other hand, considering what a god-damned fool he is, maybe not. Still, there's nothing we can do about it, Hogan.'

'No, my Lord.'

The General nodded to the Colonel of the Battalion they passed, throwing out a word of praise for his men, then looked again at Hogan. 'Sharpe had better not break into that god-damned convent, Hogan. I'd rather the bloody frogs caught him!'

'It seems he's done for either way, my Lord.'

Wellington scowled. 'He's done for anyway, man. You know that, so do I. We just strung him a little hope.' The subject of Sharpe seemed to irritate Wellington. The General no longer believed that the death of the Marqués held a mystery that threatened him, the advance into Spain and the campaign that loomed ahead had dwarfed such a worry into insignificance. He nodded at the Irishman. 'Keep me informed, Hogan, keep me informed.'

'Indeed, my Lord.'

Hogan let his horse fall behind. The Marquesa was immured in a convent, and his friend, by that fact, was doomed. A French cavalry regiment had gone hunting in the mountains, and Sharpe had only a boy to protect him. Sharpe was doomed.

The outside of the Convent of the Heavens was grey and bare. The interior was rich and brilliant. The hallway floor was of chequered tiles, the walls of gold mosaic, the ceiling painted. There were pictures on the walls. Facing him, alone in the cavernous hallway, was a single woman dressed in white robes.

'Go away.'

It seemed a hopeful thing to say to a man who had just spent twenty minutes breaking down a door. Sharpe stepped over the rock that had fallen in the doorway and smiled at her. 'Good morning, ma'am.' He brushed his jacket down and politedly took off his shako. 'I wish to speak with La Marquesa de Casares . . .'

'She is not here.' The woman was tall, her face lined with age. She had a splendid dignity that made Sharpe feel shabby.

He took one pace forward, his boots unnaturally loud in the cavernous hallway. 'You may force me to bring my men and search the whole convent.' That struck him as the right thing to say. The woman was frightened, and rightly, by the incursion of one man into this building where no man but a priest was ever supposed to tread. She would surely fear a whole company of soldiers.

She looked at him, frowning, 'Who are you?'

The truth would not do. When the tale got about that an Englishman had broken into a convent there would be hell to pay. Sharpe smiled. 'Major Vaughn.'

'English?'

He thought how often Wellington had insisted in his orders that the Roman church in Spain must be respected by the British. Nothing, the General believed, was more damaging to the alliance than insults to Spain's religion. Sharpe smiled. 'No, ma'am. American.' He hoped Colonel Leroy would forgive the lie, and he was glad that he did not wear a red coat that was always thought to be the only uniform of Britain.

She frowned. 'American?'

'I have come a long way to see La Marquesa.'

'Why do you wish to see that woman?'

'Matters of policy.' He hoped his Spanish was correct. She tossed her head. 'She will see no one.'

'She will see me.'

'She is a sinner.'

'So are we all.' Sharpe wondered why on earth he was swapping theological small talk with a Mother Superior. He supposed she was the Mother Superior.

'She is doing penance.'

'I wish only to talk with her.'

'The Church has ordered that no one should see her.'

'I have come from North America to see her.' He liked the lie. Even in this remote convent the news must have arrived that the Americans had joined the war that burned about the world. 'My President demands that I see her. He will send many coins to Rome if I can see her.' Why the hell not, he thought? The Americans had declared war on Britain, so why should the Pope not declare war on America? He embroidered the lie. 'Many, many gold coins.'

'It is against God's law to see her.'

'God will forgive me.'

139

'You are a sinner.'

Sharpe frowned. 'I am an American!'

The Mother Superior turned away, her voice superb. 'You cannot see her. Go away.'

She had reached a door and Sharpe feared breaking through another barrier in this place, for he needed all the time he could scrape together for his battle against *El Matarife*.

He ran forward, his boots loud on the chequered tiles, and the noise made the woman turn. For the first time she showed fear. It seemed for a moment that she would try to stop him as she lifted her thin hands from beneath the strip of white cloth that hung from her neck, but as he came close she twisted aside and snatched up a brass bell that stood on a dark oak table. Sharpe thought she was going to hit him with the bell, but instead to began to ring it. She fled from him, through the door, the bell clanging as a warning for the nuns to hide.

He followed. It was as if a wildcat had come into a hen run. He was on the top floor of a double cloister and the sound of the bell was driving white-robed women in desperate flight towards stairs and doors. Despite their panicked, fluttering scattering, they were all silent, only the clanging bell telling Sharpe that he had not been struck deaf as a punishment for his terrible sin. His was the only voice in the place. 'Helene!'

There were a dozen doors to choose from. Somewhere in the recesses of the building the bell still clanged. He decided to follow it. 'Helene! Helene!'

He found himself in a long corridor hung with huge, gloomy pictures that showed martyrs undergoing the kind of fate that the bell now warned the nuns against. The corridor smelt foully of soap.

He pushed open doors. In the chapel there was a huddle of nuns, their backs to him, their robes quivering as their hands counted beads. The candles flickered. 'Helene?'

There was no answer. The bell still tolled. He ran down a flight of stairs and heard the soft sound of slippered feet fleeing on flagstones. He wondered who repaired the old buildings. Did the nuns plaster the walls and put up new beams? Perhaps men were allowed in to do the heavy work, just as a priest undoubtedly visited to give the sacraments. 'Helene!'

He pushed open doors of empty cells, losing himself in the maze of small passages and musty rooms. He pushed open one door to find himself, aghast, in a bathroom. A woman, dressed in a white linen shift, sat in a tub of water. She stared at him, her mouth dropped, and he shut the door quickly before her scream deafened him.

He went through another door and found himself in a walled kitchen garden. The clouds were grey overhead. It had begun to rain, soaking some scrawny chickens who miserably flocked at one end of the walled garden. 'Helene!'

Back in the convent he found the refectory, the long tables set with dull metal plates. The Virgin Mary, in a vast picture, raised her eyes to the beamed ceiling. 'Helene! Helene!'

And this time there was a scream in reply, the first human voice Sharpe had heard since the Mother Superior had lifted the brass bell, and Sharpe crossed the great room to push open a door beside the empty, cold fireplace.

A chicken carcass missed his head by inches. It was only half-plucked and the feathers settled on the shoulder of his Rifleman's jacket.

He was in a huge kitchen, the vaulted stone ceiling blackened by the centuries of smoke, and facing him were a dozen nuns who had none of the demure fear that filled the rest of the convent. The half-plucked chicken had been hurled by a great, ham-faced woman with forearms like pontoon cables, who now seized a second chicken and drew back her arm.

Sharpe ducked. The body thumped on the wall behind him. 'Helene!'

He saw her, and even here, imprisoned and drab, her beauty checked him. She made the breath stop in his throat and his heart race with the surge of desire.

141

The widowed Marquesa de Casares el Grande y Melida Sadaba stared at him. She was dressed in a shapeless grey shift, her hair caught up and tied by a hank of grey rag, her face devoid of any cosmetic. The nun who held her had a hand over La Marquesa's mouth, but Helene must have sunk her teeth into the woman's palm for the hand jerked away and she struggled against the other hand. 'Richard!' Her eyes were huge, as though he was a ghost.

A great flabby ball of dough was hurled at him, he ducked again and went forward, and the nun who had started the artillery bombardment picked up a rolling pin that was as big as a cannon's axle. Sharpe ignored her. He looked at the nun holding La Marquesa. 'Let her go.'

The rolling pin was tapped once into a huge hand. The woman, Sharpe thought, looked big enough to be Patrick Harper's twin. It was a good job she had chosen the Church, he reflected, for otherwise she would have made some poor man's life a flaming hell. She stepped towards him, no fear on her face, the rolling pin ready to strike.

Yet how to fight a nun? He could not draw the sword, and he dared not strike her with his fists, but one blow from the rolling pin would shatter his skull. La Marquesa still struggled. She seemed to understand his plight and shouted at him in Spanish. 'Take your trousers down!'

The suggestion checked the woman, and Sharpe used her pause to move right and pick up an unthrown chicken by the neck. He whirled the carcass, threw, and the half-drawn giblets flailed bloodily across the room and slapped the woman over the face and she snarled, raised the pin, and Sharpe heard the screams of the other nuns. He watched the great weapon, ducked, side-stepped, and ran towards the pinioned Marquesa. His approach scared her captor, she let Helene go, and Helene ran desperately to Sharpe's side.

'This way!'

The rolling pin missed his body by inches, brushing his

sleeve as the nun hammered it onto the table with a thump that would have stirred the coffined dead.

'Come on!' He had the Marquesa's hand in his, he was running, and then the rolling pin slammed past his head to crack on the door of the kitchen.

They ran. Another chicken thumped on his back, something metallic clanged on the flagstones behind him, but then he was in the refectory, he had Helene's hand in his hand and he hurried her towards the far end. He was laughing, she was laughing, and somewhere in the convent the bell was ringing still.

It could, he thought, be a difficult retreat. He had penetrated deep into enemy country, seized his prize, and he now had to regain the front door. But no one appeared to bar their withdrawal, and the huge nun of the kitchens was not prepared for pursuit. He looked at the woman beside him, her eyes bright with excitement. 'Did you want to be rescued?'

'Don't be a bloody fool.' She laughed and led him down a long corridor. 'Christ, Richard! I was told you were dead!' He laughed with her and her hand was warm in his. 'How did you know I was here?'

'An angel told me.'

She led him upstairs. The bell had stopped. 'I must look awful.'

'You look wonderful.'

'The bitches took my clothes! God! You should see the lavatories here, Richard! You have to hold her breath if you want to piss. I've been constipated for a week! You can't bathe, you can't wash! I haven't washed my hair since I got here. No wonder they don't marry, no man could bear them. Oh Lord!' This last was to greet the Mother Superior who waited in the front hallway. She was alone. She frowned.

'You cannot go.'

La Marquesa ignored her. 'Richard? Open that door.' She pointed at a solid oak door at the side of the hall.

'Open it?'

'For Christ's sake, do it!'

It was locked. The Mother Superior protested, but Helene insisted, and Sharpe kicked it with his heel, shaking it, then kicked again to splinter it open. Helene pushed past him. 'They took my jewels, my clothes, everything! They've got a thousand dollars worth of my jewellery in there!'

Sharpe listened as she raked through drawers and opened cupboards. He heard the rustle of cloth, the chink of coins, and he smiled wanly at the Mother Superior who stood frowning and unable to stop the desecration. Sharpe shrugged. 'My President will make reparations, madame. Just write to him.'

La Marquesa swore cheerfully in the room, then, holding a bundle, came back to the hall. She smiled at the Mother Superior. 'I'm going to commit adultery again. Lots of it.' She laughed, held her hand out to Sharpe, and he went with her to the broken front door.

She stepped over the rock that still blocked the opening. 'Christ! It's raining! My hair will be ruined!'

'You said it needed a wash.' He remembered to retrieve his shako from the hall table.

She laughed. 'Are those our horses?'

'Yes.'

'I haven't ridden a horse in years.' She walked outside and put her face back as if to let the rain drench away the smell of the convent. She laughed with pure delight. 'Where are we going?'

'I don't know.'

'Then let's go there!' She chose Carbine for herself, unerringly picking the better horse. She mounted, her bundle given to Sharpe, and she waited for him to mount Angel's horse. Then she turned Carbine towards the open grass of the rain-swept plateau, pushed her heels back, and urged the big, black horse into a gallop.

Sharpe caught up with her. Her face was bright with the rain and with the sudden joy of freedom. This was not the time, he thought, to talk of *El Matarife*. She looked at him,

144

laughed, then fumbled at her neck. She untied the hank of grey, drab rag, tossed it away, and released the great golden mane of her hair. She was free, she was beautiful, and Richard Sharpe followed her into his uncertain future.

CHAPTER 12

He checked La Marquesa at the top of the path. She was cold now. The rain had soaked the woollen shift so that it clung to her body. Sharpe pulled out his cloak that was strapped behind her saddle and draped it about her shoulders, then took his telescope and trained it down the hill. He could see the hairpin bend in the road where Angel was hidden. He could see more. There were two pine branches beside the road. They lay parallel to the track and they told him that at least six men, but less than nine, had climbed past Angel's hiding place. If they had been at right angles the message would be that the men were waiting in ambush higher on the road, but instead Angel had seen them reach the summit of the hill.

Sharpe closed the telescope. He twisted in the saddle and stared behind him. The convent was out of sight. This northern side of the plateau was broken country, the small trees lashed by the rain, and somewhere in the damp wasteland of rocks, grass and bushes was hidden the enemy. He grinned at her. Her hair was flattened now by rain. 'We've got company.'

'What do you mean?'

'Enemies.'

She used a word that Sharpe would not have expected a lady to know, even one like the Marquesa who spoke perfect English, just as she spoke a half dozen other languages to perfection. 'So what do we do?'

'Ride down.' *El Matarife* was doing what Sharpe would have done. He was planning to trap Sharpe on the steep, twisting roadway. There would be men blocking off the track at the foot of the hill, and once Sharpe was committed to the road, the men who had reached the top would follow him down.

She stared at him reproachfully. 'Are we in trouble?'

'I'll take you back to the convent, if you like.'

'Christ, no! Who are these bastards?'

'Partisans.'

She shook the reins and went forward. 'You know what they'll do to me?'

'I know what they'd like to do.'

He followed her. The road zig-zagged sharply down the hillside. It was rutted, showing that carts had used it, but it must have been a nightmare journey to bring a cart or carriage up the track with the steep drop always threatening to one side. She frowned at him. 'Do you know what you're doing?'

'I spent all of last night planning this.'

She shivered. 'I'm cold.'

He found it hard to take his eyes from her. Her hair, pale as the palest gold, was normally full and shining, but under the lash of rain it had fallen flat like a shining helmet on her head. It somehow gave her features more prominence and strength. She had a wide, generous mouth, big eyes, and high bones. Her skin was as white as paper. She caught him looking at her. 'Forgotten me?'

'No. I thought you might forget me.'

'You were supposed to think that.' She laughed.

He twisted and looked behind. The track was empty. 'What were you doing there?'

'Finding God. What do you think I was doing there?'

'You were kidnapped by the Church?'

'Yes.'

'Why?'

'They want my money, God damn them.'

'Why did you write that letter to your husband?'

She turned her grey eyes to him, wide and innocent. 'Don't be a bore, Richard.'

He laughed. He had ridden across half of Spain for this woman, beaten down the doors of a convent, and now risked disembowelling at the hands of the Slaughterman, all to be told not to be a bore. She smiled at his laughter. 'Is that why you came?'

'Partly.'

'What was the other part?'

He felt clumsy and shy. 'To see you.'

He was rewarded with a smile. 'How very nice of you, Richard. Did you kill Luis?'

He supposed Luis was her husband. 'No.'

'So why did they say you were hanged?'

He shrugged, it seemed too complicated to explain. He turned again and, in the shifting curtains of the rain, he saw movement behind. She must have sensed something for she turned as well. 'Is that them?'

'Yes.'

'Shouldn't we gallop?'

'They'll have blocked the road off below.'

'Jesus Christ!' She was staring at him. 'Are you sure you know what you're doing?'

'Yes.' At least six men were behind him. Two would die for certain; he could be reasonably sure of a third, which would leave at least three to be tackled. He kept his voice confident. 'You'll have to move fast in a few minutes.' She shrugged. He could see how cold she was. 'And you've got a long cold day ahead of you.'

'I suppose it's better than eternity with those lavatories. They wanted me to clean them! Can you imagine that? It was bad enough being a kitchen skivvy! Let alone a bloody cleaner!'

He went into a trot. The men behind were two hundred yards away, not hurrying, safe in the knowledge that they were herding Sharpe down the zig-zag road towards the waiting ambush. He turned a corner and, ahead of him, a hundred paces down the track, was the place where Angel was hidden. 'You see that overhang of rock?'

'Yes.'

'You're going to dismount and you're going under there. You'll find a boy there; get behind him and keep quiet.'

She mockingly tugged her wet hair. 'Yes, sir.'

Sharpe had walked up and down this stretch of road in the night, even waiting for the first light of dawn to see the tangle of rocks from the enemy's point of view. Now, staring ahead, he could see no sign of Angel, but that was good.

He looked behind him. The enemy were out of sight, hidden by the twist in the road and by the overhanging junipers. He hurried the horses. 'You know what to do?'

'You just told me, for God's sake. I'm not a complete fool.'

In the dawn what he had planned seemed foolhardy. Now, in the cold rain, it seemed a desperate hope, but he had to try. He wondered if he should give her instructions what to do if he failed, but decided against it. If he failed she would be caught, however frantically she scrambled across the hillside. He must simply give her confidence now. He came to the turn in the road, leaned over for her reins, and told her to dismount.

He watched her run clumsily under the overhang and press her way between the rocks. From here it looked like a cave, though it was no more than a heap of great, fallen boulders that faced the road's hairpin bend. She disappeared.

Sharpe took the horses down the road, hurrying them twenty yards to a tiny patch of flat ground where they could be half hidden. He tied their reins to a root of juniper, tying the knot doubly tight so that, in the sudden scare of gunfire, they could not jerk loose. Then he climbed the rocks.

He had done this in the night, he could do it again now, but the rocks were slippery with water and numbingly cold. He dragged himself up, his boots slipping once to jar his thigh against stone, then he was over the lip and in the foul, slippery leaf mould beneath the bushes.

He wriggled uphill, almost to the level of the roadway above. He listened for the enemy. He wanted them to ride past the boulders, past the dark overhang and turn the corner before they knew they had been ambushed.

He could hear nothing except the hiss and spatter of the

rain. He drew his sword, then lay on his stomach beneath the bushes.

A hoof sounded on stone, another, and then he could hear the Partisans laughing. The rain was slashing down and he was glad of it. The water would make their muskets useless, while Angel, crouching in the dark overhang of rock, was armed with two dry and loaded rifles.

Sharpe wondered if the boy could shoot at his own countrymen. He would see in a moment, and he would discover whether Angel truly did trust him. The sounds came closer, came to the road immediately above Sharpe, and he heard one of the men say that he could not see the Englishman.

'They're there somewhere,' another man said, but nevertheless Sharpe heard the horses go into a trot as they rounded the corner.

Sharpe drew his legs up slowly. He could see them now. Seven men with heavy cloaks dripping with rain. They carried muskets, but he could not see whether the locks had been wrapped with cloth against the damp. He could not see *El Matarife* among the small band.

The leading man was beneath him now. Sharpe waited.

Angel should fire now, he thought, before they see the tethered horses. The rain dripped from the leaves about his ears, the men were passing him, and still there was no rifle shot. The grip of the sword felt slippery in his hand.

A man cursed the rain beneath him, another guessed that the Englishman, knowing he was to die, had stopped to pleasure the whore. They laughed, and the first rifle fired.

Sharpe's boots slipped. He told himself not to hurry, he pushed again, and he was standing on the steep slope, his boots level with the heads of his enemies, and jumped.

One man was down, a bullet in his back, while the others were turning, their mouths open, their hands fumbling with their guns and Sharpe was falling, shouting, the sword heavy as it fell on the rearward man who could only lift a hand and scream as the blade cut down to the bone.

Sharpe landed heavily, fell, and he came up with the

sword flailing at the man he had wounded. The man's horse reared, the sword was at his breast, and the Partisan fell and Sharpe was gripping the reins and pulling the horse towards him. He flailed with the sword at another man, striking his horse on its rump and frightening it downhill. Sharpe was shouting like a demon, trying to drive the men down the track by the sheer ferocity of his voice.

The leading man had turned, had drawn a sword, and he shouted at his companions to make way. His mouth stayed open as Angel put the second bullet into it. He went backwards, the rain suddenly crimson, and the shock of the second bullet checked the men and gave Sharpe enough time to put his foot into the rope stirrup and swing himself into the saddle. He wheeled the horse and took his heavy sword against the remaining Partisans.

He supposed he ought to be ashamed of this kind of joy, of the fierce, singing joy of battle, yet he had known, from the moment that he had mounted the horse, that his ambush had worked.

A flint clicked uselessly on steel, the musket's powder turned into a grey porridge by the rain. Four men faced Sharpe and he drove his horse towards them, sword lifted, shouting, and he swept the grey blade down on a raised sabre, lunged into the man's ribs, and twisted the blade free. A musket butt slammed into his left arm, he pulled the reins with numbed fingers, stood in the saddle and screamed a challenge as the sword came across and down to shear into the man's face. A third rifle shot banged from the wet rocks.

God bless the boy, Sharpe thought. Angel had reloaded as fast as any Rifleman and another man was down, being dragged by the stirrup of his frightened horse, and Sharpe parried a swinging musket, sliced wood from the butt, and lunged at the enemy's throat, twisting the blade as it went home, and the blood was warm on his hands as he parried right, hacked down, and the enemy was going downhill. They were running!

He pushed his heels back. 'Go! Go! Go!' They heard him

coming, they were frightened, and one man pulled the reins, his horse slipped, screamed, and Sharpe swerved past him and lunged forward with the sword at the spine of the last unwounded man. The man screamed, arched his back, and Sharpe let the blade come free.

He pulled on the reins.

His attack had been so sudden and so savage, as an attack should be, that the enemy was gone, all but their dead. Sharpe leaned left, snatched the reins of another horse, and turned back up the hill. Now was the time for speed.

'Angel!'

'*Señor?*'

Sharpe was galloping the horses uphill. 'You're a marvel! A bloody, bloody marvel!' He had shouted it in English. He tried an approximation in Spanish and was rewarded by seeing the boy's broad grin as he squeezed out of the rocks. Sharpe was laughing. 'You're as good as any Rifleman!'

'Better!'

'You're better!' They both laughed. 'Get the horses!'

Angel threw Sharpe's rifle to him and he slung it on his shoulder. 'Helene!'

She came slowly out of the crack in the rocks. She stared at the men who lay crumpled on the road, their blood already diluted by the rain and trickling down the ruts of the track. Her eyes came up to Sharpe. She was smiling. 'I've never seen you fight!'

'You'll see more if you don't hurry.'

'You're wonderful!'

'Helene! For God's sake! Hurry! What are you doing?'

She was running past him. 'I want one of those cloaks! I'm god-damned cold!'

She dragged a fur cloak from one of the dead men, grunting at the weight of the corpse. Sharpe leaned from his saddle to help her. He laughed when she draped it about her shoulders because it seemed so odd to see such delicate beauty swathed in such a brutal great fur.

El Matarife had not been among the seven men, so

presumably the Partisan leader was at the foot of the mountain. He would have heard the shots, but it would be several minutes, maybe a half hour, before he knew what had happened. Then, though, he would realise what Sharpe was doing and guess that his enemy was escaping him. Sharpe chivvied Helene into Carbine's saddle, knowing that every moment was precious.

Sharpe had four horses now and he led them upwards, away from the dead men, up to the plateau. 'Where are we going, Richard?'

'Down the other side. There's a small path, a goat track.' He had ridden round the plateau before going to the convent, sure there must be another path, fearful that he would not find it.

'Then what?'

'We ride as far as we can! We've stolen half a day's lead on the bastards, but they'll follow us!' He did not tell her that no one moved faster across country than Partisans. Their pursuit would be grim, their revenge terrible unless he hurried.

She watched as he clumsily wiped the blood from his sword on the saddle-cloth of his captured horse. 'Thank you, Richard!'

'Thank Angel! He got three of them.'

Angel blushed. He was staring at La Marquesa with dog-like devotion. Sharpe laughed, then led them back up the mountain and south towards the far valleys.

He felt an extraordinary surge of life in him. He had done it! He had crossed Spain and snatched this woman from the Convent of the Heavens, he had fought her enemies, and he would take her to safety. He would find his answers, he would wrench his life back where it belonged, but first, first before all things, because at this moment it seemed the most important of all things, he would find out if she had changed. He looked at her, thinking that her beauty dimmed this land, and that when she smiled it was as if she held all his happiness in her hand. For the first time in months, because of this woman, he was content.

CHAPTER 13

La Marquesa moaned, her eyes shut. She turned her head on the pillow, her lips open just enough for Sharpe to see her white teeth. The fire smoked into the room. Rain rattled a crisp tattoo on the tiny window through which, dim through the rain-smeared grime, Sharpe could see a candle burning in a cottage across the street.

'Oh God, oh God, oh God.' She paused, her head turning in its gold hair on the pillow again. 'Oh God!'

He laughed. He poured wine for her and put it beside the bed. A tallow wick, held in an iron bracket, smoked above its dim flame. 'Wine for you.'

'Oh God.'

They had ridden till one horse had had to be abandoned, until even the two good British horses were heaving with tiredness, and until La Marquesa's thighs, unused to the saddle, were rubbed raw like fresh meat. She opened her eyes slowly. 'Aren't you sore?'

'A bit.'

'I never want to see a bloody horse again. Oh Christ!' She scratched her waist. 'Bloody place. Bloody Spain. Bloody weather. What's that?'

Sharpe had put a metal pot on the rough table. 'Grease.'

'For God's sake why?'

'For the sores. Rub it on.'

She wrinkled her nose, then scratched again. She was lying on the bed, too tired to move, too tired to take any notice as Sharpe had ordered the fire lit, food prepared and wine brought.

They had come to this town, a tiny place huddled in the mountains where there was a church, a marketplace, an

154

inn, and a mayor who had been impressed that a British officer should come to this place. Sharpe, fearing *El Matarife*, would have preferred to have ridden on, to have found a place in the deep country where they could have hidden for the night, but he knew that La Marquesa could take no more. He would risk the town's inn and hope that *El Matarife*, if he reached this far, would be inhibited by the townsfolk from trying to seize back La Marquesa. This was not the time, Sharpe thought, to tell her that he planned an early start in the morning.

She pushed herself up on her elbows and frowned about the room. 'I don't think I've ever, ever, stayed in a place so awful.'

'It seems comfortable enough to me.'

'You never did have elevated tastes, Richard. Except in women.' She flopped back. 'I suppose that hoping for a bath here is futile?'

'It's coming.'

'It is?' She turned her head to look at him. 'God, you're wonderful.' She frowned again as she scratched. 'This bloody shift! I hate wearing wool.'

Sharpe had hung the dress she had rescued from the convent by the fire. Her jewels were on the table. She looked at the dress. 'Not very suitable for a wild flight, is it?' She laughed and watched Sharpe peel off his wet jacket. 'Is that the shirt I gave you?'

'Yes.'

'Don't you have a laundry in the British army?'

'It couldn't come with me.'

'Poor Richard.' She tasted the wine and grimaced. 'One day, Richard, I'm going to have a house on the River Loire. I shall have an island in the river and young men will row me to my island where we will eat lark pâté and honey and drink cold, cold wine on hot, hot days.'

He smiled. 'Which is why you want your wagons?'

'Which is why I want my wagons.'

'And that's why the Church arrested you?'

She nodded. She closed her eyes again. 'They arranged it

155

all. Luis had no one to leave his money to but me, and they found the bloody will and the clause which said they'd get it all if I became a nun. Simple.' She gave a wan smile. 'It's rather clever of them.'

'So why did you write the letter?'

She waved a hand airily. 'Oh, Richard!' She looked at him and sighed impatiently. 'They had to have Luis dead, didn't they? They told me they wanted him punished, I don't know why. I didn't know what was happening, and I didn't think you'd mind killing him. He never was much use to anyone.' She smiled at him. 'I never thought it would get you into trouble, darling. Truly! I'll write you a letter for Arthur, telling him you're innocent. What a lot of trouble you went to!' She frowned again, scratching at the grey shift.

'Helene.'

She looked at him, struck by the seriousness in his voice. She hoped that he was not going to question her lies, she was too tired. 'Richard?'

'It isn't the wool.'

'What isn't the wool?'

'Your scratching.'

'What on earth are you talking about?'

He gestured at the discarded fur cloak she had taken from the dead Partisan. 'You've got guests.'

She stared at him suspiciously. 'Guests?'

'Fleas.'

'Christ!' She sat up with sudden energy and hauled the shift above her knees. She frowned at her bared skin. 'Fleas?'

'Probably.' He looked at her thighs, wondering why she had lied to him. He was sure that she had, he was certain that there was more to the letter she had written to her husband than the mere request of a church that wanted her riches, yet he sensed that he would have to accept her explanation because he was not clever enough to get the real truth from her.

She twitched the shift higher, peering at her legs. 'God and hell and damnation! Fleas? I can't see any.'

'You won't.'

She pushed the shift down. 'I'll never get rid of them!'

'You will.'

'How?'

'The same as the rest of us. A piece of soap.'

'Just wash them away?'

He grinned. 'No.'

Someone knocked on the trapdoor that was the entrance to the room. Sharpe unbolted it, hauled it up, and the innkeeper's wife pushed a great tin bath towards him. He took it from her and saw the buckets of water steaming at the ladder's foot. 'You have towels?'

'*Si, señor.*'

Sharpe saw Angel by the fire at the end of the inn's main room. The boy stared forlornly at Sharpe, jealous that the Rifle officer was in La Marquesa's room. 'And I want soap.'

'*Si, señor.*'

La Marquesa was sitting, legs apart, on the edge of the bed. 'What do I do with the soap?'

'You dampen a corner, chase the fleas and dab them with it. They stick to the soap. It's twenty times faster than trying to catch them with your fingers.' He pulled up the first bucket and poured it into the tin bath.

She stared at him in disbelief. 'What if they go to my back?'

Sharpe laughed. 'The innkeeper's wife will help you. She doesn't want fleas in the bed.' Privately he would be surprised if there weren't fleas already in the bed, though it was possible, this being the inn's only proper bedroom, that it was clean.

'That woman?'

'Why not?'

'Christ, Richard! I don't want her to know I've got fleas! You'll have to do it.' She shrugged. 'You've seen it often enough before.'

He poured another bucket. 'Yes, ma'am.'

'It's what you wanted, isn't it? A rescuer's reward? Isn't that why knights rode around rescuing maidens? Only they called it the Holy Grail which is a nicer name than some I've heard.'

'Yes, ma'am.'

She laughed at his smile. 'I missed you. I often wondered what you were doing. I imagined you scowling through life, scaring all the rich young officers.' She made a face at him. 'I don't even have a comb, let alone a brush! Is that all the water they're giving me?'

'There's more coming.'

'Thank God for that.' She leaned back on the bed. 'I could sleep for a month. I never want to see a bloody horse again.'

Sharpe lifted more buckets into the room. 'You'll have to ride one tomorrow.'

'No I don't.'

'I could leave you for *El Matarife*.'

'He couldn't make me more sore than this.' She turned her head and watched him through the billows of steam. 'I was sorry about your wife, Richard.'

'Yes.' He did not know what else to say to such abrupt sympathy.

She shrugged. 'I can't say I'm sorry about Luis. It doesn't seem real, somehow, being a widow.' She laughed softly. 'A rich widow, if that bastard doesn't steal everything.'

'The Inquisitor?'

'The bloody Inquisitor. Father Hacha. Is it ready?'

'Just the towels.'

He took the thin linen cloths from the woman downstairs and closed the trapdoor. 'Your bath, ma'am.'

'You make a bloody awful lady's maid, Richard.'

'I think I'm relieved to hear that.'

'Let it cool a bit. I don't fancy being scalded as well as flea-bitten and sore.' She sat on the side of the bed, her chin cupped in her hands, and looked at him. 'What do we do now, Richard?'

'What do you want to do.'

'I want to go to Burgos.'

He felt disappointed. He had somehow, and he knew stupidly, hoped that she would come back to the army with him. 'If the French are still there,' he said dubiously.

She shrugged. 'Wherever they are, that's where I want to be. Because wherever they are, that's where the wagons are.'

'Won't they arrest you again?'

She shook her head. 'The Church can't do it twice.' She was thinking of General Verigny. 'I won't let the bastards do it twice.' She reached over and put a hand in the water. 'You've got the soap?'

'Ready and willing, ma'am.'

She grinned, then crossed her arms to draw the shift over her head. She laughed at his expression, then pulled the grey wool up and over her head. 'I'm cold.'

'Nonsense. Just stand in the bath.'

For ten minutes, to unseemly laughter, he hunted her skin. She complained that it tickled as he explored for the fleas, dabbed them onto the soap, then pinched them between his fingernails, and by the time the last flea had been found she insisted on searching him for fleas and by the time she had done that she was on the bed, cursing the raw skin of her thighs, and his face was in her hair and her arms were on the scars where he had been flogged so long ago. She kissed his cheek. 'Poor Richard, poor Richard.'

'Poor?'

'Poor Richard.' She kissed him again. 'I'd forgotten.'

'Forgotten what?'

'Never mind. Do you think that bloody bath's cold?'

It still had enough warmth and she soaked herself, washed her hair, then put her head back on the wall. She was looking at him where he lay naked on the bed. 'You look happy.'

'I am.'

She smiled sadly. 'It doesn't take much to make you happy, does it?'

'I thought it took a lot.'

Later, when they had eaten and when each had a bottle of wine inside, they lay in the bed. The fire was hot, the chimney warmed and drawing well, and La Marquesa smoked a ragged cigar that she had bought from the innkeeper. Sharpe had forgotten that she liked to smoke. She had a hand on his belly, twisting the small hairs with her fingers. 'Will that man come into the town?'

'I don't think so. The *alcalde* said not.' The mayor had said that the town fell into the fief of another Partisan leader, a man not fond of *El Matarife*.

She looked at him. Her hair had dried soft and golden to spread about her face. 'Did you ever think you'd see me again?'

'No.'

'I thought I'd see you again.'

'You did?'

'I think so.' She blew a smoke ring and looked at it critically. 'But not in a nunnery.' She laughed. 'I couldn't believe it was you! I thought you were dead for a start, but even so! I think that's the nicest thing anyone's ever done for me.'

They spoke of what had happened in their lives since the summer in Salamanca, and he listened in awe to her descriptions of the palaces she had seen, the balls she had attended, and he hid the jealousy he felt when he imagined her in the arms of other men. He tried to persuade himself that it was useless to be jealous about La Marquesa, a man might as well complain of the wind veering.

He spoke about his daughter. He told her about the winter in the Gateway of God, the battle, the death of Teresa.

She sat up to drink wine. 'You weren't popular with us.'

'Because of the battle?'

She laughed. 'I was quite proud of you, but I didn't dare say so.' She gave him the bottle. 'So you gave all your money to your daughter?'

'Yes.'

'Richard Sharpe, you are a fool. Some day I'll have to teach you how to survive. So you're poor again?'

'Yes.'

She laughed. She spoke of the money that was with the retreating French army, not her own money, but the hundreds of wagons that had been collected at Burgos. 'You can't believe it, Richard! They looted every monastery, every palace, every bloody house from here to Madrid! There's gold, silver, paintings, plate, more gold, more paintings, jewels, silks, coin . . .' She shook her head in amazement. 'It's the fortune of the Spanish empire, Richard, and it's all going back to France. They know they're losing, so they're taking everything with them.'

'How much?'

She thought about it. 'Five million?'

'Francs?'

'Pounds, darling. English pounds.' She laughed at his expression. 'At least.'

'It can't be.'

'It can.' She threw the cigar into the fire. 'I've seen it!' She smiled at him. 'Your dear Arthur would like to get his fingers on that, wouldn't he?' Undoubtedly, Sharpe thought, Wellington would dearly like to capture the French baggage train. She laughed. 'But he won't. That's what our army's protecting.' She raised her wine glass. 'All for us, dear. Loser takes all.'

'Will you get your wagons back?'

'I'll get my wagons back.' She said it grimly. 'And I'll write a letter that will get you your job back. What shall I write? That the Inquisitor killed Luis?' She giggled. 'Perhaps he did! Or his brother.'

'His brother?'

She turned her head to him. '*El Matarife*,' she said it as if to a child.

'They're brothers!'

'Yes. He came and looked at me in the carriage.' She shuddered. 'Bastard.'

Sharpe supposed it made sense. Why else would the Partisan come to these far, inhospitable mountains except to do his brother a favour? But even so, he was astonished that the bearded, brutal man was brother to a priest. He looked at the beauty beside him. 'For God's sake write that your other letter wasn't true.'

'Of course I will. I shall say a nun threatened to rape me unless I wrote it.' She smiled. 'I am sorry about it, Richard. It was thoughtless of me.'

'It doesn't matter.'

'It does really. It got you into trouble, didn't it? I thought you'd survive though.' She smiled happily. 'And if it wasn't for that letter we wouldn't be here, would we?'

'No.'

'And you wouldn't be able to put grease on my thighs, would you?' She handed him the pot, and Sharpe, obedient as ever to this woman of gold, obeyed.

He lay awake in the night, one arm trapped beneath her waist, and wondered if the letter she would write would be sufficient. Would it restore his rank or vindicate his honour?

The glow of the fire was on the yellowed ceiling. Rain still tapped at the window and hissed in the chimney. Helene stirred on him, one leg across his, her head and one hand on his chest. She had murmured a name in her half sleep; Raoul. Sharpe had felt jealous again.

He touched her spine, stroking it, and she muttered and pushed her head down on his chest. Her hair tickled his cheek. He thought how often in the last year he had dreamed of this, wanted this, and he ran his hand down her flank as though he could impress the sensation in his memory to last forever.

She had lied to him. He did not for one moment believe that the Church had murdered her husband, or made a plan to take her money. Something else was behind it all, but she would never tell him what it was. She would do what she could to save his career, and for that, he thought, he should be grateful. He looked at the tiny window and saw nothing but the dark reflection of the room, not a hint of a lightening sky. He told himself that he must wake in an hour, turned towards her warm softness, brushed his lips on her hair, and slept with her body tight in his arms.

He came awake suddenly, the small window showing grey, knowing he had slept longer than he should have. He wondered why Angel had not thumped on the trapdoor.

He rolled from the bed, making Helene grunt, and he saw that it had stopped raining. The fire was dead.

Then he froze with a sudden gut wrench of fear within him, and knew that he had failed utterly. A noise had woken him, and now he could hear it again. It was the noise made by horses, by many horses, but not horses in motion. He could hear their breathing, their hooves stirring, the jingle of curb chains. He reached for the rifle, thumbed the cock back, and went to the small window.

The grey-dawn street was filled with horsemen. *El Matarife* was there, and about him, the dew glistening on their shaggy cloaks, were his men. Next to *El Matarife*, on a superb horse, was a tall man in a silver cloak with a sabre at his hip. About the two men, crowding the narrow street, were at least two hundred horsemen.

'Richard?' Her voice was sleepy.

'Get dressed.'

'What is it?'

'Just get dressed!'

El Matarife spurred forward on an ugly roan horse. He looked up at the inn windows. 'Vaughn!'

'Jesus!' La Marquesa sat up. 'What is it, Richard?'

'*El Matarife.*'

'Jesus.'

'Vaughn!'

Sharpe pushed the window open. The air was cold on his naked skin. '*Matarife?*' He saw the *alcalde* of the town behind the horsemen, and next to him was a priest. He knew suddenly what had happened.

The Partisan leader rode close beneath the window. He stared up. His huge beard was beaded with moisture. Strapped on his back, next to a musket, was a great poleaxe, the weapon of a slaughterman. He grinned. 'You see the man in the silver cloak, Major Vaughn?'

'I see him.'

'He is Pedro Pelera, my enemy. You know why today we are friends, Major Vaughn?'

Sharpe could guess. He could hear La Marquesa dressing, swearing softly under her breath. 'Tell me, *Matarife*.'

'Because you offend our holy place, Major Vaughn. You fight the nuns, yes?' *El Matarife* laughed. 'You have ten minutes, Major Vaughn, to bring us *La Puta Dorada*.'

'And if I don't?'

'You die anyway. If you come gently, Major, then I will kill you swiftly. If you do not? We shall come for you!' He gestured towards his men. Sharpe knew he could not fight so many, not even by staying at the top of the ladder. They would merely blast the trapdoor with musketry. *El Matarife* drove the point home. 'There's no help coming, Major. Your boy fled. You have ten minutes!'

Sharpe slammed the window. 'Christ!'

La Marquesa was wearing the dress she had fetched from the convent, a confection of blue silk and white lace. She was putting the jewels about her neck. 'If I'm going to die I'll die in bloody jewels.'

'I'm sorry, Helene.'

'Christ, Richard, don't be so god-damned stupid!' She said it with sudden, vivid anger.

He went to the back wall and thumped it, as if it might be thin enough to break through, yet he knew that the Partisans would have the inn surrounded. He swore.

'Are you going to die naked?' Her voice was bitter. 'How the hell did that bastard find me?'

Sharpe cursed himself. He should have known! He should have guessed that by breaking into the convent he would stir the whole countryside against him, and instead he had been so eager to share this bed that he had not given the danger a single thought.

He dressed swiftly, dressing as if for battle, yet he knew that it was over. This mad escapade in the hills would end

164

in blood on a muddy street, with his death. He should have been hanged these four weeks ago, and instead he would die now. At least, he thought, it would be with a sword in his hand. 'I'll go and talk to them.'

'For Christ's sake, why?'

'To get a promise for your safety.'

She shook her head. 'You are a fool. You really believe there's decency in the world, don't you?'

'I can try.' He pulled up the trapdoor. The room beneath was empty. He turned to look at her one more time and thought how splendid she was, how lovely even in anger. 'Do you want my rifle?'

'To shoot myself?'

'Yes.'

'The Holy Grail isn't that bloody precious.' She looked at his face and shook her head. I'm sorry, Richard, I keep forgetting that you think it is. What are you going to do?'

'Fight them, of course.'

She laughed, though there was fear in the laugh. 'God help you in peacetime, Richard.'

He fingered the sword hilt and hesitated. He knew he should not say it, but in ten minutes he would be dead, butchered by the Slaughterman or his men. He would take some of them with him, he would give them cause to remember fighting against a lone Rifleman. 'Helene?'

She looked at him with exasperation. 'Don't say it, Richard.'

'I love you.'

'I knew you'd say it.' She was putting the diamond earrings into her lobes. 'But then you are a fool.' She smiled sadly. 'Go and fight for me, fool.'

He went down the ladder, drew the great sword, and opened the door to the street where his enemies had gathered for his death.

CHAPTER 14

Angel had woken before dawn. He had slept in the stable, wrapped by warm straw and his thick cloak. He had shivered as he yawned, wriggled from his bed, and went into the yard. He splashed water on his face and looked up at the dark roof beneath which Sharpe slept with the golden woman.

Angel had polished the saddles the night before. He had brushed the horses and made everything ready for this morning. Not just ready, but gleamingly ready. He had done it for a woman more beautiful than his dreams had dared imagine, and now, in yet more homage to her, he saddled Carbine and folded a blanket over the saddle in an effort to give La Marquesa a more comfortable seat. He knew she was French, and he hated the French, but no woman so lovely as she could be evil in Angel's worshipping eyes.

He tried out his makeshift attempt at her comfort, riding out of the inn yard, and turning Carbine towards the south. The wind was at his back, bringing a chill to his thin body. The shapes of the townspeople were dark where they moved in alleys and courtyards. He put a hand on the butt of his rifle that he had pushed into the saddle's holster.

The eastern mountains were edged with light. Angel put his heels back, letting Carbine go into a trot. He revelled in the feel of the big, black horse that lifted its hooves high and tossed its mane with impatience. Angel straightened his back, imagining that he was *El Arcangel*, the most feared Partisan in Spain, riding to battle. A woman of great beauty, with golden hair and grey eyes, waited for his return, though she did not believe that any man would return from so suicidal a mission.

He pulled the rifle from its holster, then twitched the reins to take Carbine down to the stream where the women of the town washed their clothes. He would let the horse drink there, and let his daydream run on to the delicious moment when he returned from battle, not too severely wounded, and the golden haired woman would run from the house, her arms wide; then Angel saw the horsemen over the stream.

He was in the darkness beneath chestnut trees. He checked Carbine and saw the grey shapes in the grey light and he thumbed back the cock of the rifle, thinking that he should fire a warning shot for Sharpe, then thought that the sound of the rifle would bring the men galloping over the stream for his blood.

He pulled the reins, knowing he must ride back to the town and warn Sharpe, but as Carbine moved, so the men over the shallow stream saw the movement, one shouted, and Angel saw the water splash white as they drove their horses towards him.

They were ahead of him, cutting him off from the town, and the boy, now no longer the feared *Arcangel*, but merely Angel riding for his life, let the black horse have its head.

Carbine easily outstripped *El Matarife's* men, carrying Angel south in the valley, away from the town. Angel discarded the folded blanket, pulled the reins left, and hid himself among pines that grew on a small knoll. He watched from their cover, wondering what he could do to help, and then he saw more horsemen coming from the south and he knew there was nothing he could do except to wait, watch, and hope. He remembered Major Hogan's urgent warning that his job was to protect Sharpe, and he felt failure with all the passion of his sixteen years. He patted Carbine's neck, sheathed the unfired rifle, and shivered.

A murmur greeted Sharpe, a murmur that rose to a chorus of hate. The horses in their semi-circle about the inn's facade came forward and *El Matarife* raised his hand and bellowed for silence and stillness.

El Matarife looked down on Sharpe. 'Well, Major Vaughn?'

'What happens to the woman?'

The Partisan laughed. 'That's no worry of yours.'

Sharpe was in the doorway, ready to leap inside at the first sign of an attack. He held his sword low, and now, with his left hand, he brought the rifle into view. 'If you want to fight me, *Matarife*, I am ready. The first bullet will be for you. Now tell me what happens to the woman.'

The bearded man paused. From somewhere in the town came the smell of a kitchen fire. The street was slick and thick with mud from the night's rain. *El Matarife* licked his lips. 'Nothing happens to her. She goes back to the convent.'

'I don't believe you.'

El Matarife's horse pranced in the mud. The bearded man quieted the beast. 'She goes back, Englishman, to where she belongs. Our quarrel is not with her, but with a man who dared to frighten nuns.' Slowly, his eyes not leaving Sharpe, he reached down to his saddle. Sharpe knew what was coming and he did not move.

El Matarife produced a looped chain. He held onto one end of it and tossed the rest towards Sharpe. The chain lay in the mud. The Partisan took from his belt a long knife and that too he threw towards the inn door. 'Do you dare, Englishman? Or do you only have courage against nuns?'

Sharpe stepped forward. He had small choice. He remembered the speed of this man, he remembered how he had speared the eyes from the French prisoner, but Sharpe knew he must accept the challenge. He stooped, picked up the last link of the chain, and a musket sounded to his left.

The musket's report was curiously flat in the chill morning. *El Matarife* stared up the street, then suddenly threw down the chain and shouted at his men. He rowelled his spurs back and Sharpe was forgotten in the sudden panic.

Hooves galloped. A trumpet was splitting the valley with sudden urgency, and Sharpe heard a whoop of glee from the upstairs room of the inn, a shriek of pure joy from La Marquesa, and then more muskets hammered and he smelt the acrid powder smoke as he ducked into the inn and knelt with his rifle ready.

Lancers swept into the street. French lancers. Some had pennants on their blades that were already stained with blood. A riderless horse galloped with them.

The Partisans were running. They were not ready for the charge, not formed up to meet the shock of the heavy horses. They could only turn and run, but the street was crowded and they could not move as the lancers tore into them.

Sharpe watched the French riders grimace as they leaned into their long spears, as they ripped the enemy from their horses, as they rode over the dying to strip the long blades free in gouts of blood and screams.

The blades came up again, aimed for new targets, and the trumpet drove a second squadron into the street, horses' teeth bared, hooves slinging the mud high to stain the uniforms of the riders, and Sharpe watched two cornered Partisans raise their muskets, but Frenchmen rode at them, lunged, and a lance pinned one man to the wall of a house with such force that the lancer left the weapon there with the spitted man wriggling and screaming and dying. The lancer drew his sabre to pursue the second man who had leaped from his horse and now fell as the sabre was back-sliced into his face.

Some Partisans had escaped as far as the market place, but now Sharpe heard another trumpet from the plaza's far side, and more lancers came from the north to drive the fleeing Partisans into a melee of turning horses, shouts and fear. The townsfolk were running for shelter, the children, brought to watch the Partisans, screamed as the lancers rode knee to knee into the panicked mass.

Pistols banged, muskets coughed smoke, and another squadron cantered at the trumpet's command to take their long blades into the dull press of cloaked Partisans. The lance blades, razor sharp, dipped at the officer's order, the

169

horses were urged on, and the level blades were driven into the enemy. The green and pink uniforms were darkened by blood. One lancer came running from the melee, his square-topped hat in one hand, his other hand pressed to a running wound in his scalp. Another of the bright uniforms was in the mud, but for every Frenchman down there were a dozen Partisans, and still more lancers thundered towards the marketplace, and still the trumpet urged them on, and still the long blades were rammed home to scrape on ribs and tear the guts from the panicked horsemen.

Sharpe thought he could hear *El Matarife* shouting, he thought he saw the poleaxe raised once in the churning mass of men and screaming horses, and then he saw a fence fall at the far side of the marketplace and, as if a whirling flood had been released by a broken dam, the Partisans fled over the broken wattle of the downed fence leaving the square to the triumphant, blood-stained cavalry. The marketplace stank of blood. The wounded pulled themselves through the mud, crying out for Jesus, screaming as the lancers rode at them and, with surgical precision, pushed down with the stained blades. The French laughed as they inflicted pain on their elusive *guerrilla* enemies. One wounded man was pierced again and again, and still no lancer tried to kill him. A woman, crouching over a still body, screamed at the French troops until a cavalryman kicked her with his heavy boot and she fell onto her dying man.

The trumpets took three squadrons in pursuit, two stayed to deal with the wounded and prisoners. Sharpe had gone to the back door of the inn, thinking to go up into the trees behind the stable yard, but the small yard was full of Frenchmen who were leading the captured horses from their stalls. One saw him, shouted, but Sharpe barred the door and turned back.

La Marquesa was at the ladder's foot. She stared at the sword in his hand. 'You won't get away, Richard.'

Sharpe sheathed the sword. There were hands hammering on the barred door, shaking it. 'My name's Vaughn.'

She smiled. 'What?'

'Vaughn!'

'And you slept in the stable, Richard!'

He saw the intensity in her eyes, the warning there, and he nodded wearily. He slung the rifle on his shoulder, and then a tall man ducked into the front door of the inn, Helene screamed with delight, and ran to his arms. Sharpe, a prisoner of the French, could only watch.

General Raoul Verigny was six feet and two inches tall. There could not have been an ounce of fat on his body. His uniform was tailored tight as a drumskin.

He had a thin, dark face with a small, neatly upturned moustache. He smiled often.

He had shouted at the men at the back door to stop their noise, bowed to Sharpe, and accepted the gesture of surrender. He had spoken with La Marquesa for two minutes, bowed to Sharpe again, and returned the sword. 'Your bravery, Major, makes it imperative to return the sword. You have my most wonderful thank you.' He bowed a third time. 'The rifle, Major, I have it my duty to take.' He pronounced it 'Riffle'. He gave it to an aide-de-camp who gave it to a Lieutenant who gave it to a Sergeant.

Now, an hour later, Sharpe was an honoured guest at breakfast. About them the town burned. The inn was spared, so long as it provided shelter.

General Verigny was solicitous of Sharpe. 'You must be dishevelled, Major Vaughn.'

'Dishevelled, sir?'

'To fail in this hope.' He smiled, touching the points of his moustache.

'Indeed, sir.'

La Marquesa had told Verigny that Sharpe had been sent by the British to take her from the convent to Wellington's army where she would have been questioned. Verigny poured Sharpe some coffee. 'Instead we take Helene home, and you prisoner.'

'Indeed, sir.'

'But it is not to worry to you.' Verigny offered Sharpe a leg of chicken, pressing him to accept. 'You will be changed, yes?'

'Exchanged?'

'Exchanged! I do not practice my English so much. Helene speaks it so well, but she does not speak it at me. She should do so, yes?' He laughed, and turned to La Marquesa, pouring her wine. He was, Sharpe judged, a man of his own age, darkly handsome. Sharpe was jealous. The General turned back to Sharpe. 'You speak French, Major?'

'No, sir.'

'You should! It is the very beautifullest tongue in the world.'

The table was crowded with French officers who grinned with the happiness of men who had won a great victory. It was rare for French cavalry to surprise the Partisans, and this morning they had reaped a grim harvest of their enemies. The silver-cloaked man was a prisoner, doubtless screaming beneath a blade as his captors sought answers to their questions, but *El Matarife* had escaped into the eastern mountains. Verigny did not mind. 'He is ended, yes? His men broken! Besides, I come for Helene, not him, and you have released her for me.' He smiled and toasted Sharpe.

The assembled officers looked curiously at the Englishman. Few had seen a captured British officer before, and none had seen one of the feared Riflemen as a prisoner. If they caught his eye, they smiled. They offered him the best food on the table, one poured him wine, another brandy, and they urged him to drink with them.

Verigny sat close to La Marquesa. She fed him scraps with her fork. They touched each other, laughed privately, and seemed to fill the room with their gaiety. At one point there was a roar of laughter and the General smiled at Sharpe. 'I tell her she should be marrying me. She says she might become a nun instead, yes?' Sharpe smiled politely. Verigny asked whether Sharpe thought La Marquesa would make a good nun, and Sharpe said that the nunnery would be a fortunate place.

Verigny laughed. 'But what waste, Major, yes?' He gestured at her. 'I ride here to rescue her. I insist they make me come here, I demand it! You think she deserves marriage to me as a return, yes?'

Sharpe smiled, but inside he felt sick. He had been a prisoner before, back in the Indian wars, and then too he had been captured by lancers. He would remember to his last day the face of the Indian leaning towards him, teeth gritted as he drove the blade into Sharpe's waist to pin him to the tree. Now he had been captured again, and he could see small hope of freedom.

He listened to the loud laughter of the officers, saw their eyes fastened on La Marquesa, watched her coquettish gestures as she played to her audience. She pouted at him once, raising more laughter, and he hid his despair beneath a wan smile.

General Verigny had said that Sharpe could be exchanged, but Sharpe knew it would not happen. Even if the British had a captive French Major to exchange, they would not recognise the name Vaughn on the French proposal. Every few weeks the two sides exchanged lists of prisoners, but Wellington's headquarters would query Major Vaughn. The French would presume that the British did not want 'Vaughn' back and he would be sent to the fortress town of Verdun where officer prisoners were kept.

Nor could Sharpe reveal his real name. To do that would be to prompt a dozen questions, each nastier than the last. He must stay Vaughn, and as Vaughn he would go to Verdun, and as Vaughn he would sit out the war, rotting behind Verdun's walls, wondering what kind of bleak future peace would bring.

Or he could escape, yet not till Verigny had safely escorted him from these mountains with their vengeful Partisans. Even as he thought it, Verigny turned and smiled at him. 'Helene she tells me you break into the convent, yes?'

'Yes.'

'You are brave man, Major Vaughn!' Verigny lifted a glass to him. 'I owe you my thank you.'

Sharpe shrugged. 'You can let me go, sir.'

Verigny laughed, then translated the exchange into French to provoke more friendly laughter from his officers. He shook his head. 'I cannot let you go, Major Vaughn, but you do not cause yourself to worry, no? You will be changed at Burgos.'

Sharpe smiled. 'I hope so, sir.'

'You hope! It is certain! But however! You must give me your parole not to escape before then, yes?'

Sharpe hesitated. By giving his parole he promised to make no effort to escape. He would keep his sword, he would be free to ride with the Lancers without guard, and he would be treated with the respect due to his rank. If he did not give it, then he would be able to make an attempt to escape, but he knew that he would be well guarded. He would be disarmed, he would be locked up at night, and if there was nowhere to lock him he could even be tied to his guard.

Verigny shrugged. 'Well?'

'I cannot give you my parole, sir.'

Verigny frowned. The table was silent. The General shrugged. 'You are a brave man, Major, I do not want to treat you bad.'

'I cannot accept, sir.'

'But I want to help, yes? Helene say you treat her with honour, so I do the similar for you! You will be changed! Why do you not let me do this?'

Sharpe stood. The whole table watched him. He stepped over the bench. In his head he could hear Hogan's insistent words that he must not be captured. He cursed himself. He had sought a warm bed last night when he should have insisted in sleeping in the open air, hidden by woods and night mists.

La Marquesa watched him. She shook her head, is if to tell him that he must not do what he planned. At least, Sharpe thought, she had kept her word. So far the French did not know that they had captured Richard Sharpe.

Verigny smiled. 'Come, Major! You will be changed!'

In answer Sharpe unbuckled his sword belt. The slings jangled harshly. He leaned forward and put the great sword on the table. The dull metal scabbard scraped on the wood as he looked at the General and pronounced his own failure. 'I am your prisoner, sir. No parole.'

Beyond the inn door the town burned. A woman screamed. A child sobbed. The lancers searched the houses before torching them, and Richard Sharpe was led under guard and locked into a stable. He had failed.

CHAPTER 15

There was nothing in the cell, no blanket, no cot, not even a bucket. The floor was thick with slime. Each breath made Sharpe want to gag on the stench that was thicker than musket smoke. There was no window. He knew he was deep inside the rock on which Burgos' castle was built.

He had been brought through the outer courtyard, past walls still scorched from the explosions of British howitzer shells fired in last year's siege, through the packed, loaded wagons of treasure that crammed the yard, past the roofless, burned out buildings, to the massively walled keep.

He had been pushed down stairs, down a dank, cold corridor, and into this small, square room with its slimy floor and the incessant drip of water onto stone outside. The only light was a faint glow that come through a small hole carved in the thick door.

He shouted that he was a British officer, that he wished to be treated accordingly, but there was no reply. He shouted it in Spanish and English, but his voice faded in the cold echoing corridor to silence.

He touched his temple and winced with the pain. It was swollen where the infantry Sergeant had struck him with a musket butt. The blood was drying to a crust.

Rats moved in the corridor. The water dripped outside. Once he heard voices far away, and he shouted again, but there was no reply.

He had been given no chance to escape on the journey south. The lancers had ridden fast, and Sharpe was put in the centre of a whole squadron, the men behind him with their lances ready to thrust. At night he had been locked up, twice in churches, once in a village jail, and guarded by men who stayed wide awake with loaded muskets on their knees. La Marquesa had travelled in a coach that General Verigny had confiscated in the town where he had found her. Once or twice she would catch Sharpe's eye and shrug. At night she sent him wine, and food cooked for the lancer officers.

His telescope, his pack, all his belongings except the clothes he wore, had been taken from him. Verigny, who could not understand why Major 'Vaughn' was so stubborn, had promised that the belongings would be returned to him. Verigny had kept the promise. When Sharpe was taken up the steep road and into Burgos Castle, his property was given back.

He had been handed over to the fortress troops. Verigny's men left him in the courtyard, standing under the guard of two infantrymen as the sun climbed higher.

Sharpe had stared at the wagons in the yard, trying to see beneath the roped tarpaulins a clue to confirm La Marquesa's tale that the treasure of the Spanish empire was here. He waited. Men of the garrison passed him, staring curiously at the prisoner, and still no administrative officer arrived to arrange his future. Once, at one of the high windows in the keep, Sharpe saw a man with a telescope. The glass seemed to be aimed directly at himself.

It had been shortly after he had seen the man with the spyglass that the four infantrymen, led by a Sergeant, had run towards him. He had thought that they were going past him, had stepped back, but one of the men had bellowed at him, swung a fist, and Sharpe had hit back, one punch, two, and then the Sergeant had cracked him on the temple with the musket butt and he had been unceremoniously brought to this cell where he could pace three steps in each direction and where there was no light, no stool, no bed, no hope.

He was thirsty. His head throbbed. He leaned on the wall for a time, fighting pain, darkness and despair. The hours passed, but what time it was he did not know. No bells penetrated to this room hacked in the rock beneath the old castle.

He wondered if he had been recognised, but even if he had then it made no sense for him to be treated this way. He thought of La Marquesa, imagining her in the arms of her General, her head on his chest, her hair golden against his skin. He tried to remember the night in the inn, but it seemed unreal. All that seemed real was this cell, his hurts, and the thirst. He found a wet patch of wall and he licked the stone for moisture. The stench in the cell was foul. Night-soil had been thrown in here, or left by other prisoners, and each breath he took was foetid.

Time passed and passed, measured only by the dripping of water onto stone. They wanted him to despair, to be dragged down by this foul, stinking place, and he fought it by trying to remember the names of every man who had served in his Company since the beginning of the war in Spain, and when he had done that he tried to call aloud the muster-roll of the very first Company he had joined in the army. He paced the cell against the cold, back and forth, his boots splashing on the floor, and sometimes, when the smell was too much, he put his mouth against the spyhole in the door and sucked deep breaths.

He cursed himself for this capture, for oversleeping in the dawn, for accepting the challenge of a duel.

He sensed that the day had passed, that night had come, though the glow at the door did not change. He propped himself in a corner, squatting on his heels with his back to the wall, and tried to sleep. Four nights ago he had been in a real bed, between sheets, with La Marquesa warm against him and over him and he tried to sleep, jerked awake, and listened to the rats outside and the drip of water. He shivered.

He sensed that the prisoner put in this cell was supposed to lie down. They wanted the prisoner here to soil his clothes and be stained with faeces. He would not oblige them.

Three men came for him eventually, two armed with bayonet-tipped muskets and the third the same great hulk of a Sergeant who had first struck Sharpe. The man was huge. He appeared to have no neck and his arms bulged the uniform sleeves with muscle. The Sergeant shouted at him in French, then laughed at the smell of the room.

Sharpe was tired, desperately so, and the thirst had half closed his throat. He stumbled in the sudden light of the flaming torch held by one of his guards and the Sergeant pushed him so he fell, and then hauled him up with a strength that took Sharpe's weight easily.

They marched him down the corridor, up the stairs, along a second corridor and up more stairs. There was daylight here, coming through small windows that looked into the keep's central courtyard, and then the Sergeant pushed Sharpe into a room where a fourth soldier waited.

It was a room about twelve feet square. One window, high and barred, let a grey, unhappy light onto the stone of the walls and floor. A single table was in the room, behind it a chair. The guards positioned themselves on either side of him. The Sergeant, the only unarmed Frenchman, was one of the two men on Sharpe's right. Whenever Sharpe tried to lean against the wall he was shouted at, pulled forward, and then there would be silence again.

They waited. The two men immediately closest to Sharpe faced him with bayonets. Sharpe closed his eyes. He swayed slightly with tiredness. His head throbbed.

The door opened.

Sharpe opened his eyes and understood.

Pierre Ducos stepped into the room. For a second Sharpe did not recognise the small, pock-skinned man with the round spectacles, and then the Christmas meeting in the Gateway of God rushed back to him. Major Pierre Ducos, who had been described to Sharpe as a dangerous man, a clever man, a man whose hands stank with the slime of politics, was responsible for this treatment, for the filthy cell, for what, Sharpe knew, was about to happen.

Ducos wrinkled his nose then stepped almost delicately behind the table and sat. A soldier followed him and put Sharpe's sword on the table, then his telescope, then some papers. Not a word was said until the soldier had gone.

Ducos fussily aligned the edges of the papers before looking up at the English officer. 'You slept well?'

Sharpe ignored the question. 'I am an officer of His Britannic Majesty's army, and I demand the treatment proper to my rank.' His voice came out as a dry croak.

Ducos frowned. 'You're wasting my time.' His voice was deep, as if it belonged to a much huger man.

'I am an officer in His Britannic . . .'

He stopped because the huge Sergeant, on a nod from Ducos, had turned and planted one vast fist into Sharpe's stomach, doubling him over, driving the wind from him.

Ducos waited until Sharpe was upright again, until his breathing was normal, then smiled. 'I believe, Mr Sharpe, that you are not an officer. By a Court-Martial decision, of which I have a record here,' he tapped the papers, 'you were dismissed the army. In brief you are a civilian, though masquerading as a Major Vaughn. Am I right?'

Sharpe said nothing. Ducos unhooked the spectacle from his ears, breathed on them, and began to polish their round lenses with a silk handkerchief he took from his sleeve. 'I believe you are a spy, Mr Sharpe.'

'I am an officer . . .'

'Do stop being tedious. We have already ascertained that you were cashiered. You wear a uniform to which you are not entitled, carry a name not your own, and by your own admission to General Verigny you were trying to abduct a woman in the hope that she could provide information.' He carefully hooked the wire spectacle frames onto his ears and smiled unpleasantly at Sharpe. 'It sounds like spying to me. Did Wellington think that by faking your execution you would become invisible?' He laughed at his jest. 'I will admit, Mr Sharpe, that it fooled me. I could hardly credit it when I saw you in our courtyard!' He smiled triumphantly, then picked up the top sheet of paper. 'It seems from what that fool Verigny has told me that you rescued La Marquesa from the convent. Is that true?'

Sharpe said nothing. Ducos sighed. 'I know you did, Mr

Sharpe. It was inconvenient of you, to say the least. Why did you go to such lengths to rescue her?'

'I wanted to go to bed with her.'

Ducos leaned back. 'You're being tiresome and my time is too valuable to listen to your filth. I ask you again, why did you rescue her?'

Sharpe repeated the answer.

Ducos looked at the Sergeant and nodded.

The Sergeant turned stolidly, his face expressionless, glanced up and down Sharpe and then brought his right fist hard again at the Rifleman's stomach. Sharpe moved from the blow, his own hand going for the Sergeant's eyes, but a bayonet chopped down on his arm and the Sergeant's left fist crashed into his face, banging his head back on the stone wall, then the right fist was in his belly, doubling him over, and suddenly the Sergeant, as woodenly as he had turned to Sharpe, turned away and slammed to attention.

Ducos was frowning. He watched Sharpe straighten up. Blood was coming from the Rifleman's nose. Sharpe leaned on the wall and this time no one stopped him. The Frenchman shook his head. 'I do dislike violence, Major, it upsets me. It has its uses, I fear, and I think you now understand that. Why did you rescue La Marquesa?'

Sharpe gave the same answer.

This time he let himself be hit. He had only one weapon, and he used it. He pretended to be weaker than he was. He fell to the floor, groaning, and the Sergeant disdainfully pulled him up by his jacket collar and threw him against the wall. The Sergeant smiled in victory as he turned back to Ducos.

'Why did you rescue La Marquesa?'

'I needed a woman.'

This time Ducos did not nod to the Sergeant. He seemed to sigh. He took off his spectacles again, frowned, polished them with his handkerchief, then, with a small wince, hooked the wires back on his ears. 'I believe you, Major. Your appetite would run to women like Helene, and doubtless you rut her capably. Tell me, did she ask the British for help?'

'Only for a rut. It seems the French don't do it well enough for her.'

Sharpe braced himself for the blow, but again Ducos did not give the signal. He sighed again. 'I should tell you, Mr Sharpe, that Sergeant Lavin is remarkably efficient at exacting words from reluctant talkers. He usually practises his art on the Spanish, but he has long wanted an Englishman.' Ducos' spectacles flashed two circles of grey light. 'Indeed, he has wanted an Englishman for a long, long time.'

Sergeant Lavin, hearing his name, turned his squat, hard-eyed head and looked at Sharpe with disdain.

Ducos stood up and walked round the table, picking up Sharpe's telescope as he came. 'Before you are in no state to appreciate it, Major, I have a score to settle with you. You broke my spectacles. You put me to a deal of trouble!' Suddenly, astonishingly, Ducos sounded angry. He seemed to control it, straightening his small body and frowning. 'You deliberately broke my spectacles!'

Sharpe said nothing. It was true. He had smashed Ducos' glasses in the Gateway of God. He had done it after Ducos had insulted Teresa, Sharpe's wife. Now Ducos held Sharpe's telescope. 'A very fine instrument, Major.' He peered at the brass plate. 'September 23rd, 1803. We called it *Vendemiaire* Second, Year Ten.' Ducos, Sharpe knew, regretted the abolition of the revolutionary calendar.

Sharpe pushed himself up from the wall. 'Take it, Ducos, your army's stolen everything else in Spain.'

'Take it! Of course not. You think I'm a thief?' He looked back at the brass plate. 'The reward for one of your acts of bravery, no doubt.' He pulled the telescope open, revealing the polished inner brass tubes. 'No, Major Sharpe. I'm not going to take it. I'm simply going to pay back the insult you offered me.'

With gritted teeth and sudden frenzy, Ducos swung the telescope by its eyepiece, slamming it on the stone floor and then swinging it again and again. A fortune in finely ground glass was being smashed by the small man who went on beating it, bending the tubes, scattering thick glass fragments on the stone floor. He dropped the telescope and stamped on it, splitting the brass tubes apart, then he kicked at them viciously, skittering them about the floor until, nothing left to kick at, he stood panting. He straightened his jacket and looked with a smile of pitiful triumph at the Rifleman. 'You have paid me your personal debt, Mr Sharpe. An eye for an eye, so to speak.'

Sharpe had watched the destruction of his telescope, his valued telescope that had been a gift from Wellington, with mounting anger and frustration. He could do nothing. Sergeant Lavin had watched him and the bayonets had been in his ribs. He forced his anger down and nodded at the sword. 'Do it to that, Ducos.'

'No, Mr Sharpe.' Ducos was behind the table, sitting again. 'When they ask me how you died, I shall say that I offered you parole, you accepted, and that you then attacked me with the sword I had politely returned to you. My life will be saved by Sergeant Lavin.' The Frenchman smiled. 'But I truly hate violence, Mr Sharpe. Would you believe me if I said I do not wish you dead?'

'No.'

Ducos shrugged. 'It's true. You can live. You can walk out of here with your sword. We won't exchange you, of course, you'll spend the rest of the war in France. We might even civilise you.' Ducos smiled at his joke and looked down at the papers. 'So tell me, Mr Sharpe, or even Major Sharpe if it makes you feel better, did Helene seek British help?'

Sharpe swore at him.

Ducos sighed and nodded. Lavin turned, stolid and unstoppable, and this time he punched Sharpe's face, cutting his lips open and slashing a bloody line over his forehead with a ring he wore. Sharpe fell again, deliberately, and this time boots slammed into his back. He cried out, also deliberately, scrabbled with his hands, and suddenly knew hope.

A twisted, bent tube of brass from his telescope was by the wall. He shouted again as a boot landed, grabbed the tube, and concealed it in his fist. A hand grasped his collar, hauled him up, turned him, and pushed him back to the wall.

It was the smallest tube in his hand. He could feel the torn, knurled rim that had held the small lens of the eyepiece. The tube was six inches in length and one end was split and jagged where Ducos had stamped on it.

Ducos waited for Sharpe's breathing to slow, for the battered, bleeding face to face him again. 'It may help you to know, Major, that I will ask you a number of questions to which I already have the answers. You will, therefore, suffer pain unnecessarily. Eventually you will understand the futility of that course. You were accused of murdering Helene's husband, true?'

'You know I was.'

Ducos smiled. 'I arranged it, Mr Sharpe. Did you know that?' Ducos was pleased by the jerk of Sharpe's head, the sudden surprise in the bruised eyes. Ducos liked his victims to know who was responsible for their misfortune. 'Why did Wellington fake your death?'

'I don't know.' Sharpe's lips were swelling. He was swallowing blood. He made his breathing ragged. He was judging distances, planning not the first death, but the second.

Ducos was enjoying the spectacle of his enemy trampled and broken. It was not the physical beating that gave Ducos pleasure, but Sharpe's realisation that he had been outmanoeuvred. 'You were sent to rescue Helene?'

Sharpe's voice came out thickened and slurred by his bleeding lips. 'I wanted to know why she lied in her letter.'

The answer checked Ducos, who frowned. 'The rescue was your own idea?'

'My idea.' Sharpe spat a gob of blood onto the floor.

'How did you know where she was?'

'Everyone knew. Half of bloody Spain knew.'

Ducos accepted that truth. Her fate was supposed to have been a secret, but nothing was secret that happened in Spain. Even Verigny, a gaudy fool, had eventually discovered where his lover was held. None of that worried Ducos. All that worried Ducos was the security of the treaty. 'So you rescued her five days ago?'

'Something like that.'

'And General Verigny discovered you the next day?'

'Yes.'

'Did you sleep with her, Mr Sharpe?'

'No.'

'But you said that's why you wanted to rescue her.'

'She wouldn't have me.' Sharpe shut his eyes and leaned his head on the wall. The last two times he had been attacked the armed soldiers had not bothered to use their bayonets to stop him retaliating. They could see he was beaten and defenceless. They were wrong, but he must wait for his moment and he was planning it carefully. He had fallen to his right the last time and the man there had stepped back and away to give Lavin room. He must be made to do it again.

'Did you sleep with her?'

'No.'

'Did she tell you why she was in the convent?'

'She wanted a rest.'

Ducos shook his head. 'You are a stubborn fool, Mr Sharpe.'

'And you're a filthy little bastard.'

'Mr Sharpe,' Ducos leaned back in his chair, 'tell me what explanation she offered to you. She must have offered you some reason for her arrest?'

Sharpe shook his head as though he was having difficulty with his senses. 'She said she had a dream about you. She was ordered to marry you by the Emperor and she saw you naked and it was the most horrid thing she'd ever . . .'

'Sergeant!'

The first blow landed on Sharpe's skull, a glancing blow, but then there was a pile-driving thump in his belly and the air rushed out of him. He forced himself to the right, was helped by a blow to his head, and then he was on the ground. 'Stop!'

A boot thudded at his kidneys. He pulled the brass tube out of his sleeve, turned it, and gripped it with his right hand. He would have one chance only, just one.

'No!' He shouted it desperately, as if he was a child begging to be spared a beating, and then yelped as a boot hammered on his thigh. Ducos spoke a word in French.

The blows stopped. The Sergeant leaned down to haul Sharpe up by his collar. The other three men were standing back, weapons lowered, grins on their faces.

Lavin pulled Sharpe up and never saw the hand that struck up with the jagged brass tube.

Sharpe bellowed in anger, the war shout. They thought him weak and beaten, but he had one fight in him and they would learn what a Rifleman was in a fight.

The tube, jagged brass edges splayed at its end, struck Lavin's groin and Sharpe twisted it, pushed and gouged as the Sergeant let go of him and screamed a horrid, high scream and dropped his hands to the blood and pain, but already Sharpe had let the tube go, was rising to the Sergeant's right, was moving with all his speed and filling the room with his battle-shout.

The Sergeant's body blocked two men. The third raised his musket, but the muzzle was seized, pulled, and the heel of Sharpe's right hand struck the man's moustache, break-ing bone, snapping the head back, then Sharpe dropped his bleeding hand to the musket's lock, turned the gun, and pulled the trigger.

The two remaining men had dared not fire for fear of their own comrades. Seconds only had passed since the Sergeant had stooped to pick up the broken English officer. Now a musket belched smoke and noise.

One man fell, the musket ball in his lungs, and Sharpe hammered back with the brass butt at the man whose musket he had taken and who still grappled with him. The butt hit the man's head, but he dragged Sharpe down, close to the bleeding, sobbing Sergeant, and the room echoed to a second musket shot, hammering louder than thunder in the room, drowning even the agony of Sergeant Lavin.

Sharpe twisted, heaved, flailed with the musket at the man who had fired as he fell. He still shouted, knowing that men are frightened by noise, by savagery, and he wrenched his right foot free from the man who held it, rose snarling from the bloody floor and lunged with his captured bayonet in short, professional strokes at the last of his enemies still standing. Ducos, his mouth open, was standing terrified at the door. He had no weapon.

The bayonets clashed, Sharpe pushed his opponent's aside, lunged again, then broke to his right, to the table, seized the sword and his voice was triumphant as he swung it, the scabbard scraping free and flying across the room, and he sliced down with the blade, shouting in savage victory, and cut into the last man's neck, dragging the blade back against bone and blood. He saw the man begin to fall, then finished him off with a lunge that was dragged downwards by the dying man. In seconds, just seconds, he had killed two men and wounded two others.

He twisted and jerked the sword free, then turned to the door. 'Ducos!'

The door was empty.

He went to it, the sword bloody in his hand. His face was a mask of blood, his uniform soaked with Lavin's blood. One man against four, and that a Rifleman! Sergeant Harper would say they were fair odds.

'Ducos! You bastard! Ducos!'

He walked into the corridor. Behind him the Sergeant sobbed and wailed and bled into the hands cupped over his groin.

'Ducos! You filth!'

'*M'sieu?*'

The voice came from his right. Sharpe turned.

A group of French officers stood there. They were elegant and clean, staring aghast at the bloody man with the swollen face and the savage voice and the sword that dripped blood.

The French officers wore swords, but none was drawn.

One man stepped forward, a tall man in green and pink, a man who frowned. 'Major Vaughn?'

It was Verigny. His face was screwed up, either because of the smell of blood, or the sight of Sharpe. 'Major?'

'My name is Sharpe.' There was no point in concealment any longer. 'Major Richard Sharpe.' He leaned on the wall. The tip of the sword rested on the flagstones and made there a small pool of thick blood.

Verigny seemed to stand to attention. 'I came from honour, Major, that you would be treated in accord with honour.'

Sharpe jerked his head towards the door. 'The bastards tried to kill me. I had no sword then. I fought back.' Sergeant Lavin was sobbing in high, pitiful cries from within the square, stone-walled room.

Verigny looked through the door. He stepped back and stared in awe at the Rifleman who had made the room look like a slaughterhouse. 'You will be treated good, Major. You have need of a doctor?'

'Yes. And water. Food. A bed.'

'Of course.'

'These clothes washed. A bath.'

'Of course.'

Sharpe pulled his right hand from the sword. His palm was a bloody mess. It hurt. He held the sword out with his left hand. 'I am your prisoner again, it seems.'

'You will do me the honour to keep the sword, *M'sieur*, till we have discussion on what we do to you.'

Sharpe nodded, then turned back into the room. He retrieved his scabbard and sword belt, but could not fasten them with his wounded hand. He went and stood over the moaning, sobbing Sergeant Lavin who looked up at him with eyes that seemed to mix pain with an astonishment that he had been beaten. Sharpe looked at the French General. 'Sir?'

'Major?'

'Tell this eunuch he got his wish.'

Verigny was chilled by the Rifleman's voice. 'His wish, *M'sieu?*'

'He wanted an Englishman. He got one.'

CHAPTER 16

Sharpe was led to one of the buildings in the castle yard that was still in a state of repair, then helped upstairs to a limewashed room, decently furnished with a bed, table and chairs, and with a view from a barred window into the fortress' biggest courtyard. He could see across to the squat keep, past the castle church, and every spare inch of the courtyard was crowded with the treasure wagons.

A doctor came. Sharpe's wounds were washed and bandaged. He was bled with lancet and cup, then given food and brandy.

A great tub was brought to his room, filled by a succession of buckets, and he soaked his body in it. His uniform was taken away, laundered, mended, and returned.

He was still a prisoner. Two guards were outside his door, at the head of the stairs which led down into the courtyard. One of the guards, a cheerful young man no older than Angel, shaved him. Sharpe could not hold a razor in his bandaged right hand.

His sword was propped by the bed. He had cleaned the blade with difficulty. In the ridges of the wooden handle, that should have been wrapped with leather and bound with wire, there was blood that he did not have the energy to clean. He slept instead; a sleep of bad dreams and intermittent pain.

His guards brought him food, good food, and two bottles of red wine. They tried to tell him something, grinning good-naturedly at his incomprehension. He heard the name Verigny and supposed that the General had sent the food. He smiled, nodded to show he understood, and the guards left him with candles and his own thoughts. He paced the floor, thinking only that soon all Spain would think that Wellington had released the murderer of a Spanish Marqués. He had failed Wellington, Hogan, and himself.

In the morning the doctor came again, unpeeled the bandages, and muttered to himself. He examined Sharpe's night-soil in the bucket, seemed pleased by it, then bled Sharpe's thigh into a small cup. He did not re-bandage Sharpe's head, only the cut hand that was still painful.

His lips were swollen. Their insides were coated with congealed blood. Rather that, he thought, than the Sergeant's wound.

He sat by the window all morning, watching the wagons roll out of the courtyard. Wagon after wagon left, their oxen prodded by drivers with pointed staves. The axle squeals never stopped as the courtyard slowly emptied. The French retreat, that had begun in Valladolid, had started again and Sharpe knew that the British must be advancing still, and that the French were sending the treasure wagons back on the Great Road towards France. He wondered if Helene's six wagons were among the ones that left. He wondered why Ducos had arranged for him to be accused of the Marqués' death, and why Helene had lied about it.

The castle church had been used as an ammunition store. As the wagons made space in the big courtyard, squads of infantry began carrying shells and canister from the church towards the keep. Sharpe, with nothing else to do, watched.

After an hour the shells were no longer being carried into the keep, but instead were being piled in the courtyard. Pile after pile was made, starting by the keep door and working slowly down the courtyard towards him. He wondered if this was a punishment detail, forced to do one of the pointless chores that all armies gave their defaulters, but then, curiously, he saw French engineer officers running white fuses to each of the conical heaps, fuses that led back into the keep.

He realised suddenly that the French must be abandoning Burgos, that they were blowing the castle apart rather than delivering such a fortress intact to their enemies, yet it struck him as odd that they should go to the trouble of piling the shells in the courtyard instead of blowing them in one great mass in the magazine. Then, hearing footsteps on the stairs, he turned from the window and forgot the strange piles of ammunition.

He made sure the sword was within reach. He was half expecting Ducos to return and finish what he had begun, but it was a smiling French lancer who opened the door. On the man's arm, incongruously, hung a basket covered with a linen cloth.

More such men came, men who arranged food and wine on the table in Sharpe's room. None spoke English. They finished their job, left, then Sharpe heard her voice on the stairs. It was La Marquesa, looking as if she had bathed in dew and sipped ambrosia, her eyes bright, her smile welcoming, and her concern about his battered, blood-marked face oddly touching. With her was the tall, dark figure of General Verigny, while behind came another French officer, a plump Major called Montbrun who spoke fluent English and trusted that Major Sharpe was not in any great pain?

Sharpe assured him he was not. Major Montbrun nevertheless hoped that Major Sharpe would realise that his treatment at the hands of Sergeant Lavin had not been worthy of the great French army, and that Major Sharpe would forgive it, and offer Major Montbrun the pleasure of joining him in a small, light luncheon?

Major Sharpe would.

Major Montbrun knew that Major Sharpe had the honour of already knowing La Marquesa and the General. Montbrun explained that he was an aide to King Joseph himself, Napoleon's brother who was the puppet King on the crumbling Spanish throne. Montbrun hoped that Major Sharpe would not take it amiss if he said that His Majesty King Joseph was flattered that so redoubtable an enemy as Major Sharpe should have been captured. Sharpe did not reply. La Marquesa smiled and brushed the crusted wound on Sharpe's head with her fingertips. 'Ducos is a pig.'

Montbrun frowned. 'Major Ducos has explained what happened, my Lady. I'm sure we must believe him.'

'What did he say?' Sharpe asked.

Montbrun held a chair for La Marquesa, then for Sharpe, then sat himself. 'Major Ducos explained that Sergeant Lavin lost his temper. Most sad, of course. You'll forgive us serving ourselves, Major Sharpe? I thought we might be more intimate without orderlies.'

'Of course. And how is Sergeant Lavin?'

Montbrun frowned, as though the subject was deeply distasteful. 'He, of course, faces disciplinary charges. Can I suggest some of this cold soup? It's most tasteful, I'm sure. May I have the honour of assisting you?'

He could. La Marquesa, dressed in lilac silk with a low, lace frilled neckline, smiled at him. Sharpe agreed with Montbrun that the spring had been wet, and that this summer had more rain than most in Spain. He agreed that the soup, a *gazpacho*, was delicious. Montbrun wondered if there was too much garlic for his taste, but Sharpe assured him there could not be too much garlic in anything for his taste, and Montbrun agreed how wise that view was.

Verigny grinned. His moustache was stained with the soup. 'I think you demi kill that *mighou* Lavin, yes?' He looked at La Marquesa. '*mighou*?'

'Bugger, darling.'

'Ah! You kill the bugger Lavin, yes?'

Sharpe smiled. 'He tried to kill me.'

Verigny shrugged. 'You should kill him. I hate buggers.'

Montbrun hastened, with a courtier's smoothness, to recommend the red wine which, though Spanish, had a certain plangency, he thought, which Major Sharpe might find pleasing. Major Sharpe, who was thirsty, found it very pleasing. He drank.

La Marquesa toasted him with her glass. 'You should have more champagne, Richard.'

'I shall save it.'

'Why? There's plenty!' There was, too. The bottles of wine and champagne stood in ranks at the end of the table.

Montbrun poured a separate glass of champagne for Sharpe. 'I hear it's scarce in your country now, Major, because of the war.'

Sharpe, who had never drunk champagne in England, and only in Spain when he was with La Marquesa, agreed it was scarce.

'Indeed,' Montbrun poured himself a glass, 'I was told by an Englishman we took prisoner that you're paying twenty-three shillings a bottle now in London! Twenty-three shillings! Why that's nearly thirty francs a bottle!'

La Marquesa looked astonished and wondered how anyone could possibly live with prices like that, and asked why there were not riots in the street by a champagne-starved populace. What did the English drink instead?

'Beer, my Lady.'

Montbrun helped Sharpe to some cold ham and cold chicken. He apologized for such simple fare. The ham had been baked in a glaze of honey and mustard.

La Marquesa wanted some English beer and seemed unhappy that there was none immediately available in Burgos castle. General Verigny promised to find some. He grunted as he drew the corks of two more bottles of the red wine. 'We have to drink it. We cannot take it with this bloody army.'

Montbrun frowned.

Sharpe smiled. 'Bloody army?'

Verigny tossed back a glass of wine and poured himself another. 'It is not an army, Major, not a true army. We are a – ' he paused, frowned, '*un bordel ambulant!*'

'I think you'll find the terrine especially good, Major.' Montbrun smiled. 'You'll allow me to cut you some bread?'

'A what?' Sharpe asked.

'A walking brothel, Major.' La Marquesa smiled brightly. 'There do seem to be rather a lot of ladies with us. Especially since King Joseph joined us.'

'Allow me, Major.' Montbrun put some of the terrine onto Sharpe's plate. 'More wine? Champagne, perhaps?'

'Wine.'

When the meal was over, and when the peel of oranges littered the table among grape-stalks and the rinds of cheeses, Major Montbrun brought the talk to Sharpe's future. He took from the tail pocket of his gilt-encrusted jacket a folded sheet of paper.

'We're most pleased to offer you parole.' Montbrun smiled and put the paper in front of Sharpe. 'General Verigny will count it an honour, Major, if you will let him provide you with all your necessities. A horse, your expenses.' Montbrun shrugged as though the generous offer was a mere nothing.

'The General has done me enough honour already.' Verigny, in addition to providing this room and Sharpe's food, had given Sharpe a new razor, a change of shirt, new stockings, and even a fine new tinder box; all to replace the articles stolen from Sharpe since he fell into Ducos' hands.

Sharpe opened the paper, not understanding the French words, but seeing his own name, misspelt, on the top line. He looked at Montbrun. 'Is my name to be submitted for exchange?'

They must have expected the question. An officer was rarely kept as a prisoner of war if he was captured close to the battlelines. Montbrun frowned. 'We fear not, Major.'

'May I ask why?'

'You have, *M'sieu*, a certain notoriety?' Montbrun smiled. 'It would be foolish of us to release so formidable a soldier to wreak further damage on our cause.'

It was a pretty enough compliment, but not the answer Sharpe wanted. If he was not to be exchanged, then he faced a journey to the frontier, where he would be released on his parole to make his unescorted way across France. Verigny, speaking eagerly, explained that it would be his pleasure to provide Sharpe with the means to stay only in the best hotels, that he would, indeed, furnish him with introductions and the Major would be welcome to linger on his journey north to savour the summer delights of France. 'Take the entirely summer, Major. You can drink, there are women, there are more drink!' He demonstrated by finishing his glass. Already, Sharpe noted, Verigny was slurring his words.

There was yet more. Once at Verdun, the great northern fortress where officer prisoners were kept, Montbrun explained that the General would ensure that Sharpe had money to take rooms in the town, servants, and membership of all the best clubs organized by the captured British officers. Even, he said, the Literary and Philosophical Association, which was neither literary nor philosophical, but provided the wealthiest British captives with the discreet pleasures a man needed.

Sharpe thanked him.

Montbrun reached into his pouch and produced a quill and ink bottle. He pushed them to Sharpe. 'You will sign, Major?'

'When will I be leaving Burgos?' Sharpe had not touched the quill.

'Tomorrow, Major. The General is with the rearguard. You may travel by horseback or, if your wounds are troublesome, in the Marquesa's coach. We will leave, it is expected, at nine o'clock.'

Sharpe looked at Helene and knew the temptation to yield now, to sign the paper, and share the journey with her.

She smiled. 'Do, Richard.' She shrugged. 'We're not going to let you go, you do know that.'

Verigny belched, Montbrun frowned. Sharpe smiled. 'I may have to escape then.'

That shocked them. There was a second's silence, then Verigny exploded into words, pleading words. If there was no parole then they would be forced to heap indignities upon a brave man who had suffered enough indignities at the hands of Frenchmen who were a disgrace to their country, their Emperor and their sacred flag. It was unthinkable that he should be marched as a common criminal to prison. Verigny would not hear of it! He must sign!

Yet if he signed he could not attempt an escape.

He looked at the paper again. 'I will give my decision in the morning. Say at eight o'clock?'

It was the best they could do. They tried to persuade him, but he would not change his mind. 'In the morning. Eight o'clock.'

Two more bottles were opened. Sharpe's head was already feeling the effects of the first six, but he let Montbrun pour him more wine. They toasted Helene, they toasted her chances of recovering her wagons. It seemed, she said, that they had been sent to Vitoria already, but that General Verigny was confident that he would take them back for her. More wine was poured. Major Montbrun, his plump face gleaming with sweat, asked Sharpe's permission to toast the Emperor which, the permission having been graciously given, they duly did. Out of courtesy to their guest they proposed the health of King George III, and then various other Kings including Arthur, Alfred, Charlemagne, Louis I to Louis XIV inclusive, Caesar Augustus, Old King Cole, the King of the Castle, Nebuchadnezzar, Wilfred the Hairy, and finishing with Tiglath Pileser III, whose name they could not by then pronounce, but who had the honour to take the first of the brandy.

General Verigny was asleep. He had slept ever since he had proposed the health of Richard the Lionheart.

'He was a *mighou*,' Montbrun had said, then blushed because he had said it. Now, as the sun was setting and casting long shadows on the conical piles of shells in the castle courtyard, Montbrun decided they must leave. 'You will give us your decision in the morning, Major?' His words came out slowly. He tapped the parole.

'In the morning.'

'Good. I shall leave it with you, if I may.' He stood, and his eyes showed alarm at the effects of the wine on his balance. 'Good gracious!'

Two lancers were fetched to carry the General downstairs, and one to assist Montbrun. La Marquesa, who gave her hand to Sharpe to be kissed, seemed unaffected by the drink. There were still six untouched bottles on the table. She smiled at him. 'Don't escape, Richard.'

He smiled. 'Thank you for coming.'

'Poor, foolish Richard.' She touched his cheek and followed the two officers to the stairs.

Sharpe sat. He listened to the General's feet drag on the stairs, listened to the door open and close, heard the carriage creak, then clatter away. He stared at the parole, at the odd French words, and felt the temptation to share Helene's coach.

The door opened.

She smiled 'I've told them to come back for me in three hours.' She knocked on the door and Sharpe heard the bolt slide across outside.

She stared at him, her head on one side, then she walked to the bed, sat, and lifted one foot to untie the half boots she wore under her dress. 'Come to bed, Richard, for Christ's sake come to bed.'

He took a champagne bottle with him and she laughed. 'You see how good it is to be a prisoner of France?'

He smiled and lifted his bandaged right hand. 'You'll have to undress me.'

'I intend to, Richard. Come here.'

He went. He saw the white lace go, the dress fall, and she was naked in the red sunlight. Her hands reached for his jacket, then pulled him down to the bed and to her arms.

She smoked a cigar. She lay on her back and blew smoke rings at the ceiling. 'I practised those for months.'

'You're very good.'

'At blowing smoke rings too.' She giggled. 'You're not very drunk.'

'Nor are you.' He was dribbling champagne into her navel and sipping it. 'Can you feel the bubbles?'

'Yes.'

'I don't believe you.'

She said nothing for a few seconds, then, in a suddenly changed voice that made him stop his game to look at her, she told him that Major Ducos had made her sign the letter that had provoked the duel.

Sharpe stared into the grey eyes. 'I know.'

'Come here.' She gestured at the pillow beside her, and when he was there she pulled the sheet over them both and hooked a leg over his. 'Are you drunk?'

'No.'

'Then listen.'

She talked. She spoke of a treaty that was being made between the imprisoned Spanish king and the Emperor Napoleon. She spoke of Pierre Ducos' part in the making of the treaty, and she described the terms of the treaty and how, if it was signed, it would force the British from Spain. 'You understand?'

'Yes. But what . . .'

'. . . Has it got to do with that letter?' She finished his question for him, then shrugged. 'I don't know.' She threw her cigar onto the floor and put her hand on his waist. 'I just don't know, except that I think the Inquisitor must be helping Ducos, and I'm guessing that my money is the price of that help.'

He stared into her lustrous, beautiful face and he tried to sense whether this was the truth. He could not tell. It made more sense than her last story, but he knew this clever woman was a liar of practised fluency. 'Why are you telling me?'

She did not answer the question, instead she asked if he had liked Major Montbrun. Sharpe shrugged. 'I suppose so.'

She propped herself on one elbow, the sheet falling to her waist. It was almost dark, and Sharpe lit the candle beside the bed. She leaned over him to light a fresh cigar from its flame and he reached up with his tongue to touch her breast. 'Richard! Will you be serious?'

'I am.'

'Why do you think Montbrun was here?'

'I don't know.'

'Christ! Think, you stupid bugger!' She was half leaning over him. 'Montbrun is one of Joseph's men, and Joseph is King of Spain! He rather likes it, he likes being called

"Your Majesty"! He doesn't want to give up Spain. Even if we can keep a bit of Spain he's got a kingdom, but now his brother's planning to pull the throne out from underneath him and give it all back to Ferdinand. You understand?'

'I understand. But why tell me?'

'Because you're going to stop it.' She took a shred of tobacco from her lip and wiped it onto his chest. 'You're going to sign that parole and come with me. Then you're going to escape. Montbrun will help, he knows about it. All that talk of crossing France was for Raoul's benefit. Instead we want you to escape.' Her fingers were stroking his chest. 'You go to Wellington. I'll give you a letter and Montbrun will sign it.' She was staring at his wide eyes. 'You escape with our help, you go to Wellington, because if he makes a public announcement now then he can stop the treaty. No one will dare support it yet. Only Ferdinand can make the stupid bastards accept it, but if Arthur gets the Spanish to make an announcement now that it wouldn't be accepted, then it will never get signed. So you stop it, do you understand?'

He frowned. 'Why doesn't Joseph stop the treaty?'

'Because his brother will crucify him! They're all scared of Napoleon. But if you tell Wellington, then no one can blame Joseph.'

'Why don't you just exchange me?'

She seemed exasperated by his questions. 'We can't. Ducos won't allow it. He wants to parade you in Paris as proof of Britain's bad faith. Besides, do you think we'd ever exchange someone like you?'

'But you'll let me escape.'

'Because then Ducos loses. Because Joseph keeps a bit of Spain and gives me my wagons back!' Her eyes flicked between his, judging him. 'Montbrun will pay you, too.'

'But didn't you say the treaty would save France?'

'Christ on the true cross! And I'll be poor, and half of Joseph's men will be ruined! We need this summer, Richard, that's all! Besides, it was that bastard Ducos who

199

arranged this, who had me arrested, who almost had you hanged! I want Ducos to be stood against the wall, I want that so badly, Richard, I can feel it in my guts. Next year they can make their god-damned treaty, but not now, not till Pierre Ducos is dead.'

'And you want your money.'

'I want that house.'

'Lark pâté and honey?'

'And you can visit me from England. We'll pay you, Richard. Two thousand guineas, in gold, or paper, or whatever. Just sign the parole and we do the rest.' She watched him as he stood, as he walked naked to sit in the window. 'Well?'

'If I break my parole I have no honour.'

'God spits on honour. Three thousand!'

He turned to her. She was leaning towards him, naked, her face alive with the moment. Her body, that was so beautiful, was lit and shadowed by the candle. He wondered if she felt anything when he embraced her. 'You want me to sign away my honour?'

She threw the cigar at him. 'For your country. For me! Anyway, it isn't dishonourable!'

'It isn't?'

'Montbrun misspelt your name on purpose. It's not your parole.'

He turned away from her. Beneath him a carriage was coming into the courtyard between the strange piles of ammunition.

She heard it, swore, and began to dress. 'Can you hook me up?'

'Just about.' He fumbled with his bandaged hand at the nape of her neck, then turned her. He looked into her eyes and she reached up and kissed him. 'Do it for me, Richard. Finish Ducos and that bastard Inquisitor, and go back to your career.' She put his hand on her breast and pressed it. 'The war will be over in two or three years. Over! Come to me then. Promise me?'

She was more beautiful than a dream, more lovely than

the stars in winter, softer than light. She kissed him, her lips warm. 'Come to me when it's all over.'

'Come to you?'

She half smiled. She was heart-breakingly beautiful, and she whispered into his ear and her cheek was warm on his. 'I love you, Richard. Do this for me and come to me.'

There was a knock on the door. She shouted at them to wait and dragged a hand over her hair. 'Will you come to me?'

'You know I will.'

She gestured at the parole. 'Then sign, Richard. For both of us! Sign!' She smiled at his nakedness, motioned him to stand behind the door, and then was gone into the night.

Sharpe drank steadily, his mood worsening. He was thinking of honour betrayed, of a woman who had promised herself to fulfil his wildest dream, of a treaty to expel Britain's army from Spain. He had pulled on his overalls and jacket, lit more candles, and still he had not signed the parole.

He decided he was too drunk to sign the parole. Since Helene had left he had finished two bottles of wine.

He went to the table, amazed that he could stand upright, and took two bottles back to the window, reasoning that by carrying two he would save himself another complicated journey across the room when he had finished the first. The reasoning struck him as extremely clever. He was proud of it. He rested his head on the window bars. Somewhere a woman laughed, a low sound of pure pleasure, and he was jealous.

'Helene.' He said it aloud. 'Helene, Helene, Helene.'

He drank more, not bothering with the glass. If he was to sign the parole, he thought, then he would be with her for a few days. Verigny could not be there all the time. They could make love in her carriage, the curtains drawn.

He would break his honour. He would break his parole. There would be no honour left to him if he did that, none.

Yet he would save Britain from defeat at the price of his

honour. He could make Helene rich for his honour. And, by forcing failure onto Ducos, he could disgrace the man, maybe even, as Helene had said, have him stood against the wall and shot. All at the price of his honour.

He thought of Ducos and lifted the bottle against the night. 'Bastard.' He yawned hugely, drank more, and tried to concentrate his vision on a lit window of the keep, but it kept sliding diagonally up to the right. He frowned at it. Perhaps she meant it, he thought, perhaps she did love him. He sometimes thought she was a treacherous bitch, beautiful as hell, but even treacherous bitches had to love someone, didn't they? He wondered if love was a sign of weakness, and then he thought that it was not, and then he could not remember what he was thinking and he drank more from the bottle.

He wondered if Antonia would like to have a French aristocrat as a stepmother. He drank to the thought. He drank to lark pâté and honey and white wine and her body in his arms and her breath in his throat and he wished she was still here and he drank more wine because it might take away the loneliness because she had gone.

Beyond the window, to the north west, it seemed as if there was a glow in the sky. He noticed it, frowned at it, and thought the glow in the sky might like to be toasted. He raised the bottle and drank. He felt sick. He thought he might feel better if he was sick, but he could not be bothered to go to the bucket that was decently hidden behind a wooden screen made from an old packing case. They had all laughed when Montbrun had used the bucket and had seemed to piss forever. He laughed again now. She loved him. She loved him. She loved him.

He closed his eyes.

Then he jerked his head up, eyes open, and stared at the great red smear in the sky. He knew what it was. It was the camp fires of an army, seen far off, reflected on the clouds that threatened rain. The British were to the north and west, close enough for their fires to be seen on the clouds, close enough to be forcing a further retreat from this French army, this walking brothel. He laughed and drank again.

He threw the empty bottle into the courtyard, hearing it smash on the stones and provoke a shout from a sentry. Sharpe shouted back. '*mighou! mighou!*'

He picked up the next bottle. 'You shouldn't drink it,' he told himself, then decided that it was a terrible waste if he did not. He thought he might drink it in bed and stood up.

He held onto the wall. It all suddenly seemed clear with the marvellous prescience of the drunk. King Joseph and Montbrun wanted him to escape. Montbrun was a courtier. Montbrun knew more about honour than Sharpe, so it would be all right to break his parole. He would escape. He would go to the British army and he would be rich and he would marry La Marquesa when the war was done because even treacherous bitches had to love someone and he could not bear to think of her loving anyone else. He drank to the thought. Lark pâté and honey, he thought, and wine. More wine. Always more wine, and then he pushed himself off the wall, aimed for the bed, and collapsed just short of it. He managed to save the bottle.

He sat by the narrow bed where he had loved her just this day. 'I love you,' he said. He pulled the blankets about his shoulders, and drank some more. It was all so easy. Escape and victory, marriage and riches. Luck was with him. It always had been. He smiled and raised the bottle.

He drank more wine, just to prove that he could do it, and then, when he was solemnly thinking he ought to work out a detail or two of the decisions he had made, his head went back onto the bed, the bottle dropped, and he slept the sleep of the drunk.

CHAPTER 17

Morning came like a sad groan. He was still tangled in blankets beside the bed. The dawn light was depressing.

He swore and closed his eyes.

Someone was using a sledgehammer within the castle, the blows were ringing through his skull.

'Oh God.'

He opened his eyes again. A bottle of wine lay close to him on the floor, the wine trapped by the bottle's neck dark with sediment. He groaned again.

He leaned his head on the bed and stared up at the whitewashed ceiling. The hammering seemed to be coming from the very walls of the room. He could not believe it was possible to feel this ill. His eyes felt as if they were trying to burst from his head, his mouth was fouler than the cell Ducos had first put him in, his stomach was sour and his bowels were water. 'Oh God.'

He heard the bolts on his door shoot back, but did not turn round. *'Bonjour, m'sieu!'* It was the cheerful young guard.

Sharpe turned slowly, his neck hurting. 'Jesus.'

The guard laughed. *'Non, m'sieu. C'est moi.'* He put the bowl on the table and mimed shaving. *'Oui, m'sieu?'*

'Oui.'

Sharpe stood up. He staggered on aching legs, and wished he had stayed on the floor. He held a hand up to the guard. 'A minute! Wait!' He went to the wooden screen, held it, and vomited. 'Jesus!'

'M'sieu?'

'All right! All right! What time is it?'

'M'sieu?'

Sharpe tried to remember the word. He snapped the fingers of his left hand. '*L'heure?*'

'*Ah! C'est six heures, m'sieu.*'

'Cease?'

The soldier held up six fingers, Sharpe nodded, then spat through the window.

The young guard seemed happy to shave the English officer. He did it skilfully, chatting incomprehensibly and cheerfully as he lathered and scraped and washed and towelled. It occurred to Sharpe that he could elbow the boy in the belly, take his musket, shoot the man outside, and be in the courtyard within ten seconds. There had to be a damned horse there and, with luck, he could be through the gates and away before the guards knew what was happening.

On the other hand he did not feel up to morning mayhem, and it seemed distinctly churlish to attack a cheerful man who was shaving him with such skill. Besides, he needed breakfast. He needed it badly.

The boy patted Sharpe's face dry and smiled. '*Bonjour!*' He backed out of the door with the bowl and towel, came back a moment later for the musket he had left beside Sharpe. He waved farewell and shut the door, not bothering to bolt it.

The hammering still echoed in the room. He went to the window and saw, where the sentries paced their monotonous beats on the ramparts, that the guns which had defied Wellington last year were being destroyed. Their trunnions, the great knobs that held the barrels to the carriages, were being sawn through. When the hacksaws were halfway through, a man would give a great blow with a sledgehammer to shear the bronze clean. The blows rang dolorously through the courtyard. To make sure that the guns were far beyond repair they were being spiked as well, then heaved over the ramparts to fall onto the precipitous rocks below. The noise was shattering. He groaned. 'Oh God!'

Sharpe lay on the bed. He would never drink again, never. On the other hand, of course, the hair of the dog that bit you was the only specific against rabies. Half the British army went to their rest drunk and could only face the next day by drinking the night's dregs. He opened one eye and stared gloomily at an unopened bottle of champagne on the table.

He fetched it, frowned at it, then shrugged. He jammed it between his legs, and twisted the cork with his left hand. It popped boomingly. The sheer effort of pulling the cork seemed to have left him weaker then a kitten. The champagne foamed onto his overalls.

He tried it. It took the taste of vomit from his mouth. It even tasted good. He drank some more.

He lay back again, holding the champagne in his left hand, and remembered the parole on the table. He was supposed to sign it, then his escape would be engineered by those people in the French army who did not want peace with Spain. It all seemed so complicated this morning. He only knew that by signing the paper and then escaping he was sacrificing all honour.

The door opened again and he lay still as the breakfast, supplied by courtesy of General Verigny, was put onto the table. He knew what it would be. Hot chocolate, bread, butter, and cheese. 'Mercy.' At least, he thought, he was learning some French.

An hour later, with the breakfast and half the champagne inside him, he decided he was feeling distinctly better. The day, he thought, even had promise. He looked at the parole. He could not sign it, he told himself, because it would be unworthy of him. He would have to escape instead. He would have to go to Wellington with this news, but not by sacrificing his honour. Captain d'Alembord had said that honour was merely a word to hide a man's sins, and La Marquesa had laughed at the word, but Sharpe knew what it meant. It meant he could never live with himself if he signed the paper and let Montbrun engineer his escape. Honour was conscience. He walked away from the table, from the temptation of the parole, and carried the champagne to the barred window.

He stared down, bottle in hand, at the piles of artillery shells that glistened faintly from the rain that had fallen in the night. An officer was checking the fuses. It would be a hell of a bang, Sharpe thought, and he wondered if he would get a view of it from the Great Road.

He could hear womens' voices. There were an extraordinary number of women with this army. What was it that Verigny had said yesterday? Sharpe frowned, then smiled. This army was a walking brothel.

He turned from the window and crossed to the table where the parole, splashed with red wine stains, still waited for his signature. He tried to make sense of the French words, but could not. Even so, he knew what it said. He promised not to escape, nor in any way assist the forces of Britain or her allies against the French armies until he was either exchanged or released from the bond.

He told himself he should sign it. Escape was impossible. He should sign it and refuse to accept La Marquesa's offer of escape. He thought of travelling in her coach, the curtains drawn, and he remembered her saying that she loved him. He looked at the quill. Was it dishonour to sign the parole and then carry news of the secret treaty to Wellington? Did his country come before honour? Had Helene spoken the truth? Would she want him when the war was over, when he was a discarded soldier? She had spoken of three thousand guineas. He shut his eyes, imagining three thousand guineas. A man could live a whole life on three thousand guineas.

He picked up the quill. He dipped it in the ink and then, with quick strokes, scored it again and again through the paragraphs of the parole. He tipped the ink bottle onto the paper, obliterating the words, destroying the parole. He laughed and walked back to the window.

Beneath him, from a doorway, a cavalry officer emerged into the dawn light. The man was gorgeously uniformed, his white breeches as skin-tight as General Verigny's. Sharpe wondered if such men greased their legs with oil or butter to achieve so tight a fit. He would not be surprised.

Cavalry officers would do anything to look like palace flunkies.

The man straightened his pelisse, tilted his hat to a more rakish angle, then blew smoke into the air. He took a cigar from his mouth, inspected the sky to judge the weather, then strolled towards the keep. The weak light was reflected from his gold scabbard furnishings and from the gold wire that was looped and braided on his blue jacket. He walked slowly, forced to the pace by the tightness of his breeches, but looking languorous and confident. He avoided the puddles that still remained in the courtyard, jealous of the brilliant shine on his spurred boots.

Smoke dribbled back from the man's cigar. He stepped over one of the fuses, then tapped ash onto a pile of shells. Sharpe watched, disbelieving. The cavalryman walked on, disdaining his surroundings. Another cloud of smoke drifted up from his cigar and then, with superb unconcern, the man tossed the cigar stub behind him onto the tangle of fuses. He disappeared into the keep.

No one seemed to have noticed. The Engineer officer who had been examining the fuses had gone. The sentries on the walls stared outwards. Two infantrymen who carried a great, steaming pot over the yard were busy with their own thoughts.

Sharpe looked back at the piles of shells. Was it his imagination, or was there a small wisp of smoke coming from where the cigar had landed?

It was just his imagination, he decided.

He noticed that, despite the wound, he was gripping the bars of the window with his right hand. He uncurled his fingers.

Some men walked beneath his window. They laughed loudly.

It was not his imagination. The cigar stub was burning through to the powder core of the fuses. Smoke drifted up more thickly.

Sharpe froze. If he gave the warning he would stay a prisoner. If he did not there would be death and chaos, quite possibly his own death. But if he risked that, then the chaos would be on his side. He could use it to escape, he could forget the parole, he would be free and his honour would be intact.

The smoke was thickening now, rising up to drift eastward. An artilleryman crossed the yard from a magazine against the far wall. He passed within ten feet of the smoke, but noticed nothing. He was eating a hunk of bread and staring up at the sky which threatened rain. There were men on the walls, on the keep's roof, yet none of them saw a thing.

Sharpe bit his lip. His left hand gripped the champagne.

The smoke turned to fire. One moment there was a grey haze, the next there was the hiss of fuses and the sparks were shooting up from the fire that snaked along the white line.

The gunner, the bread held to his mouth, stopped. He stared unbelieving at the fire-snakes. One disappeared into a pile of shells, would be eating at the first shell's fuse, and then the gunner shouted, pointed with his loaf, and started to run.

The shell exploded.

It lifted the other shells into the air, fuses spinning, and then a second exploded, a third, and suddenly the courtyard was a maelstrom of fire and shell casing, and men were bellowing at each other to run, and Sharpe went back from the window. There were fuses leading into the keep and he had just seen, through the smoke, a streak of bright fire dart into the massive stones.

He backed slowly away. There was no safety in leaving the room. The stairway led only to the courtyard where the shells exploded. He had to stay in the room and survive whatever happened.

He tipped the cot bed over, sheltering himself behind the straw mattress, and, just as he had done so, the hill of Burgos Castle moved.

Deep beneath the keep, in the cellars and in the mine shafts that had been dug to oppose the British mines of the

209

year before, the powder had been stacked. Barrel after barrel was down there, packed in the rock, and now the fire found it.

It blew.

It did not shatter outwards. There was more than enough powder to scythe the hilltop bare, to obliterate the walls, church, bastions, guns, and gates, but the rock-bound cellars acted as a giant mortar and hurled the blast upwards into the air until the flame spikes touched and pierced the low cloud, and still it went on, hurling stones and shells high into the air beyond the cloud and following with the rumbling, billowing, dark cloud that was fed by new blasts and pierced through by new flames as more stacks of powder were reached by the fire that destroyed the keep and thundered the sound miles out into the countryside.

Sharpe huddled against the wall.

The bed seemed to thump on him, the air was like a great, warm fist that pounded all about him and left only silence where there had been nothing but sound.

He was deafened.

He could feel shock after shock thudding the stone floor. He guessed that the shells were cracking open in the courtyard, and then there was a bigger blast, a thunder that pierced even his deafness, and he felt fragments spatter on the mattress that shielded him.

Silence again.

He was breathing dust. The thudding had stopped, but the room seemed to be shifting like the cabin of a ship under way.

He stood up, pushing the bed away, and saw the air was filled with white fog. It was not smoke, but powdered lime shaken from the walls and ceiling which now hung suspended in the room and stung his eyes.

He spat the dust out of his mouth.

The bottle of champagne was still in his hand. He swilled his mouth with it, spat again, then drank. The whole world seemed to be moving. The door was open, blown flat by the blast. The table had fallen and he saw, yet did not

210

understand, that the ink bottle was rolling back and forth on the floorboards like the weight of a pendulum.

He went to the window. The room seemed to lurch as a ship lurched when caught by a sudden wind.

He had seen Almeida after the explosion and this reminded him of the Portuguese fortress. There was the same stench of roasted flesh, the same fire and dust in the silence.

The keep was a boiling cauldron of flame and smoke. He could not imagine how so much smoke could be roiled out of stone. There was a ringing in his ears, insistent and annoying. He hit the side of his head with his hand.

A man screamed beneath him. His clothes were gone, his body was blackened, and blood showed on his back. The sound made Sharpe aware that he could hear.

Time to go, he thought, and the realisation was so odd that he did not move. A magazine exploded somewhere and spewed a lance of flame into the boiling smoke. The floor shifted again.

He heard a rumble to his right, felt the sudden shock of the floor tilting, a movement that made him drop the champagne and grip the window bar for support. A crack had appeared in the wall, a crack that widened as he watched. Jesus! The old houses built against the courtyard wall were slumping down!

Go, he thought, go! He frowned, turned, and slapped his waist to check his sword was in its slings. It was.

Walking to the door was like walking the deck of a ship. He feared that even his footsteps might tip the precarious balance of the fragile house, that at any moment he would be felled by the falling masonry and collapsing floors.

The building shuddered again. A man shouted outside, then another, and Sharpe stepped over the threshold to see the young, cheerful guard lying dead. A shell had come through the landing window and blown him apart.

Masonry rumbled. A crack sounded like a whiplash. He jumped recklessly down the rubble and dust-choked stairs. His uniform was thick with the white dust. Instinctively, as he reached the door to the courtyard, he began to beat it off, then stopped. It was as good a disguise as he could hope for.

Masonry fell somewhere, provoking shouts, and Sharpe knew that soon men would be in the castle who were not dazed, men who would begin the process of rescue and recovery. He hurried into the courtyard and turned left, towards the gate, and saw there a knot of men who stared aghast into the glimpse of hell that had been the keep.

He turned. He walked away from them, going towards the fire, but keeping the wall close to his right. He passed dead men, wounded men, men who cried, men who were past crying. The flesh smelt thick. He wished he had kept hold of the champagne to clear the taste of dust and smoke from his mouth.

Then a crash, a splintering, growing, hellish noise erupted to his right in the building where he had been prisoner, and he had a glimpse of the walls falling, of roof beams coming like lances through the breaking stones, and then it was blotted by dust and he was running, the stones falling, and he felt a massive blow on his leg that twisted him to his side, threw him down, and his mouth, nose, ears and eyes were thick with the dust and the noise and he was crawling blindly towards the light.

He felt his leg. It seemed whole. He drew it up, pushed, and staggered to his feet. Someone shouted, but Sharpe could barely help himself. He felt sick again, choking on dust, limping from the bruise on his leg.

He went on. He was going away from the gate where the enemy were gathered, going ever closer to the fire. He could feel the heat, a scorching, terrible, searing heat that made him swerve back to his right and there, in a tunnel of the wall, he saw daylight.

He went down the tunnel, cannoning off the walls, his scabbard scraping the stone. At the far end there was a shattered door, and beneath it steps that led down to a ruined church that clung high on the rock hill of the castle.

He sat on the steps. He had not quite gathered that he

was free, that he was outside the fortress, that the wide world was spread before him and that he was breathing warm, clean air. He wiped his eyes that were stinging with dust and stared at the view.

The city was spread beneath him along the banks of the River Arlanzon. The spires of the great cathedral dominated the houses, and Sharpe, blinking from the dust and smoke, saw that there were holes torn in the roof of the huge building, holes from which smoke came, and that there was more smoke in the town, buildings burning, and he guessed that the shells had been blasted up and outwards to fall randomly on the city. He knew he must move.

The castle hill fell two hundred steep feet to the houses. He stumbled down, falling twice, sliding one section in a scrabble of soil, loose stone, and pain. When he got up he saw that the bandage on his right hand was soaked through with fresh, bright blood. Blood was sticky on his face too, the wounds reopened. His leg felt as if it had been struck by a musket ball. He limped the last few yards to the shelter of an alleyway. A woman watched him from a window.

There were shouts and screams in the city. He could hear the fires burning. 'Jesus.' He spoke aloud. He was feeling dazed, his ears ringing. He could hardly remember leaving the castle. He leaned on the wall.

The woman spat through the window. She would think he was a Frenchman.

He walked down the alley that stank of the nightsoil that was indiscriminately thrown from the bedrooms. He knew he was free now, but he knew little else.

He came to the plaza before the magnificent cathedral. He saw civilians running with buckets through the great doors and he glimpsed, as he went forward, the glow of fires deep in the gloom inside. Then he looked right.

A division of French troops had been forming in the plaza before beginning their march north eastwards. They looked now as if they had been in a battle. Shells had fallen into their ranks and the dead and wounded were scattered on the cobbles. Some screamed, some wandered dazed, others tried to help. Above him the sky was dark with the smoke. Ashes fluttered in the air and fell soft as snow onto the shattered ranks.

He suddenly felt alarm. He had escaped the castle, only to walk like a fool into a city of the enemy. He went back into an alley, leaned on the wall, and tried to make plans, tried to force the ringing from his ears and sense into his head. A horse. For God's sake, a horse. What was it Hogan had once said to him? For some reason the strangeness of the words had stuck. 'A horse, a horse, my kingdom for a horse.' The Irish Major was always saying odd things like that. Sharpe supposed they were lines of poetry, but had not liked to ask.

He felt sick again. He bent down, his back against the wall, and groaned. He should hide, he decided. He was in no state to steal a horse.

There were footsteps to his right. He looked and saw men in the darkness of the alley. They wore no uniforms. They stared at him suspiciously.

He straightened up. '*Inglés*.' The word was choked by the dust in his throat.

The man closest to him carried a wooden mallet. He stepped forward, his face twisted with hatred. Sharpe knew they took him for a Frenchman and he shook his head. '*Inglés!*'

He could not draw his sword with his bloody, bandaged right hand. He tried, but the mallet struck him on the head, there was a rush of feet on the cobbles, hisses of anger and curses, and then dozens of boots and fists thumped into him, the mallet swung again, and he was dragged away, beaten half insensible, the blood flowing from his opened wounds.

They kicked him, dragged him deeper into the alley and into a small, foul courtyard. A man produced a long butcher's blade, Sharpe tried to ward it off, felt the edge sear into his left hand, then the mallet smashed onto his head again and he knew nothing more.

* * *

214

The French left Burgos that day, marching north east and leaving the city with its great spire of smoke that drifted up as a mark of their retreat.

It began to rain as they left, a steady rain that helped extinguish the fires in the city. It seemed the kind of rain that might last for ever.

The French would have liked to have held Burgos and to have forced Wellington to try once more to take the high fortress on its hill, but Wellington had marched his army to the north, into the hills which common wisdom said were impassable for an army. Wellington's army was passing the impassable hills, threatening to come south and cut off the French army in Burgos, cutting its supply lines, and so the French went backwards. Back towards the hills about Vitoria where other French armies would join them and they could turn and offer battle.

The British army saw the smoke rising from the city. They were far away. A few British cavalrymen, their horses smeared with mud. rode into the city and confirmed that the French were gone. They stayed long enough to water their horses and buy wine from an inn, then, the city abandoned by their enemy, its castle ruined, and nothing else in Burgos to hold their interest, they rode away. The war had come, taken its toll, and passed on.

CHAPTER 18

The British army left the pyre of smoke over Burgos far behind them. They marched in four great columns. At times two columns would come close, joining for a river crossing before they split again and took their separate paths in the hills. Always the order was speed. Speed to get ahead of the enemy, speed to cut the Road, speed to turn the French right flank, speed to meet the French before the enemy armies joined to outnumber Wellington's men.

And fighting against speed were the wagon wheels that broke, the horses that went lame, the sick who fell out on the road, the gun-axles that broke, the rain that made the tracks slippery, the flooding of a stream making a ford become a rapid. Yet still they went on, hauling at guns, at wagons, beating the mules on, the infantry driving their weary legs to climb one more hill, cross one more valley and ever into the teeth of wind and rain in the worst summer of memory. They had left their winter quarters with the promise of a fine, though late, summer, but now that they had reached the northern hills the weather had broken into a miserable, cold enemy.

Yet old soldiers had never seen an army march as well. The men marched as though the winds brought the smell of victory and they pushed through difficulties that, in normal times, would have turned men back or caused hours of delay. If a ford was high the cavalry drove their horses in to make a breakwater and passed the infantry down the sheltered side, urging them on, telling them the frogs were waiting for the slaughter, telling them there was one more march and then the victory.

They had been scenting that victory for days. Many had

expected to fight at Burgos, but the plume of smoke which marked the French retreat had driven the army on another stage. It was rumoured the French would guard the crossings of the Ebro, the last great river line before the Pyrenees, but the French were nowhere to be seen when, on a cold, chill day, the columns crossed the river unopposed and heard, at last, the orders given for the swing south and east, the swoop down to the enemy.

The columns closed up. A Spanish column stayed to the north, fending off any approach by the French troops on the Biscay shore, but the other columns merged about a single road so they could concentrate swiftly for battle. The infantry, as ever, had the worst of it. The road had to be left for the baggage, the guns, the cavalry, and so the infantry marched on the hills either side, the slopes thick with men and mules, the air noisy with their marching songs.

That they had the energy to sing was astonishing, that they sang so well was more so, that they wanted a fight was obvious. Rumours had gone through the army that the enemy guarded a convoy of gold, that each man would be rich if he did his duty, and perhaps that rumour, more than pride, drove them on. They joked that the froggies were on the run now, that Johnny-Frenchman would not stand till he was past Paris, that this army would march on and on and on till every man jack in it had a Parisian girl on his elbow and a bag of gold in his hand, and the General, who would sometimes just sit on his horse and watch them pass, would feel his soul full of pride and love for these ranks that he led, that marched in such spirits to a battle that would leave some of them broken like bloody rag dolls on a Spanish field.

Three nights after the Burgos explosion, Major Michael Hogan sat in the uncomfortable stable that was his billet. He was lucky, he knew, to have even this place to sleep. A lantern hung over his head, its light showing the map that was spread on a makeshift table made from an overturned byre.

A man sat opposite him. The man was a Jew named

Rodrigues. He was a corn dealer who travelled with the army, unpopular with the quartermasters who dealt with him, suspected by them, because of his rapacity, to be sympathetic with the French. Why not, they said? Everyone knew the Spanish church hated the Jews. Surely, they reasoned, Rodrigues would have a better life if the French ruled in Spain?

Hogan knew better. Rodrigues drove a harsh bargain, but so did every other corn factor who travelled with the army, Jewish or not. Yet this corn merchant, this despised man, had a genius of a memory and ears that seemed to hear the quietest whispers from far away. He talked now of one such whisper, and Hogan listened.

'A man broke into a convent.' Rodrigues smiled slyly. 'That must have surprised the sisters.'

'What kind of a man?'

'Some say English, some say American! Others say French. He was rescued from the Partisans by the French.'

'And you say?'

Rodrigues smiled. He was a thin man who wore his hair, summer and winter, beneath a fur hat. 'I say he was your man. He took the woman.' He held up a hand to stop Hogan interrupting. 'But the news is not good, Major.'

'Go on.'

'He went to Burgos with the woman, but he was killed there.'

'Killed?'

Rodrigues saw the look on Hogan's face and suspected, rightly, that the un-named Englishman had been a friend of the Major's. 'There are a dozen stories; I tell you what I think.' The corn merchant fidgeted with the coiled whip he always carried. It was not much of a weapon, but enough to deter the children who tried to steal from his carts. 'They say he was in the castle and that he killed a man. Then they say that he was treated with respect.' Rodrigues shrugged. 'I don't know. What I do know is that he was still in the castle when it blew up. He died with the others.'

'They found his body?'

'Who can tell? It was difficult to tell what was a body in that place.'

Hogan said nothing for a while. He was wondering if it was true, but he had learned to trust Rodrigues and so he feared that it must be so. He had heard that the explosion in the castle had been an accident that had taken the lives of scores of Frenchmen, but was it possible, he found himself wondering, that Sharpe had engineered it? He could believe that. 'And the woman?'

'*La Puta Dorada*?' Rodrigues smiled. 'She went with the French army. Escorted by lancers.'

Hogan thought of Wellington's fear that Sharpe would break into the convent. It appeared he had done just that. 'What do people say about the convent?'

The Jew laughed. 'They say it must be the French. After all the man rescued a Frenchwoman and went off with French cavalry.'

So it was over, Hogan thought, all over. Sharpe had failed. But it had been a better death than hanging, he reflected.

'So what happens now, Major?'

'Now? We march. Either the French try to stop us or they don't.'

'They will.'

Hogan nodded. 'In which case there'll be a battle.'

'Which you'll win.' Rodrigues smiled. 'And if you do, Major, what then?'

'We'll pursue them to the frontier.'

'And then?'

Hogan smiled. Rodrigues never asked for payment for information, at least not payment in gold. The Irishman tapped his map. 'A new supply port. There.'

Rodrigues smiled. The information was worth a small fortune. He would have men at that port, and warehouses ready, before his competitors even knew that the British supplies no longer were being dragged up the long roads from Lisbon. 'Thank you, Major.' He stood.

Hogan saw Rodrigues to the door, safely past the sentries, and he leaned on the doorpost and watched the rain seethe in the light of the campfires. Sharpe dead? He had thought that before and been wrong. He stared into the eastern darkness, thinking of ghosts, knowing Sharpe to be dead, yet not believing it.

And in the morning, when the rain still fell and the wind felt more like winter in Ireland than summer in Spain, the army marched on. They marched willingly, going towards the battle that would end the march, marching towards the city of golden spires; Vitoria.

'You eat!'

Sharpe nodded. The girl spooned soup into his mouth; a thick, warm, tasty soup. 'What is it?'

'Horse. Now sit up! The doctor's coming.'

'I'm all right.'

'You're not. You're lucky to be alive. Eat!'

His uniform hung against the wall, the uniform that had saved his life. Dozens of lone Frenchmen had been beaten to death in Burgos after the explosion, but Sharpe, just as the knife was about to cut his uniform away, had been recognised as an English officer. The men had not been certain. They had argued, some saying that the man's overalls and boots were French, but other men were sure that the dark green jacket was British. The buttons, with their black crowns, decided the day. No Frenchman had crowns on his buttons, and so they had let Sharpe live.

The girl laughed at him. 'Eat.'

'I'm trying!' Both hands were bandaged. He was bruised all over. His head was bandaged. 'What day is it?'

'Tuesday.'

'What date?'

'How do I know? Eat.'

This, he knew, was the house of the carpenter who had hit him so effectively with the mallet. The man was eager to make amends, had given Sharpe this room, had even sharpened the sword on a stone and propped it beside Sharpe's bed. The girl was a housemaid, black-haired and plump, with a bright smile and a teasing manner. One of her eyes was blind, a white blankness where there should have been a pupil. 'Eat!'

The doctor came, a gloomy man in a long, stained black coat. He bled Sharpe's thigh. He had raised his eyebrows on his first visit, scarcely believing the scars on Sharpe's body. Beyond the doctor, through the window, Sharpe could see the smoke still hazing the grey clouds above the castle. Rain was soft on the window. It seemed to have been raining ever since he had woken in this room. The doctor wiped the small cut and pulled the sheet down. 'Another two days, Major Vaughn.'

'I want to go now.'

The man shook his head. 'You're weak, Major. You lost much blood. The bruises.' He shrugged. 'Two days of Pedro's food and you'll be better.'

'I need a horse.'

'The French took them all.' The doctor threw the cupful of blood into the fireplace and wiped the bowl on the skirts of his coat. 'There may be a mule for sale tomorrow at the market.'

'There must be a horse! They're feeding me horsemeat soup!'

'That horse died in the explosion.' The doctor spat on his lancet and wiped it on his cuff. 'I will come tomorrow if God wills it.' He turned to go, but Sharpe called him back.

'*Señor?*'

Sharpe grimaced as he tried to sit up on the bolster. 'Did you ask about the Inquisitor, Doctor?'

'I did, *señor*.'

'So?'

The doctor shrugged. 'His house is at Vitoria. There was a time when the family had land throughout Spain, but now?' He shrugged and hefted his small bag. 'Vitoria. That is all our priest knew. You will forgive me, Major?'

When he was alone Sharpe sat on the edge of the bed. He felt dizzy. He wondered how hard the blow on his head

221

had been. It throbbed still and the lump was like a hen's egg. He swore quietly. The rain fell.

He pulled on the linen shirt that he had worn ever since Helene had given it to him at Salamanca. There was fresh blood on the collar.

He put on the French overalls that he had taken from her brother. The rip in the bib had been made by Sharpe's sword. The tear had been mended, but he could still see how he had twisted the great blade when Leroux fell.

His head hurt as he leaned down and tugged on the big French cavalry boots. He felt better with the boots on. He stood and stamped his feet into comfort. His legs were stiff. There was a vast black bruise on his left thigh.

The jacket felt good. He buttoned it from the crotch to his chin, forcing his bandaged hands to do the fiddly work. The fingers of his left hand were not wrapped and with them he picked up the sword. It jangled as he buckled the snake clasp. He had no shako. He had nothing now but the clothes he wore and the sword that hung at his side. He had no cloak, no razor, no tinder box, no telescope. He had a secret that could win the war for France that he must take to Wellington.

'What are you doing?' Consuela, the maid, stood in the doorway.

'I'm going.'

'You can't! You're weak as a kitten! Go on! To bed.'

He shook his head stubbornly. 'I'm going.'

They tried to stop him, a gaggle of women at the foot of the stairs shouting at him and fluttering like the nuns in the convent. He thanked them, pushed gently past them, and went into the yard of the house. The yard was filled with wood shavings. The rain was cold on his face.

'You mustn't go!'

'I have to go.'

He had no horse so he would walk. It was hard at first, his bruised muscles refusing to make the stride easy. He crossed the great plaza, still smeared with the marks of the exploding French shells, past the cathedral that had been saved from the flames, and the townspeople watched him silently. He looked an odd figure, a soldier with a slashed head, black eyes, walking stiffly like a man going to his death. He had not been shaved this day and he thought for a moment of stopping at one of the barbers who waited for trade by their chairs in the street, then remembered he had no money.

He crossed the Arlanzon, seeing the water pitted by the rain, and already the water was cold where it had soaked through his uniform.

'*Señor! Señor!*'

He turned. Consuela, the half-blind maid, was running after him. He stopped.

She pushed a package wrapped in oil-paper into his hands. 'If you must go, Major, take this.'

'What is it?'

'Cold chicken. Cheese.' She smiled. 'Go with God.'

He kissed her on the cheek. 'Thank you, Consuela.' He walked eastwards on the Great Road, following the French army that had long gone, walking to a war.

He stopped that afternoon in an orchard. He ate half of the chicken, and wrapped the rest of the food in the paper. Then, every muscle aching, he went to the stream that ran through the thick orchard grass. He knelt at its edge.

He used the fingers of his left hand to undo the bandage on his right. It came stickily away, the last tug hurting like fire and ripping the crust from the wound. He hissed with the sudden pain and thrust his hand into the water.

He flexed his fingers. He watched the blood dilute and go, wispy red, downstream. He spread his fingers wide, let the water flow into the cut, then took off the bandage that covered the wound made by the knife. The cut was on the ball of his left hand. It too bled into the water. He left his hands in the stream till they were numb.

He unwrapped the bandage from his head and dipped his skull into the water, holding his breath to let the stream flow about his hair. He drank. He took his head out, flicked the wet hair back with a jerk, and saw the horsemen.

He stayed still. He was on all fours. The horsemen were on the Great Road. hunched beneath their cloaks against the rain. They were Partisans and they rode to battle. Sharpe could see corks stuck in their musket muzzles, see the rags wrapped about the locks, see the sabres protruding from the wet cloaks.

He could have called out, he could have shouted for help and asked for a horse, but he did not. The men were fifty yards away, visible through the twisting trunks of the stunted apple trees, and Sharpe had seen their leader. He had seen the black beard that grew up to the high cheekbones, the small eyes, the broad blade of the poleaxe on the man's shoulder. It was *El Matarife*. Sharpe stayed rock still as they passed, then settled back on his haunches.

El Matarife was following the French, hoping to be present when the armies met, and *El Matarife* was now between Sharpe and his goal.

He stayed by the stream and the rain fell on him as he thought what to do. He could only press on, he decided, and when he had waited long enough for the Partisans to be well out of sight, he stood, groaned with pain, and went back to the muddy road.

He walked. He seemed alone on the road. The fields either side still showed the damage caused by the trampling French army. Sharpe walked on the crushed crops because they gave firmer footing than the slick, muddy road.

He went through small villages, always checking first that no horsemen lingered at a wine house. By dusk he was in a wide land, no houses or horsemen in sight, with the road stretching damp before him towards the darkening east. The rain blocked his view of the hills that he knew should be on the horizon.

He was looking for shelter, hoping for a farm or, at the least, a bush to keep the worst of the rain from him. There was nothing. He walked on, trying to force his pace to the fast Rifleman's march, persuading himself that by ignoring the pain it would go away. His feet squelched in his boots and rain trickled into his eyes.

He heard a horse and turned to see a single horseman a hundred yards behind him. He cursed himself for not looking before, though there would have been nowhere to hide in this bare land even with ten minutes more warning. It was possible, he knew, that the man was simply a farmer on his way home, but the horse was bigger and stronger than a farmer's mount. Sharpe suspected it was one of *El Matarife's* men, left behind for some reason on the road.

Sharpe gripped his sword-handle. His right hand was still stiff because of the gouging of the brass telescope tube. He saw the horseman spur into a trot, then the man waved, and suddenly Sharpe was laughing and stumbling back down the road. 'Angel! Angel!'

The boy was laughing. He jumped from Carbine's back and put his arms round Sharpe. 'Major!' He was slapping Sharpe's back. 'You're here!'

'Where did you come from?'

'Your face!' Angel took off his cloak and insisted on putting it round Sharpe's shoulders.

'How the hell did you find me?' Sharpe took the proffered flask of wine and tipped it to his lips. It felt good.

Angel had done no more than follow orders. Major Hogan had told him not to leave Sharpe and so, when the lancers took Sharpe south, Angel had followed. He had hidden himself outside Burgos, watching the Great Road to see if Sharpe was taken eastwards.

The boy had seen the explosion. Afterwards, when the last of the French had left the city and he had seen no prisoners with them, he had tried to get news of Sharpe. 'They said you were dead.'

'Who did?'

'The people who worked for the French. There was one English prisoner in the castle, but the building he was in collapsed.'

Sharpe grinned. 'I got out first.'

'So I looked in the ruins.' Angel shrugged. 'Nothing. Then *El Matarife* came so I hid again.'

'What did he want?'

'There was a rumour that the French left their wounded in a hospital. It wasn't true.' Angel nodded up the road. 'He went on.'

'I saw him.'

The boy grinned. 'So now what?'

'We find Wellington.' Sharpe looked at Carbine and suddenly knew that everything would be all right. He laughed aloud, his tiredness forgotten. 'We're going to win the bloody war, Angel. You and I, just you and I!' He patted the patient, strong horse. Carbine would take him to Wellington, he would vindicate himself and, he laughed at the thought, do everything that Helene wanted him to do, but with his honour intact. 'We're going to win the god-damned war!'

The army tried to sleep. Some men succeeded, others listened to the rain on canvas, to the owls calling in the valleys and, from the hills, the howling of wolves that made the horses nervous. Children cried and were soothed by their mothers.

An hour after midnight the rain stopped and, slow and ragged, the sky cleared. Stars showed for the first time in weeks. The wind was still cold, shivering the picquets who stared into the shadows and thought of the morning.

The bugles called the army awake when the stars were still bright. The breakfast was cold. The tents were collapsed and folded. Men muttered and shivered and thanked God it was not raining. Sufficient unto this day was the evil that awaited them.

Captain d'Alembord, stumbling through the mud and long grass with a mug of tea in his hand, shouted into the darkness for his Company. Sergeant Harper's voice answered.

The Captain stood shivering by the small fire. 'Thank God it's not raining.'

'Aye.' Harper looked pleased.

'The Colonel says it's true.'

'Might as well get it over with.' The huge Sergeant was rolling up his blanket. The South Essex had marched without tents.

Captain d'Alembord, who had never fought in a real battle, was nervous. 'They reckon they're waiting over the hills.'

'But not far away, eh?' Harper laughed. 'So there'll be a fight, yes?'

'So they say.'

'With all the trimmings, sir. It'll be a grand day for it, if it doesn't rain.'

'I'm sure we'll acquit ourselves nobly, Sergeant.'

'We always do, sir.' Harper was strapping the blanket to his pack. 'Farrell!' The roar of Harper's voice made d'Alembord jump.

'Sarge?' A plaintive voice sounded from the darkness.

'Get up, you protestant bastard! We've got a battle to fight!'

Some men laughed, some men groaned. Harper grinned reassuringly at Captain d'Alembord. 'The lads will be all right, sir, don't you fret.' Captain d'Alembord, quite understandably, was fretting whether he would be all right. He smiled.

'Finish the tea, Sergeant?'

'You're a grand man, sir, so you are. I thank you.' Harper tilted the mug and swallowed what was left in great gulps. 'Would you be a betting man, sir?'

'I am.'

'I have a feeling we'll be seeing an old friend today.' The Sergeant said it comfortably, his voice utterly confident.

Captain d'Alembord, who had come to trust Sergeant Harper, sighed. He knew that the Irishman had never accepted Sharpe's death and the Captain feared what would happen when it dawned on Harper that the Major was truly dead. There were stories that, before he met Sharpe, Harper had been the wildest man in the army and

227

d'Alembord feared he would become so again. The officer chose his words carefully. This was the first time that Harper had spoken of Sharpe to him since the hanging, and d'Alembord did not want to be too savage in breaking the Irishman's hopes.

'What if you don't see him, Sergeant?'

'I've been thinking about it, so I have, sir.' Harper thumped his shako into shape with a fist. Isabella was rolling her own blanket beside him. Harper smiled. 'There's no way Nosey would hang him, not after Sharpe saved his life, sir. And there's no way the frogs can kill him, so he has to be alive. He'll be back, sir, and if we're in a fight, that's where he'll be. A pound says I'm right.'

'D'Alembord grinned. 'You haven't got a pound.'

'I will tonight, though. Farrell! You heathen bastard! Get up!' Harper looked back to his officer. 'A pound?'

'You need your money, Harps. You're getting married.'

'Christ! Don't talk about it.' Harper sounded gloomy. 'I'll still lay the pound, sir.'

'I accept.'

In the valley a trumpet sounded. In the darkness thousands of men prepared themselves. Behind them was a epic march through the hills, and beyond the next hill was Vitoria.

They marched before dawn, the columns splitting again, but all going eastwards, going towards the enemy. The columns twisted through the misted valleys, going towards Vitoria, going towards the treasure of an empire, and going to battle.

CHAPTER 19

The rain, at last, had stopped, and the dawn of Monday, June 21st, 1813, brought a dazzling, blinding sun that lanced over the Pamplona valley, over the spires of Vitoria, and into the eyes of the few British horsemen who had climbed the hills to the west of the city.

They could see nothing of the French beneath them. The wide valley in which Vitoria stood was shrouded in mist, a mist that was thickened by the smoke of myriad camp-fires. The watching horsemen appeared to be alone in a wild, dazzling landscape.

The sky was brilliantly clear. The valleys were hidden by mist, and the east was filled with the searing glory of the rising sun, yet to north and south the British horsemen could see the successive ridges of the hills etched in startling clarity against a pale sky. After the days of rain and low cloud it seemed almost indecent to be fighting on such a day as this. Yet fight they must, for, by the will of Marshal Jourdan and General Wellington, one hundred and forty thousand men had come to this misted plain from which, like a strange island in a white sea, the spires of Vitoria's cathedral jutted golden in the sun.

From the west, in the valleys that were mysterious with shredding mist and shadow, the British army marched. They were cold from the night and few men spoke or sang as they marched, waiting for the sun and the smell of powder to warm their spirits. In every Company the sibilant hiss of stone on steel could be heard. The sharpening stones were handed round and the men honed their bayonets as they marched and prayed they would not need to use them.

They had marched across the roof of Spain, coming from Portugal to this place where, like a knife put to a throat, they threatened the Great Road that was France's lifeline in Spain. The men knew, because their officers had told them, that a battle was imminent. Some, who had stood in the battle-line before, tried not to think of what was to come while others, who had never before seen an enemy army, wondered if they would live to remember the sight. Some, remembering the long hard marches in the high inhospitable hills, feared defeat, for, if this army was broken today and forced to retreat, they would face days of being hunted in the high valleys by the long-bladed French horsemen.

Wellington, this day, commanded Spanish, Portuguese and British troops. With him, too, was the King's German Legion. They marched towards the valley of Vitoria, and with them went their women and children who would wait at the field's edge while their men fought. With the army, too, were sutlers and merchants, salesmen of patent medicines, friars and priests. There were whores, beggars, horse-thieves, and politicians, and, like a lumbering, ponderous beast, the whole great mass curled and heaved itself towards the valley, towards Vitoria and towards a fight.

The French were confident this day. Their enemies had an edge in numbers, it was true, but numbers were not all in warfare. The French had picked their battlefield, chosen where to stand, and they defended their chosen place with the greatest concentration of artillery that had ever been assembled in Spain.

To the north of their position was the River Zadorra, and to the south the Heights of Puebla, and the constriction of river and highland would force the British to a frontal attack in the valley that would bring them into the face of the great guns that, in this morning of drifting mist, looked like fearsome monsters in wait for their victims.

The guns that gave the French such confidence were placed on a low north-south ridge called the Arinez Hill. The French high command, knowing that soldiers, above

230

all humankind, are superstitious, had spread the story of the Arinez Hill, and the story, on this dawn of waiting, added to the French confidence. The hill was a place of ill-luck for the English.

Centuries before this dawn, on a day of searing heat, three hundred English knights, marauding for plunder, had been surrounded by a Spanish army on the Arinez Hill. The English had dared not take off their armour, for then they would have been meat for the Spanish crossbows, and so they fought, the day long, roasting like pigs, their tongues swelling with thirst, their eyes blinded with sweat, and time after time the Spanish came up the hill to be thrust down with the long, heavy swords or beaten back with the maces and clubs. The stolid clay of the hill was slick with blood and loud with the screams of horses and men.

The English refused to surrender. They fought till the last man was choking in his own blood, and the last banner was trampled in the gore. For the English, then, this hill was a place of ill-luck, and the French knew it.

There was even more cause for the French to hope, for the war's tide was at last turning in France's favour again.

The Empire had reeled from the defeat in Russia, had waited in trepidation for news that the Russians and the Prussians were marching into northern France, but just two days since had come the glorious news. The Emperor had won his campaign.

The bells had been rung in Vitoria, bells that carried the message to all the troops bivouacking on the plain. The news followed the clamour, news of two battles, at Bautzen and Lutzen, battles that had repelled both the northern enemies who had now signed a truce. Soon, the news promised, Bonaparte would come south. Only the British were left in the field and Bonaparte would come down and drive them in ragged defeat from Spain and the tricolour would rule again from the straits of Gibraltar to the edge of the steppes.

The waiting French were confident. The river here was rich in bridges, some going back to the Romans who had built their own city on this plain, yet none of the bridges had been destroyed. Let the British cross them, the French reasoned, and that way the gunners would know where to fire and the redcoats would walk into the killing ground, and the blasting, tearing canister would make each bridge into a blood-soaked arch of masonry to drip red into the Zadorra.

Yet, if the French Engineers had not blown the bridges, they had not been idle. They had worked for two days on a strange contraption on Vitoria's western wall. It was built high on the ramparts so it looked over the suburbs and orchards towards the great plain where the army waited for battle. The Engineers had built tiers of seats so that the women who followed the French army could watch this French victory in comfort. To those seats the women came and there, too, came the sellers of lemonade, pastries and fruit.

The French were confident enough to order Vitoria's largest, best hotel to prepare a victory feast for this evening. Even now, as the mist lifted and the British came towards the guns, the cooks were at work.

The French were confident enough to send troops away from the battlefield. Just that morning a whole division marched north on the Great Road, back towards France, and with the Division went a convoy of heavy wagons loaded with the treasures of the Escorial, Spain's royal palace. What was left in Vitoria was worth far more, but the French needed to make a start and they were sure that they could beat off Wellington's attack and escort the rest of the plunder safely to the border.

And, as if to make up for the paintings, tapestries and furniture that had gone north, a smaller convoy had come south bringing five million golden francs to give the army its arrears of pay. The wagons of coin were put into the baggage park. The coins would be paid after the battle.

A hundred and forty thousand men had come to one place for the purpose of battle. The sun burned the valley's mist away and those British horsemen who had climbed the

232

western hills saw, beneath them, the might of France drawn up in its battle-lines. They saw the guns. They saw the ranks of men waiting beneath their splendid banners and glinting eagles. As yet no cannon or musket smoke drifted to hide the glory that was an army in array. The river, beneath its bridges, sparked silver in the dawn. The fields, where they had not been trampled by the soldiers, were bright with poppies and cornflowers. A kingdom was at stake, and a battle to be fought.

The French headquarters, strangely empty now that the Generals were on the plain, were high on the hill that rose to Vitoria's cathedral. On the topmost floor of the head-quarters building, in a large, plain room that looked west towards the battlefield, a lone man worked at papers spread on a huge table.

Pierre Ducos had worked all night, yet the sleeplessness had not lessened his efficiency. He sorted papers, some going into a great leather travelling chest, others into a sack for burning. Though he had told no one, Pierre Ducos planned for defeat.

He had considered going north with the convoy that had left before dawn, but there were rumours that the British had sent part of their army to cut the road and there would be more safety, Ducos decided, in staying with the army. Better, he thought, to face defeat with the main army than with the single division that had gone towards San Sebastian.

He was not certain why he was sure of defeat. It was, perhaps, that he admired Wellington. The English General had a mind of fine calculation that appealed to Ducos, who did not believe that the vainglorious Marshals of France had the measure of the Englishman. The Emperor, now, he was different. He would outcalculate and outfight any man, but the Emperor was not yet in Spain, nor was it certain that he would come.

The Emperor had won a great victory in the north, and his enemies had signed a truce, yet if Wellington won today

233

then the victory could encourage the other enemies of France to fight again. And if, and Ducos loved the ifs of the future that he explored so ruthlessly, the northern war recommenced, then the treaty would be needed.

He had the treaty now. Last night a messenger from the Inquisitor had delivered letters to Ducos, letters that he now kept in a haversack attached to his belt. They were letters from eminent men of Spain, from soldiers and churchmen, politicians and aristocrats, lawyers and merchants, and the letters all spoke of the desirability of peace with France. For the good of trade, for the good of the Church, for the good of Spain's empire, and above all, for the glory of Spain, the letters encouraged Ferdinand VII to accept a peace treaty. The Inquisitor, Ducos granted, had performed a wonderful piece of work. And now, Ducos knew, the Inquisitor was coming to ask a favour.

He heard the footsteps on his stairs, waited for the knock on his door, shouted in answer, and leaned back in his chair.

The skirts of the Inquisitor's cassock bore two white smears of dust where he had knelt in his morning prayer. His dark face was heavy as though he, too, had spent a sleepless night. He glanced out of the window to where the army waited for battle, then sat opposite Ducos. 'You received the letters?'

'I received the letters.'

The Inquisitor waited, as though seeking approval for his work. When it did not come he gestured abruptly. 'Your soldiers are confident.'

'I imagine the British are too,' Ducos said drily. In truth he had been astonished by the surge of morale in the French army. The news of the Emperor's victories had filled them with a desire to do in Spain what Napoleon had done in the north.

'Victory for you today,' the Inquisitor said, 'would make the treaty unnecessary.'

'For the moment,' Ducos said, 'but I would not be so certain of our victory, father.' He stood and walked towards the window. On a table beside it, in a small bowl, he kept breadcrumbs that he now put on the ledge for the birds. 'It has been my misfortune to spend much of my life with soldiers. They are boastful creatures, noisy, crude, and unthinking. They believe in victory, father, because they cannot bear the thought of defeat.' He turned from the window and stared at the priest. 'I do not think your work will prove to be wasted.'

'But unrewarded.'

'Your reward,' Ducos said as he walked back to his table, 'is Spain's glory and the survival of the Inquisition. I congratulate you. You also, I believe, have the Marquesa's wagons safely locked in your courtyard.' He said the last words with heavy mockery.

'The money,' Father Hacha spoke uncomfortably, 'is not legally ours.'

'True. But it is not my fault if you cannot keep a woman locked in a nunnery.'

The Inquisitor said nothing for a few seconds. From the window ledge came the small scratching sounds of beaks and claws. From much further away, made tiny by the distance, came the thin call of a trumpet. The Inquisitor brushed at the dust on his cassock. 'If there is to be peace between our two countries, then there will also have to be diplomatic relations.'

'True.'

'I have hopes that, in those relations, I might be of further use to you.'

Ducos said nothing. He had expected the Inquisitor to offer him a threat that, unless the Marquesa was arrested, he would betray the proposed treaty's existence to the enemy. Indeed, Ducos had been prepared for that threat, and would have met it with the death of this priest. Instead, though, the Inquisitor was offering a bargain of a different kind. 'Go on,' Ducos said.

'There will be a new beginning in Spain.' The Inquisitor seemed to be gaining in confidence as he spoke. 'There will be a need for new men, new advisers, new leadership. With wealth behind me, Major, I can rise to that challenge. But not if the wealth is tainted. Not if a woman is challenging me in the courts, or spreading rumours in the chanceries of Europe. If you let me rise as I intend to rise, Major, then in the years to come you will find France has a friend in the Spanish court.'

Ducos liked the suggestion. He liked such an excursion into the far future, the promise that, in a new Europe, the Inquisitor would be his informant and ally. He shrugged. 'I cannot have her arrested.'

'I don't ask you to.' From far away came a sound like thorns burning. The Inquisitor looked out of the window, but Ducos dismissed the musketry.

'They're clearing their barrels, nothing more.' He stroked his finger down a quill. 'You want to kill her?'

'No!'

The sharpness of the reply made Ducos look up. 'No?'

'She will have made her own will. If she dies then her inheritors become my enemy. No.' The Inquisitor frowned. 'She must go to a convent. She must learn the humility of religion.'

Ducos smiled thinly. 'You failed once.'

'Not again.'

'Perhaps not.' Ducos sounded dubious, but he reflected that Richard Sharpe was dead, and could not repeat his impudent rescue of the woman. Sharpe's death had pleased Ducos. He had been given nightmares by his memory of the fight in Burgos Castle, of the battered, beaten, bleeding Rifleman suddenly roaring his challenge and turning the room into a shambles. Yet Sharpe had died in the explosion and that fact gave Ducos some small happiness. Ducos looked at the priest. 'Yet it is not the duty of the Emperor's forces to put women into convents.'

'I don't ask that.'

'Then what do you ask?'

'Just this.' The Inquisitor leaned forward and put on the table a piece of paper. 'That you sign a pass allowing those men into the city today.'

The paper was a list of names. It was headed by the name of the Slaughterman, *El Matarife*, and Ducos knew that the others would be members of his band. There were thirty names. 'What do you expect of them?'

The Inquisitor shrugged. 'Both victory and defeat will bring chaos to the city. Within chaos there is opportunity.

'A slight hope, I would have thought?'

'God is with us.'

'Ah,' Ducos smiled. 'It was a pity he was not with your brother in the mountains.' He took a clean piece of paper, uncapped his ink, and wrote swiftly. 'Will you want these men to carry weapons in God's service?'

'Yes.'

Ducos wrote that the bearers of this paper were servants of the diocese of Vitoria and were to be allowed, with their weapons, into the city. When it was written he stamped it with the seal of King Joseph, then pushed it across the table. 'I have your word that these men will not bear arms against our forces?'

'You have my word, unless your forces defend her.'

'And you will ask nothing more of me in this matter?'

'Nothing more.'

'Then I wish you well, father.'

Ducos watched the man go, and when he was alone again he walked to the window, stepping gently so as not to frighten the sparrows on the window ledge, and he could see, far on the plain, the waiting French army.

He frowned. It was not right, he thought, that the fate of nations and the affairs of a great empire should be left to the boastful, childish bravery of soldiers. Victory this day would mean the treaty might not be needed, and all this fine work wasted. Yet Ducos did not believe in a French victory today. He almost, and he acknowledged it only to himself, wished for a French defeat, for then, in the chaos of a shattered kingdom, he would produce the treaty as a diplomatic triumph and save France. He would show the soldiers, the foolish, vain, brave soldiers, that their power was as nothing to the subtle mind of a clever, calculating man.

He turned from the window. He had no more duties to do, nothing now to engage him except to wait for the lottery of the day. So, on this day of sunshine and battle, Ducos slept.

The Marquess of Wellington, Generalissimo of the Allied army in Spain, looked at his watch. It showed twelve minutes past eight. 'We shall dine at the usual hour this night, gentlemen.'

His aides smiled, not sure if he was joking. They had come with him to the lower slopes of the western hills and could see, two miles to the east, the dark line of the French guns.

The General looked to his right where the Great Road came from a defile and he watched, on the river's far bank, a column of infantry begin climbing the slopes of the Puebla Heights. The column was led by Spanish troops, who would, this day, have the honour of first engaging the enemy. He snapped the watch shut. 'Gentlemen.' His tone was distant, almost sour. 'I wish you all joy of the day.'

The battle of Vitoria had begun.

CHAPTER 20

The guns, the great French guns, the guns that were the Emperor's love and the weapons most feared by France's enemies, fired.

The sound died and the smoke drifted.

The French had shot at no target. They had merely warmed the barrels and watched the fall of the roundshot in the killing ground. As yet the battle had no pattern. Some Spanish troops clawed their way up the Puebla Heights and fought the French skirmishers on the steep slope, but no infantry and cavalry had appeared on the plain to become meat for the gunners who now had the range perfectly judged. The smoke from the cannons drifted southwards, dissipating in the small breeze. The ladies who sat on the tiers of seats built by the French Engineers on Vitoria's wall felt faintly disappointed that the sound had stopped.

La Marquesa climbed to the topmost tier. She smiled at the wife of a cavalry Colonel, knowing that the woman eagerly spread gossip about her. 'Your husband's piles are better, dear Jeanette? Or is he riding to battle in a cart again?' She did not wait for an answer, but climbed on upwards then waited as her maid spread cushions on the bench. She felt in her reticule for some coins and nodded towards one of the pastry sellers. 'I want some of the lemon pastries.'

'My Lady.'

She sat. She carried a small ivory spyglass. There was little to be seen on the plain. The killing ground was hidden from her beyond the Arinez Hill. On a lower ridge that was closer to the city she could see troops drawn up in close order. Over their heads floated the great purple and white banner that told her they were King Joseph's household guards.

She wondered where General Verigny was. He had left her eagerly, exhilarated at the thought of battle. With victory this day, he assured her, Pierre Ducos would be defeated. Joseph would keep the Spanish throne and La Marquesa's wagons could be taken from the Inquisitor. Helene had smiled at her lover. 'And what if we lose today?'

'Lose? We can't lose!'

Just days before, she reflected, the French army had expected nothing but retreat and the abandonment of Spain. Suddenly, with a volatility brought by news of Napoleon's victories, the army was replete with confidence. Today, they were sure, they would revenge themselves on Wellington.

It was all so unexpected. At Burgos she had tried to persuade Richard Sharpe to betray his honour in order to defeat Ducos' scheming. She wondered whether Sharpe would have signed the parole, then dismissed the thought because he was dead and the question was irrelevant. Instead King Joseph was fighting for his throne and victory today would mean an end of bribing Spaniards for favours. France would crush Spain again. The world would watch an Empire rear back to greatness.

A Captain, in the green and pink uniform of General Verigny's regiment, appeared at the bottom of the steps. He had one arm in a sling, and one eye bandaged. He limped. He could not fight this day and he had been ordered to attend on La Marquesa instead. It was typical of General Verigny, La Marquesa thought, to make sure that her escort was of an unbelievable ugliness. She raised her fan, caught his eye, and smiled as he joined her. 'You're looking for me, Captain?'

'Are not we all, my dear lady?' He bowed over her hand, kissed the gloved fingers, and smiled. 'Captain Saumier, at your obedient service.'

He really was extraordinarily ugly, with a face like a

grumpy toad. 'Do sit down, Captain. You must be desolated not to be fighting today?'

'There'll be other days, my Lady, but this one is yours. How can a man regret such a thing?'

'So prettily said. A lemon pastry?'

She sent the maid for more, and ordered wine to be brought from her coach. 'How did you fetch your wounds, Captain?'

'Falling from the balcony of a lady. Her husband objected.'

No doubt, La Marquesa thought, at his wife's egregious taste. She waved her fan at the battlefield. 'You must tell me what is happening, Captain.'

She could see the small clouds of musket smoke on the Puebla Heights. Captain Saumier borrowed her glass, stared through it for a few seconds, and delivered himself of the opinion that Wellington was attacking on the Heights because he dared not attack on the plain.

'But if they take the hills,' she paused as her maid brought her the fresh pastries and wine, 'won't they have to come down to the plain?'

'Oh indeed, my Lady. How very true!'

'And what happens then?'

'We beat them with the guns.' Saumier grinned, showing long, yellow teeth.

'As simple as that?'

Saumier smiled. 'War is simple.'

'No wonder men like it so much.' She smiled. 'Perhaps Wellington will do something you don't expect?'

Captain Saumier shook his head. He subscribed to the view commonly held in the French army, a view he stated now with manly certainty to reassure this nervous, beautiful, wide-eyed woman. 'Wellington can't attack. He puts up a reasonable defence, my Lady, but he can't attack.'

'You were at Assaye?'

'Assaye?'

She did not enlighten him. 'Argaum?'

He shrugged.

She smiled. 'Salamanca?'

Saumier smiled. 'These are most excellent pastries, my Lady.'

'I'm so glad you like them, and I'm so looking forward to your enlightenment today, Captain. It's so rare to watch a battle with a guide beside one.'

Saumier had been told by his General that the Marquesa was intelligent and well informed. He rather feared that he would be enlightened this day. 'You're comfortable, my Lady?'

'Eminently.' She turned from him and trained the glass on the Puebla Heights. She could see nothing of interest. The battle was being fought below the skyline. She hoped, she hoped passionately, for a French victory this day, or else the wealth that she had accumulated so carefully and with such good planning would be lost. She remembered her lover's certainty, and took heart that Captain Saumier was also so replete with assurance. It seemed that the French army were sure of their coming triumph. No one had ever beaten Wellington in battle, but neither had Wellington ever fought an army commanded by Marshal Jourdan. She ate her pastry, accepted a glass of wine, and hoped for victory.

Her hope that was devoutly shared this day by Don Jose, by the grace of God, King of Castile, of Aragon, of the Two Sicilies, of Jerusalem, of Navarre, of Granada, of Toledo, of Valencia, of Galicia, of Majorca, of Minorca, of Seville, of Sardinia, of Corsica, of Cordoba, of Murcia, of Santiago, of the Algarves, of Algeciras, of Gibraltar, of the Canary Islands, of the East and West Indies, of the Ocean Islands; Archduke of Austria; Duke of Burgundy, of Brabant and of Milan; Count of Hapsburg, Tyrol and Barcelona; Sire of Biscay and of Molina. The titles were ones he had given to himself. His younger brother, who was the Emperor of France, merely called him Joseph Bonaparte, King of Spain and the Indies.

If he lost today's battle he would be king of nothing.

Which was why, as the sun rose higher and the guns waited, Joseph Bonaparte was troubled by the evident success that Wellington's troops were having on the Puebla Heights. He expressed his concern to his military commander, Marshal Jourdan, who merely smiled. 'Let the British have the Heights, sir.'

'Let them?' King Joseph, a kindly, anxious man, looked worriedly at his military commander.

Jourdan's horse was restless. The Marshal calmed it. 'They want the Heights, sir, so they can march safely through the defile beneath. And that's where I want them.' If the British came from the defile where the river left the plain then they would be marching towards his great guns. He smiled at Joseph. 'If they come from the west, sir, they're beaten.'

Jourdan hoped to God he was right. He had planned on a British attack from the west and when the cannons had smeared the killing ground with British dead he would release the cavalry to become the first of France's Marshals to defeat Wellington. He did not care about the Heights. No man there could influence the battle on the plain. The British could take every damned hill in Spain so long as they marched into his guns afterwards. He could almost taste the victory.

There was only one place that worried Marshal Jourdan, and that was the flat land north of the river. If Wellington did not attack from the west, but instead tried to outflank the plain by marching about the French right, then Jourdan would have to turn his battle-line and resite his guns.

He looked anxiously northwards, to the land across the river where the wind stirred the crops in long, pale, rippling waves. Two marsh harriers flew above the trout-rich Zadorra, gliding out of sight behind the hill that hid the river's bend. He had not fortified that hill. He wondered if Napoleon would have put men there. No. No. He must not have doubts! He must behave as if he knew exactly what would happen, as if he was controlling the enemy as well as his own army.

He made himself smile. He made himself look confident. He complimented the King on his tailor and tried not to think of British troops coming from the north. Let them come from the west! Pray God, from the west!

'Sir!'

'Sir!'

A chorus of voices sounded. Fingers pointed west towards the defile that was still deep shadow.

'Sir!'

'I see it!' Jourdan spurred forwards.

From the defile, marching towards the small village that lay before the Arinez Hill, marching onto the great killing ground dominated by the French guns, were British infantry.

Their Colours were flying. They marched like parade soldiers towards their deaths.

'We've got him! We've got him, by God!' Jourdan slapped his thigh.

So Wellington was not being clever. He was coming straight on and that was what Jourdan wanted. Straight on to death and glory to the Emperor! He spurred his horse forward, waving his plumed hat at the artillerymen. 'Gunners! Wait!'

The linstocks were lit. In each of the great guns, more than a hundred of them, the priming tubes had pierced the powder bags and waited for the fire.

King Joseph rode alongside his Marshal. Joseph was terrified of his younger brother's displeasure, and the terror showed on his face. If he lost this battle he would be a king no more, and to win it he had to see Wellington beaten. Joseph had witnessed the British army fight at Talavera and he had seen how their infantry had snatched victory from certain defeat.

But Marshal Jourdan had seen more. He had fought as a private in the French army that went to help the American Revolutionaries. He had seen the British defeated, and he knew he would see it again. He beamed at the King, the Emperor's brother. 'You have a victory, sir. You have a victory!'

'You're sure?'

'Look!' He waved his hand at the empty north, then to the troops that spread out before his guns. 'You have a victory!'

It was the last moment that men could look at the field and see what happened, the last moment before the smoke of the guns hid the struggle. Jourdan drew his sabre, the steel bright as the sun, and swept it down.

The guns began.

The defile where the Great Road entered Vitoria's plain was crowded. Troops waited to be ordered forward. Wounded, from the Heights of Puebla, had been brought to the road. Surgeons, their aprons already gleaming red, tried to work their saws and blades as men crowded the narrow verges waiting to go towards the gunfire that had suddenly started.

Men joked about the sound of the French guns. They joked because they feared them.

Young drummer boys, their voices unbroken, watched the veterans and tried to take comfort from their calmness. Young officers, sitting on expensive horses, wondered whether glory was worth this nervousness. Staff officers, their horses' flanks already white with sweat, galloped along the columns looking for Generals and Colonels. The Colours, untouched in the defile by any wind, hung heavy on staffs. The first Battalions were already on the plain. The first wounded were already dragging themselves back towards the surgeons.

Men broke from the ranks to go down to the river and fill their canteens with water. Some had prudently saved their ration of wine or rum. It was better, they said, to go into battle with alcohol inside.

An Irish regiment, their red coats faded and patched to show their long service in Spain, knelt to a chaplain of a Spanish regiment who blessed them, made the sign of the cross above them, while their women prayed anxiously behind. Their Colonel, a Scottish Presbyterian, sat in his saddle and read the twenty-third psalm.

Some Highland troops were climbing the Puebla Heights,

going to take over from the Spaniards. The sound of the pipes, wild as madness, came to the defile mixed with the roar of the French guns.

Men asked each other what was happening, and no one knew. They waited, feeling the warmth coming into the day, and they listened to the battle sound and prayed that they would live to hear the sound of victory. They prayed to be spared the surgeons.

At the rear of the column, where the women and children waited for the day's lottery of widowhood to be drawn, and where the local villagers stared wide-eyed at the strange, huge tribe that was packed into their valley, two horsemen reined in. One of the two men, a tall, dark-haired, scarred man shouted at a group of soldiers' women who sat at the river's edge. 'Which Division is this?'

A woman who was suckling a baby looked up at the Rifleman who had shouted the question. 'Second.'

'Where's the Fifth?'

'Christ knows.'

Which answer, Sharpe reflected, he deserved. He spurred Carbine forward. 'Lieutenant! Lieutenant!'

A Lieutenant of infantry turned. He saw a tall, suntanned man on a horse. The man wore a tattered uniform of the 95th Rifles. At his hip was a sword, which seemed to suggest that the unshaven man was an officer. 'Sir?' The Lieutenant sounded tentative.

'Where's Wellington?'

'I think he's over the river.'

'Fifth Division?'

'On the left, sir. I think.'

'Are you the right?'

'I think so, sir.' The Lieutenant sounded dubious.

Sharpe turned his horse. The defile was jammed with men and he could hear the sound of guns that told him this road led only to the battlefield.

He did not care about Wellington. Now was not the time to find the General and speak of the treaty that La Marquesa had betrayed to him in Burgos. He had written down everything that she had told him, and he would make sure that the letter reached Hogan. But now Sharpe had caught up with the army on a day of battle, he was a soldier, and vindicating his name could wait until the fighting was done. He looked at Angel, mounted on an ugly horse that they had stolen in Pancorvo. 'Come on!'

He led the boy back to the village where a bridge crossed to the western bank. He would find the South Essex, he would come back from the dead, and he would fight.

CHAPTER 21

The French guns fired all morning. Their sound rattled the windows in the city. It was like a thunder that had no ending.

The smoke grew like a cloud. The women who sat on the tiers of seats above the city wall grumbled because their view was obscured. They could not see the enemy. They could only see the great cloud that grew and spread and drifted southwards with the breeze. Some of them strolled on the ramparts, flirting with the officers of the town guard. Others, their parasols raised against the sun, dozed on the benches.

The gunners fired, aimed and fired again. They dragged the guns forward after each shot, levered the trails round with handspikes, and pushed the ammunition into the hot muzzles that steamed from the sponging out. Men were sent to the small streams of the plain for buckets of water to soak the sponges. The roads from the city were loud with the galloping limbers that brought new ammunition to feed the guns that hammered at the killing ground.

The French infantry sat on the ridges, slicing sausage and bread, drinking the raw, red wine that filled their canteens. The guns were doing their work. Good luck to the guns.

The guns bucked, their wheels jarring from the ground with each shot. As each gun thudded down the gunner ran forward to put his leather-covered thumb over the smoking touch-hole. With the touch-hole covered if was safe to ram the wet sponge down the barrel and kill the last red sparks before the next powder charge was pushed home. Without the touch-hole blocked the rush of air forced by the plunging sponge could flare pockets of unexploded powder that had been known to erupt with enough force to blast the sponge back and impale its handle through the body of a gunner.

The guns had names embossed on the barrels beneath the proudly wreathed "N"s. *Egalité* fired next to *Liberté*, while *Fortune* and *Defi* were being sponged out.

The gunners sweated and heaved and grinned; listened to their officers call the aim and they knew they were filling the western plain with death. They could not see their enemy, the smoke hid all to the west, but each shot lanced a spear of flame into the smoke that would twitch with the canister's passing and then the gunners would reload, would haul the gun back into a true aim, then stand back as the chief gunner rammed his spike through the touch-hole into the canvas bag of powder, as the second man pushed the quill of fine powder into the hole made by the spike. The quill carried the fire down to the powder from the linstock held by the chief gunner.

'*Tirez!*'

All gunners were deaf, they said. They were the kings of the battlefield and they never heard the applause.

Sometimes, rarely, a battery would pause. The smoke would clear slowly from its front and the officers would peer at their target. The British had been stopped.

The red lines were cowering in the crops, hiding behind stone walls or crouching in ditches filthy with the summer's rain. The gunners knew the British were beaten. No troops in the world would dare advance into the horror of round-shot and canister that the guns poured into the killing ground.

For the British it was a nightmare of sound. The round-shot rumbled like giant barrels on planks overhead, the canister whistled, the screams of the wounded riding over it all. The musket balls from the broken canister rattled on stone or cracked through corn or thudded into flesh and always there was the rolling thunder from the white cloud ahead. Sometimes, when a gun was short of shot or canister, a shell would be fired instead. The shell would land in the broken crops. It would spin, its fuse smoking wildly, then the casing would crack apart in flame, smoke and iron fragments to add to the noise of death.

The British died in ones and twos. They sheltered where they could, but sheltering men won no battles. Yet these men could not go forward. No man could go into that storm of shot. They crouched, they lay in shallow scoops of land, they cursed their officers, they cursed their General, they cursed the French, they cursed the slow, crawling time, and they cursed the lack of help on the plain's edge. They were alone in a storm of death and they could see no help. The Colours were shredded with shot.

The lucky ones were in the small village, the first village of the plain, for there the stone walls were a shield. Even so, some roundshot smashed the houses flat, carving bloody paths in the packed rooms, and always the air outside the hovels was loud with the sound of death.

The attack was stalled.

'We have him, by God, we have him!' Marshal Jourdan, who like all the French Marshals had begun to think of Wellington as unbeatable, knew that his enemy had underestimated him. Jourdan guessed that Wellington, secure for the first time by having greater numbers than the French, had committed his army to a frontal attack. The guns, the pride of the French army, were shredding the enemy.

He looked north. A few English cavalrymen were in sight on the river's far bank and the sight of them had alarmed some of his officers. Jourdan clapped his hands for attention and raised his voice.

'Gentlemen! The cavalry is a feint! If they planned to attack from there they would have done so already! They want us to weaken our left! We shall not!'

Indeed, he strengthened it. The reserves who guarded the northern river bank were marched south, behind the Arinez Hill, to reclaim the Puebla Heights. Jourdan planned more for them. When the British broke, and when he unleashed his lancers and sabres onto the killing ground, the men from the heights could sweep down to block the defile. The

British, broken and bloodied, would be trapped. But first, Jourdan knew, he must let Wellington send more men onto the plain, more men to be killed and cut off, more corpses and prisoners for the Emperor's glory. Jourdan knew he must wait. In another two hours, perhaps, the heights would be retaken and the moment would have come when he would destroy Wellington's reputation for ever. The Marshal called for food, for a little wine. Another two hours, he thought, and he would send the Eagles forward to take Spain back for France. He smiled at King Joseph. 'I trust, sir, you have invited no one to sit on your right this evening?'

Joseph frowned in puzzlement, not understanding why Jourdan spoke about the victory feast which had been ordered in Vitoria. 'I hope you will take that place of honour, my dear Marshal.'

Jourdan laughed. 'I shall be pursuing the enemy, sir, but you may have the Lord Wellington to entertain. I hear he likes mutton.'

Joseph understood and laughed, 'You're that hopeful?'

Jourdan was that hopeful. He had won, he knew it, and he could taste the victory already.

The guns made the silver cutlery quiver on the white linen in Vitoria's grandest hotel. The waiters had laid one hundred and fifty places in the dining room. The bottles of wine, standing in thick groups on all the tables, clinked together and sounded like a thousand small bells.

Flowers had been cut and were now being put on the high table. That was where King Joseph would sit for this feast of victory ordered by the French. A tricolour was hung from the ceiling. The crystal chandeliers vibrated with the sound of the cannon. The whole great room was filled with clinking, ringing, shaking things.

The hotel's owner looked at the room and knew his men had done well. He wrung his hands. He should have dared ask the French to pay for this feast in advance. They had ordered the best Medoc, burgundy and champagne, and

251

the kitchens were preparing five bullocks, two score sheep, two hundred partridges, and a hundred chickens. He groaned. The patriot in him prayed for a British victory, but the businessman feared that the British might not pay for what their enemy had ordered. He listened to the guns and, his purse more important than his pride, prayed that they would win the day.

The Marquess of Wellington, sitting his horse on the lower slopes of the western hills, watched the French gun line flame and smoke and shatter his men in the killing ground. None of Wellington's staff officers spoke to him. The whole sky seemed to vibrate with the great blows of the guns.

Staff officers spurred on the slope beneath him. To a casual eye the western hill and the defile seemed like chaos. Wounded men dragged themselves towards surgeons, while other men waited for battle. To someone who had never seen a battle, there seemed no order in the casual disposition of men. They might have hoped for a plan to help them understand.

There was a plan. Jourdan planned to stop the attack with his guns, and Wellington planned to grip those guns in a fist and squeeze.

The English General thought of his plan like a left hand placed palm downwards on the map.

The thumb was the attack on the heights.

The index finger was the troops who had advanced beneath the heights into the guns' thunder, the troops who had been stopped by the French artillery, the troops who suffered minute by horrid minute.

The thumb and index finger were supposed to do no more than pin the enemy's attention, to draw his reserves across to the south and west, and, when that was done, the remaining three fingers would curl in from the north.

But where were they? The men on the plain were dying because the left hand columns were late and Wellington, who hated to see men die unnecessarily, would not even allow himself to be consoled by the fact that the longer he waited, the more his enemy would be convinced that the main attack was coming from the west.

He rode a small way up the slope and stared northwards. The land seemed empty. He clicked his fingers. An aide spurred forward.

The General turned. 'Hurry them!'

'My Lord.'

There was no need to explain who should be hurried. There should be three columns coming from the northern hills, columns that would trample the crops over the river, carry the bridges, and fall on the French right. Wellington wondered why in God's name the French had left the bridges intact. His cavalry scouts had reported no signs of powder ready to blow the arches sky high. It made no sense. The General had feared that his northern attacks would have to wade the fords, their bodies drifting downstream in bloodied water, but the French had left the bridges open.

Yet the three columns which, like fingers, would squeeze the life from the French army, had not appeared and their lateness meant that the French guns were taking a heavy toll on the plain. The fingers of Wellington's right hand drummed on the pommel of his saddle. He waited, while beneath him the guns shivered the warm morning.

'Dear Captain Saumier?'

'Ma'am?' He sounded tired. Eight times La Marquesa had sent him limping down the crowded tiers, either for more wine or more pastries.

'In my coach there is a parasol. Would you be very gallant and fetch it for me?'

'Entirely my pleasure, ma'am.'

'The white parasol, not the black.'

'There's nothing else I can fetch you at the same time?' her escort asked hopefully.

'Not that I can think of.'

He edged down the crowded bench, his ugly face reddening because he knew that the other women had observed him running errands like a small boy for La Marquesa.

She stared at the battlefield, seeing only the great cloud of cannon smoke. For some reason she found herself thinking about Sharpe, wondering whether he would have been as malleable as this Captain Saumier. Somehow she doubted it. Richard had always been ready to frown and growl his displeasure. He had been, she thought, a man of immense pride, a pride made fragile because it had come from the gutter.

She had felt regret when she had heard he was dead. She was glad then that she had lied to him, had told him that she loved him. Richard, she thought, had wanted her to say that and he had been eager to believe it. She wondered why soldiers, who knew death and horror better than anyone, were so often soggily romantic. Send them to their deaths happy was what the women of this army said; and why not? She tried to imagine being in bed with Captain Saumier, and the thought made her shudder. She cooled herself with her fan. The sun was tryingly hot.

A cavalry officer reined in at the wall's foot. There had been a succession of such officers all morning who had come to show off to the ladies and shout up news from the fighting that was still hidden by the great bank of smoke. The cavalry officer swept off his hat. All was well, he said. The British were beaten. Soon Jourdan would order the line forward.

La Marquesa smiled. Victory today would mean Ducos' defeat. A beat of pure malicious pleasure went through her at the thought of that defeat.

She looked away from the smoke. She looked at the empty northern fields, bright with poppies and cornflowers, a scene of innocence on this day of guns and smoke. Far off there, at the foot of the northern hills and too far away to play any part in today's battle, was a small, story-book castle. She pulled her ivory spyglass open and stared at the tiny old fortress.

And instead she saw troops. Troops trampling the crops flat. Troops spilling from the gullies of the hills, troops swarming southwards towards the right of the French line.

She stared. The troops wore red. She knew what she saw; it was the despised Wellington proving to the French yet again that he could not attack. Beneath her the cavalry officer caught a thrown handkerchief, wheeled his horse, and galloped back to the battle.

'Sir!'
'Sir!'

Marshal Jourdan, who a moment before had been thinking that the battle would be won by two o'clock, and had been thinking regretfully that his pursuit would mean he could not attend the victory dinner that night, stared to his right.

He could not believe what he saw.

The columns were coming towards him, towards the unguarded flank, and the British Colours were bright over their heads. He had already taken his reserves from the right to re-assault the Puebla Heights, now Wellington had unleashed the weight of his real attack. For one brief, horrid second, Jourdan admired Wellington for waiting this long, for letting his men suffer under the guns long enough to convince the French that the frontal attack was the real attack, then the Marshal began shouting.

The right flanks of the French lines were to turn outwards. There would not be time to stop the British crossing the river, so Jourdan knew he must fight them on the near bank with his guns.

King Joseph, who had retired into his carriage to use his silver chamber pot, came hurrying back into the sunshine. 'What's happening?'

Jourdan ignored him. He was staring north, watching the most easterly enemy column that was not coming towards him. It was striking for the Great Road, trying to cut him off from France. He shouted for an aide. 'What's the village on the river bend there?'

'Gamarra Mayor, sir.'

'Tell them to hold it! Tell them to hold it!'

'Sir!'

King Joseph, his breeches flap held in his hands, watched in horror as the aide spurred his horse into a gallop. 'Hold what?'

'Your kingdom, sir. There!' Jourdan's voice was savage. He was pointing at the river bend and the small village of Gamarra Mayor. 'You!' He pointed to another aide. 'Tell General Reille I want his men in Gamarra Mayor. Go!'

If the river was crossed, and the road taken, then a battle, a kingdom and an army were lost. 'Tell them to hold it!' he shouted after the officer, then turned back to the west. A gun sounded, no great thing on this day, except this was a British gun and it had been brought to face the French, and the roundshot landed on the slope of the Arinez Hill, bounced, and came to rest a few yards from Jourdan's horse. It was the first enemy shot to reach the Arinez Hill and it spoke of things to come.

Marshal Jourdan, whose day of triumph was turning sour, tossed his Marshal's baton into his carriage. It was a red velvet staff, tipped with gold and decorated with gold eagles. It was a bauble fit for a triumph, but now, he knew, he had to fight against disaster. He had sent his reserves to his left, and now his right was threatened. He shouted for news and wondered what happened beyond the bank of smoke which hid this battle for a kingdom.

Richard Sharpe, though he did not know it, galloped within two hundred yards of Wellington. He went north, following the river, shouting at the villagers who watched the battle from the track to clear a path. Across the water he could see the smoke pumping from the French gun line. The canister twitched and tore at the trampled crops.

He slowed at the river bend, forced to negotiate a village street crowded with Battalions who waited to cross the bridges. He shouted at one mounted officer, asking where the Fifth was, and the man waved Sharpe on. 'The left!'

A Rifle officer, lighting a cigar from the pipe of one of his men, saw Sharpe and his mouth dropped open. The cigar fell to the ground. Sharpe smiled. 'Morning, Harry. Good luck!' He put his heels back, leaving the man stupefied by the sight of a disgraced, hanged, and buried man come back from the dead. Sharpe laughed, cleared the village, and put Carbine into a canter that took them due east along the Zadorra's northern bank.

Ahead of him the Third and Seventh Divisions were launched at the river. They attacked at the double, skirmishers in front, the huge formations splitting apart to stream over the unblown bridges and unguarded fords. Angel was awed by the sight. More than ten thousand infantry were moving, a red tide that assaulted the southern French positions.

A Major galloped towards Sharpe. Behind him a Brigade of infantry were standing, their General impatient at their head. 'Are you staff?'

'No!' Sharpe reined in.

'God damn it!' The Major's sword was drawn. 'The Peer's forgotten us! God damn it!'

'Just go!'

'Go?'

'Why not?' Sharpe grinned at the man. 'Where's the Fifth?'

'Keep going!' The Major had turned his horse and now waved his sword towards the river in a signal to his General. The Brigade picked up its muskets.

'Come on, Angel!' Sharpe feared the battle would be over before he could join it.

To Sharpe's right, as he circled the rear of the now advancing brigade, the British attack reformed on the Zadorra's southern bank. Ahead of the attack, spread out in the untrodden wheat that was thick with flowers, the Rifles, men of the 95th, went ahead in the skirmish line. They could see the French guns on the Arinez Hill and they knelt, fired, reloaded and advanced.

The bullets, flickering out of the smoke cloud and clanging on the black-muzzled barrels of the French guns, were the first warning the battery had of their danger. 'Spikes!'

The gunners desperately slewed the guns round, the men heaving on the handspikes as yet more bullets came from the north. 'Canister!' the officer shouted, and then a bullet span him round, he clapped a hand to his shoulder, and suddenly his men were running because the Riflemen were charging up the slope. 'Load it!'

It was too late. The Riflemen, their weapons tipped with the long sword-bayonets, were in the battery. The blades stabbed at the few Frenchmen who tried to swing rammers at the British Riflemen. Some gunners crawled under the barrels of their guns, waiting for a prudent moment to surrender.

Behind the Rifles, spreading in the wheat with their Colours overhead, came the lines of red-jacketed men.

'Back! Back!' A French gunner Colonel, seeing his northern battery taken, shouted for the limbers and horses. Men hurled ready ammunition into chests, picked up trails, the trace chains were linked on, the horses were whipped, and the French guns went thundering and rocking and bouncing back towards the second line.

'Ready!' Now the French infantry, who had thought the guns had done their task, had to come forward to blunt the British attack. 'Present! Fire!' Over the fields that had been flayed with canister came the sound of musketry, the clash of infantry.

The Marquess of Wellington opened his watch case. He had his lodgement on the plain, he had driven the first French line into confusion, but now, he knew, there would be a pause.

Prisoners were being herded back, the wounded were being carried to the surgeons. In the smoke of the battlefield Colonels and Generals were looking for landmarks, seeking out units on their flanks, waiting for orders. The attack had worked, but now the attack had to be re-aligned. The men who had suffered under the French guns must be relieved, new Battalions marched onto the plain to link up with the northern attacks.

Wellington crossed the river. He spurred forward to take

command of the next attack, the one that would drive the French army due east, towards Vitoria, and he wondered what was happening to the small finger of his plan's hand. That finger was the Fifth Division. It marched to a village called Gamarra Mayor, and if it could take that village, cross the river, and cut the Great Road, then it would turn French defeat into a rout. There, Wellington knew, the battle would be hardest, and to that place, as the sun rose to its zenith, Sharpe rode.

CHAPTER 22

Lieutenant Colonel Leroy fiddled with his watch. 'God damn them!'

No one spoke.

To their right, three miles away, the other columns had struck over the river. The battle there was a roiling cloud of musket and cannon smoke.

The Fifth Division waited.

Three Battalions, the South Essex one of them, would head the attack on Gamarra Mayor. Ahead of Leroy's men was a gentle slope that led down to the village, beyond which was a stone bridge that crossed the river. Beyond the river was the Great Road. If the Division could cut the road, then the French army was cut off from France.

He snapped open the lid of his watch again. 'What's keeping the bloody man?' Leroy wanted the General of Division to order the attack quickly.

The French were in Gamarra Mayor. This was the only river crossing they had garrisoned, and they had loopholed the houses, barricaded the alleys, and Leroy knew this would be grim work. Three years before, on the Portuguese frontier, he had fought at Fuentes d'Onoro and he remembered the horrors of fighting in small, tight streets.

'Christ on his cross!' Across the river, where the lane from the bridge rose to the Great Road, he could see French guns unlimbering. The attack would now be harder. The guns were just high enough to fire over the village and, even if the British took Gamarra Mayor, the guns would make the bridge murderous with canister.

'Sir?' Ensign Bascable gestured to the right. A staff officer had ridden to the centre Battalion of the attack.

'About god-damned time.' Leroy rode forward, his face, scarred dreadfully at Badajoz, looking grimmer than ever. 'Mr d'Alembord?'

'Sir?'

'Skirmish line out!'

'Sir!'

Then the Colonel of the centre Battalion waved his hat, the band of that Battalion struck into a jauntier tune, and the Light Companies were going forward. Leroy looked at his watch. It was one o'clock. He closed the watch's lid, thrust it into a pocket, and shouted the orders that would march the South Essex's line towards the enemy. Leroy was taking them into battle for the first time.

The Colours had been unsheathed. The silk looked crumpled after its long confinement in the leather tubes, but the Ensigns shook the flags out so that the tassels danced and the great emblems spread out above their heads. On the right was the King's Colour, a huge Union Flag that was embroidered with the badge of the South Essex at its centre. The badge showed a chained eagle, commemorating Sharpe and Harper's capture of the French standard at Talavera.

On the left was the Regimental Colour, a yellow flag that listed the South Essex's battle honours about the badge at its centre and with the Union flag sewn into its upper corner. Both flags were holed, both scorched, both had been in battle before, and it was to the flags, more than to King or country, that a man gave his love and allegiance. Around the two Ensigns who carried the standards were the Sergeants, halberd-blades shining in the sun. If the French wanted to take the flags they would have to get past the men with the long, savage, axe-headed spears.

The Battalion marched with bayonets fixed and muskets loaded. They trampled the wheat flat.

Ahead of them, spread out like beaters, was the Light Company. Sergeant Patrick Harper shouted at them to spread out more. He had waited all morning for an officer to come with black hair and a scar on his left cheek, but there had been no sign of Sharpe. Yet Harper refused to give up hope. He stubbornly insisted that Sharpe was alive, that he would come today, that Sharpe would never let the South Essex fight without being present. If Sharpe had to come out of the grave, he would come.

Captain d'Alembord listened to the thunder of guns to his right. British guns were on the plain now, firing from the Arinez Hill at the second French line. D'Alembord, who was at his first great battle, thought the sound was more terrible than any he had ever heard. He knew that soon the six French guns across the river would open fire. It seemed to Peter d'Alembord, as he marched ever closer to the silent, barricaded village, that each of the French guns was pointing directly at him. He glanced at Harper, taking comfort from the apparent stolidity of the huge Irishman.

Then the guns disappeared in smoke.

Lieutenant Colonel Leroy saw a pencil line go up and down in the sky and knew that a roundshot was coming towards him. He kept his horse going straight, held his breath, and watched with relief as the ball thumped into the grass ahead of the Battalion, bounced overhead and rolled behind them.

The shots came over the village and plunged onto the meadow that the British Battalions crossed. The first volley did no damage, except for the ball that had bounced over Leroy's head. It bounced again, once more, and rolled towards the South Essex's bandsmen who waited at the rear for the wounded. A drummer boy, seeing the ball roll slow as a cricket ball that might not make the boundary, ran to check it with his foot.

'Stop!' A Sergeant shouted at the boy, but he was too late. The drummer put his foot in the ball's path, it seemed to roll so innocuously, so slowly, and, as the boy grinned, it took his foot off in blood and pain.

'You stupid bastard!' The Sergeant slapped him and hauled him upright. 'You stupid god-damned bastard! How many god-damn times have you been told?' The other drummer boys watched silently as their comrade was carried sobbing back to the surgeons. The drummer's foot, still in the boot that he had polished in honour of the battle, lay in the grass.

The guns fired again and this time a ball plucked through the South Essex's number six Company, throwing two men sideways and down, spattering blood onto the wheat and poppies. The line stolidly closed up.

The Light Company had opened fire. The rifles cracked. The French cannon smashed back again, and once again the lines had to close and once again the meadow behind the attackers was littered with bodies and blood.

Leroy lit a cheroot with his tinder box. The men were doing well. They were not flinching from the artillery, they marched silently and in good order, but still he feared the village. It was too well barricaded, too thickly loopholed, and he knew that the muskets of Gamarra Mayor's defenders could do far more damage than the six field guns on the far side of the river. Not a French musket had sounded yet. They waited for the British to get close. Leroy had begged for permission to attack in column, but the Brigadier had refused. 'We always attack in line, man! Don't be a fool!' The Brigadier, knowing Leroy to be an American, wondered if he was touched in the head. Attack in column, indeed!

Leroy put his tinder box away and spurred past the Colours. 'Captain d'Alembord?'

'Sir?'

'Form on us!'

The South Essex was now protected from the field guns by the houses in the village. Still the French did not fire. The Light Company scrambled to their place on the left of the Battalion. They marched forward.

Leroy frowned. He knew what would happen when the defenders fired. He feared it. The South Essex was still under strength, and the next few moments could destroy his command. He muttered at the enemy under his breath, begging them to fire too soon, begging them to give his men a chance.

But the French waited. They waited till every shot could

count, and when the fire order was given Leroy almost flinched from the sound and from the destruction.

The heavy musket bullets tore at the British line, jerking and twisting men, chopping them down, spinning them, and then new men took over at the loopholes and more bullets came tearing into the red-jacketed attack and it seemed to Leroy that the air was filled with the noise of muskets and bullets as he shouted into the wind of fire to keep his men going forward.

'Forward,' the officers shouted, but they could not go forward. The musketry from the village had jarred the South Essex backwards. Men fired their muskets in reply and wasted the bullets against the stone walls and barricades. The Colours fell, the Ensigns shot by French marksmen.

'Forward! Come on!' Leroy spurred ahead of the line. 'Forward!' His horse reared, screaming, was struck by another bullet, and Leroy cursed as his right boot would not leave the stirrup. His cigar fell, he flailed for balance, then his right foot was free and he slid clumsily over the rump of his falling, dying horse. He climbed to his feet, drew his sword, and shouted the men on.

The meadow was laced with smoke. Men crawled backwards, blood staining their tracks. Men cried for God or their mothers. Officers' horses, wounded, died in the wheat or stampeded towards the rear. Some men, seeing a chance to escape the carnage, helped the wounded towards the bandsmen and the surgeons. Other men reloaded and aimed at the loopholes, and still the French fired at them and still the enemy bullets twitched the thickening musket smoke and made the meadow a place of death and screams and wounded.

'Forward!' Leroy shouted. He wondered when new Battalions would be sent up to help his men, and he felt a rage that a Battalion under his command might need help. 'Forward!'

The Colours were lifted up by new men. They went into the fire, and the King's Colour fell again, was lifted again, and it twitched like a live thing as the bullets plucked at it.

The smoke was spoiling the French aim. From the village

they could see a mist that surrounded their positions and, at the far side of the mist, the dim shapes of men who came forward, were thrown back, and still the French fired, thickening the mist, sending their bullets to pluck at the British line that had wrapped itself about the village but could not break in.

The Regimental Colour fell; this time a Sergeant picked it up, but the movement in the mist attracted a dozen French marksmen and the Sergeant was hurled back and the flag was down again.

'Forward!' Leroy ran, sword in hand, and he heard the shot plucking at the grass and thrumming in the air, and he heard the cheer behind and knew the companies were coming with him, and the wall ahead of him flickered with flame, someone screamed behind him, and suddenly Leroy was at the village, safe between two loopholes in a barn wall, and more men joined him, crouching beneath loopholes, feverishly reloading their muskets.

Leroy grinned at them. 'We've got to go for a barricade.'

'Yes, sir.'

He wondered again, for the hundredth hundredth time, why these men, reckoned by their country to be the dregs of society, fought so well, so willingly, so bravely.

Leroy recongised a Lieutenant from Three Company. 'Where's Captain Butler?'

'Dead, sir.'

A French musket sounded deafening beside Leroy. He ignored it. They were safe here, hard against the wall, though he glanced up to make sure that no Frenchmen were on the barn roof. To his right he could see a farm wagon on its side. If enough men could drag it out of the way then he could lead a party into the alley. He organized a firing party, their job to fire over the barricade while other men pulled at it. Then, with fixed bayonets, the rest of the Company would follow Leroy into the alley. He grinned at them. 'Are you ready, lads?'

'Yes, sir.'

They looked nervously at him. The battle, for them, had become ten yards of murderous wall, nothing more.

Lieutenant Colonel Leroy, who had no intention of being defeated in his first battle as Battalion Commander, wiped his hand on his breeches and regripped his sword. 'First man in gets a guinea!' He listened to their cheer, knew they were ready, and straightened up. 'Come on!'

He ran to the barricade. Behind him the men came, cheering, but a single bullet, planted in Leroy's brain, finished the attack before it began. The Company, demoralised by his death, huddled back against the wall and wondered if they dared run back through the smoke before the victorious French, sallying from the village, slaughtered them with bayonets. Gamarra Mayor was being held. Ten yards from the alley, his scarred face spattered with blood, Thomas Leroy lay dead. His watch, ticking in his pocket, gave the time as ten past one.

'You're staying here!' Sharpe said to Angel.

'No!'

'If I die no one else knows about the god-damned treaty! You stay here and make sure the letter reaches Hogan!' Sharpe saw Angel nod reluctantly

The Band Sergeant was staring at Sharpe with a white face. 'Mr Sharpe?'

'You make sure this boy doesn't move, Sergeant!'

'Yes, sir.' The Sergeant was shaking. 'It is you, Mr Sharpe?'

'Of course it's me!' Sharpe was watching the village, seeing a Battalion broken. 'You two!' he pointed at two unwounded men who helped a comrade back.

'Sir?'

'You're not bloody wounded! Get back! Sergeant?'

'Sir?' The Band Sergeant was staring at Sharpe in utter disbelief.

'Shoot the next unwounded bastard who comes back here.'

'Yes, Mr Sharpe.'

Sharpe drew the sword. He went forward into the wheat that was trampled and blood-stained, littered with broken bodies, the scene of disaster. He had come back.

Captain d'Alembord never knew who first shouted for the line to retreat. The panic seemed to spread from the centre of the line, he heard an officer shout for the men to stand, to fire, to attack again, but the shouting was no good. The smoke isolated the men, they could not see the Colours, then came the news that the Colonel was dead, and suddenly the South Essex was running back through the smoke and the French cheered and sent them on their way with another volley of bullets.

D'Alembord ran with them, out of the smoke, running across the village meadow and into the wheatfield. He knew this was wrong, he knew that he should form the men into a skirmish line, or into close order, and he saw Harper bellowing at the Light Company and he knew he should do the same, then, suddenly, another voice was shouting on the battlefield, a voice forged long ago on forgotten parade grounds, and d'Alembord, looking left in the tangling smoke, saw a ghost.

A ghost who swore at them, who threatened them with his sword, who bellowed at officers, and promised to cut down the next man who went backwards.

They stared at him in shock. The big black horse carried a dead man among them, an unshaven ghost they thought dead and buried. A ghost whose anger was livid, whose voice flayed them into ranks and made them lie down so that the French bullets went high. 'Captain d'Alembord!'

'Sir?'

'Skirmish line forward. Edge of the smoke! Lie down. Keep the bastards busy! Move!' Sharpe saw the shock on d'Alembord's face. 'I said move!' He turned back to the other companies.

He would form them into a column. He would attack in the French manner. God alone knew why they had not attacked in column in the first place. He shouted the orders, ignoring the bullets that flickered out of the smoke.

Patrick Harper had tears in his eyes. If anyone had dared ask him why he would have said that the musket smoke was irritating him. He had known, he had always known, but he had not truly believed that Sharpe was alive.

'Sergeant Major!'

MacLaird gaped at Sharpe, then managed to speak. 'Sir?'

'Where's the Colonel?'

'Dead, sir.'

Christ! Sharpe stared at the staring RSM, then the flutter of a bullet snapped him to his duty. 'Take six men from Two Company. Stay at the back. You shoot any man who falls out. 'Talion! Move! Colours to me!'

To his right Sharpe could see that the other two Battalions were checked at the village's edge. They formed a ragged line about the houses, a line held by the French volleys. But a line would not pierce defences like this. It would take a column, and the column must go like a battering ram at the village, must take its losses at its head and then carry the bayonets into the streets.

He formed them into a column of four ranks. Some men were laughing like madmen. Others simply stared at a man come back from the grave. Collip, the Quartermaster, was shaking with fear.

The bullets still plucked about them, but Sharpe had formed the column a hundred yards from the village, far enough to take the sting from the French marksmen.

He rode down the column, telling them what to do, and he suddenly had to shout because the fools were cheering him, and he had to turn his face away and pretend to stare at the other two Battalions. He knew he should stop them cheering, but he could not. He thought how stupid it was to cheer a man who would lead them back to death, and how splendid it was, and he laughed because the Battalion was suddenly cheering in unison and he knew the cheer would carry them to victory.

The Grenadier Company was at the front. Sharpe picked ten men whose job was to fire a volley at point blank range when they reached the barricade. He would lead them, following a track of beaten earth that disappeared in the smoke but which, he knew, must lead to one of the barricaded alleys.

'Raise the Colours!'

There was a cheer as the flags were hoisted by two Sergeants. Sharpe stood in his stirrups. He would dismount for the attack, but for this moment, as the French bullets hummed about his ears, he wanted the South Essex to see him.

He raised the sword, there was silence, and he could see that they were straining to get the attack done. He smiled villainously. 'You're going to fight the bastards! What are you going to do?'

'Fight!'

'What are you going to do?'

'Fight!'

He beckoned at a man and ordered to him to hold Carbine till the fight was done, then Sharpe dismounted, turned, and stared at the village. It was time to go, time to fight, and he thought suddenly of the golden-haired woman who waited beyond the enemy lines, and he knew there was only one way that he would ever reach her. He hefted his sword and gave the command. 'Forward!'

CHAPTER 23

It was odd, Sharpe thought, but at that moment, as he led the Battalion forward, he wished La Marquesa could see him.

He was not in love with her. He might be jealous of her, he might seek her company, but he did not love her. He had said so, on that morning when he thought he went to death at *El Matarife's* hand, but he knew it was not true. He wanted her. He flickered about her as a moth flew about a bright flame, but to love someone was to know them, and he did not know her. He wondered if anyone knew her.

She had said she loved him, but he knew she did not. She had wanted him to break his honour for her, and she had thought the word love would make him do it. He knew she would use him and discard him, but nevertheless he now walked, sword in hand, towards the waiting muskets and he did it for her.

The sword felt heavy in his hand. He wondered why every new battle was harder than the last. Luck had to stop somewhere, he supposed, and why not here where the French had already broken one attack and waited for the next? He thought, as he shouted the column forward, that he lived on borrowed time. He wondered, if he died, whether Helene would hear that he had lived a few more days for her, and that he had died in the stupid, vain, selfish hope of seeing her again.

His boots swished in the meadow grass. Bees were busy at the clover. He saw a snail with a black and white shell that had been crushed by an infantryman's boot. The grass was littered with cartridges, spent musket balls, discarded ramrods, and fallen shakos.

He looked up at the village. The Light Company was provoking the musket fire, keeping the acrid smoke thick. Behind him the column marched in good, tight order. He took a deep breath. "Talion! Double!'

The bullets plucked the air about him. He heard a scream behind him, a curse, and he was running fast now, the village close, and, through the smoke, he could at last see the alley's mouth. It was blocked with a cart, with furniture, and flames stabbed from the barricade and he shouted for the firing party to break to one side.

He heard their volley. He saw a Frenchman go backwards from the barricade's top and then there were only a few yards to go, more bullets flamed from the village, but instead of a thin line attacking it was a column thick enough to soak up the French fire. Sharpe gathered himself for the jump. He would not wait to pull the barricade down. 'Jump!'

The air was filled with the hammering of muskets. Sharpe jumped onto the cart, swept down with his sword at a stabbing bayonet, while about him the British were clawing up the barricade, dragging the furniture down, trying to scramble over the heaped timber and screaming at the enemy. A musket fired beside his ear, deafening him, a bayonet tore at his sleeve as more men pushed behind, forcing him over, and he fell, flailing with the sword, rolling down the French side of the barricade as the enemy bayonets reached for him.

He twisted sideways and suddenly men of the South Essex were jumping over him, driving the French back, and he scrambled up, went on, and shouted at the men to watch the rooftops. No one heard him. They were mad with the battle-lust of fear, wanting to kill before they were killed, and it was that spirit that had driven them over the barricade and which drove them now into the tight, small streets of Gamarra Mayor.

A door opened in a house, a man stabbed with a bayonet and Sharpe lunged, twisted, and he could feel the warm blood on his hand as his sword found the enemy's neck. He dragged the blade clear of the falling body. 'Kill the bastards!' The alley was thick with men, pushing, shouting, swearing, stabbing, screaming. Men were trampled when they were wounded. The front rank clawed at the enemy. The close alley walls seemed to magnify every shout and shot.

There was a volley of muskets from the alley's far end and a French counter-attack, readied against just such a breakthrough, came towards them.

'Fire!'

The few men still loaded fired. Two Frenchmen fell, the rest came on, and Sharpe took his sword forward and swept it like a scythe at the leading bayonets. He was shouting the war shout, letting the anger frighten the enemy, and he felt a blade sear his thigh, but the sword flicked up into the man's face; there was a scream, and it was British bayonets that went forward; twisted, stabbed, tore the enemy counter-attack into shreds.

Sharpe was treading on bodies now. He did not notice. He watched the rooftops, the windows, and always shouted at his men to follow him, to keep moving forward.

The bayonets went forward, the British were shouting like madmen, like men who know that the best way to get rid of terror is to get the damned job done. They were clawing at their enemy, trampling them, screaming and lunging, cutting, slashing, driving them back.

'Into the houses! Into the houses!'

There was no point in piercing the village's centre, there to be surrounded by the enemy. This first alley had to be cleared, the houses emptied of the French and Sharpe kicked a door open and ducked under the lintel.

He was in an empty room. Men crammed in behind him, bayonets red. Opposite them was a closed door.

Sharpe looked round. 'Who's loaded?'

Three men nodded at him. Their eyes were bright in the darkness, their faces, stained by powder burns, were drawn back in permanent scowls. Sharpe dared not let these men catch their breath or feel safe here. He had to keep them moving.

'Fire through that door. On my order!'

They lined up, they levelled their muskets.

'Fire! Go! Go! Go!'

He was still shouting as he kicked the door and led the way through the musket smoke. He had to stop himself from flinching as he went through the door, so strong was his certainty that a volley waited for him on the far side.

He found a French soldier sprawled, twitching and bleeding, in a small yard that was strewn with straw. Other Frenchmen were backing into the yard, defending an alley at the far side that must have been penetrated by other men of the South Essex. Sharpe bellowed a triumphant shout, the sword struck again while, either side of him, his men went forward with bayonets and the Frenchmen were shouting for quarter, dropping their muskets and Sharpe was yelling at his men to hold their fire and to take prisoners.

A thatched roof had caught fire across the alley. Beneath it men were running, driving the French back, and Sharpe joined them, all control of the Battalion gone. They were hunting the defenders out of the houses, blasting closed doors with musket fire, kicking the shattered doors open and searching the small rooms. They did it savagely and quickly, avenging the dead American who had wanted this victory.

A trumpet sounded and Sharpe, turning, saw through the smoke in the village street the flag of another Battalion. The rest of the Division was coming through and he shouted at his own men to take cover, to clear the alleys. Let other men carry on.

He picked up some straw in a farmyard and scoured at the blood on his sword blade. Two prisoners watched him. All about him the village echoed to muskets and screams. The French garrison, prised from the houses, ran back over the bridge. A Sergeant watched Sharpe. 'It is you, sir?'

Sharpe tried to remember the man's name and Company. 'Sergeant Barrett, isn't it?'

'Yes, sir.' The man smiled, pleased at being remembered. Men of his Company gaped at Sharpe.

'It is me.' Sharpe grinned.

'They bloody hung you, sir.'

'This army can't do anything right, Sergeant.'

The men laughed, as he had meant them to. Barrett offered him some water that Sharpe took gratefully. Burning wisps of straw, blown from the thatch, threatened to start more fires. Sharpe ordered them to find rakes and get the prisoners to pull the burning thatch down. Then he set off to look at the village he had captured.

Marshal Jourdan could only fear and wait. The news from Gamarra Mayor said that the British had taken the village, but had failed to cross the river. He sent a messenger to say that the bridge had to be held at whatever cost. He felt the frustration of being outmanoeuvred, of trying to double-guess the hook-nosed, blue eyed General who opposed him.

Jourdan had glimpsed Wellington once, glimpsed him through a ragged hole in the smoke curtain and he had watched his opponent calmly dressing the line of a British Battalion. A General had no business doing that, Jourdan thought, and what made it worse was that the Battalion had then thrown the French from the southern flank of the Arinez Hill.

Marshal Jourdan, his great guns outflanked and his infantry defeated, had been thrown back on his second line. If the new line, and if the troops across the river from Gamarra Mayor both held, then all was not lost. Indeed a victory could still be his, but he had the horrid sensation of control slipping from his hands. He shouted for information, demanding to know where General Gazan's troops were, and no one could tell him. He sent aides galloping into the smoke and they did not come back, or if they did they had no news, and Jourdan felt a shrinking horror that the second line was not complete, and what there was of it was suffering terribly from the enemy guns.

Suffering because Wellington had done what Wellington was reputed never to do. He had taken a leaf from the Emperor's book and concentrated his artillery and now the

British, Portuguese and Spanish guns were pounding from Arinez Hill, pounding and pounding, stopping a man thinking, and carving great furrows of blood through the waiting French infantry.

King Joseph, his horse nervous, came close to Jourdan. 'Jean-Baptiste?'

Jourdan frowned. He hated his Christian names, he hated the familiarity that he knew was being used to disguise fear. 'Sir?'

'Should we advance?'

Christ on his bloody cross! Jourdan almost snarled at his monarch, but bit the blasphemy back. He forced himself to look calm, knowing that the eyes of the staff were on him. 'We shall let our guns gnaw at him a bit, sir.' Jesus wept! Advance? Jourdan spurred his horse away from the King, noting wryly that the royal coach was ready for flight, coachman aloft and postilions mounted on horses. The truth was that Wellington conducted the music of battle now, god-damned Wellington, and Jourdan was praying that his men would hold on long enough to let him dream up a response. Troops! He needed fresh troops. 'Moreau! Moreau!' He called for an aide. There must be reserves somewhere! There must be!

The afternoon had come, and it had brought an artillery duel on the plain. Jourdan shouted for more troops, but he knew his enemy, behind the curtain of smoke, was regrouping for a new attack. He demanded news, always news, and he asked for reassurance from staff officers who could not give it. Panic was beginning to infect the French command, while behind their guns the British prepared a new attack. The infantry were in their ranks, fresh cartridges issued, an army readying itself for victory.

On the walls of the city the ladies watched. They frowned when the carts brought the bloodied wounded back from the battle, but they believed the handsome cavalry officers who came to give them news. Jourdan, the cavalry officers said, had merely pulled his line back to give the guns more room. There was nothing to be worried about, nothing. One woman asked what happened to the north, and an officer reassured her that it was merely a few enemy who had come to the river and were learning the power of French guns. The officers caught the flowers tossed to them by the women, gallantly fixed the blooms to shining, plumed helmets, and trotted away through Vitoria's suburbs leaving the womens' hearts fluttering.

Captain Saumier knew that Marshals of France did not yield ground to give the guns space. 'Are you packed, my Lady?' His voice was low.

'Packed?'

'In case we have to retreat.'

La Marquesa stared at the ugly man. 'You're serious?'

'I am, my Lady.'

She knew defeat. If Sharpe had still lived, she thought, she would have been tempted to stay in Vitoria in the sure knowledge that Sharpe would dare to do what General Verigny dared not; snatch her wagons back from the Inquisitor. But Sharpe was dead, and she dared not stay. She consoled herself that in her coach, prudently concealed beneath the driver's bench, there were jewels enough to save her from utter poverty in France. She shrugged. 'There's still time, surely?'

'I hope so, my Lady.'

She smiled sadly. 'You still think Wellington can't attack, Captain?'

He frowned, not at her question, but at her face. She had turned from him and now stared in horror and puzzlement at the crowd who stood at the foot of the tiered seats. Saumier touched her arm. 'My Lady?'

She took her arm away. 'It's nothing, Captain.' Yet she could have sworn, for one instant, that she had seen a bearded face, a face so covered in beard as to resemble a beast, a face that had stared at her, turned away, and which she had seen on a cold morning in the mountains. The Slaughterman. She told herself she imagined it, for no Partisan would dare show himself in the heart of the French army, and she looked back to the plain where the battle still thundered and where that army fought for its existence.

Regimental Sergeant Major MacLaird reported that the burning thatch was now extinguished. 'And we've got forty-one prisoners, sir. Half the buggers are wounded badly.'

'Where's the surgeon?'

'Outside the village, sir.'

'Lieutenant Andrews!'

'Sir?' The Lieutenant still did not seem to believe that Sharpe was alive.

'My respects to Mr Ellis. Tell him there's work in the village and I want him here now!'

'Yes, sir.'

The South Essex had been ordered to rest while other Battalions streamed through the village to attack the bridge. Sharpe thought of the guns just up the slope. His hopes of reaching Vitoria seemed slim so long as the French battery was unmolested.

'Mr Collip!'

'Sir?'

'I want an ammunition check on all companies.'

'We've lost the limber, sir.'

'Then god-damned find it! And if you see my horse, send it here!'

'Horse, sir?'

'Black, undocked tail.' Sharpe had taken over a house in the village plaza. Its furniture had all gone to the barricades. He listened to the French guns open fire again, and knew that the attackers would be dying as they struggled to cross the bridge. 'Paddock!'

The Battalion clerk grinned from the kitchen door. He had been speechless when he saw Sharpe and he still grinned like a madman. 'Sir?'

'Someone must have some bloody tea.'

'Yes, sir.'

Sharpe ducked out into the street. A dog ran past with a

cut of meat in its mouth. He preferred not to wonder what kind of meat it was. The smoke of the French cannons drifted over the village roofs, low enough to touch the belfry. Once or twice the bell would clang as a fragment of canister bounced from the bridge to strike the instrument.

'Sir! Sir!' Sharpe looked left. Harry Price was running towards him. 'Mr Sharpe!'

'Harry.' Sharpe grinned.

Lieutenant Price, formality forgotten, thumped Sharpe on the back. He had been Sharpe's Lieutenant in the Light Company. 'Christ! I thought the buggers had hanged you!'

'This army can't do anything right, Harry.' It was the twentieth time he had said it.

Price was beaming. 'What in hell's name happened?'

'Long story.'

'Here.' Price thrust a bottle of brandy at Sharpe. 'Found it in their headquarters.'

Sharpe smiled. 'Later, Harry. There might be more to do.'

'God, I hope not! I want to live to be thirty.' Price tipped the bottle to his mouth. 'I suppose you're the commanding officer now?'

'You suppose right.' Leroy's body had been brought into the village. His death had at least been quick. Leroy would have known nothing. The other consolation was that he had left no family, no letters that needed to be written or widow to console.

The guns still fired at the bridge. Sharpe frowned. 'Why in hell haven't we got guns?'

'I heard they got lost,' Price grinned. 'This bloody army never does anything right. Jesus! It's good to see you, sir!'

And, oddly to Sharpe, it seemed the whole Battalion thought the same. The officers wanted to shake his hand, the men wanted to look at him as if to prove to themselves that he still lived, and he grinned shyly at their pleasure. Angel, who had come into the village with Sharpe's horse, basked in the reflected glory. Dozens of bottles were thrust at Sharpe, dozens of times he claimed that the army couldn't hang a curtain if they tried. He knew he was smiling idiotically, but he could not help it. He shook Harry Price off by ordering him to set up picquets at the village's northern edge and took refuge from embarrassment in his temporary headquarters.

Where someone else found him.

'Sir?'

The doorway was shadowed by a huge man who was festooned with weapons. Sharpe felt the smile coming again. 'Patrick?'

'Christ!' The Sergeant ducked under the lintel. There were tears in his eyes. 'I knew you'd be back.'

'Couldn't let you bastards fight a war without me.'

'No!' Harper grinned.

There was an odd silence, which both men broke together. Sharpe waved at the Irishman. 'Go on?'

'No, sir. You?'

'Just that it's good to be back.'

'Aye.' Harper stared at him. 'What happened?'

'Long story, Patrick.'

'It would be.'

There was silence again. Sharpe felt an immense relief that the Sergeant was alive and well. He knew he should say something to that effect, but it would be too embarrassing. Instead he waved at the window-ledge. 'Paddock made some tea.'

'Grand!'

'Is Isabella well?'

'She's just grand, sir.' Harper tipped the cup up and drained it. 'Mr Leroy gave us permission to get married.'

'That's wonderful!'

'Aye, well.' Harper shrugged. 'There's a wee one on the way, sir. I think Mr Leroy thought it would be best.'

'Probably.'

Harper smiled. 'I had a bet with Mr d'Alembord that you'd be back, sir.'

Sharpe laughed. 'You'll need money if you're going to marry, Patrick.'

'Aye, that's true. Nothing like a woman for spending a man's money, eh?'

'So when's the wedding?'

'Soon as I can find a priest. She's got herself a dress, so she has. It's got frills.' He said it gloomily.

'You'll let me know?'

'Of course!' Harper was embarrassed. 'You know what women are like, sir.'

'I've seen one or two, Patrick.'

'Aye well. They like marrying, so they do.' He shrugged.

'Especially when they're pregnant, yes?'

Harper laughed. There was silence again. The huge Sergeant put the cup down. 'It is grand to see you, sir.'

'You won your bet, eh?'

'Only a bloody pound.'

'You had that much faith in me, eh?'

They laughed again.

A horse's hooves were loud outside. A voice shouted. 'South Essex!'

'In here!' Sharpe shouted back, glad suddenly of the distraction from the emotion he felt.

A staff officer dismounted and ducked under the lintel. 'Colonel Leroy?' He straightened up.

It was Lieutenant Michael Trumper-Jones, in his hand a folded order for the Battalion. He stared at Sharpe, his mouth dropped open, and, his head slowly shaking and his eyes widening, he fell backwards in a dead faint. His scabbard chains clinked as he slumped on the floor. Sharpe nodded at the prostrate body. 'That's the bugger who defended me.'

Harper laughed, then cocked his head. 'Listen!'

The French guns had stopped. The bridge must have fallen, and suddenly Sharpe knew what he wanted to do. 'Angel!'

'*Señor?*'

'Horses! Patrick?'

'Sir?'

'Grab that fool's horse.' He pointed at Trumper-Jones. 'We're going hunting!'

'For what?' Harper was already moving.

'Wedding presents and a woman!' Sharpe followed Harper into the street, looked around, and spotted a Captain of the South Essex. 'Mr Mahoney!'

'Sir?'

'You'll find orders in that house! Obey them! I'll be back!' He gave the mystified Mahoney the letter for Hogan, swung onto Carbine's saddle, and rode towards the bridge.

To the north of Gamarra Mayor, at a village called Durana, Spanish troops cut the Great Road. The defenders at Durana had been the Spanish regiments loyal to France.

Countrymen fought countrymen, the bitterest clash, and Wellington's Spaniards, faithful to Spain, won the bridge at five o'clock. The Great Road to France was cut.

The Spanish troops had climbed barricades of the dead. They had fought till their musket barrels were almost red hot, till they had savaged the defenders and won a great victory. They had blocked the Great Road.

The French could still have broken through. They could have screened themselves to the west and thrown their great columns at the tired, blood-soaked Spaniards, but in the confusion of a smoke filled plain no one knew how few men had broken through in the rear. And all the time, minute by minute, the British Battalions were coming from the west while the great guns, massed wheel to wheel by Wellington, tore huge gaps in the French lines.

The French broke.

King Joseph's army, that had started the day with a confidence not seen by a French army in Spain for six years, collapsed.

It happened desperately fast, and it happened in pieces. One Brigade would fight, standing fast and firing at their enemies, while another would crumble and run at the first British volley. The French guns fell silent one by one, were limbered up and taken back towards the city. Generals lost touch with their troops, they shouted for information, shouted for men to stand, but the French line was being shredded by the regular, staccato volleys of the British Battalions while overhead the British shells cracked apart in smoke and shrapnel and the French troops edged backwards and then came the rumour that the Great Road was cut and that the enemy came from the north. In truth the French guns still held the British at Gamarra Mayor and the Spaniards further north were too tired and too few to attack south, but the rumour finally broke the French army. It ran.

It was early evening, the time when the trout were rising to feed in the river that flowed beneath the now unguarded bridge at Gamarra Mayor. The French who had guarded the bridge so well had seen their comrades run. They joined the flight.

The men who watched from the western hills or from the Puebla Heights were given a view of magnificence, a view granted to few men, an eagle's view of victory.

The smoke cleared slowly from the plain to show an army marching forward. Not in parade order, but in a more glorious order. From the mountains to the river, across two miles of burned and bloodied country, the allied Regiments were spread. They marched beneath their Colours and the sun lanced between the smoke to touch the ragged flags red, white, blue, gold, and red again where the blood had soaked them. The land was heavy with the men who marched, Regiment after Regiment, Brigade after Brigade, climbing the low hills that had been the French second line. Their shadows went before them as they marched towards the city of golden spires.

And in the city the women saw the French army break, saw the troops come running, saw the cavalry heading the panicked flight. The tiered seats emptied. Through the city, from house to house, the news spread, and the camp-followers and families and lovers of the French began their own headlong flight from Vitoria. They were spurred on their way by Marshal Jourdan's last orders in Vitoria, orders brought by harried cavalrymen who shouted at the French to make for Salvatierra.

The Great Road was cut and the only road left for retreat was a narrow, damp track that wound its way towards Salvatierra and from there to Pamplona. From Pamplona, by tortuous paths, the army might struggle back to France through the high Pyrenees.

The chaos began. Civilians, coaches, wagons and horses blocked the narrow streets while, to the west, beneath a sun hazed by the smoke of battle, the victorious Battalions marched in their great line towards the city. The victors darkened the plain and their Colours were high.

While to the south three horsemen crossed Gamarra Mayor's bridge. They had to pick their way through the corpses, which were already thick with flies, onto the Zadorra's northern bank.

Sharpe touched his heels to Carbine's flank. He had his victory, and now, with Harper and Angel beside him, he would ride into the chaos of defeat to search for the Marquesa.

CHAPTER 24

The road to Pamplona was wide enough for a single wagon or gun. The verges and fields either side of the road were too softened by the rain to take either.

Onto that road the whole of the French army, with more than twenty thousand camp-followers, three thousand wagons and over a hundred and fifty guns and limbers, was trying to reach safety.

All day the baggage park had listened to the thunder and watched the smoke over the spires of the cathedral. Now came the orders to retreat, not up the Great Road, but directly east towards Salvatierra and Pamplona.

Whips cracked, oxen protested the iron-shod poles that prodded them into motion, and from a half dozen field tracks and from the crowded city streets the vehicles started towards the single, narrow road. Into the confusion came the guns, thundering from the battlefield and adding their weight to the press of baggage and animals.

The first wagon stuck just a hundred yards beyond the place where the field tracks converged on the road. A carriage, trying to go round it on the soft verge, overturned. A gun swerved, skidded, and the two tons of metal slammed into the carriage, horses screaming, gunners falling beneath the metal, and the road was blocked. Oxen, horses, carriages, wagons, carts, cannon, howitzers, portable forges, ambulances and limbers, all were trapped between the road block and the British.

The wagons swarmed with people. Soldiers fleeing the city, drivers, camp-followers, all ran through the wagon park. Some began to slit the tarpaulins and drag boxes from the loads. Muskets fired as guards tried to protect the

Emperor's property, and then the guards realised that the Emperor had lost this property and whoever took it now might keep it. They joined the looters.

Thousands of French troops were streaming past the blocked wagons, trampling the crops and running eastwards. Generals rode with the cavalry, rehearsing the excuses they would make, while other men swerved into the wagons and searched desperately for wives and children.

King Joseph was in his carriage, fleeing towards the road block, and then there was the thunder of hooves, the sight of lifted sabres, and the first British cavalry, sent around the city, descended on the panicked, fleeing mob.

The King escaped only by abandoning his carriage. He scrambled from the right hand door as the British cavalry wrenched open the left. He abandoned his belongings and ran with his erstwhile subjects.

Women and children screamed. They did not know where their men were, only that the army had dissolved into a mob and they must run. Hundreds stayed in the baggage park, tearing the wagonloads down, not caring that the British cavalry were coming. Better to be rich for just a few minutes than eternally poor. From the city came the Spaniards, many with long knives ready for the slaughter.

Captain Saumier heard the shout for the army to go to Salvatierra and guessed that the city's single eastern gate would already be cramming with desperate people. He shouted at the coachman to go for the north gate.

It was a sensible move. The narrow eastern streets were filled with carriages and wagons, with men shouting and women screaming in fear. Saumier would take La Marquesa through the northern gate and then turn east.

The wheels bounced on the cobbles, skidded at one corner, but the driver held the balance and cracked the long whip over the horses' heads.

Saumier, his one good hand holding a pistol, leaned from the window and saw the city gate ahead. 'Go on! Go on!' His voice was loud over the harsh sound of the wheels and hooves, over the crack of the whip and the shouts of other fugitives. General Verigny had told Captain Saumier to protect this woman, and Saumier, who thought her more beautiful than any woman he had ever seen, hoped that his protection would merit a reward.

The carriage slowed to pass the narrow gate, a soldier tried to jump onto the step and Saumier hit the man with the brass butt of his pistol. The man fell under the wheel, screaming, the carriage leaped into the air, jarred down, and then it was through the archway and rattling down the street of houses that lay outside the wall. The coachman turned the horses eastwards at a crossroads, shouted at them, cracked the whip again, and the carriage picked up speed as Saumier leaned back on the upholstered cushions and pushed his pistol into his belt.

La Marquesa, her maid nervous beside her, looked at him. 'Where are we going?'

'Wherever we can, dear lady.' Saumier was nervous. He could see the men running from the battle and could hear the heavy noise of the gun wheels coming from the plain. As the coach cleared the last houses of the northern suburb he leaned again from the window and was appalled by the chaos he saw. It was as if a whole army ran a panicked race. Then he heard the brakeshoes slap on the wheels, he lurched as the carriage slowed, and he looked ahead to see the massive jam of wagons, guns and carriages that blocked the eastern road. 'Go round! Go round!'

The coachman pulled on the reins, bumping the carriage off the road and onto the verge. He shouted at the horses, cracking the whip above their ears, and the carriage seemed to surge and heave its way over the wet ground, yet whip the horses as he could, the coachman knew the carriage was slowing.

The rear of the coach dipped and Saumier, opening the door to lean out, saw people clinging to the baggage rack. He threatened them with his pistol, but their weight had slowed the carriage too much, the wheels were already sinking into the morass, and, slowly, finally, it stopped.

Saumier swore.

A dozen people were running towards the horses, knives drawn to cut the traces and use the animals for their own escape. He reached for La Marquesa, politeness forgotten, and pulled her out of the coach. 'Come on!'

The maid was hunched into a corner, refusing to go out into the panicked mass of people. La Marquesa, made of sterner stuff, jumped onto the wet ground. Saumier saw she had a pistol. 'Stop them!'

A man was hacking at the silver trace chains of the horses. La Marquesa aimed at him, her teeth gritted, pulled the trigger, and the man screamed, blood spurting from his neck, and Captain Saumier, his own pistol thrust into his sling, finished the man's work by hacking down with his sabre. He led the horse from the harness. 'My Lady?'

'Wait!' She had climbed onto the driver's seat, lifted the coachman's bench, and now dragged a leather sack from the compartment beneath. She gestured Saumier to lead his horse closer, then, modesty gone and not caring who saw her legs, she slithered across from the driving perch onto the horse's back. Saumier climbed up behind La Marquesa and shook the long driving rein with his good hand. Behind them, sabres raised, the British cavalry swept towards the road block. The coachman had taken another horse and galloped eastwards.

Saumier kicked back with his heels and the horse, frightened and lively, went into a gallop that took them past the stuck wagons. La Marquesa, mourning the fact that she had been forced to abandon all her belongings and her wealth, saw the soldiers and their women scattering silver dollars on the ground and scrambling at the wagons for more plunder. There were riches to be made here this day, but the British were coming fast from the west, and she would ride eastwards to safety. Saumier, the bandage on his eye flecked with mud thrown up by the hooves, took her to the north of the road and galloped onwards.

Pierre Ducos, in the stables of the French headquarters, had kept a swift, English horse taken from a captured officer. He had mounted it when disaster struck, had taken his precious papers, and was already a mile beyond the blockage on the road. He paused where the road climbed a small rise and looked behind.

A rabble swarmed towards him.

Soldiers, bloody soldiers! Trust the soldiers to lose a country which could have been kept by politics and guile. He smiled thinly. He did not feel any desperate sadness at defeat. He had become used to military defeat while in Spain. Wellington against the Emperor, he thought, that would be a battle worth seeing! Like ice meeting fire, or intelligence meeting genius.

He turned east again. He had planned for defeat, and now France would find its salvation in his plans. The fine intricate machine he had wrought, the Treaty of Valençay, would be needed after all. He smiled thinly, spurred his horse, and rode towards the greatness he had so long planned.

Saumier had chosen to go north of the road, well clear of the panic, but he had chosen wrong. A great ditch faced him, full of dirty water, but without a saddle and with the horse double-ridden, he knew he could not jump it. He slid from the horse's back. 'Stay there, my Lady.'

'I'd not planned on leaving you, Captain.'

Saumier gripped the long driving reins with the fingers of his injured arm and walked to the ditch's edge. He plumbed it with his sabre and found that it was shallow, but with a soft, treacherous bottom. 'Sit tight, my Lady! Hold onto the collar!'

The horse was nervous so Saumier would have to lead it through the ditch. He stepped into the water and felt his boot sucked into the slimy mud. He slipped, held his balance, then tugged on the reins.

The horse nervously came forward. It put its head down and La Marquesa gripped the mane.

Saumier smiled at her with his yellow teeth. 'Don't frighten it, my Lady! Gently, now, gently!'

The horse stepped into the water.

'Come on! Come on!'

A horseman took the ditch in one stride a few yards to Saumier's left. The Frenchman looked up, fearing a British cavalryman, but the man wore no uniform. Saumier tugged on the reins again. 'Come on, boy! Come on!'

La Marquesa screamed and Saumier looked up at her, ready to chide her for frightening the horse, then he saw why she had shouted in fear.

The horseman had stopped beyond the ditch. The man grinned at Saumier.

More horsemen were behind La Marquesa. One of them was a huge man with a beard that seemed to grow from every part of his face.

The bearded man came forward and smiled. From his belt he drew a pistol.

Saumier let go of the reins. He had his sabre drawn, but his boots were stuck in the filth at the ditch's bottom.

El Matarife still smiled. He had followed the carriage from the city and now he had found the woman he had been ordered to capture. She was to be taken to a nunnery, those were his brother's orders, but *El Matarife* planned to give her one taste of the joys she would miss in the close confinement of a convent. He glanced at her, and she was more beautiful than a man could wish for, even screaming in horror at the sight of his face. The man in the ditch dropped his sabre and fumbled for the pistol in his holster.

El Matarife pulled his trigger.

Captain Saumier jerked backwards, hands flying up and pistol falling.

He splashed into the ditch, his boots slowly sucking up from the bubbling mud.

He floated.

His blood drifted in the dirty water, spreading as he died, choking on ditch-water and blood.

El Matarife smiled at La Marquesa, at the woman whose golden hair had been like a beacon in the havoc. 'My Lady,' he said. He began to laugh, the laugh getting louder and louder until it blotted out the screams of the chaos. 'My Lady, my dear lady.' He reached for her, dragged her belly-downwards over his saddle. She screamed, and he slapped her rump to keep her quiet, then headed back towards the wagons. As he had followed her carriage here he had seen the gold and silver scattered like leaves upon the ground. There would be time, he knew, to take some for himself before he delivered the golden whore to her new prison. He went into the chaos with his prisoner.

CHAPTER 25

'God save Ireland!' Patrick Harper's favourite oath, saved only for the things that truly astonished him, was hardly sufficient to describe what he saw as he crossed the shallow crest where the grass was still scorched from the French guns that had made the slaughter on the bridge. He tried another. 'God save England, too.'

Sharpe laughed. The sight, for a few seconds, had taken his mind from La Marquesa.

Angel stared open-mouthed. An army was running a race. Thousands and thousands of Frenchmen, all order gone, ran between the river and the city, streaming eastwards, abandoning muskets, packs, anything that would slow them.

From Sharpe's right, cavalry approached, British cavalry who stared and laughed at the tide of panicked men. Their Major came towards Sharpe and grinned. 'It's cruel to charge them!'

Sharpe smiled. 'Do you have a glass, Major?'

The cavalryman offered Sharpe a small spyglass. The Rifleman opened it, trained it, and saw what he thought he had seen with his naked eye. The road was blocked. There were hundreds, perhaps thousands of wagons that were stuck in the fields east of Vitoria. He could see carriages there, their windows red from the setting sun. There was a woman there, and a treasure there. He closed the glass and gave it back to the cavalryman. 'You see those wagons, Major?'

'Yes.'

'There's a god-damned fortune there. The gold of a bloody empire.'

The cavalryman stared at Sharpe as if he was mad, then slowly smiled. 'You're sure?'

'I'm sure. It's a king's ransom.'

The cavalryman looked at Angel, ragged on his stolen horse, then at Harper, huge on his. 'You think you can keep up with us?'

'Think you can keep up with *us*?' Sharpe smiled. In truth he needed these Hussars to help cut through the panicked mass of fugitives who still streamed between them and the city.

The Major grinned, brushed at his moustaches and turned to look at his men. 'Troop!'

The trumpeter challenged the sky, the troopers drew their sabres and walked the horses forward. The men were in ranks of ten, knee to knee. The Major drew his sabre and looked at Sharpe. 'This is going to be better than a strong scent on a fine day!' He looked at his trumpeter and nodded.

The trumpet sounded the gallop. There was no other way to go through the flood of fugitives and the Hussars shouted, raised their sabres, and plunged into the fleeing army.

If Sharpe had not been so concerned for the fate of La Marquesa he would have remembered that ride for ever. The Hussars cut into the French retreat like men going into a dark river, and, just as in a river, the current took them downstream. The French, seeing their enemy coming, parted before the horses and only those who could not move fast enough were cut down by the curved blades.

They went like steeplechasers. They crossed a small stream, hooves shattering water silver in the air, scrambled up a field bank, jumped a stone wall, and the men whooped like maniacs and the French split before them. The hooves hurled mud higher than the guidon that was held aloft by the standard bearer.

There were guns everywhere, abandoned field guns with blackened muzzles, their wheels mired in the soft earth. The cavalry rode in the middle of their enemies and not a hand was lifted against them.

There were carts overturned, mules running free,

wounded men crawling eastwards, and everywhere there were women. They called for their men, for their husbands or lovers, and their voices were forlorn and hopeless.

The Major, breaking free of the French rout, cut his men towards the wagons. Sharpe shouted at Harper and Angel, pulled left, and reined Carbine in. He had stopped by a dark blue carriage, its wheels sunk into soft turf, its varnished panels spattered with mud. He stared at the coat of arms that was painted on the carriage door. He knew it. He had seen it first on another carriage in Salamanca's splendid square.

It was La Marquesa's carriage, and it was empty.

The upholstery had been split open and the horses led away. One window was broken. He peered inside and saw no blood on the torn cushions of the seats. One silver trace chain was left in the mud.

He stared into the havoc of wagons and carriages. She could be anywhere in that chaos of shouting and theft, of musket shots and screams, or she could be gone.

Harper looked at the carriage and frowned, 'Sir?'

'Patrick?'

'Would that be her Ladyship's?'

'Yes.'

'Is that why we're here?'

'Yes. I want to find her. God knows how.'

The Irishman stared at the baggage park. 'You say there's treasure here?'

'A god-damned fortune.'

'Seems a good place to start looking, sir.'

Sharpe urged his horse towards the wagons. He was looking for the great mane of golden hair amidst the chaos that had once been King Joseph's baggage train. 'Helene!'

A box of fine porcelain was spilt ahead of him, the plates smashed into a thousand gilded shards. A woman, blood streaming from her scalp, hurled a second dinner service out of its packing cases, looking for gold.

A French soldier lay dying, his throat half cut by a Spaniard who ripped with his knife at the man's pockets.

He found a watch, a stolen masterpiece made by Breguet in Paris. He put it to his ear, heard no tick, and furiously smashed the crystal with the hilt of his knife.

'Helene!'

Sharpe's horse trampled on leather-bound books, books that had been made before the printing press had been invented, books made by patient men over months of work, with exquisitely painted capitals that were now ground into the mire.

A tapestry that had been made in Flanders when Queen Elizabeth was a child was torn by two women to make blankets. Another woman, wine bottle in hand, danced between the wagons with the gilded coat of a Royal Chamberlain on her shoulders. She wore nothing else. A French soldier, drunk on brandy, plucked the coat from her and tore at the gilt braid. The naked woman hit him with her bottle and snatched the coat back.

'Helene!'

Silver Spanish dollars, each worth five English shillings, were strewn like pebbles between the wagons. No one wanted silver when there was so much gold.

'Helene!'

Two men bent, twisted, and hacked apart a golden candelabra, one of a set of four that had been given to King Phillip II by Queen Mary of England when she had married the Spanish King.

'Helene!'

Two Frenchwomen, abandoning their army and their children for the sake of a box of jewels, prised the stones from a reliquary that contained the shin-bone of John the Baptist. The jewels were glass, replacements for the real stones that had been stolen three centuries before. They dropped the shin-bone into the mud where it was snapped up by a dog.

One man shot another to get a wooden box that the victim had been dragging away. The murderer took it beneath a wagon, reloaded his musket, and blew the lock off. It contained horseshoes and nails.

'Helene!'

It was hopeless. The wagons seethed with people. He could see nothing. Sharpe swore. A four year old child, abandoned by its mother, was trampled by a rush of men towards an untouched wagon. The child cried, unheard and unseen, its ribs broken.

'Helene!'

A Frenchman ran at Sharpe, musket held like a club, and tried to knock the Rifleman from his horse. Sharpe snarled, chopped down with the sword, knocked the musket aside, and chopped again. The man screamed, the sword cut into his neck, shearing his ear off, and then Harper's gun butt slammed into the other side of his head. The man fell, golden francs spilling from his pockets, and in an instant he was set on by a score of people who slashed with knives and scrambled in the mud for gold.

There were acres of wagons! Hundreds of them. Many as the plunderers were, there were still scores of untouched wagons.

'Helene!'

He galloped down between a row of wagons, turned into the next row and galloped back. Silver dollars were beneath Carbine's hooves. A woman tossed and unrolled a bolt of silk, scarlet in the failing sunlight, silk that arched and fell into the mud.

A man threw crates of silver cutlery off a wagon, spilling them into the mud, searching for gold.

'Helene!'

A woman staggered towards Sharpe, blood flowing in a dozen rivulets down her head and matting her hair. She had found her box of gold, but a man had taken it from her. She cried, not from the pain, but from loss. She picked up some silver forks and thrust them into her dress.

'Helene!'

A man, trousers at his knees, was on top of a woman by an overturned coach. Sharpe hit him with the flat of the sword, trying to see the woman's face. She had none. It was just blood from a cut throat. The man tried to scramble away, but Sharpe sliced the sword in a backswing and cut the man's throat as he had cut his victim's.

A pretty girl, incongruously dressed in tight French cavalry uniform, danced on top of a wagon and whirled a rope of pearls. A British cavalryman laughed with her, protecting her, and then bent to scoop more pearls from a box. A horde of people, seeing the treasure, scrambled like rats up to the wagon's top.

'Helene!'

Sharpe put his heels back, shouting at the plunderers to clear the way. A drunk, a bottle of priceless wine in each hand, staggered in Carbine's path and the horse threw the man down. Sharpe held his balance, urged the horse on, and never noticed the painting that the hooves trampled. Van Dyck had worked long on the canvas which was pulled out of the mud by a man who needed a tarpaulin to cover a mule-load of plunder.

'Helene!'

A box of *Legion d'Honneur* medals was tossed to the crowd. The Spaniards, laughing, attached the medals to hang beneath their horses' tails. Angel caught one and laughed at the trophy.

A British cavalryman ripped a tarpaulin from a wagon to find pictures beneath. They had been cut from their frames. He pulled a Rubens from the top of the pile to see if it concealed gold. It did not, and he rode on, looking for better plunder.

A golden clock, made in Augsburg three hundred years before, that showed the houses of the zodiac, the phases of the moon, as well as the time, was hacked apart by men with bayonets for the sake of its golden case. One of them, piercing his palm with the clock's dragon hand, smashed at it with the butt of his musket. The brass and iron clockwork, that had been cared for over centuries, was scattered in the mud. Its jewelled astrolabe was carried off by a British sergeant.

'Helene!'

They searched row after row of wagons until Sharpe felt

296

the hopelessness rise in him. He reined in and looked at Harper. 'It's no good.'

The Irishman shrugged. He looked eastwards into the valley of the Pamplona Road that was thick with fugitives. 'She'd have been foolish to stay around here, sir.' That had been his private opinion ever since they began this frantic, useless galloping amongst the stranded wagons. He wondered just what had happened to Sharpe in the last weeks. Somehow he was not surprised that the golden-haired woman was involved; Sharpe always had been a fool for women.

Sharpe swore. He wiped his sword on his leg and sheathed it. A bare-footed British infantry Captain walked past. He carried his boots carefully, both boots filled to the top with gold twenty franc pieces. Three of his men cheerfully guarded him.

Another woman dressed in French cavalry uniform called to Sharpe for protection. Sharpe ignored her. He was staring about him, watching the plunderers tear at wagons. He tried to see La Marquesa's golden hair. A British infantryman, one of the many who now swarmed into the baggage, grabbed the woman's hand. She clung to him and went happily enough with her new guardian.

Harper edged his horse close to the nearest wagon. If Major Sharpe wanted to look for a woman, Harper might as well look for a marriage settlement. The wagon had words stencilled on its backboard. *Domaine Exterieur de S.M. L'Empereur*. He wondered what they meant, then drew his knife, slashed the tarpaulin, and started working at the first box.

Sharpe watched the British infantry come like children into this wonderland of treasure. He thought of La Marquesa's wagons and wondered if they too were being stripped and if she was trying to protect them from the muskets and bayonets. He stood in his stirrups. God damn it! Her carriage was here, she must be close by; and then he supposed that she must have fled eastwards and abandoned her wealth. Or perhaps Ducos had taken her. He swore again. He wished he would meet Ducos in this chaos for one brief moment, a moment long enough to use the heavy sword.

'God in his Irish heaven! Jesus! Mary, Mother of God, would you be looking at this. God save Ireland!'

Sharpe turned. Harper held up a diamond necklace. The Irishman looked at Sharpe with pure delight. 'Open your haversack, sir.'

'Patrick?'

'For Christ's sake, open your haversack!'

Sharpe frowned. He was thinking of La Marquesa.

'Mr Sharpe, sir!'

'What?' He snapped the word, still trying to see the golden mane of hair in the failing light.

'Give us your bloody haversack!' Harper shouted it as if he was addressing a particularly stupid recruit. 'Give it to me!'

Sharpe obeyed, hardly knowing what he was doing.

Harper called to Angel to help him. They tethered their horses to the wagon and stood on the load to lever open the locked chests. Harper was emptying the first chest of small leather boxes, each lined with white silk. He tossed the leather boxes away, keeping the jewels that they contained. He worked fast, knowing as a soldier to take swift advantage of good luck. He opened leather box after leather box, taking out necklaces, tiaras, bracelets, earrings, drops, brooches, scabbard furniture, enamelled decorations studded with stones, enough pieces for Sharpe's haversack, his own, and Angel's pockets. He buckled Sharpe's haversack and tossed it to his officer. 'A welcome home present, sir.'

Sharpe slung the haversack on his shoulder. 'Where the hell is she?'

'Jesus knows.' Harper wrenched open another box and swore. The box had velvet napkins folded carefully between tissues. Harper spilt it onto the ground and worked his knife beneath a new lid. 'God in his heaven!' The box had gold altar furniture in it; ewers, cups, candlesticks, a jewelled monstrance, and a great golden crucifix. He took the smaller items. Angel had found a set of duelling pistols, their butts chased with gold. He pushed them into his belt.

'Patrick!' Sharpe's voice was urgent.

'Sir?'

'Follow me!'

Sharpe had put Carbine into a gallop, disappearing into the chaos. Harper had caught a glimpse of his officer's face, and he thought that never had he seen Sharpe look so grim and savage. The Irishman looked at Angel. 'Come on, lad.'

Harper mounted his horse. He had made himself rich beyond the wildest dreams of the wildest Irishman that ever marched to war, and, like a true friend, he had made Sharpe rich too. Of course the Englishman had not noticed, but that was Mr Sharpe. Mr Sharpe was thinking of someone else, of another treasure. Harper looked into the seething mass of plunderers. 'Where the hell is he?'

Sharpe had disappeared. Harper stood in his stirrups and stared about the seething mass of people who swarmed around the half-stripped wagons. The setting sun bathed the whole scene in a vivid, blood-red light. There was laughter and tears all about him. 'Where the hell is he?'

'There, *señor*!' Angel was still standing on the wagon. He pointed south. '*El Matarife*!'

'What?'

The boy was pointing at a band of horsemen. In their lead was a man who looked half-beast, a hulking brute with a face of thick hair, a man who had a woman held on her belly over his saddle. The woman, Harper saw, had hair the colour of fine gold.

Harper urged his horse through the crowd. He saw how many armed men were with the bearded man. He saw too, that Sharpe was riding alone towards them and he knew that Sharpe, in this savage mood, would think nothing of taking on all those horsemen with his sword. Only one thing puzzled Harper and that was the presence, in Sharpe's left hand, of a great length of silver chain. Harper cocked his seven-barrelled gun and rode, a rich man, to the fight.

CHAPTER 26

Sharpe had seen *El Matarife*. The Partisan, with a group of his men, was stripping one of the French wagons that had brought the defeated army's arrears of pay. Some of his men unloaded the gold twenty franc pieces, the rest kept other looters away. *El Matarife* had La Marquesa over his saddle.

Sharpe knew he could not defeat all of them. There were twenty muskets there that would snatch him from the saddle and leave her to the mercy of the bearded man. Yet *El Matarife*, Sharpe knew, would not be able to resist a challenge to his manhood. There was one way, and one way only, that this fight must be fought.

He swerved Carbine towards La Marquesa's abandoned carriage. He drew his sword and, reaching the vehicle, he leaned down, grasped the last trace chain, and hacked with his sword at the leather strap which held it to the splinter-bar.

He looped the chain in his left hand, and turned towards his enemy.

Weeks before, he thought, he had been foolish enough to accept a challenge to a duel. Now he would issue the challenge.

He rode towards the wagon, and the men who ripped at the chests stopped when they saw him coming. They called to their leader and *El Matarife*, who had been told that this man was dead, crossed himself and stared at the tall Rifleman who came out of the scarlet lit chaos. 'Shoot him!'

But no one moved. The Rifleman had tossed a silver chain onto the ground into the mud that was thick with unwanted silver dollars, and he stared with savage loathing at the bearded man. 'Are you a coward, *Matarife*? Do you only fight women?'

Still none of them moved. Those who had been scooping handfuls of gold from the broken chests stared at the tall Englishman who, slowly, his eyes on *El Matarife*, dismounted. Sharpe unbuckled his sword. He laid it, with his haversack, beside the wheel of the wagon.

El Matarife looked down at the chain, then back to Sharpe as the Rifleman looped the silver links about his upper left arm. Sharpe left a length of the chain to swing free from his arm. 'Are you a coward, *Matarife*?'

El Matarife's answer was to swing himself from his saddle. He dragged La Marquesa down and pushed her towards his men, shouting at them to hold her and keep her. She cried out as she stumbled, as a man reached down and seized her golden hair and held her against the flank of his horse, and as she turned and saw Sharpe standing in the wheel-churned mud and silver.

'Richard!' Her eyes were huge, staring in disbelief. Like her captor, in a half-forgotten gesture from her past, she touched her face, her belly, and her breasts in the sign of the cross. 'Richard?'

'Helene.' He smiled at her, seeing her fear, her astonishment, her beauty. Even here the sight of that unfair loveliness struck into his soul like a dagger.

Behind Sharpe, Harper curbed his horse. He took Carbine's rein, then leaned down and retrieved Sharpe's sword and haversack. 'Behind you, sir!'

'Watch the bastards, Patrick! Put a bullet into them if they take her away!' Sharpe had spoken in Spanish, a language that Harper had learned from Isabella.

'Consider it done, sir.'

The Partisans were awed by the huge man who sat on his horse with his two guns, one of them larger than any gun they had ever seen held by a man. Beside Harper was Angel with his rifle in his practised hands. Angel was staring at the woman he thought more beautiful than lust.

The sky was darkening towards night, the west reddened with the sun's setting. Skeins of smoke, dark blue-grey against the cloudless sky, stretched above the field of plunder in delicate rills. They were the gun's detritus, the drifting remnants of the battle that had been and gone on Vitoria's plain.

El Matarife shrugged off his heavy cloak. 'You can ride away, Englishman, You will live.'

Sharpe laughed. 'I shall count the ways of your death, coward.'

El Matarife stooped, picked up the chain, and knotted it about his upper arm. He drew his knife and, with a patronising smile on his wet lips that showed through the thick hair of his face, threw it to Sharpe.

It turned in the air, catching the dying sun, and landed at Sharpe's feet.

It was bone handled, with a blade as long as a bayonet's. The blade looked delicate. It was thin, needle pointed, and its two edges were feathered where it had been sharpened on the stone. This weapon, Sharpe knew, would draw blood at the lightest stroke. In *El Matarife's* comfortable grip, taken from one of his lieutenants, was a similar blade; as bright, as sharp, as deadly.

El Matarife stepped backwards and the silver chain slowly lifted from the mud. The links clinked softly. The Partisan smiled. 'You're a dead man, Englishman.'

Sharpe remembered the terrible skill with which his enemy had taken the eyes from the French prisoner. He waited.

El Matarife's men were silent. From the city came the jangling of church bells, announcing that the French were gone and that the first Allied troops were in the narrow streets.

The chain tightened. The sun reddened its links.

The Slaughterman smiled. His poleaxe was stuck into the ground at the edge of the circle made by his men. He pulled against Sharpe's strength until the silver links were as taut as a bar of steel, and the only evidence of the huge strengths that opposed each other were the scraps of mud that fell from the tight links.

Sharpe felt the pressure on his arm. *El Matarife* was pulling with extraordinary force. Sharpe pulled back and saw the Slaughterman's eyes judging him.

The Slaughterman jerked. Sharpe's arm came up, he jerked back, and the Slaughterman was grunting and pulling, and Sharpe was jarred forward. He pulled back, knowing he did not have the same brute strength as his enemy, but when he saw the Slaughterman smile and gather his strength for a massive pull, Sharpe jumped forward to throw the man off balance.

The Slaughterman was ready, he had expected it, invited it, and he closed the ten foot gap with lightning speed and his knife slashed up towards Sharpe, bright in the dusk light. The Rifleman swerved, not bothering to reply, backed away, and his left hand caught the chain for greater leverage and he pulled on it with all his power and the Slaughterman did not move.

El Matarife looked at Sharpe's gritted teeth and laughed. 'Your death will be slow, Englishman.'

The crowd, swollen by people from the city, shouted an abrupt, brief shout in appreciation of the Slaughterman's skill. *El Matarife* acknowledged the cheer with a wave of his knife and then hooked his left hand over the chain. He stepped back, tightening it.

The power came. It pulled Sharpe forward. He could not resist it and he saw the Slaughterman smile with the ease of the task. Sharpe braced his feet, but his boots slid in the mire and he was being dragged towards his opponent. Then the jerking began, the vicious, hard jerks that pulled him off balance and he tripped, fell, and the chain was pulling his arm from his socket and when the pressure stopped he rolled to one side, knowing the knife was slicing down, only to hear the Slaughterman laughing.

'The Englishman is frightened!'

Sharpe stood up. His jacket and overalls were smeared with mud. The crowd was catcalling, jeering him. The

Slaughterman had simply made a fool of him to demonstrate his strength. *El Matarife* was smiling now; smiling with relief and triumph. He had made this kind of fighting his speciality, and he would play with Sharpe as Sharpe had watched him play with the French prisoner.

El Matarife beckoned Sharpe forward. 'Come, Englishman, come! Come on! Come to your death.'

Sharpe dropped his left arm and flexed it.

He went forward.

El Matarife waited. He was crouching, the knife low. He began to shake the chain, trying to loop it about Sharpe's blade, but Sharpe simply held his left arm out and the chain went away from him.

'Come, Englishman.'

They were close now, four feet from each other, both men staring into the other's eyes, both knives held low. Neither moved. The crowd was silent.

When *El Matarife* moved it was as fast as a scorpion's strike, but Sharpe had fought all his life and his own speed matched that of the Spaniard. Sharpe stepped back and the blade hissed past his face. Sharpe smiled.

El Matarife bellowed at him, trying to frighten him, and then looped the chain high so it would fall over Sharpe's head. Sharpe caught the loop as it came, jerked on it, and sliced up with his knife as the Spaniard's guard was lifted, and Sharpe saw the sudden fear on the beast's face as *El Matarife* realised Sharpe's speed and as the Rifleman's knife whipped upwards.

'*Uno!*'

El Matarife's right forearm was bleeding.

The crowd was silent.

Sharpe had gone back as fast as he had moved forward. The Spaniard growled. He had underestimated the Englishman, even let him live as a boast to the crowd, but now *El Matarife* planned Sharpe's death. He stepped back, tightening the chain, and began again to try and tug Sharpe off balance, jerking the silver chain with massive strength, but this time Sharpe stepped into the pull, letting himself be dragged forward, and the Slaughterman had to step back and keep stepping back until he was at the edge of the fighting space with nowhere to go and Sharpe laughed at him. 'You are a traitor, Spaniard, and your mother whored with swine.'

El Matarife roared and leaped forward. The knife seared high, coming at Sharpe's eyes, dropped, and slashed upwards.

'*Uno!*' *El Matarife* was shouting it in triumph and the crowd shouted with him.

Sharpe would have waking nightmares about that moment for ever. The knife was within a half inch of slicing his belly open, slicing from his groin to his ribs and spilling his guts onto the silvered mud, and he would never know how his body moved so fast or how his right hand, seeing the opening, slashed in to chop at the Spaniard's passing arm. He shouted as he jumped back.

'*Dos!*'

La Marquesa had cried out and hidden her eyes with her hands.

The crowd breathed out a great sigh. The Englishman was not touched. *El Matarife* was panting, his great chest heaving beneath his black leather coat. Both his forearms were cut.

Harper breathed a huge sigh of relief. 'God save Ireland.'

'Will he win?' Angel asked.

'I don't know, lad. I tell you one thing.'

'What?'

'I'll shoot that fat bastard through the gut before he kills Mr Sharpe.'

Angel hefted his rifle. 'I kill him. I'm Spanish.'

The chain tightened as Sharpe stepped back. In his left hand he held the loose end of the chain. He watched *El Matarife's* eyes, saw the moment when the Partisan would challenge the pressure of the chain, and Sharpe went suddenly forward. He lunged with the knife, going low, still watching the eyes between their mats of hair, and as the Slaughterman brought up his knife arm to spear the point

305

into Sharpe's face, the Rifleman whiplashed the silver chain.

The end struck the bestial face, slashing across his eyes to sting and momentarily blind him. and Sharpe turned, kicked, and his right boot-heel was going where he had wanted it to go, thumping into *El Matarife's* left knee with sickening force, tearing down and away, grinding kneecap and flesh, and the Slaughterman's eyes widened in pain as his knife came desperately down in defence.

Sharpe was falling. He saw the blade come, felt it razor into his skin, slicing through his leather boot as if it was cotton, and then he was scrambling away from the huge man and the roar of the crowd was like thunder among the wagons.

'*Uno! Uno! Uno!*'

El Matarife jumped forward and Sharpe heard the cry of pain as his weight went onto the wounded knee. The pain gave Sharpe time to roll to his feet and the crowd, that had been noisy with anticipation, fell into uneasy silence.

Harper, who had seen the boot-heel slam into the knee, smiled to himself.

El Matarife had not shouted the number with the crowd. His knee was on fire, the pains shooting up to his groin and down to his ankle. He had never faced a man this fast.

Sharpe laughed. 'You're slow, *Matarife*.'

'God damn you, Englishman.' *El Matarife* leapt at Sharpe, knife going to the Englishman's groin, but his knee crumpled on him, he stumbled forward, and Sharpe stepped back.

Patrick Harper laughed.

El Matarife tried to stand. Sharpe jerked back, pulling him forward. The Spaniard tried again, and again the chain jangled as Sharpe tugged it, and again the Slaughterman was pulled forward into the mud and coins.

El Matarife tried again, and again the Rifleman wrenched him down, and this time Sharpe jumped forward and his foot was on the Slaughterman's right wrist, pinning the knife into the mud. The Slaughterman looked up at his enemy, seeing death.

Sharpe stared at the man. 'You let me live a moment ago, *Matarife*. I return you the favour.'

He stepped away. He let the Spaniard stand, then pulled again, pulling all the huge man's weight onto the knee so that the bestial face screwed in pain and the great, leather-clad body fell once more to the mud. The crowd was silent. The Slaughterman was on his hands and knees, staring up at Sharpe, and, as the Rifleman came close, the Partisan lunged again with his knife at Sharpe's groin, but Sharpe had moved faster.

The loose end of the chain whipped and curled about the Slaughterman's hand, was jerked back, and *El Matarife* cried out as the chain crushed his fingers and snatched the knife from his grip. Sharpe kicked it under the half-plundered wagon.

The Rifleman went behind his enemy. He gripped the Slaughterman's hair and jerked his head up.

The crowd watched in silence. Sharpe raised his voice. 'You hear me, *Matarife*?'

'I hear you.'

Sharpe spoke even louder. 'You and your brother work for the French!'

'No!'

But the blade was at the side of *El Matarife's* neck. 'You work for the French, Slaughterman. You whore for the French.'

'No!' And the big, bearded man tried to seize Sharpe's wrist, but the blade moved away and Sharpe's hand jerked back on the thick, greasy hair and his knee ground into the Slaughterman's spine so that the huge beard jutted out above his throat.

'Who killed the Marqués?'

There was silence. Sharpe did not know what answer he expected, but the lack of any answer seemed to suggest that the question was not foolish. He pulled on the hair and let the blade rest on the skin of *El Matarife's* neck. 'Who killed the Marqués?'

The Slaughterman suddenly wrenched forward and his hands reached for Sharpe's wrist, but Sharpe hauled back and flicked the knife sideways to slash the reaching hands of his enemy. 'Who killed him?'

'I did!' It came out as a scream. His hands were soaked in blood.

Sharpe almost let him go, so surprised was he by the answer. He had expected to be told that the Inquisitor had done it, but it made sense that this man, the brother of the clever, ruthless priest, would be the killer.

He put the knife back on the neck. He spoke lower now, so that only the Slaughterman could hear him. The Partisans were watching Sharpe, and Harper was watching the Partisans. Sharpe bent down. 'You killed that girl to fool me, *Matarife*.'

There was no answer.

Sharpe remembered the hanging, turning, bloodied body. He remembered the prisoner blinded. He paused, then struck.

The knife was as sharp as a razor, honed to a wicked, feather-bladed edge, and, tough as a man's throat is, with its gristle and tubes and muscle and skin, the knife cut the throat as easily as silk. There was a gasp as the blood gushed out, as it splashed once, twice, and then the heart had nothing left to pump, and Sharpe let go of the black hair.

The Slaughterman fell forward and his bearded, brutal face fell into the mess of blood, mud and silver.

There was silence from all who watched.

Sharpe turned and walked towards La Marquesa. His eyes were on the man who held her, and in his eyes was a message of death. Slowly, his head shaking, the man let go of her.

Sharpe dropped the knife. She ran towards him, stumbling in the mud and silver coins, and his left arm was about her and she pressed herself against his mud smeared chest. 'I thought you were dead.'

308

The first stars were visible above the plunder of an empire.

He held the woman for whom he had ridden across Spain, for whom he had ridden the field of jewels and gold, of silk and diamonds.

She could never be his, he knew that. He had known that even when she had said that she loved him, yet he would ride the fields of silver and pearls again for her; he would cross hell for her.

He turned from *El Matarife's* men and Harper threw down his sword and haversack. Sharpe wondered why the bag was so heavy. He buckled. the sword and knew he would have to go into the city and find the Inquisitor. There were questions to be put to that Inquisitor, and Sharpe would be as delicate as the Inquisition in his search for the answers.

He would go into Vitoria, and he would take the answers to the mystery that Hogan had asked him to solve, but that, he knew, was not the reason that he had come to this place. Not for victory, and not for gold, but for the woman who would cheat him, lie to him, never love him, but who was the whore of gold and, for this one night at least, Sharpe's woman.

EPILOGUE

The army had gone, following the French towards the Pyrenees, and Vitoria was left to the Spanish Battalions. Of the British only a few staff officers and the South Essex were left; the South Essex to guard the French prisoners who would soon start their journey to Dartmoor or the prison hulks.

On a warm night brilliant with starlight, Sharpe was in the hotel where so many British officers, on the night of the battle, had enjoyed a free meal. He was in a vast room with windows that looked towards the cathedral on its hill.

'What is it?'

'Open it.' Helene smiled at him. She was dressed in cream silk that was cut so low that one deep breath, he was sure, would tip her breasts over the lace-trimmed collar.

She had given him a box. It was made from rosewood, polished to a deep shine, and it was locked with two golden clasps that he pushed aside.

'Go on,' she said, 'open it.'

He lifted the lid.

The box was lined with red taffeta. Lying in a trough that ran the length of the box was a telescope. 'God! It's beautiful.'

'Isn't it?' she said with satisfaction.

He lifted it. Its barrel was of ivory, its trimmings of gold, and it slid apart with extraordinary smoothness. There was a plate engraved and inset into the ivory. 'What does it say?'

She smiled, took the glass from him, and tipped it to the candlelight. '"To Joseph, King of Spain and the Indies, from his brother, Napoleon, Emperor of France".' She laughed. 'A king's telescope for you. I bought it off one of your cavalrymen.'

'It's wonderful.' He took it from her, drew the tubes fully out, and stared with it at the sickle moon that hung over the northern hills. His last telescope, destroyed by Ducos, had been good, but it had been nothing compared with this instrument. 'It's wonderful,' he said again.

'Of course! It's French.' She smiled. 'My thank you to you.'

'For nothing.' He put the telescope into its box, and she laughed at him.

'For nothing, then. Just for my wagons, my life, little things like that. Nothing.'

He frowned, clasping the box shut. 'You'll take nothing from me?'

'You are a fool, Richard Sharpe.' She walked to the window, raised her bare arms to the curtains, and paused as she stared into the night. Then, abruptly, she pulled the curtains closed and turned to him. 'You keep those diamonds. They have made you rich. And don't give them away, not to me, not to anyone. Keep them.'

He smiled. 'Yes, ma'am.'

'Because, Richard,' and she touched his face with her finger. 'this war will not last for ever, and when peace comes, you will need money.'

'Yes, ma'am.' There was a thump on the door, a hearty, loud, hammering of a thump, and Sharpe raised his voice. 'Who is it?'

'Officer of the day, sir!' It was Captain d'Alembord's voice

'What is it?'

'I need you, sir.'

La Marquesa smiled. 'Go on. I'll wait.'

Sharpe unlocked the door. 'I only just got here, Peter!'

The tall, elegant Captain, who was more than a little drunk, bowed lavishly to Sharpe. 'Your presence is demanded, sir. You'll forgive me, ma'am?'

They stopped at the stair's head. Half the Battalion were

in the dining room that was littered with broken plates and discarded cutlery. Sharpe doubted whether three-quarters of these men had ever eaten in such style. Someone had discovered, in a locked chest, a French tricolour that was being paraded noisily about the room. Most of the men were drunk. Some were asleep. Only at the head table was there a hint of decorum, and even there, not much.

Sergeant Patrick Harper presided. Next to him, resplendent in white, with a veil of lace that had been taken from the French baggage park, sat Isabella. About her throat was a necklace of diamonds. Sharpe doubted whether her husband would let her wear it again, at least not till they were safely away from the thieves of the British army.

Sharpe had never seen a man so frightened as Harper. He had shaken in the cathedral. Sharpe had given his Sergeant two big glasses of whisky, but even they had not stopped his fear. 'It's ridiculous, sir! Getting married.'

'Women like it, Patrick.'

'Why do they need us? Why don't they just do it and tell us afterwards. Christ!'

'Are you sure you want to go through with it?'

'And let her down? Of course I'll do it!' He was indignant. 'I just don't have to enjoy doing it!'

He was enjoying himself now. He was drunk, better fed than a soldier had a right to be, and with a pretty, pregnant, dark-eyed girl beside him.

'It's astonishing,' Captain d'Alembord observed, 'how she keeps him in order.'

Sharpe smiled. He was a Major again, reinstated to his rank, and in temporary command of the South Essex. The command would only be temporary. He had not served long enough as a Major to be given the next rank, and so he must wait, with these men, to see who replaced Lieutenant Colonel Leroy.

Wellington, furious almost beyond words at the looting of the baggage park, had spared praise for Sharpe. The Inquisitor, his bruises explained as a tumble down his stairs, had provided the Generalissimo with a list of those

313

men who had offered support to a peace with France. Already those men were being visited, were listening to quiet arguments that were not quite threats, but which were unmistakeable just the same.

The Inquisitor had offered another explanation of the Marqués' death, an explanation listened to in silence by those Spanish officers brought to hear it. They had looked at Sharpe, at Wellington, and a few, seeing the jest inherent in what they saw, had laughed.

La Marquesa, who had provoked a smile from Wellington's anger, had taken her fortune from the Inquisitor's house. She had been promised safe conduct as soon as the roads to the frontier were cleared of the last French garrisons. Wellington, as ever susceptible to a pretty face, had listened to her account of the treaty and rewarded her treachery by restoring her wealth. She would go home, and Sharpe was back where he belonged; with his men.

He had eaten with them this night, made an embarrassing speech to them, and laughed when they had cheered the Marquesa and, because of her dress, shouted at her to jump up and down. Now, standing at the stair's head with Captain d'Alembord, he felt a surge of affection for these soldiers whose life was so hard and whose pleasures so few and who knew how to take both hardship and pleasure in their stride. He looked at Captain d'Alembord. 'Why did you need me?'

'We just thought you'd gone to bed early, sir. Thought you might like to drink another toast.'

Sharpe laughed. He went down the stairs and listened to the cheers and laughter of his men, saw the worried hotel proprietor who winced every time another plate or glass broke, and he walked up to the head table, reached for a bottle of champagne, smiled at Angel who had been given a place of honour, then turned back to the stairs.

'Where are you going, sir?' a voice shouted.

He did not reply, instead he waved the champagne, took the stairs two at a time, and the cheers, jeers, and whistles wafted him up to the landing, and the suggestions were

314

thick about him as he turned at the top, raised the bottle, and bowed to them. He motioned for silence that was a long time coming, but finally the faces stared up at him, flushed with drink, and grinning broadly at the Major who had come back from the dead to lead them to victory.

He wondered what he should say. Wellington, in his rage at the men who had plundered the baggage park, had called his army 'the scum of the earth'. Sharpe laughed aloud. He was proud of them.

'"Talion?' He paused. They waited. 'Morning parade at seven o'clock, married men included. Goodnight.'

He turned, laughed, and their insults followed him to the door of his room.

He went inside. The first thing he saw was a pair of shoes lying on their side. Beyond the shoes was a cream dress, fallen on the floor.

She was in bed. She smiled at the champagne, then at him, and Richard Sharpe, leaning on the locked door, thought that this was what had driven him across Spain to this city. This woman, treacherous as sin, who would love and betray him in the same moment. She was as faithful as a morning mist, as hard as a sword-bayonet, and that, he thought, made her a suitable reward for a soldier.

He unbuckled his sword, dropped it on a chair, and sat on the bed. The Marquesa pulled his face to hers, kissed him, and put her hands to the buttons of his jacket. She was the whore of gold, she was the enemy, and she had known that this man, in the cause of her greed, would give to her his sword, his strength, and even his life. He would give her all that he had, all but for the one small thing that she had wanted; the one small thing she could not take; Sharpe's honour.

HISTORICAL NOTE

"The material captured," wrote Charles Oman in his great *History of the Peninsular War*, "was such as no European army had ever laid hands on . . . since Alexander's Macedonians plundered the camp of the Persian king after the battle of Issus."

"Many of our men," wrote Commissary Schaumann, "and particularly those who found diamonds, became rich people that day."

Edward Costello, a Rifleman, reckoned that he made about a thousand pounds on the evening of the battle, helped by a "few whacks of my rifle".

The plunder of Vitoria was truly spectacular. In military terms it was stunning; all the French guns save two, a hundred and fifty-one in all, and of the two guns the French did manage to salvage, one was lost during the retreat. But it was not the guns that the soldiers were interested in acquiring.

No one truly knows the value of the plunder. I suspect the figure of five million pounds is a low estimate, and it could well have been seven million. In today's money that translates to something like £154,000,000 ($234,000,000). Much of it was in such 'non-negotiable' items as paintings by Rubens, though even those had their uses as tarpaulins. Eventually the paintings were recovered and some of them, presented to Wellington by the restored King Ferdinand VII, can be seen at Stratfield Saye or at Apsley House in London. One object that was never recovered was the Crown of Spain.

Some of the plunder was extremely negotiable, and not just the gold. Schaumann, a German officer in Wellington's army, who was one of the men who enjoyed the victory feast in the hotel, particularly noted the number of captured women, many of them dressed in specially tailored cavalry uniforms. Schaumann, who had a particular and discriminating eye for women during the campaign, noted how, in the plunder, the French women instinctively found one enemy soldier to whom, in exchange for protection, they offered their allegiance. Those who, like the Marquesa, wanted to return to France with their belongings, were given safe conduct and an escort. The words, "we are a walking brothel" were spoken to Wellington by a captured French officer.

Wellington himself reckons that the British soldiers took one million pounds worth of gold coin (and they were *third* into the baggage-park after the fleeing French and the citizens of Vitoria), while he, for the military chest, received only one hundred thousand silver dollars. Among the other trophies were King Joseph's silver chamberpot (still used, though for drinking purposes, by the cavalry regiment that captured it), and also Marshal Jourdan's baton which Wellington sent to the Prince Regent. The Prince returned the compliment, "you have sent me the staff of a French Marshal, and I send you in return that of England". Except that no such English 'staff' existed, one had to be designed, and thus Wellington became a Field Marshal.

An extremely unhappy Field Marshal after his victory. He was furious with the men for plundering the baggage, describing them in a phrase for which he has been attacked ever since; "the scum of the earth". Many of his soldiers doubtless were (but by no means all) and those people who cite the phrase as evidence that Wellington despised the men who fought for him usually forget that he was fond of adding, "but it is wonderful what fine fellows we have made of them". Wellington had cause to be angry (he was hoping to use the French treasure to pay for the campaign), but in defence of the "scum" it is very hard to see how any soldier, paid a shilling a day, could resist the field of gold that waited for them to the east of Vitoria. Yet many did; some regiments kept their order and marched straight through it, so I have no excuses to offer for Sharpe and Harper.

The Inquisition was banned by the Spanish Junta, and reinstated by King Ferdinand in 1814. I have no evidence that the Inquisition was involved in the politics that accompanied the restoration of Ferdinand, but it seemed a fitting idea. The Spanish Inquisition was finally dissolved in 1834.

The thought that a restored Ferdinand VII might make peace with France and expel the British is not fiction. It formed the basis of the Treaty of Valençay, signed by Ferdinand and Napoleon, and there was support for it among those Spaniards who wished to restore their Empire and defeat the new liberals. In the end the treaty was never fulfilled. Napoleon kept his side of the bargain (by restoring Ferdinand and releasing all Spanish prisoners), but Ferdinand VII was prevented (by public opinion as much as anything else) from making the peace with France that would have expelled Wellington's army and allowed his own to reconquer the Spanish empire abroad.

The battle of Vitoria was not the largest battle fought in the Peninsula, but it had the most far-reaching consequences. At a time when the fortunes of Napoleon seemed to be rising after his huge defeat in Russia, the battle encouraged the northern allies to continue the fight, leading to the great northern victory at Leipzig in the following year.

The battle also ejected the French from Spain, except for the garrisons of three fortresses. Eight thousand Frenchmen and five thousand of Wellington's men were casualties. The plundering of the baggage and the night of drink that followed the battle effectively stopped any pursuit by the British and so the remnant of Joseph's army managed to reach France, struggling up the steep tracks of the Pyrenees north of Pamplona.

Burgos Castle is still in ruins (it was mined for destruction and the mines, as described in the novel, went off prematurely, though no one knows why). Vitoria is now a much enlarged industrial city, though the central hill, with the narrow streets circling about the cathedral, looks much today as it did in 1813. The battlefield is still recognisable, at least to the west of the town. The river follows the same course, the bridges are there, and the Arinez Hill provides a superb viewpoint. The area of Gamarra Mayor, where the fighting was among the heaviest (the British lost 500 casualties in taking the village and trying to cross the bridge) is sadly much changed.

One happy circumstance to note is that Vitoria, rare among cities in Spain, marks the contribution Wellington's army made to the liberation with a quite magnificent statue that shows Wellington with his men. It is a truly fantastic confection, appreciated by an army of pigeons, and also by the citizens of Vitoria who are fond of it in the same way that Londoners like the Albert Memorial. In most cities in Spain, where Wellington's men died for that country's freedom, you look in vain for any memorial that acknowledges the gratitude that Vitoria so lavishly bestows.

It was a great victory. Wellington, when he started the campaign, had turned at the border of Portugal, raised his hat, and prophetically said goodbye to a country. "I will never see you again." Now, as a result of the battle of Vitoria, he is threatening a different country; France itself.

So Sharpe and Harper will march again.